book one ✦ THE LAST PUBLISHERS

the VISION

DEBI PEARL

Pearl Books

BE SURE TO READ THESE OTHER BOOKS BY
MICHAEL & DEBI PEARL

Created To Be His Help Meet

To Train Up A Child

No Greater Joy I, II & III

Good & Evil

Holy Sex

Joy of Training DVD

Making Herbs Simple DVD

Available from No Greater Joy, www.nogreaterjoy.org

SPECIAL THANKS

A writer's greatest pitfall is self-doubt. God blessed me with a true friend, so that when I faltered she firmly insisted, "You can do this; I will help you." And she did. So here's to my friend, SC Lady. I hope I made you proud.

-Debi

FIRST EDITION, JUNE 2009

Copyright © 2009 by Debi Pearl

All rights reserved. Published in the United States.

Scripture quoted from the Authorized King James Bible.

Cover and interior photos designed by Clint Cearley.

Front cover characters and interior photographs taken by
Elizabeth Stewart.

Back cover photo of author taken by Laura Newman.

ISBN: 978-0-9819737-0-8

www.DebiPearl.com

NOTE ON FOOTER TEXT

The gray boxes at the bottom of some of the pages found in
this book contain spot research. I wanted my readers to know
that much of what they are reading is based on facts.
Yellowstone is truly a threatening monster. Muslim honor
killings do happen regularly, including here in the USA.
The White Supremacist type groups are growing in numbers.
Some herbs and berries have amazing healing powers.
The end is near.

The web addresses and additional information cited were
accurate at the time of this printing, however, I encourage you
to visit www.debipearl.com for updated links and info.

-Debi

TABLE OF CONTENTS

1

Asher Joel felt strangely detached, staring at the thick, gray morning fog cloaking the world beyond the diner's window. A single droplet of water, released from the window's condensation, captured his attention as it zigzagged down the inside of the plate glass, finally dropping onto the windowsill. He glanced down to the lightly rolled newspaper lying by his left hand. Last night's bombing in Atlanta dominated the headlines, but Yellowstone's latest series of earthquakes competed for the public's attention. Funny—they were getting used to the bombings.

He unconsciously murmured as he thought of the irony of the big deal the news was making of a few small earthquakes while keeping the big news of Yellowstone quiet. He understood why his brother, a government volcanologist, had told him the whole truth would not be released to the public. What use would it be to awaken the public to the knowledge that deep in the recesses of Yellowstone Park lay a waking monster? What could anyone do?

A small burst of laughter from two tables down caused him to shift his glance toward two old fishermen that had often come in to eat while he and Dan dined. Now, even in the diner people were subdued and withdrawn. Laughter had become a strange sound that caught your attention. Again a mumbling groan escaped from Asher's clinched lips as he mulled over a more local threat. The locals called it The Muslim Invasion. This threat tempered the locals' usual ready laughter, their interest in politics, even their fishing.

It muffled every aspect of their lives.

It happened gradually, the influx of Arabic speaking Muslims into their small coastal area of Washington State ... but now the fear subdued all of life's joys and trials.

Even grief.

Quickly Asher turned again to face the window. A solitary tear slid down his face, a manifestation of his loss. Old Dan had been a good friend—more than a friend. Dan had been almost like a father.

A rush of the cold morning dampness accompanied the sound of the door opening. Another pair of old fishermen pushed through and took their customary seats, each turning stiffly to Asher, offering silent condolences with the meeting of eyes and the slightest of nods. It was a gesture that expressed their shared sorrow, only understood and appreciated by proud alpha males. Asher's cold blue eyes acknowledged their tribute before turning back to look at the gray swirl.

He stared at the reflection of the hardy fishermen seated around him. *What will become of this world of simple fishermen and small diners?* Men like Dan, who worked hard all their lives, had old time values and were American to the core. Men like Dan died when they stood up for what they believed. The young man clenched his jaw as his ears seemed to fill with a roar.

Too much knowledge is deafening. It screams at your soul, not allowing you to enjoy music, laughter, dreams, or even the thought of a good woman. With trembling hands he carefully laid aside the salt shaker he had been casually pushing back and forth.

Almost as if it were an omen, he caught a fleeting glance of scurrying Muslim men rushing off to where they would kneel together toward Mecca. A deep furl appeared between his eyes. His hands doubled up into hard fists.

The Puget Sound region has become particularly attractive to Muslims. Almost 90% of the area's Muslims are immigrants, said Nazeer Ahmed, editor of the Northwest Islamic Journal. An average of 10,000 to 12,000 people move into the Puget sound from overseas each year.

These many families are changing the face of the community by getting involved in politics and changing the laws to suit their religious beliefs. Islamic schools, centers, mosques, and eating spots reflect the new face of Seattle. ✑

www.islamfortoday.com

This much anger was not good for the soul.

The watery reflection in the window of the waitress bearing down upon him, carrying his smoked salmon eggs benedict, caused Asher to turn again toward the room. His lips smiled his appreciation to the old woman as she slid the plate in front of him with the familiar clatter unique to diners. But he couldn't keep the turmoil out of his eyes.

Looking up at the familiar, gum-smacking, smiling face, Asher took in the highly arched, painted brows and the compassionate, kind eyes. "Thank you, Louise. This is my favorite breakfast. It looks good—as usual."

The lumpy older woman pulled at the bodice of her stuffed dress and flushed, pleased with the compliment. "Sho-wah, Honey; it's goo-ahd fooahd." Her voice always surprised newcomers with its distinctive New England 'Kennedy' clip and its touch of Old World class, in odd contrast to her appearance. Asher smiled as the stranger sitting in the opposite booth quickly looked over his shoulder to see who was talking. Louise, still cracking her gum, never noticed the curious glance as she stood staring intently at Asher.

Louise looked as if she were born to be a waitress in a low-class diner. Her hair color and style changed almost as frequently as her penciled-on eyebrows. Old Dan had called her a character, but he had always said it with a fond smile as if it were a fine compliment.

"You really miss the old man, ayuh." Her opening had the sound of a planned, practiced speech.

"We," she fluttered her hand toward the counter, indicating the girls working there, "knew you'uhd be bahck at least one more time. Like a memorial ta Dan." Her voice caught for a moment before she continued, "We needed you ta come jus once more so's we could say goodbye to 'im too." This time a tear ran slowly down her rouged face,

Scientific American
www.sciam.com/article.cfm?id=magma-on-the-move-beneathMagma
On The Move Beneath Yellowstone
By David Biello

Much of Yellowstone National Park is a giant collapsed volcano, or a caldera. In an enormous eruption roughly 640,000 years ago, this volcano spit out around 240 cubic miles of rock, dirt, magma and other

>

provoking her to quickly turn so the other waitresses would not see. She sounded stressed as she said, "I know t'was his wish not ta have a funeral, but we ahll needed clo-shah."

Louise fidgeted with her apron pockets, pulling her order pad out and flicking her pencil as if waiting to take his order before finally asking, "Do you mind if I join you foh-wah a minute? I know it's not good waitress manners, but yo-wah truck looks loaded, so I guess yo-wah leaving this area, and I wanted to tell you something befo-wah you go." He watched her spit her gum into her hand and fold it into a slip of paper before dropping it into her pocket. She meant to talk.

He had been quietly salting and peppering his eggs as Louise talked, but now Asher smiled and motioned for her to sit. As he spread the napkin in his lap, he politely asked her, "Mind if I eat while you talk?"

Her face registered appreciation for his polite manner. "Gosh, Honey, mah favorite thing in life is watchin' a man eat. So eat up! It will make it easier fo-wah me ta tell you about me'n Dan." She waved her hand for one of her workers to bring her a cup of coffee as she slid into the booth.

Asher had a biscuit half in his mouth, but her statement stopped him mid-chew. "What?"

Glancing down at the napkin in her hand she stammered, "Well, we nevah ... that is he nevah ... it was just I had always hoped." The older woman smiled, lifting her shoulder in a shrug, "You know ... oldah single man comes in ta eat mah food every morning fo-wah seven years, so I naturally hoped, but ... well, anyway, that's not what I was going to tell you."

She reached into her pocket as if to pull out a cigarette but retrieved a pencil instead. "I quit smoking five yeahs ago, and it still drives me crazy not havin' one in mah hands ..."

The coffee arrived. Louise welcomed the distraction and busied

material. Around 70,000 years ago its last eruption filled in that gaping hole with flows of lava. The area has enjoyed an uneasy peace since then, the land alternately rising and falling with the passing decades. New satellite data indicate that this uplift and subsidence is caused by the movement of magma beneath the surface and may explain why the northern edge of the park continues to rise while the southern part of the caldera is falling.

herself with the cup for a few seconds, collecting her thoughts while Asher finished his meal. He pushed aside his plate, then leaned back, picking up his warm cup, cradling it in his big hands as he waited for Louise to say what she obviously needed to tell him.

"I—uh—once I offered ta give 'im some ... comfaht," Shame washed over her as Asher's expression registered shock. She shifted her eyes away. Her raspy cigarette-scarred voice hurriedly continued, "Oh, don't worry. He set me straight on that, ayuh." She waved her hands in the air, fending off the young man's apparent distaste. "I know," she explained, "I know, it was wrong of me; but at the time it was who I was, and he was a nice man, so ... I like ta feed the guys and I, well ... but that is no-what I was tryin' to say!"

Louise looked perturbed with the turn the conversation had taken, as if it were somehow Asher's fault. He calmly raised his hand, casually motioning for a refill of coffee. The girl came immediately. Louise used the interruption to regain her composure.

When they were again alone, she restarted with a rush. "So, anyway, about Dan. You know in all these yeahs, he nevah once forgot ta pray and thank God for his food. Me and the girls ... we watched. No mattah who was in heah, he just prayed right out loud, Muslims or no Muslims ... he paid them no mind and certainly no honor. I know you already know the only time he didn't stuttah was when he prayed."

She set her elbow on the table and brought her right hand up to her mouth, pinching her painted lower lip with her thumb and index finger, a longstanding nervous habit of hers. The woman stared out the window as if seeing the past. "I loved him. I loved him for the good man that he was. I loved him because for the first time in mah life I saw God in somebody. Lawd, I needed ta see God in somebody. I sure have seen enough fake religion in mah time."

He turned towards her reflection in the window and saw that her

Although previous studies had hinted at new magma moving beneath Yellowstone, this represents the first compelling evidence, according to Dzurisin. Such magma movement would also explain recent surface phenomena including new cracks and hot springs as well as the more frequent eruption of Steamboat Geyser. "If you do pressurize or increase the volume of a source [seven miles] deep, you put the ground in tension and that would be conducive to new fractures giving access to the surface for hot waters that previously hadn't had that access," he adds.

>

blue eyes were bright with unshed tears. They stared at each other's reflections in mute, mutual grief.

"When I first came heah, I had been on the streets doin' drugs off and on for over 25 years. He signed me up for rehab at this Christian dry-up house. Then, when I proved to Dan I was off the drugs and had a knack at this kind of work, he gave me a loan, interest free, so I could buy this place from Rosy. Rosy still helps me do the books even though I baht it from her."

She turned from the window, looking straight at Asher with a satisfied look. "Bet you didn't know Dan helped like that, ayuh?"

Asher's eyes twinkled at her assertion. His voice confirmed his amusement. "You're right there; he never told me."

Louise picked up her spoon and stirred her cooling coffee, "He wasn't much of a talkah, but he sho-wah introduced us ta God. All us girls ..."

The old face momentarily collapsed as tears eroded her makeup. She again motioned towards the girls at the counter. Her broken voice was barely audible. "Ahll us."

Asher lifted his eyes to view the counter where four weeping women stood staring at him as if he were the one they wanted to thank. He could feel his throat tighten as he nodded to them. Their tear-streaked faces lightened with smiles, relieved that he now knew how they felt.

In that instant, tension seemed to take hold of Louise. Like a scared child she leaned forward, whispering while staring straight into Asher's eyes, "Just look at me ... not the window ... I see that Arab man outside again. The one that was always watching Dan. I think he's the one that killed Dan. Theys hated Dan's guts."

This new magma does not mean that Yellowstone will erupt again in the near future; much more significant signs such as more earthquakes, more focused ground deformations and the escape of volcanic gases would point to that. But it does point to continued activity at one of the world's largest volcanic systems. "We don't know if the next event will be a continuation of the series of lava flows that filled in the caldera or the beginning of a new cycle that will create a new caldera," Dzurisin says. "Eruptions are far enough apart that there is a very low probability of the next eruption happening in our lifetimes or anytime soon. The flipside is: the system has been active for millions of years and it's going to erupt again sometime." ∞

A strangled, panicky giggle escaped from Louise at the memory of Dan's bold challenge to the local Muslim mosque. Her head turned almost against her will toward where the man stood across the street. "I told Dan he shouldn't oughta keep pushin' theys buttons ... he was just askin' for trouble."

Asher could feel the hairs on the back of his neck stand up at the thought of the danger of the last few weeks. The old man had proven he cared deeply for the Muslim youth by cashing in all his stocks and using the money to finance the translation of the *God's Story* book into the Arabic tongue. Then he had hired a webmaster to create a site with *God's Story* in all five dialects of Arabic. Unhesitatingly, old Dan passed out thousands of business cards in the local school containing the web address where Muslim youth could read the truth. Asher dropped his head as he thought of the many hours the old man had prayed for the Muslim teens that now constituted a substantial minority in the local schools.

Now Dan was dead.

They said it was a gas leak in his kitchen that caused the explosion. The investigators said there was no evidence left to say otherwise.

Yet ...

The old woman's voice broke into his reverie. "I still can't understand why he went into the mosque to preach the gospel. He knew theys was after him, but you know Dan ... he wouldn't stop until evar one of them had heard of the one God and his only Son Jesus." Asher chuckled wryly at the memory of his unstoppable friend. Old man Dan had been a strange mixture of militant and mild. He was as gentle as a soft spring rain to the broken ladies in the diner, yet he would risk

>

all to get the gospel to the emigrant Muslim sect that had taken over their neighborhood.

Louise's whispered voice croaked on. "You know, several months ago Dan told me that I might oughtta consider sellin' out and movin' back east. Us girls ... we've seen that man standing there behind the light post watching Dan. We knew he was scared for us girls." The older woman twisted her hands in distress. "Ayuh, them takin' over this area so fast is awful. Last year this time wahrn't none to be found, and now ..."

Her dramatics caused several of the regulars to turn their heads to look, their troubled faces reflecting their uncertainty in this odd turn of life. Louise was too much in turmoil to notice.

Asher's expression clouded. "It's not going to get better. I think Dan would tell you it would be wise to leave even if you can't sell."

For a long moment the two sat quietly trying to separate what had always been from their new reality. Louise broke the silence with a deep, cleansing breath followed by an unexpected laugh. Surprised by the sudden noise, Asher looked up questioningly. She gently shook her head and smiled sadly as she sat staring down at her hands. "I tell you, when it rains, it po-ahs. Theyah's so much to be scared of, it's plain confusin'. Ayuh ... no use ta cry ovah spilled milk. At least I know what I need ta do. I gotta little stash. Me and tha girls'll be fine."

Asher couldn't help but admire the woman's fortitude, knowing she would start over without complaint. He noticed also that she included the other girls in her plans. She was a survivor; she was a giver. For the first time he could clearly see what Dan had so appreciated in her, not only as a cook but also as a friend.

She had grit.

The two sat in silence, lost in thought, until Louise finally spoke again as if the new troubles were no longer an issue. Her mind had returned to matters of the heart. "We will showly miss him ... both of you.

"I know Dan was intrahsted in the Hmong people over in Thailand gettin' that *God's Story* book. With Dan gone, we figyahd you'd head to the hills of East Tennessee ta be a paht of the The Last Publishahs ministry."

Asher raised his eyebrows.

"Oh, we know ahll about The Last Publishahs. He signed us up ta receive TLP magazines yeahs ago, so we have been readin' all about the diffrahnt translations of that Bible story book he's been givin' out to the Muslim kids. Hey, we ahll figured you would court that gal in the magazine ... now, shc is cute!"

Asher's mind was on memories of Dan. Louise's last statement re-gained his attention. "I'm sorry. I missed that ... what were you saying?"

Louise leaned forward over the table with a silly little girl grin. She lowered her head as if she were about to tell a secret.

"I've been prayin' for that Tennessee girl, Cheyenne, that's a part of the TLP ministry." Louise's face twisted as she winked, then grabbed his hand in delight of the moment. "I think she is the one for you. I really believe she is!"

Asher's tension kept him from smiling. Louise was a good-hearted matchmaker, and she wasn't the only one that had noticed the pictures of Cheyenne. He had noticed them too. Louise was right: she was a beauty. He had found her on www.threadtree.com and corresponded with her after he had decided to move to Tennessee. At least, that had been his excuse to correspond with her.

At that moment a strong protective instinct came over the young man. He wanted to safeguard Louise. He wanted to get her out of this place.

Her soft sigh interrupted his thoughts. "Ayuh, we will showahly miss all the fine hullahbaloo you and Dan managed to bring us, but we will pray for you and the folks at TLP." Then she added teasingly, "I wondah if The Last Publishers might need a cook?"

For a few seconds the young man stared empty-faced at the older woman. Then he stood, taking her hand. He pulled her up and wrapped his big arms around her short chunky frame, rocking her back and forth in his embrace. Finally he kissed the top of her head, and whispered in a voice thick with emotion, "Thank you, Louise. It was good of you to tell me all this. I needed you to tell me. You will be hearing from me. I promise." He felt her patting his back as if he were a child.

Finally he let her go and reached for his wallet, but she put her hand on his wrist, stopping him as she wiped the tears from her face with her other hand. Smiling, she told him, "No charge; the last meal is free. But, son, you fawght to thank God for yo-wah salmon egg benedict. With you headin' ta Tennessee, it will probably be the last one you will eat for a wicked long time. Old Dan's probably fussin' up a storm about you not thankin' God."

Asher studied the shadows before stepping out of the diner. The middle eastern man that was following him had gone or had slipped deeper into the shadows. The city street light shone dimly. He kicked the tires, checking one last time for air, and then wiggled the clamps holding the small camper to the frame of the dually four-wheel drive F-350.

Asher's unease returned as he looked around. He was tired of watching the shadows and wondering if he would be the next victim, weary of setting alarms to ensure his safety. The thought of living in quiet, rural Tennessee made him sigh with relief.

A recipe for Salmon Egg Benedict can be found in the back of this book. ✆

2

OUR LITTLE MARY, SATURDAY, ONE YEAR EARLIER

An elderly couple sat down to Sunday supper. They quietly bowed their greyed heads to give thanks to God for their dinner of fresh baked trout and wheat rolls. The little garden that Mary tended had provided them a nice salad and herbs for hot tea. In spite of the delectable fare, neither of them were very hungry. With the passing of years, their bodies weary, food no longer seemed important.

Henry looked up at his sweetheart. "Darlin', let's go out tonight. I know these old eyes don't do well after dark, but God will help us, and we'll stay on familiar roads." He patted her hand and gave her a reassuring wink.

Mary smiled and asked in her sweet, delicate voice, "That sounds so nice, Henry, but where are we to go?"

Henry hesitated. His love for her was as deep as the ocean. Tenderly he said, "Mary, dear, somewhere out on the street this evening there is another Mary who needs our prayers. I know we promised to place the past behind us and never mention it, but so often I think of how your dear grandmother prayed for you. I remember how God miraculously pulled you out of the miry pit of sin. Well," he squeezed her hand, "to-night I feel that God has revealed to me that there is a little Mary out on the streets that needs our prayers. We're going to find her. Although we don't know her, I believe God will guide us to the right one. To-night it's her turn for someone to pray."

Mary flushed; even after 62 years, the regret she felt for her youthful sins still brought shame. "Oh, Henry, I'm so ashamed. I do want to help some other little girl before I die." The old woman's head dropped and her voice now was barely audible, "I should have been out helping wayward girls my whole life … it's just such a shameful thing. My self-reproach has held me captive all these years." She blinked back tears and sat up straight, taking on a no-nonsense air. "Oh Henry, I think regret is the ugliest, most debilitating word in the English language. I know it will be erased when we are in the presence of our Lord." The old woman stood; her aged hands rested on the table. "I'll not waste any more time with regrets. I'll put the dishes away later."

Henry blinked. He looked at the food still on the table, marveling that a lifelong habit of cleaning up first, regardless of the circumstances, was finally to be broken. "We've got a more important clean up job tonight, right, Mary dear?"

She gently smiled her answer.

That first evening, Henry and Mary found a quiet place to park their ancient black car in the shadows in a very run down section of town. Across the street girls paraded their wares, waiting to be picked up by men. A very young, childlike girl with very long pale hair stepped up to the curb. "That's our little Mary." Henry spoke softly, "I wonder what her real name is? No matter. God knows. We can call her our little Mary."

Henry's dear Mary began to pray as tears rolled down her lined face. She prayed for the young girl, knowing as if it were yesterday all of the pain, shame, and sorrow that her path brought. With those terrible memories came an overwhelming thankfulness of knowing her sins were forgiven.

"Merciful God! Redeem this poor child for your own! Reach down your loving hands and snatch her from the hell she is making for herself. Prepare your people to love her as their own. God, merciful, loving, forgiving Savior, save this wretched little Mary who now stands on the street of Sodom."

John 15:7 "If ye abide in me, and my words abide in you, ye shall ask what ye will, and it shall be done unto you." ∽

3

ASHER, SATURDAY, APRIL 5TH, 6:40 A.M.

Four young fawns jostled together, trying to nurse from one mother doe as she moved slowly to the edge of the valley floor still deep in the early morning shadows. The overtaxed doe frantically snatched at the dew drenched grass, racing the morning sun that was soon to steal over the high eastern ridge, spreading its glorious, warming light over the land. With the dawn, she would move her adopted fawns deep into the woods to sleep through the day. Asher stood riveted to the magnificent scene from 300 yards up the ridge on the far side of Malachi Freeman's property where The Last Publishers ministry resided.

Two years earlier there was a terrible drought in East Tennessee which stressed nature, but the 'blue tongue fly' had flourished, descending on the deer population, crawling into and biting their ears. This spread a disease called Blue Tongue from deer to deer. Until autumn that year the springs and creeks had been full of dead deer, trying in vain to quench their thirst. Over 40% of the deer population had perished in East Tennessee.

Asher briskly rubbed his hands together for warmth, then ran his hands over the stubble of his day old beard as he scanned the ridge top for the first golden rays. The mama deer silently shepherded her adopted fawns into the shadows. The show was over.

Blue-tongue Fly Disease is a viral hemorrhagic disease of domestic and wild ruminants that can be transmitted by insects known as midges.

www.ncwildlife.org   www.mainehuntingtoday.com ∽

In one smooth movement Asher placed the binoculars his brother had sent him from Israel into its pouch and stood to his feet, stretching. Reaching up, he removed his worn leather hat, revealing a thick shock of red hair. He wiped the moisture from his forehead with his sleeve and set his hat back in place. With a small notepad and a pencil stub he carefully marked the count he was keeping for the local Fish and Game Department. He grinned as he tallied his results.

He softly cheered, "Go, Mama, go." The sound of his deep bass voice spilled out into the shadowy pre-morning chill. He was still grinning as he leaned his body back against the ancient oak tree, the sole of his big boot up against the trunk and his face turned skyward.

Tracing the high ridge to the east, he could see the golden flecks of dawn beaming like jewels as the first rays peeked over the top of the tree line and glimmered off the leaves. As the moments passed, he watched the shimmering grow in dazzling brilliance. The first penetrating light spilled over the rim. A gentle breeze stirred the new poplar leaves. The hilltop fluttered with dancing sounds and trembling shadows. Asher's face was toward the light as he worshipped his Creator. "God, Father, how great and mighty is your name."

Asher's spirit quickened; his pulse raced. He faltered. Old tensions of being watched, of living in a world of fear, came flooding down on him. His voice became urgent as he questioned, "God, what is it?"

The young man tensed. Retrieving the binoculars from the pouch, he again scanned the area for any possible change. Standing almost at the northernmost point of the west side of the long, horseshoe shaped ridge, he could look over more than half of the twenty-seven acre valley. The old farmhouse where Malachi and Hope Freeman lived was partly visible, perched high on the side of the ridge; the TLP Ministry offices and warehouses lay deep in the valley, out of view. Other than the absent deer, nothing had changed from the last hour.

Asher turned his back to the farmhouse. He gazed due north out of the valley, studying the narrow entrance. The gravel road lay undisturbed. Not even the smallest dust cloud billowed. Closing his eyes,

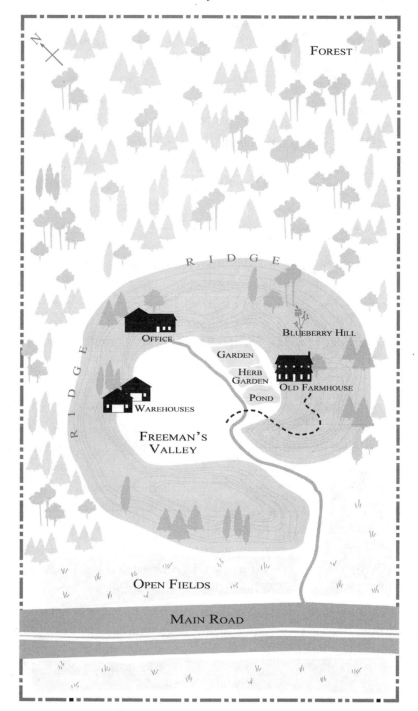

he swept the air with his nose, sniffing for smoke, checking for a forest fire, but he caught only a brief wood stove odor so familiar to this area. Putting the binoculars to his eyes again, he slowly surveyed the top of the ridge.

His brows knit with concern as he contemplated. Nothing seemed out of order. It was a nice, quiet Saturday morning. No one was at The Last Publishers' warehouse. He had watched the headlights of Malachi Freeman's car as he left for his prison ministry some twenty minutes earlier. Asher felt his heart race as his mind fastened on Malachi's youngest daughter.

PROTECT HER – "God, don't let anything happen to her." He shook his head, trying to throw off the anxiety. He wondered if his agitation didn't come from his preoccupation over that lovely young woman. He grinned. That girl always made his heart beat fast.

Again he felt an undeniable apprehension as if it came on the wind. The young man lifted his hat and bowed his head.

"What is it, Lord?"

Some of the urgency dissipated as he stood quietly scanning the wooded valley. Except for the distant sound of a small barking dog, the valley seemed to be sleeping. Returning his hat to his head, he yet again examined the valley through his binoculars, swinging in a widening circle. Following the road that entered the valley, Asher studied the rickety wooden bridge at the northernmost edge of the Freemans' property.

An involuntary smile stole across his face when he caught the distant sound of grinding gears complaining about their misuse. He watched, transfixed, as the ancient pink panel truck rattled across the wooden bridge, dislodging bits of dirt which fell splashing into the creek below. He chuckled with pleasure, feeling again his heart race. "Well, Cheyenne's come to visit her mama. Can't miss that girl's ridiculous huge pink panel truck.

"Oh, but Lord," his mouth went dry as he continued his prayer, "that gal is fine! She is mighty, MIGHTY fine."

The brief thrill of the moment was stolen as the troubling, urgent sense of danger washed over him again. This time the intensity of the alarm took hold of him with a tremor. Never in all the time he had lived in Seattle had such a sure sense of dread filled his being, not even when he and Dan were being stalked by Muslims.

A cold sweat prickled onto his brow. "God, protect her. God, help me see what evil is present so I can protect her. What is going on? Why do I feel like something terrible is about to happen? God, please take care of Cheyenne and her mama this morning, and Malachi as he travels to prison."

Asher remained in a posture of prayer, expecting direction from God. None came. "Lord, I sure would like to know now what is going on and what I need to do. Well, Lord, since I never had anything like this happen to me before, and since I have no idea what it means beyond making me alert to evil, I believe you want me to check out the woods on these ridges. God, cause me to be keen and alert to your will."

Asher reached down with practiced ease and extracted the .38 stub-nose pistol Dan had left him. He quickly checked its load and replaced it into his ankle holster before he began walking a wide loop across the high, rough ridge that rimmed the valley.

As he walked, he continued to pray, focusing on Cheyenne. "Keep her safe, Lord. I'm asking, Lord, keep that sweet girl safe." He urged with unguarded emotion, "Please, God."

4

CHEYENNE, 6:49 A.M.

Cheyenne Freeman was full of delight as her truck approached the old bridge that led into the Freeman's property. "Whew! I love my new truck." She patted the truck's dashboard, talking to it as if it were a new friend she wanted to reassure. "Everybody loves you, even Asher. He just has a problem with pink ... Pinky ... yes!" She roared above the truck's rumbling noise. "I'll call you Pinky! Wow! We are sooooo cool!"

Her brows knitted as she tried shifting again, ignoring the rattle of some just-loosened part. At the bottom of the steep drive, the panel truck jerked to a sudden halt. Slumping in her seat, she considered trying the 200 foot incline. "Nope," She muttered to herself. "Not today. I'll walk." She gracefully exited the vehicle and confidently loped up the steep drive. The hope of finding true love, the joy of being alive, and youthful hormones pulsed through her body. On impulse, she screamed with pleasure as she ran, announcing her arrival to her mother.

Lustful, beady eyes drank in the young woman's form.

She had no clue.

"Mom! M-O-O-O-M! Where are you?" Cheyenne called out as she walked to the back door of the house.

"Down here in the lab. Come on in, Shy," Hope's muffled reply drifted up from the basement.

The younger woman smiled at her childhood nickname. She lithely navigated the steps and found her mama in the basement lab.

Hope was garbed in her customary long bohemian dress, her gray-streaked, dark hair hanging loosely braided down her back. Huddled over a table full of dried berries and jars of foamy liquid brews, Hope looked just like what she was, a classic flower-child of the 60s with dominant Indian ancestry.

In contrast, Cheyenne was what her mama called a "newfangled" flower child. She was a riot of color with a bright orange silk scarf tied around the top of her head and a haphazard assortment of clothes finishing out her attire. She looked both artistic and trendy without any conscious effort.

Cheyenne's Indian heritage was easily seen in her features. Small children that had seen animated movies about Pocahontas sometimes mistook Cheyenne for a living, breathing version of the Indian maiden.

Her mama's greeting was a predictable tease: "How's your boyfriend? Planning on getting married yet?"

Cheyenne grinned and shook her head at the affectionate gibe. "You never give up, do you? Here I am, 22 years old and still unmarried!" In mock alarm Cheyenne raised her eyebrows and opened her eyes wide as she reached over to poke her mother in the ribs. Hope hopped beyond her reach and chuckled as her daughter continued, "Anyways, if you're referring to TLP's newest staff member, don't hold your breath waiting for him to take me off of your hands. Asher doesn't seem to know females exist ... at least not me. Anyway, I came for more important business than my loveless life." Cheyenne tried to make it sound like a jest, but the frustration in her tone did not escape Hope's notice.

"Let's get busy." Hope smiled and continued setting out herbs, berry mash, and work papers on the lab table. Then, as she handed a jar to Cheyenne, she responded thoughtfully to her daughter's unspoken plea.

"You know, Shy, nothing is more important than love." She cast a sidelong glance at Cheyenne and winked, "Take it from a love mama." Then she turned to her computer. "Besides ... he knows. He's just trying hard to resist." Hope leaned closer and squinted at the computer screen.

Cheyenne tried to change the subject. Moaning dramatically, she exclaimed, "Oh, Mom! Where are your glasses? You are so stubborn! Start using your own brew, for crying out loud! It fixed Dad's eyesight."

Glancing outside, Cheyenne asked, "What's wrong with Wiggles? She didn't follow me inside, and she's barking like she's having some sort of a fit. What's on the ridge that's got her attention?"

Hope dismissed her question with a wave. "Ah. Who knows? Let's keep her out. We have too much to do to listen to her yapping. She's been after something all morning."

✍

EAVESDROPPER – Hidden on the slope behind the old farmhouse, the rotund man sat snickering to himself as he adjusted his listening device. "Those dumb women should listen to their doggy. They might learn something."

Sticking his ear plugs deeper into his ears, he exhaled his malevolent intentions. "Okay, Hopey-Dopey, just say where you keep your stash of miracle cure so I can get what I need to be the man again … yeah, and do your little girl. Hurry it up and say where the stuff is. I just might be gentle with her. Naw. On second thought, it ain't fun without the screams."

THE LAB, 8:10 A.M. – Cheyenne's chair squeaked in protest as she leaned back from the computer, yawning. She looked around the lab with interest. The recently cleared surfaces revealed their treasures. "This place has always been such a mess, no one would really notice how well equipped it is," Hope commented as she placed two heavy jars of berry mash on the table and prepared for the second phase of the morning's work.

Cheyenne stood and walked around the lab, running her hands

Bio-Medicine - Pomegranate juice may cut atherosclerosis risk in diabetics.

An Israeli study has revealed that the risk of atherosclerosis in diabetics may be decreased by drinking pomegranate juice. This condition is characterized by thickening and hardening of artery walls. 80% of the diabetics who die are affected by atherosclerosis.

This study, conducted by researchers at the Technion-Israel Institute of Technology revealed that there was a decrease in the risk of developing atherosclerosis in people who drank 180 ml (6 oz.) of pomegranate juice daily for a period of 90 days.

across the stainless steel work table and countertop, then over the different culture boxes. "It's a real science lab in here," she said, glancing at the tall locked cabinets and computerized testing units. "Of course, your microscope is kinda old, but at least it's mounted on its very own table. I love your willow baskets of dried herbs and flowers hanging from the ceiling. It makes the place smell like the earth. But," she wrinkled her nose, "those tiny colored dropper bottles with the weird shapes, all lined up on that shelf, give the place the air of a witches' den."

Hope scowled at the comment. Cheyenne quickly explained, "It's just the way books and films portray herb stuff, with bottles holding the magical brews. Anyways, this place is like new tech mixed with old herbal medicine … so weirdly cool."

Cheyenne reminisced, "For as long as I can remember, it seems I've been mixing herbs and making potions. When the other kids were coloring, I was doing research on toxic substances found on the backs of frogs in the Amazon. How did I get so weird?"

"It's in your blood. My side of the family," Hope offered, while locating the notebook to record their findings. "Grab that paper. It has a list of all the berries we will need for this morning's brew. Get going, girl. We've gotta lotta work to do before Malachi gets back from preaching at the prison."

When they were finished, Cheyenne reviewed the process her mama had just taught her while, wiping the splattered remains of the mixed berries from the stainless steel table. Once she was satisfied that she had memorized the berry lesson, she began updating her mother on the China shipments.

"Man alive! Here we are taking so much time and effort, making one lousy gallon of the brew, and over in China they are making millions of containers of this stuff. Wow! I have been so busy with the busi-

The uptake of oxidized LDL or "bad" cholesterol by immune cells called macrophages helps in the development of atherosclerosis. Pomegranate juice seems to prevent this uptake.

According to the lead researcher Professor Michael Aviram of the Technion Faculty of Medicine, though the sugars present in pomegranate juice were similar to those found in other fruit juices, these sugars did not aggravate diabetes.

>

HOPE &
CHEYENNE

ness end … phew wee! Anyways, can you imagine ordering container loads of berries a whole year ahead? I'm literally spending hundreds of thousands of dollars of other people's money with one purchase! Yikes! Herbs I know … but business? Now, that's a strain."

Cheyenne paused from pouring the mashed berries they had just mixed into the gallon jug. "Which is the recipe that Dad and Cohen are using?" She thrust her hand into the crock and began massaging the berry mash while listening to her mother detail the properties of the different brews. She stopped her work, distressed. "Are you sure the recipe that we are using at the China plant is going to work as well as the one Dad's using?"

Hope chuckled at Cheyenne's concern. "Relax, kid. The China brew will work fine. It does lose some potency in the mass production techniques, but it is good … real good. It's a slower cure, dependent

"In most juices, sugars are present in free – and harmful – forms," said Aviram. "In pomegranate juice, however, the sugars are attached to unique antioxidants, which actually make these sugars protective against atherosclerosis."

Though this study was conducted on a small-scale, with only 20 participants, it is a part of a bigger proposal investigating the effects of pomegranates on cholesterol oxidation and cardiovascular diseases.

DEREK, THE EAVESDROPPER

on a person's adherence to natural foods, and it will need to be taken daily to maintain healing. That will guarantee regular sales."

Hope looked up into her daughter's face and spoke with confidence. "It will be the most amazing cure the world has seen since the Garden of Eden's Tree of Life. Yeah, our brew will rock pharmaceutical companies, and that's a fact. It ain't sugar water, that's for sure."

PRETTY GOOD, 7:40 A.M. – The Eavesdropper gave a soft whistle as he listened to Hope outline the properties of the brew. "That's pretty good, Hopey-Dopey. So this is why the judge is working so hard to take control."

Whispering, he sneered his mockery. "Can't have a bunch of Jews who pretend to be Christians getting filthy rich. Boy, has the Brotherhood got a surprise coming for you clueless dummies."

"The judge won't mind if I help myself to Hope's private stash. The old man knows my arthritis has been acting up. He'll understand. And

The antioxidant and anti-atherosclerotic benefits of licorice, olive oil, onions and pomegranates have already been worked upon by Aviram and also has published his findings. He was the first to prove inhibition of cholesterol oxidation and arteriosclerosis by consumption of red wine.

Decrease in risk of Alzheimer's disease, prostate cancer and heart disease by consuming pomegranate juice has already been proved in previous studies.

>

he won't care what happens to that hot little squaw."

As if sensing the man's intent, the dog renewed her barking. Annoyed, he called sweetly to the dog in an urgent whisper while offering a bit of pastry in his extended hand. Then, to himself, "I ain't waiting for no China brew. I'm counting on you, Hopey-Dopey; tell me where you keep your old man's stash. I need a cure now. I need it today."

LIFE FORCE, 7:40 A.M. – "Mom?" Cheyenne's tone was pensive. "The Chinese chemists that work for Cohen, won't they be able to figure out we have something much more than just another health food tincture? What's to keep them from selling the recipe to some mega company? Or even using it to promote their nationalistic agenda?"

Hope twisted her lips sideways as she considered Cheyenne's words. A knowing gleam formed in her eyes as she tried to put the knowledge into words. "There's a life force in the DNA that has not been identified. Scientists have done reverse engineering to replicate a simple rice seed, making the laboratory created version indistinguishable from the ones God makes, yet the laboratory grain will not grow. It lacks life— whatever that is. It's the combination of herbs and berries that gives us the edge. Somehow, I think by the will of God, we have happened upon a combination that closely approximates the properties of the Tree of Life." Hope's hand reached out and touched an herb pack and a berry pack with her extended fingers. It's not only the combination; it's the process we employ that causes a chemical reaction, producing an entirely new substance."

Cheyenne's eyes took on a look of otherworldliness. "I still can't believe all this is happening. I know, I know, I've said it a hundred times, but it's just so ... I mean, who would think that you would figure out something so completely healing, the perfect rejuvenator?" She

The current study is published in the August 2006 issue of Atherosclerosis.

www.bio-medicine.org/medicine-news/Pomegranate-juice-may-cut-atherosclerosis-risk-in-diabetics-15061-1/ ∽

plopped back into her chair. The chair's squeak seemed to emphasize her growing excitement.

"It is surreal." Hope shook her head, chuckling as she reinserted her berry stained hand into the crock. "All the time I was working on developing the brew, I kept thinking about that verse in I Corinthians 1:27, *'But God hath chosen the foolish things of the world to confound the wise; and God hath chosen the weak things of the world to confound the things which are mighty.'* God sure has a sense of humor."

Cheyenne's eyes twinkled as she studied her mom's berry stained face, shaking her head with the wonder of it all.

WHICH WAY? 7:50 A.M. – The icy clear water of the Freemans' farthest spring trickled past Asher's feet. His mind replayed Dusty's graphic story of the six rotting deer carcasses found lying there the year before. They had contaminated the spring runoff.

Suddenly and unbidden, a vivid memory of the bombed-out Spanish church just two blocks down from Louise's diner flooded his mind and soul. The strong jaw clenched with anger and repulsion as the memories of the odor of scorched human flesh assailed him. Americans were not as proficient at gathering up the scattered remains as were the Israelis. "God Almighty, there's going to be a judgment! God ... I'm glad."

Asher knelt to drink from the water and then, every sense alert, he stood, still trembling with the need to have a hand in justice. He tried to regain his peace by taking a few deep gulps of sweet Tennessee air. Placing his hands high up on the smooth surface of a huge hollow beech tree, he prayed, "Okay, Lord, which way? Up the ridge? Yes?" He scooped his hat from the ground, pressed it firmly on his head. "Keep her safe, Lord ... just keep her safe."

HOPE'S DREAMS COME TRUE, 7:50 A.M. – Hope wiped the freshly filled jar with an old T-shirt. Her eyes glistened with gratitude as she finished the long narrative she had been carrying on with her daughter as they worked. "Just think, Shy, with the *God's Story* book a person can quickly understand the history of God's systematic program—past, present, and future. In one year, if things go as planned with the brew, we will have the gospel story on the web in every major language on earth." Cheyenne could feel the joy radiating from her mother. "And now, guess what your Dad has on his heart?" Hope's tear-choked voice cackled with delight. "He is asking other mission groups to take languages so he will be able to prioritize our outreach to the Muslims." Hope paused, lost in thought.

At the mention of Muslims, Cheyenne's knees felt weak. A cold shudder shook her insides. She looked down at her hands, trying to hide her dread. Daily there was news of bombings, personal assaults, and even poisoning from the hands of Muslim terrorists. Muslims were now focusing more of their attacks on churches and prominent Christians. Certainly this was nothing new. It had been happening all over the world; it was just new to America.

This wasn't just a faceless fear. This fear struck Cheyenne in a much more personal way.

She hadn't told anyone except Bobbie Jo. For the last three weeks she had noticed an Arabic looking man hanging around. He seemed to be watching her local store, the Herb Den. Now, with her parents on the verge of spreading the gospel to the entire Muslim world in their own language ... it was tantamount to a death sentence.

Death sentence ... those were the very words Asher had used.

He had laughed as he told them of all the different ways Dan had managed to give hundreds of *God's Story* books to Muslim kids. That was in English. It will be another matter when the books start showing up in Muslim countries in the Arabic language.

And now Dan was dead.

Asher said he was sure Muslims had killed his friend. Cheyenne's hands jerked in nervous reaction as her spirit immediately reached out to God. *Oh God ... Why is the Arabic man watching my Herb Den? Could any of this be connected? No ... no! Not possible in Hicksville.* She smirked at the community nickname. Taking a deep breath, she tried to reassure herself. Just this past week Main Street Market changed hands. It now was owned and run by a Saudi family. Cheyenne's breath came in shallow gulps as she remembered the Muslim men who sat around a table at the back of the store, watching her as she walked in for a purchase. She hadn't been back. Driving 15 miles for gas was not practical, but it was what had to be done.

I'm just getting paranoid.

Hope was unaware of her daughter's disquiet. She was lost in her own thoughts. Hope shared Malachi's vision of the impossible. "Your daddy wants to reach the whole Muslim world," she told Cheyenne. "We can make it happen. It will take a lot of money, but we'll have that when the brew hits the market. Asher says that by using the internet it won't take us near as much money as what we originally thought. He calls it smart publishing."

In a fraction of a second Hope's face went from rapture to knotted in concentration as she moved the jars to the end of the table. "But we still need to make this brew business work."

A thoughtful Cheyenne stood wiping a jar, trying to still her fear and focus on her parents' dream. Her mother had always picked up and run with any ideas Malachi had, and she had slaved to make his vision a reality. Now listening to her mother's depth of emotion stirred deep yearnings within her.

Hope continued chattering excitedly about Malachi's plans. Cheyenne abruptly interrupted with her own line of thought. "Love can make people bigger, stronger and better than anything else in the whole world."

Hope's arms dropped from the shelf where she had been reaching for a heavy crock. She turned to look at her daughter with studied puzzlement, wondering why she didn't seem as enthused about this glorious vision.

"What's stuck in yer craw, girl?" Hope's country slang underlined her concern over her daughter's shift in mood.

Cheyenne forced a smile and offered a lighthearted response as she walked three steps to the cabinet where Hope stood. "Here, let me help you, Small Fry." Stretching her long thin frame over her mother's shorter one, she responded, "What's stuck in yer craw? Don't you know we were talking about love?"

Hope's confused expression caused Cheyenne to laugh and throw her arms around her mom. "I just got to thinking of you and Dad. Because you loved him so much, you researched to discover what would make him healthy. If he had died, *God's Story* would never have been finished, and none of this would be happening. But love drove you to learn all you could to help him."

Heat flooded Cheyenne's face as a sudden memory of Asher grabbing her hand the night before provoked a surge of tingling in her limbs. It had only been to pull her out of the chair after a game of cards, but she knew he had felt the surge of what felt like electricity. A giggle spilled out as she squeezed her mom with an urgent hug. "Oh, Mama, please pray God will give me love like you've had!"

Hope chuckled. "And soon!"

Cheyenne picked up a berry stained rag and began nervously twisting it as she toyed with the idea of telling her mom about the Arabic looking man who was watching the Herb Den. Her tension was not lost on Hope.

After a few strained, silent minutes her trepidations tumbled out.

"Mom, I need to know … will there be time for me to have what you and Dad have had? There's just so much bad stuff going on, like the Muslims bombing everything and everybody. Will I have time to enjoy being loved and loving like you and Dad have?"

The happiness that had brightened Hope's countenance when they spoke of reaching the Muslims was now displaced by lines of uncertainty. "I don't know, Shy. I just don't know."

COMMITTED, 8:55 A.M. – Asher rubbed his shirt sleeve across his sweaty brow. "Lord, Tennessee is hot and humid." As he looked out over the valley, his eyes were repeatedly drawn to Cheyenne's pink truck. The color seemed to bleed through the trees. His pulse quickened, making him shake his head, almost frustrated at his need. "Just a glimpse of that silly pink color gets me every time.

"Lord, you know I would love to have that woman. God, just to hold her in my arms, talk to her, watch her expressions change. God, is it just a selfish dream? I know the Scripture says a married man must care of the things of the world, how he may please his wife, and a single man cares for the things of God. Lord God, I have committed myself to seeing that the gospel is published to every tribe and nation. Lord, I know that with a wife comes a baby carriage. Those things would slow me down, but, God, I really would like to have a good wife. God, you know my heart. If I need to stay single, so be it. But, Lord, that gal... it's getting harder and harder to resist her." Smiling as he breathed in a deep shaky breath, he threw his head back and shouted into the morning stillness, "LOVE TO HAVE THAT WOMAN!"

SUSPICIONS, 8:57 A.M. – Bored with the women's conversation, the fat man jerked the earpieces from his head. He opened his thermos and poured a fresh cup of cappuccino as he studied the small dog, trying to decide how best to silence it. The sound of a distant, echoing shout caused him to jerk upright. The cup spilled hot cappuccino over his groin and leg. "Damnation!" he cried, jumping up from his seat. "Who in blazes is in the woods?" The fat man pulled at his hot, wet pants, trying to cool his burning skin.

He listened in quiet tension for a long thirty seconds. Nothing. He pulled his ear lobe. Maybe the bad ear was making those strange sounds again.

He grunted, relieved by his own reasoning, and reinserted the earpieces.

The skittish eavesdropper held a heavy Colt .45 pistol, his arm extended, playfully sighting on the small dog, "Bang, bang," he whispered. "I bet your guts would fly all over that tree." He snickered at the mental image.

His attention wandered as the small dog cautiously approached him. When the animal was almost within arm's reach, the eavesdropper lay the gun aside and extended his hand with a donut. He spoke in quiet, high-pitched, silly baby-talk, "Doggy, would like my donut, wouldn't Doggy? Well, come closer, you noisy nuisance."

His eyes flashed with hostility as he watched the reluctant dog. With his other hand, he crammed the remains of a cream-filled donut into his mouth. He pushed the mass to one side with his tongue so he could chew as he continued to coax the dog.

He leaned over his big belly to extend the hand holding the tempting morsel closer to the dog. With his weight shift, the thin leg of the tripod stool dug steeply into the soft dirt. The unstable stool tipped forward. He struggled to regain his balance, spilling the rest of his drink.

The loss of balance and the hot drink on his hand caused him to inhale sharply. Particles of gobbled donut blocked his airway, and he began to choke. Donut spewed forth. Wiping his spoiled hands across the front of his shirt, his rage overcoming his caution, with a roar, he let go a string of cursings. "D#&# you! You old hag. Just say where the brew is!"

Having played out his anger over his lost sweets, he looked down at the partially chewed donut lying in the leaves at his feet. His eyebrows knotted together in sullenness as he wondered if that was the spot where he had relieved himself minutes earlier. "What the heck," he said, picking up a piece of the leaf covered sweet cream and flicking off bits of crud before stuffing it back into his mouth. *Blankety blank dog made me do it. Now I'm really mad.*

ALARM, 9:46 A.M. – Up on the opposite ridge, Asher had just come to a stop. Faintly, but clearly, a man's muffled, angry voice broke through the silence. Asher's back tensed in surprise. He tried to decipher where the voice had come from … but couldn't. He scanned the distant ridge with his binoculars. Nothing. "God, what is it? Where? God, I am not seeing the problem. I need your help and direction."

SEVEN WOMEN, ONE MAN, 9:55 A.M. – For the last three hours Hope had methodically shared vital berry and herbal information with her youngest daughter. "Of course," she explained, "most of the information I've used to make the brew came from several brilliant Israeli biochemists who have been working on an eternal youth brew for the last seven years."

Cheyenne stopped tapping at the keyboard where she had been taking notes. "So if a lot of your research information came from Israel, and the best berries are found there, why haven't they come up with a brew that can bring healing like the one you have?"

"Good question." Hope considered the possibility. "Who's to say they haven't? They have the added advantage of being in the part of the world where the Garden of Eden was located, which is where the Tree of Life once grew. There could be seeds or even a tree still growing that no one has discovered. Did you know that seeds have been found in tombs that are thousands of years old and still able to be sprouted?"

The young woman was shaking her head in disbelief. "No … I can't believe the Tree of Life could still be here on earth. God kicked Adam and Eve out of the garden to keep them from eating, and … well, it doesn't say it was removed from the earth. But it is too fantastic to believe."

"Why not?" Hope challenged. "I have pestered Malachi to take me to northern Iraq so I could nose around. I almost think I could recognize it, because I would know how the leaves would smell. I have worked with so many healing herbs, you just get where you know healing chemistry by the smell." The old eyes stared transfixed as she considered the possibility of such a discovery, then shrugged her shoulders in defeat. "One of the Israeli researchers wrote that he had sent a team of young workers to look for every tree they could find, so obviously he thinks it's a possibility."

Cheyenne, still looked unbelieving, "Mom, do you really believe God would allow sinful man to have access to the Tree of Life before the Millennium?"

"You are probably right, Shy, but at least we have a blend that in some small measure approximates the healing power of the Tree of Life. I bet the Jewish scientists have what we have, at the very least. You know the Israelis. They are always two steps ahead of the rest of the world in so many areas. They must … in order to survive.

"Besides," Hope continued, "if they did have something as life-giving as what I've found, why should they give it away? Most of the world wants to blow them to smithereens. Why let their enemies know about something that is guaranteed to keep them alive and healthy? Good health is the most valued treasure, far greater than oil.

"Yeah." Hope pushed her glasses higher on the bridge of her nose. "A miracle healing tonic could force the rest of the world to leave Israel alone, as a condition to obtaining a concoction that could impart perpetual health, one small dropperful at a time."

Cheyenne gasped. "Sheeeeesh, Mom … you've got a point! What earthly treasure could exceed the value of perfect health? What good is oil or riches or power if you know your only child has cancer or if you knew you were developing Alzheimer's? Imagine that celebrity with all that wealth—what was her name, Opal?—and cancer in her brain and jaw. What wouldn't she give to be healed?"

Hope's active imagination shifted into overdrive, causing her to clap her hands together as she conjured up the possibilities. "Maybe the Israelis have a brew and are planning to keep it for their own people when they are attacked, because it's certain they will be attacked again. The brew sure would come in handy if someone used some weird biological toxin or disease, like those prophesied in Scripture, to terrorize the world."

Cheyenne's head turned quickly toward her mother. "Where is that prophecy? I've heard Dad speak of it."

Hope moved to the computer keyboard and leaned over her daugh-

Isaiah 4:1-6 "And in that day seven women shall take hold of one man, saying, We will eat our own bread, and wear our own apparel: only let us be called by thy name, to take away our reproach. In that day shall the branch of the LORD be beautiful and glorious, and the fruit of the earth shall be excellent and comely for them that are escaped of Israel." *www.nogreaterjoy.org*

ter to open the Bible program to the book of Isaiah. "Well, Revelation speaks of seven different vials, which when poured out produce the seven last plagues." She looked meaningfully at the vials of brew set aside for later analyses. "Vial is an appropriate word. All of the vials are poured out during the Tribulation, when we will be gone."

Hope tapped the computer screen to emphasize her point. "But before those Tribulation plagues come to pass, there seem to be other weird diseases prophesied to occur."

The young girl quickly scanned the Scripture that was on the screen while her mother continued to talk. "Some of the more religious Jews believe the second half of Isaiah 28 indicates there will be a scourge over a good portion of the world that seems to sicken mostly just the male population, but will not touch the Israeli men. Kinda like what happened when all the firstborn males of Egypt died, but the destroyer passed over the Jews, leaving them alive. Two times God calls it his strange act. In verse 22, it's '*a consumption, even determined upon the whole earth.*'"

Cheyenne stopped her mother. "Consumption ... that's like tuberculosis, right? But how could a disease hit all the men of the world and not Jewish men? And how could it hit only males?"

Hope nodded. "How indeed? Hormones could be the key factor that causes a disease to affect only the male population. As far as not hitting Jewish men, it is my theory that blood type has something to do with it. Unlike the rest of the world's population, many Jews are B-positive, especially those from Germany. Different blood types have certain strengths and weaknesses. It is known that B-positive has stronger immune properties, which would protect against strange diseases. On the other hand, there is the possibility that the berry brew is the deciding factor in the survival of the Jewish males. It is possible that the Jews will have the berry brew readily available to them. Maybe it's both the blood type and the brew that helps them survive. Anyway, according to verse 19, this consumption kills in one day. There appears to be so much death and blood that it takes a flood to cleanse the land."

"Does it say why God sends this plague?" Cheyenne asked.

Hope bit the inside of her cheek, trying to remember what Malachi had taught her. "The Scripture suggests that it has something to do with a covenant or agreement between two political groups that decide to take over Jerusalem. God says this covenant will be disannulled due to the overflowing scourge."

"Yikes." Cheyenne shuddered. "Someone needs to tell our president that it might be wiser to leave Jerusalem alone."

Hope's nose was close to the computer, reading over her daughter's shoulder. Her voice took on excitement. "Hey, here it is; look at this. Isaiah chapter 4 talks about seven women taking hold of one man. I love how the words are strung together."

Cheyenne giggled at her mom's enthusiasm as she leaned over to read. "'And in that day seven women shall take hold of one man, saying, We will eat our own bread, and wear our own apparel: only let us be called by thy name, to take away our reproach.'"

"So ... most of the men are dead? That leaves a lot of women to fend for themselves. Without men, they won't be able to have children. That means the lady who has a man and children will be special. But it also sounds like the ladies without husbands are begging the men to become polygamists. It would take a while for the shortage of men to cause women to get that desperate, so there must be a good period of time between the plague and these events."

Hope nodded. "That's a good point. There would have to be a year or more for women to get over the horror of the plague and wish for children and a normal life. See? There are only six verses in that whole chapter. The second verse says the branch of the Lord is beautiful, glorious, and excellent. If there was some weird disease that targeted men globally, sparing the Israeli men by way of the brew, then Israel would be the only place on earth that was not filled with dead bodies. Verse 3 says, 'he that is left in Zion, and he that remaineth in Jerusalem, shall be called holy.'"

Hope grinned and gave Cheyenne a wink. "Those Israeli men would sure feel special if they were so outnumbered by women—all those ladies being left with so few men!

"There is another passage that caught my attention. Pull up Zechariah 8." Hope leaned over her daughter so she could read out loud. "You need to read the whole chapter, but look here in verse 11. God says he will deal with the residue of his people differently. Then in verse 12 God says several different ways that they will be prosperous. Then He reminds them that they were a curse to the whole world, but now they will be considered a blessing. He says don't fear.

"Ha!" Hope's unexpected outburst startled Cheyenne.

"Good grief, Mom. You scared me. What is so 'ha!' anyways?"

Hope stared at her daughter as if wondering if she had any brains. "What? Think, Shy. When has Israel ever been considered a blessing to the world? But if they had a way to bring healing to the world ... like a berry brew ... and their men were in good shape when a goodly portion of the world's male population had been decimated? Well?"

Moving her glasses back to the top of her head, Hope continued, "And you know that the Dead Sea valley grows the very best berries for our brew. I wish I could get some more of my berries from Israel."

Cheyenne skipped several beats before she spoke; her thoughts had drifted to Asher. "Anyways," she finally said, "I sure am glad we'll have all this brew in the basement just in case the plague were to hit before our fall supply gets here. I read yesterday that the President said Jerusalem is the International City. He said that the middle 3 letters of Jerusalem is USA, like that somehow made America responsible for seeing to it that Jerusalem becomes the international capital city."

Hope picked up her notepad as she spoke with gravity. "The government better walk soft. Hand me that pencil; I need to make a note."

HEALING IN THE LEAVES, 10:28 A.M. – It didn't take much longer for the women to get the step by step directions finished. Encouraged with their progress, Hope ran through her mental checklist. "Okay.

Indian Gooseberry

Indian gooseberry has undergone preliminary research, demonstrating in vitro antiviral and antimicrobial properties. There is preliminary evidence in vitro that its extracts induce apoptosis and modify gene expression in osteoclasts involved in rheumatoid arthritis and osteoporosis.

>

I've walked you through the berry mash, fermentation, the ratios, the sequence, and the timing. There's the importance of keeping the finished brewing jars sterile yet closed loosely enough so that the fermentation gases can escape. So, let's see …"

Cheyenne stood and stretched, taking a break from the computer. "I'll read the stuff about muscadine and wolfberry tonight at home and try to find a suitable substitute for next year's brew. I can sure see why the Indian Gooseberry can't be substituted with any other berry. Do you have anything else you think I need to know before we quit?" Cheyenne said, looking at her watch, "Man, time's passing. Dad will be home in an hour."

Hope didn't answer. She was standing motionless with her back turned as if lost in thought. Cheyenne watched for a moment and grew concerned. "Mom, is there something else you want to tell me?"

"There is one more thing I guess you should know." Hope's berry stained face was at once comical and serious. "I have 22 gallons over in the cellar storage, and they are all about the same as this gallon we have made here today. This will be the 23rd gallon, and it is basically the same as the product we are making commercially in China, even though we are still experimenting with substitute leaves and berries. They all work, and work well, as you can see with your dad."

Cheyenne nodded. "Yeah, I know all that. Why do you mention it?"

Hope gazed at a quart jar sitting towards the back of the cluttered countertop. She reached out, lightly touching the lid. "I need to tell you about this one. It's different."

"Different?" Cheyenne tensed.

Hope's answer was so soft it was barely audible. "Very, very different."

Cheyenne leaned forward and asked, "What are you saying, Mom?"

Hope continued speaking quietly. "Everything else—all of the research and work—could not equal this one small jar … everything."

Experimental preparations of leaves, bark or fruit have shown potential efficacy against laboratory models of disease, such as for inflammation, cancer, age-related renal disease, and diabetes.
A human pilot study demonstrated reduction of blood cholesterol levels in both normal and hypercholesterolemic men. Another very recent study with alloxan-induced diabetic rats given an aqueous amla fruit extract has shown significant decrease of the blood glucose as well as triglyceridemic levels and an improvement of the liver function caused by a normalization of the liver-specific enzyme alanine transaminase (ALT) activity.

>

Hope's lips barely moved. "This is truly the fountain of life. This is the miracle brew."

Cheyenne's ears drummed with anticipation as she considered Hope's meaning. Her mother continued, "I took some degenerating blood cells from a dead animal. The cells were already beginning to enlarge. When I applied this formula, the blood cells began to come together, regenerate, and repair. They rapidly multiplied." Hope hissed, "I mean rapidly."

Uneasy, Hope placed her index finger to her lips. She moved to the heavy exterior lab door and she closed it. Then she turned on the noisy exhaust fan. "Just in case," she whispered.

SWEETS TO DIE FOR – The fat man giggled maliciously as he listened to Hope speak of the 22 gallons she kept in her cellar. *That's good, that's real good. Just what I needed to know. But that's a lot of stuff. I'll need help. Can't get it all today as planned. Guess you ladies lucked out.*

The sound of their voices suddenly dropped. Gingerly, he adjusted his listening device, trying to get a lock on the fading voices. "D*&%, what was she saying … ?"

While he continued to bait the barking dog, he picked up the binoculars to scan the ridge yet again. That voice he had heard earlier still spooked him. Wiggles, gaining confidence, stopped barking, and inched ever closer.

ASHER SEES, 10:31 A.M. – From a shaded spot, Asher began scanning the opposite ridge, searching for the source of the barking that had now finally stopped. He stared at the tip of the horseshoe edge and continued scanning the side of the ridge in slow, short movements. Nothing seemed out of the ordinary, but something wasn't right.

As he put the binoculars back in their pouch, he muttered, "If I

Although fruits are reputed to contain high amounts of ascorbic acid (vitamin C), 445 mg/100g, the specific contents are disputed and the overall antioxidant strength of amla may derive instead from its high density of tannins and other polyphenols. The fruit also contains flavonoids, kaempferol, ellagic acid and gallic acid.
www.npicenter.com

>

want to see the west slope, I gotta go to the side of the ridge where I was earlier this morning. What is it, God? I have walked all over these ridges. I don't see anything. Am I just imagining something? Show me, Lord, what I need to do."

There was no easy way down the steep 200 foot ridge, especially in cowboy boots and oversized feet. Carefully making his way down the slope, Asher made progress, pacing his stride for the distance and not wasting energy on excess movement. At the chert gravel lane that led into the valley, he jogged across and then dog-crawled up the point of the right ridge, sending a cloud of dust overhead. He stopped halfway up the slope to catch his breath. As he wiped the sweat from his brow, he suddenly recalled that he had promised the two boys, Dusty and Ben, that he would take them to Trashville or Poxville. Both boys loved to street preach. Asher frowned with disgust at his own thought pattern. *Man ... even I've started thinking like a hillbilly.* He mentally schooled himself, *Nashville, not Trashville.*

Sweat stung his eyes and glued a fine powdering of dust to his body and clothing. He reached the crest and stood in waist-high brush. He again retrieved the binoculars from the pouch on his belt and scanned the side of the ridge he had just left. Nothing. Not a thing in sight. Slowly he rescanned the area, scrutinizing every bush or clump that could harbor any danger until he had surveyed all the way behind the old farmhouse. "What is it, Lord, that troubles my spirit?" The muscles in his jaw and neck tensed as he whispered his prayer. He lowered the binoculars. At that moment a glint of sunlight reflected off something in the wooded area halfway down the slope, behind the old farmhouse.

"What?" Asher's binoculars zeroed in on the spot. He was stunned. "Lord, what is that piece of lascivious trash doing?"

Before he could finish his thought, his eyes took in the unfolding horror. He stumbled forward shouting, "Nooooooo!" Leaping frantically back down the ridge, he raced to stop what had already occurred. **A DOG'S DAY, 10:37** A.M. – The Eavesdropper could see the fur-bag, Wiggles, crouched only three feet away, focused on a piece of donut lying in the grass. The small dog belly-crawled, inching closer to the bait. The evil man didn't move a muscle. Just as her tiny black nose touched the food his gnarled hand clamped down on her neck, forcing out one tiny whine before cutting off her air. "Gotcha," he whispered victoriously as he held the frightened little dog, enjoying the terror in her dark eyes. "Well, now, looky what I just caught. Got me a nice little yapper. Now, I could just break your neck in one clean little snap, but that wouldn't be much fun, and after all the trouble you've caused me. No, you're definitely gonna get some serious pain." He laughed as he realized the sensation of the little racing heart. "You're a little greedy pig, you are. Oh, aren't you so scared? I would love to burn you inch by inch. That would really be fun. I've done that a lot, you know. But I guess you don't know." He chuckled proudly at the thought.

"The knife will just have to do. Too bad." He picked up the pocket-knife. Relishing the moment, he held Wiggles suspended by the scruff of her neck, rocking her to and fro as he whispered in a quiet singsong voice, "Bye bye, little doggy." He moved his fingers to hold the tiny jaw and head back in case the blade slipped. He squeezed and shook the trembling dog again to terrorize her just one last time. Just as the knife sliced into the dog, she jerked loose from his arthritic fingers, but as the wounded dog bounced to the ground a heavy boot slammed down over her little body. Again and again he stomped the little dog until she moved no more. He looked down to see bright red blood splattered on his boot and pant-leg. "%# dog! You bled all over me!" Then as if creation itself had been offended, he heard a distant protest, a wounded shout, "Nooooo!"

5

ELIXIR, SATURDAY, APRIL 5TH

Just in case ... what?

There was something about Hope's demeanor and her statement that gave Cheyenne a chill of foreboding. Why had their lesson turned so clandestine? The hum of the fan seemed to fill everything in the room with its vibration, including her body. The notes written on bits of paper and tacked to the cork board fluttered in the breeze from the fan. Time seemed to slow.

"In case what?"

Hope reached into her dress pocket and removed a scrap of yellow paper that Cheyenne had seen her write on a few minutes earlier. She handed her daughter the paper and whispered urgently, "Here's the elixir recipe. It's not a brew per se ... as you can see, it's quite different, much simpler. Memorize it so I can destroy it. I will never put the recipe on this computer."

Taking the berry stained slip of paper from her mother's hand, Cheyenne scanned it. Looking up wonderingly, she quietly exclaimed, "Why, it's so simple! It's simpler than anything you've ever done. You didn't even use all your berries. This herb—I've read about it for years, but it's so rare; I've never even been able to get any of it." She studied the paper for a few moments before handing it back to Hope. Cheyenne wore a puzzled expression. "Okay, I've memorized it. Why all the drama?"

As if to enforce Cheyenne's characterization of the moment, Hope took the paper, stuffed it into her mouth, and began to chew. Forgetting their efforts to avoid detection, Cheyenne raised her voice to exclaim, "Mom, have you totally lost your mind? What are you doing? That's too dramatic." There was no hint of the playful girl.

Hope's voice was flat. "It had to be done, Shy. I couldn't risk it getting into the wrong hands. There are indications others are becoming suspicious. I think, I think ... well, it doesn't really matter what I think. I am just doing what I know to be right."

Cheyenne was incredulous. "What good would it do if they were snooping around? I don't know of any way anyone could get any of that herb. Sheesh. It only grows in one area by the Euphrates River, and who can get in there now? Anyways, a little while ago we were talking about the Tree of Life ... this couldn't be ... ?" Cheyenne's voice trailed off as she stared at her mom, almost believing the unbelievable.

The shaking of Hope's head brought Cheyenne back down to common sense. "No, no, this is not the Garden of Eden Tree of Life that keeps people from ever dying, but with the other herbs mixed properly, it must be close."

The old woman leaned down and whispered, "It even smells right." Then she straightened her mind, going back to the basics.

"I grew the herb myself and it was the most troublesome thing I ever tried to keep alive. It's a small tree, you know, but it only grows in very inaccessible areas, in highly acidic soil. And you are right—it grows only in northern Iraq. It only grew to 14 inches before it died, but I was able to harvest 20 good quality leaves. That gives us enough ingredients for several batches to combat a multitude of disease when the time comes."

"But Mom," Cheyenne queried, "you said leaves. I never heard of anyone using the leaves of this tree; only the fruit. Besides, where did you get the seeds?"

Hope nodded and explained, "Your father is always teaching that we need to think literally when studying Scripture so that the Bible can teach us something. Remember what it says in Genesis 3 and in

Revelation 22? As you know, in the original Garden of Eden, which was located in Iraq, and again in the coming Millennium, there is a special tree growing beside the rivers called the Tree of Life. It says the leaves of the tree are for the healing of the nations. It doesn't say that the healing is in the fruit; it's in the leaves. So I thought, if it is the leaves that brings healing in the Millennium, why not now? I know this is not the Tree of Life, but in combination with other herbs, it contains propertics that must be very similar."

Motioning toward the cabinet where she had put the small bag of leaves for safekeeping, Hope continued, "I didn't even use all twenty leaves, plus I have more seeds if you ever need to grow anothcr plant or two. A friend ... I won't mention names, traveling to the Far East, sent me the seeds. The locals recognize its healing properties, but it's not so special until mixed with the other berries and herbs. We will be ready when it happens."

"You mean the time when the plague kills the men?" Cheyenne asked, still puzzled and dreading the answer.

"I don't know. But we will know when it comes, and if I am gone, you will know. We will be ready." Hope pulled a leather lanyard from inside the bodice of her dress with a small key attached. She unlocked the cabinet and removed a plastic bag with several dried leaves.

Cheyenne watched her mothcr rcmove a glass dropper from a small brown bottle and dip it into the quart jar they had been discussing. Dark purple liquid moved up into the pipette as she released her pinch on the bulb. Hope transferred it to thc smaller bottle and continued to repeat the process until the smaller bottle was full.

Capping the small bottle tightly, Hope moved back to thc cabinet and put the newly filled brown bottle into the plastic zippered bag with the precious few dried leaves. Cheyenne could tell by her mother's meaningful glance that she intended for her daughter to remember this event. Replacing the precious parcel onto the shelf, Hope shut the door and locked the cabinet, returning the key to its hiding place.

"What prompted the change?" Cheyenne almost looked afraid.

Hope looked into her daughter's eyes. "I don't know," she said flatly.

"I don't know how I knew to try it. I don't even know how I know it works in combination. But trust me … I know. Maybe something in my studies finally clicked. You know your dad always says that God uses those who are moving. I would assume God would use a mind that is always studying, seeking knowledge."

"Then you think it's supernatural?" Now, Cheyenne was trying to reconcile the possibility that her practical, concrete-thinking mom was expressing confidence in something that sounded very supernatural. Hope had never had any use for hyper-spirituality, so this was feeling strange.

Hope placed her hands over her daughter's. Speaking with complete conviction, she said, "Yes, God gave it to me."

"Why now? What's going to happen?" Cheyenne had recovered enough to regain her natural, youthful curiosity. Her mind demanded answers.

Hope's years of experience told her some things were best not known. "I don't know. How can we know such things?"

"If you could get the tree to grow, would you make this elixir to sell?"

The girl was startled to hear her mother's sharp guttural response. "Never … never. Not one drop, and you must never sell it. Never tell anyone, not a single person, how it was made. God took away the Tree of Life because men turned against him. That has not changed. It would be a great ill if what I have done changed that … no … no."

Hope's tone changed, sounding almost relieved. "My China brew is healing … a wonderful healing tonic. We say our Berry Herbal Brew will make you live forever but that is not literally true. A person taking it will still grow old and die. That is important."

"Here, take this last gallon into the cellar to add to our stash. By this fall our first load of China brew will be here, and we will all have as much as we need." Then Hope handed Cheyenne the quart that held the miracle elixir to carry in her other arm. "Here, take this one too. Whatever you do, don't drop it!" Hope winked and swooshed her expression into a silly face, breaking the tension with her humor.

Hope smiled as she leaned against the doorjamb, always ready to tease her fearful daughter. "Watch for spiders."

THE TRUCK RIDE – The opposite ridge was almost a half mile away. Asher knew he had no chance of catching the evil man, but he would try nonetheless. Less than fifteen seconds after yelling "Nooooo!" he was halfway down the slope he had just climbed. He heard an old truck engine gearing down as it rattled across the wooden bridge and turned onto the Freeman's lane. Dusty! Asher almost smiled in gratitude. Good timing, boys.

Struggling for breath, he continued barreling down the slope, hoping to intercept the truck at the lane. He stumbled and fell, losing his hat. His survival training came to his aid as he instinctively tucked and rolled, regaining his feet in a kind of crab run. Gravity propelled him forward as he continued his downward race. He stumbled onto the road just in time to find himself directly in front of the oncoming truck.

Dusty was enjoying his noisy truck. He downshifted and gunned the engine, smiling as it roared. His passenger, Ben, seemed to share his enjoyment. As they rounded the sharp curve that took them toward the narrow entrance to the valley and the Freemans' property, Dusty's youthful brag defined him more than he knew. "Man!" he shouted over the engine noise. "You gotta love a five speed!"

Ben glanced through the rear window to admire the skid marks left in the loose gravel road as the truck fishtailed. "Yeah!" He shouted back. "You're gettin' good at pullin' everything out of this truck!"

Dusty guffawed.

In a cloudburst of dust, Asher spilled onto the lane immediately in front of them.

"Look out! Stop!" Ben bellowed.

Dusty's foot automatically responded to the command. He slammed on the brakes, spewing forward a storm of dust and grit as the truck took a short, sliding stop. Both boys yelled and slammed their feet down on the floorboard.

In the second that had passed since they glimpsed their mentor, their faces had drained of all color. Unable to look away, they stared through the windshield for some sign of life.

"God help us! What's happened?!" Dusty's voice caught and broke into a wail of dismay. Ben sat in stunned silence.

Asher's form suddenly rose above the hood, already moving toward the driver's side of the truck. By the time the truck skidded to a stop Asher was already grabbing for the door handle. In a single motion his hardened muscles yanked the door open and shoved Dusty sideways. "Move over!" Asher yanked the transmission into first gear, revving the engine and feathering the clutch to gain traction. The truck blasted forward down the lane without spinning the wheels. The sudden lurch forward slammed the door shut. The same movement that slammed the truck's door also slammed both boys' heads painfully into the back window of the truck.

"Whoa! Ouch! What's going on?!" Ben said, trying to make room for Dusty as they jolted along.

"Later!" barked Asher, pulling the stick shift down into fourth gear as he topped a low rise. Here, they could see the Freemans' farmhouse a quarter mile away. Asher shifted down into the third gear and popped the clutch, skidding the truck around a hard turn to the right.

A rush of adrenaline had heightened Asher's senses. The tension, anger and need for payback that he had carried for over a year now focused on a physical enemy. His fingertips tingled with the need for just retribution, causing the texture of the steering wheel to come alive in his hands.

The truck sped up the lane, fishtailing and showering gravel and dirt as Asher abruptly turned right and cut across the newly plowed garden. The old truck jumped and bumped across the uneven ground, jarring the necks of the unsuspecting boys.

Turning to view the damage out of the rear window, the boys didn't see Asher turn the rocking truck left to mount the high ditch bank. He hit it fast enough to jump the truck over the small ditch and slam into the slop on the other side. His unprepared passengers were thrown against the door. Dusty banged his head against the roof of the cab when the truck dropped. Ben slammed his head against the glass of the passenger side window, pinching his ear painfully. When he regained his voice, Dusty shrilled, "Hey! You're tearin' up my truck!"

The calm, reserved teacher both boys knew had morphed into a wild man that shouted back dismissively, "I'll buy you another one!" He shifted into second gear and gunned the truck up the steep ridge.

Now wiser, the boys braced themselves with their arms, but their heads still received another smack against the back glass. The painful yelps accompanied the noise of the straining engine as they bumped up the near vertical slope.

The truck seemed to hang suspended, standing straight up on its rear wheels, before slamming back down on all four. The force was too much for the decrepit shock absorbers and the cab bottomed out, causing Dusty to bite and cut his tongue. Again the boys screeched in annoyance and fear.

Oblivious to their discomfort, Asher cut the wheels to make a hard left. He drove another 100 feet before jamming the brakes and bringing the truck to an abrupt stop, again throwing both boys forward into the dashboard. Ben shook his hand and checked his stinging wrist. "Man, oh man, have you gone crazy?"

Dusty spit blood into his hand. "Man, I pretty near bit my tongue off. You gonna buy me a new one of those too?"

Asher paid them no mind as he jumped from the truck, then reached down to remove his gun from its ankle holster. First he dropped into a crouch, carefully surveying the area, then began studying the ground. For a long moment he studied the back side of the old Freeman farmhouse, but there appeared to be no sign of movement.

Dusty stood by the door, still spitting blood, not noticing the weapon or Asher's surveying. Ben sat in the sudden quietness watching Asher with a fearful dread coming over him. Was this his Bible teacher or a CIA operative?

Asher ran about, searching, and then stopped in his tracks, looking down, his anger obvious. There lay the bloody, lifeless body of the Freemans' beloved pet. Something had cut a groove into the soil, and some kind of object had been dragged from the scene.

Asher slid his gun into his waistband and picked up the limp body of the dog, placing it in the back of the truck. The boys gasped, "How did you know? Who did this?" Saying nothing, Asher slumped in the driver's seat. Even Dusty now fell silent, stilled by the strangeness of their leader and the sight of the bloodied, dead pet.

When Asher started the vehicle and headed toward the ridge, Dusty suddenly came to life. "Stop! Wait. Where are you going? There ain't no way to get down offen this ridge exceptin' straight down, and we ain't going down like we just commed up. This here is my onliest truck!"

"Okay." Asher's exhausted response contrasted starkly with his previous behavior and was unlike his normal military style command. The boys exchanged perplexed glances.

Asher drove in silence across the top of the ridge, carefully avoiding the trees that crowded the old forest trail, maneuvering around the washed out pot holes. The worn springs squawked with each jostle.

As the old truck rounded the creek edge, Asher gave the boys a sidelong glance. "Sorry, boys. I didn't mean to scare you silly. I do hope neither of you wet your pants."

Involuntarily both boys touched their pants to check. Each caught the other in the middle of checking and began to laugh. Dusty spoke. "Naw, it was fun. Sorta sudden and unexpected, but it was fun."

Observant, Ben took the opportunity to ask some questions. "What's going on? Did you think you were going to catch whoever did that to Wiggles? Did you see him? Do you know who it was?"

Before Asher could respond, a suddenly excited Dusty exploded. "That's it! I should'a knowed! I mean, I should have known you were trying to catch someone. Who was it?"

"This morning, after I finished scouting for deer, I began to pray. A strong sense of unease came over me, as if evil was near. I felt that God wanted me to keep walking and praying, waiting for him to show me what to do.

"I must have been all over these ridges. I bet I covered three hundred acres. Finally I caught a glimpse of something metallic reflecting sunlight over in the wood line. I looked through my binoculars and I saw this guy from town. I can't remember his name. He's the fat guy that messed with your little cousin, Ben.

"He was hiding in those bushes up the ridge behind the farmhouse. He had some sort of listening device. I watched him kill that old dog. He must have heard me, because I yelled, which was a stupid reaction. He had to have hit the trail back to the forest road, which means he was long gone before we got there."

This new information launched Dusty onto a rant about what he would have done if he had caught the guy. Ben reflected, "I know who you're talking about. That's Derek. What was he up to? Why in the world would he be up here killing an old dog?"

Asher, angered anew at the thought of the interloper, slammed his hand against the steering wheel. "I don't have any idea. He had at least a four or five minute head start, because I was on the front side of the ridge."

Dusty nodded his head energetically. "That's right! He's got that souped-up 450 dirt bike. His dad's the sheriff. A while back, his dad busted a pot dealer taking his drugs through the woods on that bike. The sheriff took it and gave it to Derek. His granddaddy's the judge, so Derek gets away with everything no matter who he hurts. He never has to give an answer to anybody. Bunch of White Supremacists ... the lot of 'em controlling this whole county." Dusty's voice was a mixture of bitterness and envy.

Asher's brows raised. "White Supremacist? Man, that group went out with George Wallace."

Dusty and Ben exchanged uneasy looks. Ben finally spoke up to straighten out his teacher's error. "Maybe in Washington State, but in our county the White Supremacists, skinheads, KKK and all the other

Supremacist groups are on the rise, according to leaders of the groups and organizations that monitor them. The nation's largest white power website has a new feature that lets members create social-networking pages. The site had as many as 42,700 visitors in one 24-hour period during November '08.

www.stormfront.org

clans rule. I heard Derek is one of what they call their 'fist'."

Asher's puzzled look caused Dusty to add, "He does a lot of their dirty work. Kinda like a paid assassin. I know he doesn't have a job, but he always has money."

Ben wisely passed on and continued to press the matter at hand. "I still can't figure why he'd want to listen in on Hope. What's she got to say that he'd want to hear?" He paused for a moment, and the light came on. "Unless ... he's after her berry stuff!"

Asher's body jolted as the idea hit him. He turned to look at the sober boy for a moment, but didn't respond.

Pulling Dusty's truck in next to the pink truck at the bottom of the drive, Asher turned the key to the off position. The boys looked with disgusted interest at the hulking panel truck. "Who dragged that thing out of the dump?" Dusty asked.

"That's Cheyenne's newest treasure," Asher replied, suppressing a grin. "Of course, she would have to choose a vehicle based on her favorite color."

Now Ben spoke for both teens. "Critters! I'd rather walk."

The three young men crawled out of Dusty's truck and started walking up the sloping drive. Ben's bruised ear was starting to swell. He rubbed it as he reasoned, "So it was Hope and Cheyenne that Derek was listening to? He must have expected them to say something he wanted to hear."

Asher slowed his pace. "I don't think I'll tell the ladies about Derek and their dog just yet. I heard the girls at the Herb Den talking the other day about all of the news headlines. What with the Muslims blowing up that church in Chattanooga last week, killing all the kids, and the news this week of Yellowstone's volcanic activity, they were saying that they couldn't take much more bad news. I regret telling them about the Muslims in Washington State ... about Dan. It was just too much. So you two keep your traps shut about Derek and the dog until I decide what to do."

Ben whistled lowly. "Cheyenne will not like being treated like a sissy. She fusses about bad things happening, but she likes to know what's going on. I know you've been teaching us to treat ladies with respect and all, but southern girls are scrappers. Cheyenne's one of the toughest. I don't know about not telling them. And Bobbie Jo, now she's a she-bear, sure-nuff. It could get ugly if they find out we kept information from them."

Amused at the young man's assessment, Asher responded, "Well, it's my call, so you can blame it on me if they find out."

Dusty grinned. "That'll not be a problem, brother."

The boys followed Asher as he led the way to the lab. "You two keep Hope serving you coffee," Asher told them, "so I can get Cheyenne aside to ask questions and see if I can figure out why Derek might have been here."

The young boys exchanged sly grins and started elbowing each other. This slowed their pace and they had to hurry to catch up to Asher. Dusty snickered quietly, "Yeah, that will be some chore taking Cheyenne off and talking ..." At that, both boys laughed at an unspoken joke.

Asher stopped abruptly, catching the boys unprepared and causing them to stumble into him. Speaking in a stern growl, he warned, "Watch where you're going, boys, both with your feet and your speech, if you get my drift." Asher looked at them unblinking. After his recent weird, violent behavior, both boys were ready to relent.

DEAD DOG – Hope was just shutting the cellar door behind Cheyenne when she heard Asher's knock and the door open just an inch. "Hello? Can we come in?"

"Come on in, boys. I'm just cleaning up after a big berry project. You can leave the door open, just close the screen. I'm trying to keep Wiggles outside. She's been a pest, barking her head off all morning, although she does seem to have finally worn herself out."

Hope's experienced mother's eye noted instantly how all three men shifted uncomfortably at the mention of her dog. Her pleasure at seeing the young men was clouded with suspicion that something was amiss.

Before she could question their behavior, all three young men began to laugh at Hope's berry-stained, smiling face. She stood there with a puzzled look, her purple hands on her hips. Dusty asked, "Have you been picking your nose, Hope?" He pointed under her nose, where the skin was purple and pink.

The old woman winked, pretending it was a compliment as she grabbed a paper towel for herself and handed one to Ben. "You boys don't look much better. Ben, your nose is bleeding and you look like you're headed towards a good case of cauliflower ear if you don't get an ice pack on that. Dusty, you have a welt coming up on your forehead and your mouth's been bleeding. Have you boys been fighting?" Hope questioned Asher with her eyes.

He quickly answered, "No, it was just a bump in the truck. Hit an unexpected turn and they hit heads. Nothing, really ..."

The boys nodded, grinning. Hope wore a skeptical expression, prompting Ben to add with his earnest and honest expression, "It's true, Hope. Asher is telling you the truth. A very unexpected turn and whack." He clapped his fist forcefully into his hand to demonstrate the event.

Still suspicious, Hope probed for holes in the story. "So if you weren't fighting, then what are you boys doing here this morning? Anything in particular?"

Asher was nearly bent double trying to see into the small storage room. Hope turned her attention to him and asked, "You looking for something, son, or is your back out of joint?" That prompted a deep reddening of his face.

Asher surmised that since Cheyenne wasn't here she must be next door at the TLP office, so he quickly brought the visit to a close. "Well, I guess we'll go," he said shortly. "Tell the Old Gent," referring to Malachi by his nickname, "that it is very, very important that I talk to him this afternoon. I will be phoning him."

The gangling boys jostled backwards out the door and began to follow Asher around the front corner of the house toward the TLP warehouse. Hope waited a few seconds, then stuck her head out the door and called after Asher, "Okay, I'll tell Malachi ... and I'll tell

Cheyenne she missed you when she comes up out of the cellar." Hope quickly ducked back into the door and enjoyed watching the effect of her words through the window.

Asher stopped short and looked over his shoulder. He was just quick enough to catch Hope's grinning, purple face duck back into the lab. Turning on his heels, he directed the boys as if he were their commanding officer, "Go look for my hat. I lost it coming down the front ridge right before I met you."

He loped back up towards the door and entered to find Hope still grinning. Asher shook his finger in admonition. "You rascal."

She continued grinning and shrugged. "Her pink truck, as big as day, is parked down the drive. You didn't ask where she was. How was I supposed to guess you were looking for her?"

Bested, Asher moved toward the cellar door. "Well, now that I know where she is, I'll just let her know we won't be at tonight's Bible study over at the Herb Den. I wouldn't want her to miss us and wonder."

Hope snorted good-naturedly. "Yeah, save that claptrap for Cheyenne. I'm not fooled for one second. I call it predestined attraction. Hormones extraordinaire! I don't know why neither one of you will just 'fess up to nature's call." Asher was so flabbergasted by the older woman's frankness that he could manage only a barked laugh.

Before he had a chance to move toward the cellar door, Hope touched his sleeve. "Wait, Asher. What's going on? You boys tried not to let on, but I could see you were all nervous and secretive." She released his arm.

"Well, ah, err ... well," Asher dropped his hands to his sides and took a deep breath. "About fifteen minutes ago I was on the front ridge counting the deer population. Through my binoculars I saw this guy from town hiding on the ridge behind your house. I believe his name is Derek. I spotted him just in time to see him kill your little dog. I tried to catch him, but he heard me and got away. I'm sorry, Hope. I have Wiggles' body down there in the truck."

As she listened, Hope's countenance clouded in anger, then changed to confusion, finally moving on to relief. "Derek? Hiding behind the house?" Hope slapped her hands together almost in glee. "So someone is spying. I figured as much."

Then she shook her head as if to cancel out her thoughts. Turning to the matter at hand, she spoke urgently. "Never mind him. Go get Wiggles and bring her here immediately!"

Asher knew there was no need to rush, but Hope's reaction prompted him to hurry. The large hands gently picked up the little dog and carried her up the hill and into the house. When he entered the lab, Hope stood patting a spot on the stainless steel work table. "Quick, put her down right here."

"She's not breathing anymore, Hope. She's gone." Asher looked sadly at his good friend.

"I'll see what I can do." Hope was too anxious to be bothered with conversation. "Just leave her on the table and go to Cheyenne." Then, more gently, "Wash your hands right there, then go." Hope stood fingering the lanyard at her neck, looking down at the dog's body. Every nerve of her body felt like it was on fire.

There was no grief ... only possibilities.

She wished the young man would stop acting like she was a tender hearted sop and just leave. "Go on, Asher," she said. "It's okay. I'm not some young fragile damsel in distress. I'm an old woman and have seen a lot of bad things over the years. I've outlived many dogs. Go. Cheyenne will appreciate the company. She's never liked being alone down in that cellar." Hope waved her hand in a gesture of dismissal. Asher relented and moved down the steps to the cellar door.

She waited a few seconds until she was sure Asher would stay in the cellar. Then she pulled the lanyard from her bodice. Moving to the cabinet, she used the key to unlock the cabinet and open the door. From the zippered bag, she removed the small brown bottle she had just filled a few minutes earlier. "Well, this is it. I soon shall know if it really does work."

Moving back to the table, she looked at her dog over the top of her glasses as she muttered, "Well, Wiggles, you're the guinea pig again. Only this time, there's nothing left to lose. You sure look like a goner. But," there was a quiver in her voice and tears stung her eyes, "let's see if this stuff can do for you what it did for those cells I saw under the microscope. If it doesn't ..." She paused, contemplating the likelihood. "Woe to that devil Derek."

THE CELLAR – Cheyenne's heart was racing, thinking of spiders, a dread since childhood.

Talking to steady her nerves, she moved cautiously among the jars and shelves. "Man, this place stinks," she said to herself. "Smells like Wiggles when she's wet." Giving her eyes a chance to adjust to the dim light, she mentally counted the 22 one gallon glass jugs sitting in a row on the dirt floor against the far back wall. She calculated how long the brew might last two people.

Cheyenne's long, slender hand reached for the first gallon jar and began to slowly spin the thick liquid until the contents clouded. Setting it down, she made sure the upside down bowl, which served as a lid, was firmly in place before she reached for the next jar. She hummed softly to pass the time. She moved her precious quart with her as she contemplated a good place to stash it while she shook each gallon jug.

The squeaking door caused her to jump. She screeched, "Oh! You scared me!" In the next instant she recognized the shock of red hair. "Oh, hi ... fancy meeting you here!" Her voice sounded more than relieved.

Asher's own heart raced when he heard her gentled response to his appearance. Stepping over some scattered clutter he made his way to Cheyenne's side. Reaching out his hand in a playful condescending manner he said, "Here, let me help you up. This place smells like ... like ... musty old grapes."

A tingling wave ran through Cheyenne's body at the feel of his fingers wrapped around her arm in support. She unfolded her legs to stand and stretch. Giggling, she tried not to appear flustered as she handed him the gallon jug she'd nearly spilled.

He looked at the line of crocks with their odd, bowl-shaped lids. "So this is where Hope keeps her stuff? Is this the potion people say she uses to make your dad a superman?"

Still holding the jug, Asher's trained eyes took in the crocks, jugs, and jars in various stages of processing. Already he had mentally calculated the volume of containers in the space. Maybe all that talk in town about Malachi's good health coming from some homemade tonic actually has a seed of truth? Asher's mind played with different ideas, wondering if this could be important enough for Derek to be spying on Hope.

When Cheyenne hesitated, Asher asked straight out, "So?"

Cheyenne still didn't speak.

Asher normally would have been impatient for her to answer, but he was momentarily mesmerized by her appearance. Again he took note of just how strong her Indian ancestral roots were. The high cheek bones, the exotic nose, the smooth olive skin, and her long lanky body folded up into a relaxed squat with her arms sticking straight out, elbows resting on her knees as she studied the jars, all spoke of Indian heritage.

Her reply broke into his reverie. "First of all, this is a secret, although you already know most of it. Anyways, I know you're safe, because I overheard Dad telling Mom that he totally trusts you, even though you have only been at TLP for seven weeks. Dad's a keen judge of character. He told Mom you had a real heart for the souls of men, so he was placing you into the ministry work at TLP this week. Right?"

Her conversation reminded him of a spider's web: it moved in several different directions at once. He didn't really know what she was asking. "Yes, he gave me the job of keeping up with translation and publishing progress in the different languages."

Pleased with his obvious befuddlement, she continued, "So you are bound to be hearing how TLP plans to raise the money. It does take money to publish. And I know that in two weeks you are being sent to Thailand to meet with several translators and to help Timothy Vick pass out the *God's Story* book to the Hmong people, so you have to be in, but you still have to promise to keep your mouth shut."

CHEYENNE

He gave up trying to follow her reasoning. Shifting the jug to one hand, Asher held his other hand up in a Boy Scout salute as he solemnly responded, "Scouts Honor. I promise to keep my mouth shut about ... what?"

Cheyenne flushed, suddenly conscious of his closeness. She dropped her eyes, blushing through her olive complexion. She quickly squatted down in front of the next jar. Clasping her hands, she pulled her shoulders up and forward, curling inward like a shy child. Asher grinned down at her squatting form. It pleased him that he was able to provoke the famous expression that won her the nickname 'Shy.' His defenses fell. "Truly, I am honored to hear your family thinks so highly of me. Really, I would love to know what is going on."

The girl struggled to regain control of her emotions, standing up straight and willing her blushing to stop. She cleared her throat and tried to sound intelligent as she answered, "Mom started experimenting with herb and berry tinctures years ago when Dad first got sick. She started working out a recipe, processing one small jar at a time and testing it until Dad began to show real improvement. That's why there are so many different jars here. She could have mixed it up in fifty-five gallon drums, but she was working smaller batches and testing the results. She's always been a chemistry buff as well as an herbalist. With Dad sick, her hobby became a serious quest to find something to heal him."

She held out her hands for Asher to pass her the jug he was still holding. "Anyways, once Rob Cohen started taking the berry stuff, he got Asian chemists involved. They helped Mom stabilize the brew, at least the brew they are going to market for retail."

Asher had been distracted watching her, but at the mention of the older man's name he became very focused. "Wait. What did you say? Rob Cohen? I thought that guy died of cancer last year! What was his treatment? ... The brew?"

Cheyenne nodded. "He did have cancer and was about dead. They even had his funeral planned, casket and everything. Creepy, huh? Mom put him on heavy doses of the brew, made him stop all sugar of any kind, forced him to eat raw vegetables and fresh fish. In less than a month he was in China making deals. She had offered the brew to him earlier in his illness, but he didn't trust a hillbilly to know anything, and only wanted to do what the doctors suggested. Anyway, he's a Yankee." Asher ignored the condescending remark, as he had come to learn it was just a reference point for Tennesseans.

Research - For up-to-date research Google search for "fermented pomegranate Israeli research". Add whatever you are interested in such as cancer, diabetes, heart disease, etc.

www.futurepundit.com/archives/003561.html ✎

Cheyenne pointed at the 22 jars and said proudly, "This is the kind of stuff Mom gave him."

Asher let out a low whistle as chills prickled up and down his spine. Cohen's cancer was advanced, but there had been many documented cases of spontaneous healing. His voice held a note of mockery when he spoke. "Really? China? What's China got to do with your mama's jars of berries?"

Cheyenne squatted back down; with her attention on the jar she missed his ragging. She continued, "Well, most of the large berry orders came before you moved here. We already have contracts signed for berry shipments for the next three years. But we have had a few last minute details ... surely you noticed something. Last year the mulberry harvest was a failure. Our whole project was set back. Anyway, this fall will be our first shipment of the finished brew."

Cheyenne leaned over and picked up a small jar that sat against the wall. With one fluid movement she came to her feet and walked over, placing her small, special jar in the far shadowy corner of the basement. Asher noted that she seemed protective of the small jar. She bent down to shake the next jar.

Asher's mind was running in fifty different directions. Could they really believe they made a miracle healing brew? Enough to invest hundreds of thousands of dollars? It must be what brought Derek here today. He must believe it. But these country folk have a tendency to be superstitious ... but Rob Cohen did have cancer. That was a fact. Malachi's health had obviously been restored, but those things do happen, brew or no brew. Had Hope convinced herself that it was the result of the brew in hopes of financing The Last Publishers' publishing ministry? Might she have gotten so carried away with her dream that she just carried Malachi along with her? It was possible.

"You know," Cheyenne shifted her feet over a few inches so she could reach the next jug, "Dad believes the brew is why you are here."

"Me?" Asher half stood with surprise, then stooped down again. "What have I got to do with it?"

"Well," she moved down another few inches to the next jug, "You are the one who is setting up the website where every language will be available, and you are the person that has set into motion our campaign to make the websites known. You know how much money it takes to publish. And for a while now we have been treading water where money is concerned; that's why Mom's so desperate to get the brew on the market. So your web thing has kept the project going."

Asher's brows knotted as he struggled to follow her wild spider web of words.

"Dad hopes to use the money that is made selling the Berry Herbal Brew to set the whole printing thing into motion. Before now, the sale of Mom and Dad's Bible teaching books generated enough money for publishing, but now it is getting too big. The publishing of the gospel would almost be stopped except for what you're doing on the web."

Asher whistled again. He looked over at her and forgot his resolve not to question the brew. The sound of skepticism was thick. "They plan on funding the entire publishing ministry with a brew?" Asher had a sinking feeling, thinking these people really are hillbillies. "I don't want to seem like a wet blanket, but why do you think people will buy it? Just because you say it's good?"

She responded with a giggle that approached mockery. He might have been offended, but he was taken again by the magic of her spontaneous joy. She smelled of mint, lemon balm, and cinnamon. Her whole person seemed to overflow with life. The thing he loved best about her was her lack of ever being offended, always taking the high ground. "Lord," the young man silently breathed as he stepped back, "You gotta help me."

Not having a clue as to his need, she stood to mischievously poke his side with her index finger, testing his resolve even further. He faked ticklishness, flinching, pretending to lose his balance. This sent her into more giggles.

"You don't really believe it works, do you? Your patronizing is so obvious." She smiled up at him, "But you will see ... you will see. Besides, you cannot deny Rob's sudden recovery."

Asher struggled to regain his balance. Forcing his mind to refocus on the conversation, he replied, "Naw ... I mean, I don't really know enough to come to a definitive conclusion, but ..."

In the lull that followed, Cheyenne resumed working. Asher examined his hands and carefully brushed the cellar dirt off each finger as he tried to focus on his next line of questioning. "So setting up a factory in China would take millions, wouldn't it? Where's the money coming from? And how many people are in on this? I mean, surely the TLP office staff knows and, of course, the Herb Den's staff. Who else?" Remembering Derek's spying, Asher's heart accelerated as his mind now shifted to matters of safety. "Do you think some of the townspeople know?"

His apprehension was met with another giggle. Cheyenne couldn't understand why he was acting so worried. "Who knows? Less than you would guess. Not even the Herb Den's staff!"

"That's hard to believe! You and Bobbie Jo and Julie are always together. Surely the Indivisible Trio knows all." Asher was only half-teasing.

Setting her jug down, Cheyenne held up her hands, ticking her fingers as she calculated the potential list of people that may have figured out the plan. "Julie doesn't really know much, and she doesn't show much interest in this kind of stuff. Bobbie Jo knows everything.

"Only the office staff that has been with TLP a number of years has been told how we are going to try to raise the money for the publishing. They saw Cohen and Dad get well, so most of the employees are excited about the plan, although even the most trusted don't realize how effective the brew is.

"To help raise the money for the factory, and to buy the berries, Rob formed a corporation. Longtime TLP employees and a few very wealthy friends were allowed to buy stock in the brew company. They were willing to invest because some of them have seen firsthand the healing power of Mom's brew. Mom and Dad have a plan to take the company public. When the IPO comes around, the TLP employees that purchased stock and the investors will reap millions, while Mom and Dad will become millionaires since they own the bulk of the shares. That is the money we plan on using to publish the *God's Story* book into every language of the world. Everyone who has stock wants to see the publishing project fully financed. They are not interested in being rich."

Asher couldn't help telling her what he thought even though he was humored by her excitement in the project. "Don't be offended, but this seems like some serious counting your chickens before the eggs hatch,"

Asher stood, stretching his legs. He shook his head, trying to clear his thoughts. How could a man as wise as Malachi leap into something so chancy?

Cheyenne moved two more feet down the line of jars. She glanced over and saw the perplexed look on his face. She wished she could hear his thoughts.

"Why brew it?" Asher seemed to struggle with a way to explain what he was wondering. "You know, it sounds like it is wine or beer or something. Why ferment the stuff?"

Her snicker caused him to wish he hadn't asked, but she finally answered, "The different levels of fermentation for each berry changes the chemistry of each; put them together to ferment and you have another chemical altogether. Pomegranate is actually estrogenic before it is brewed, which is not good for breast cancer, but after it is fermented it totally changes. Anyways, it took Mom a thousand times of mixing to happen up on one that forms the chemical combination that really works."

He fell silent as he mulled over the information she had given him. *Could it really be that good? Good enough that people would buy it? Maybe.*

Asher suddenly boomed aloud something that struck him. "What about Timothy Vick? I guess you heard he was taken to the hospital yesterday. It doesn't look good for him. If the stuff really works, even a little, then of all people Timothy Vick needs it."

"Man alive! You scared me half to death," Cheyenne screeched, nearly toppling forward on her head. "But yeah, he does need it." The

Pomegranate research: *www.oxfordjournal.org*
Gooseberry research: *www.lef.org/magazine* and *www.naturaldatabase.com* use search query "Gooseberry herb" ∽

girl stood, stretching her cramped legs for a moment before squatting back down. "We do need to rush him some as soon as possible."

"Have you conducted tests on people?" Asher was grasping at straws, hoping these good people were not getting caught up in nonsense.

"Only a little, with the few people who know what we are doing— those that have invested in the company. Two of them have reversed heart disease and one saw his wife's cancer remitted." Cheyenne reached for the last jar. "Rob advised us to opt out of clinical trials. It would be impossible to keep everything under wraps if hundreds of people became involved and started reporting similar results as Dad and Rob. There would be no way we could keep it quiet. We would have to fend off thieves and the desperate before we could even get it to market. Besides, some pharmaceutical company would end up pulling strings to get the FDA to halt our sales long enough for them to engineer and patent their own formula."

She took a clean towel from her shoulder as she spoke. She knew he greatly respected her dad's ministry, so she wanted to reassure him that they were not foolish. "Asher, we are not leaping into this without a great deal of knowledge. We have confirmed that the consumption of this brew greatly boosts the production of serotonins, which in turn stabilizes blood glucose levels and promotes DNA repair – all the things scientists have known help people to live longer and resist disease. It cleans all the body systems, liver, kidneys, and vascular systems. The only other way to produce these results, or come even close to it, is to reduce the intake of food to just enough calories and nutrients to survive. Not too many people are willing to go that far. The berry brew would certainly be easier than starving."

Cheyenne handed him the towel. "Thanks," said Asher as he began wiping the sticky juice off of his hands. "Well, that is encouraging. For a minute there I thought you might have just taken the healing of two men as the sum of your decision to move forward."

"Stop worrying. Contrary to your suspicions, we are not a bunch of dumb hillbillies." She looked one last time over the jars before she added, "We're a bunch of highly trained, intelligent hillbillies!

"By the way, thanks for all your help shaking jars. Let's see ... you shook ... none. You Westerners seem not to be able to work and think at the same time," she teased as she turned and headed toward the door. "Let's get out of this spider colony."

Asher grabbed her arm, halting her progress. "Wait! Wait. I need to tell you something."

He had such urgency to his voice that Cheyenne froze on the spot. A tingling coursed through her body like a thousand fire brands as she stared at his hand holding her arm. She looked up into his face with the thrill of expectancy. His body warmed her with his closeness. She almost felt weak as she looked up into his face.

But his eyes were full of sadness. He stumbled over his words, and then started again. "There was an incident. Your mom's little dog Wiggles has been killed. I'm really sorry."

As he spoke, Asher became aware of the look on her face and the fact that he was holding her arm. He quickly released her, stepping back in the same motion, then stuffed his hands in his pockets. Misinterpreting his body language for guilt, Cheyenne sympathetically asked, "Did you run over her?"

"No, no, nothing like that. Well, I'll explain later after we get into the light." He didn't want to be tempted to be her comforter, especially when they were alone.

They moved back up the narrow steps from the cellar into the lab. As they stepped through the door into the lab they were met by an incredible sight and sound: Hope was sitting cross-legged in the middle of the lab floor petting her dog. Wiggles was gnawing at a big bone, healthy and focused as could be, save for one small black eye looking up at them. A soft growl informed them the bone had been claimed.

Asher stared at the dog. A drumming began to fill his head. The magnitude of what he was seeing overcame him.

Cheyenne stopped, momentarily confused by the news she had just heard and the sight before her. She looked up at Asher to question him. Upon seeing his shocked face she quickly slid the squeaky chair behind his knees, pushing him to fall backwards into the seat. His head fell backwards as he stared up into her face.

A look of pure mischievousness stared down at him. Cheyenne leaned down close, looked deeply into his eyes, and wrinkled up her nose while flashing him a big dimpled smile of satisfaction.

He stared back at her. Shakily he asked, "The brew?"

Cheyenne couldn't repress a giggle. "Told you it works, city boy. Maybe you should start multiplying the chickens and the eggs."

6

HOPE'S VISITATION

Here I am Lord, speak, your servant heareth.

It took a great deal to wake Hope. During the day she was full of energy and used up life as if every drop must be squeezed out of every moment, but at night she slept like a small, worn out child. Today had been filled with making another brew, plus teaching Cheyenne the last of what Hope had learned over the years concerning the brew. Hope had easily fallen into a deep sleep as was her custom. Normally she would still have been sleeping, but now her eyes opened. She'd been awakened by the sound of a loud, commanding voice. "Hope, Wake up. Hope."

Beside Hope lay Malachi in a deep sleep. Confused, she wondered why Malachi hadn't heard the voice. Was her mind playing tricks?

Her foggy brain woke up as the voice again spoke. "Hope, wake up. I have something you need to do. Tonight, Hope! It must be done tonight."

Now she knew the voice she heard was real.

Without delay, Hope jumped out of bed and searched for her house-coat. "I am here, Lord. Tell me what to do." She trembled at the strange yet marvelous thing that was happening to her.

Again the voice spoke with firm command. "Take two clean six gal-lon buckets and one length of 36-inch tubing. You'll find it on the pan-try shelf. Take it downstairs. Siphon the juice off the top of all 22 gal-lons of brew and fill the buckets. Take the two big buckets to your lab.

Then, Hope, listen to me; this is important. You must add two drops of the contents of the small dropper bottle that is with the bag of herbs into each of the big buckets, mix it, then pour up the brew into the new, unbreakable jars that you sterilized yesterday. Seal them. Then package the jars for my servant, Timothy Vick. Go now." Hope was conscience-stricken. She had heard Vick had fallen ill. She had not sent him the brew, thinking his illness was not threatening—something he would get over soon enough without any special treatment. Now she hurried to do what she should have already done.

Leaving Malachi snoring peacefully, Hope gathered the buckets and tubing and went down the steep ladder into the lab, not bothering to go around to the easy outside entrance. Once in the lab, she proceeded through the heavy door down into the damp, dim cellar to do as commanded. God gave her both courage and strength. She looked at the long line of gallon jars and began her job. She stopped at the 23rd gallon, knowing that the fermentation had not yet finished. Her mind suddenly remembered her own man's need of the brew. Yikes ... only one gallon left for Malachi. Well, there's no sense in sending half-finished stuff, so I'll keep this one for him. Keeping him alive is just as important as keeping Vick alive. So I gotta have something to give him until the shipment comes in from China in the Fall. One measly little gallon ... I guess I will have to cut his dose down to less than one fourth ... maybe less. Her mind shifted to prayer. "Oh Lord, multiply ... multiply. I know you will do something to stretch his brew."

Hope's hands were busy. Her mind was racing. "God, I sure would find it interestin' to know why you woke me out of a heavy sleep to do this job in the middle of the night. But God, you are God, and you can wake me anytime. I'm just naturally curious since nothing like this has ever happened to me before."

∽

It was very early Sunday morning when Hope finished her task. A pastor friend was scheduled to fly out to Bangkok later that morning.

I Samuel 3 - During the night God speaks to the young Samuel. ∽

Before dawn, just as Asher was about to leave for his early morning prayer walk, his phone rang. The number on the telephone ID brought immediate anguish. Last evening Malachi had agreed to deal with the situation of Derek after Sunday service. Asher groaned a plea, "Oh, God, no! Please God, don't let it be that that slime-wad already got the brew."

It was Hope's voice instead of Malachi's on the other end of the line. She sounded strangely confident. "Asher, this is Hope." When he heard her steady tone, he relaxed. "I need you to do somethin'. Can you come here now?"

Asher answered as if he had been standing waiting for the call and the order. "I will be there in five minutes."

The boxes were addressed and ready when he walked into Hope's lab. Evidence of much activity lay all around. Hope's face looked so different that Asher remained silent. She looked resolute, confident, and resigned. Her face reminded him of old black and white photos he had seen of men who had been in a terrible battle and knew they had won.

"Take these boxes to the airport. You know that John Mark and Pastor Bellmont are scheduled to fly out around 10 A.M. I want John Mark to hand deliver these boxes to Timothy Vick in two days. Pay whatever the cost. We will cover it. Just make it happen."

Asher asked, "This is the brew?" Hope nodded. The young man quickly picked up his cell phone and headed out the door to back his truck up to the lab door for loading. He was relieved that God had gone before him.

The previous afternoon, Asher had told Malachi of Derek's activities. They agreed that he was likely after the brew. If Derek was planning on stealing the brew he would find it gone. Malachi had been confident God would intervene.

Now as Asher drove to the airport with the brew, faith and hope were born in him. Asher prayed as he drove, speaking aloud to God with great joy. "Well, Lord, this brew seems to be from you. I don't understand why. It doesn't seem to be your way." With newfound confidence, the young man was overflowing with thankfulness. "Thank you, God, for letting me be a publisher of the gospel."

⚬

Hope was staring at Malachi when he opened his eyes that morning. "Man, did I sleep well," Malachi remarked. "I can't remember a night when I slept so heavy. It must be the clean spring weather. I sure like sleeping with the window open. I'll be fresh as a daisy and wild as a tiger today." Malachi lunged at Hope, making tiger noises while rolling over and over with her in his arms. It was a child's game they had been playing every morning for 40 years. This happy wake up time first started with the babies as they came along, laughing and playing, and blowing and snorting until everyone was giggling. The small children grew up, so now it was just the two old folks, but the happy wake up time was still fun.

Malachi crawled out of bed and slipped into the bathroom, calling out, "How did you sleep, Hope? Are you all rested up and ready for a big day?"

There was a delay before she answered. "Why don't you come on back to bed and let me tell you about my night? It was quite unusual." Something in Hope's tone caused Malachi to do as she requested. He lay quietly with his hands behind his head and his eyes closed listening as Hope told him all that had happened during the night and what she had done.

Malachi sat, taking her into his arms, holding her tight for a long time, then he stared deeply into her apprehensive eyes. "So be it. Let's pray for the shipment to get through to Timothy." The lovers clasped hands, closed their eyes and began to pray.

DELIVERING BREW – Asher glanced at his watch. "Still be on time for church … maybe." He had barely made it to the airport in time to deliver the boxes to Pastor Bellmont. Asher grinned as he remembered the big man's reluctance to take Hope's heavy boxes to Thailand. Although Pastor Bellmont had demanded to know what was in the boxes, Asher had not answered. Bellmont was a good Baptist, and good Baptists did not partake of brews, nor did they deliver them to missionaries. Vick was different. He would take anything that kept him alive and in the publishing ministry.

He eased the truck off the interstate onto the country highway and was amazed at the heavy canopy of green trees this early in spring. "Green ... if I had to say what color Tennessee was I would say green." He yawned and stretched, then casually glanced in the rear view mirror. "Oh Lord, not again." Instantly he could feel the hammering of his heartbeat in his ears. It was racing, making a drumming noise. "Oh God, don't let it be him." Asher ignored his exit and kept driving, not willing to take the chance that the car following him was the same one that tailed him in Washington State. It sure looked like the same cream-colored Passat. The same darkened windows, which made it impossible to see the occupants. The same dent in the front side.

His life in Seattle seemed a lifetime away, a million miles behind him. "God ... how did they find me down here? I guess Dan really made them mad ... or maybe it was the *God's Story* books I gave to their youth that made them mad enough to hunt me down. Now they've found the source."

At the next road he turned left. His eyes narrowed. Resolve settled deep in his chest. He reached under the seat, pulling his pistol into his lap. *If they want to play ... I'm ready. I won't be an easy target.* When he looked back again the car was gone.

DEREK'S GALLON – At 11 A.M. that Sunday morning Derek and three well-paid teenagers slipped into Hope's lab and then through the cellar door. The Freemans were at church. "What the &%#.?! The lids are off! Some stupid fool has left the lids off and now the fruit flies are here!" Derek raged. Only one gallon remained. "One lousy gallon and it cost me 150 bucks to pay these goons."

At the cellar door, Derek remembered the quart he had briefly heard Hope mention. He went back to get it but found a big, nasty looking brown recluse spider crawling across its top. He shivered and stomped his foot in nervousness. "Ha, they can have that jar. I can come back in the fall and help myself to the little fancy bottles coming in from China." Derek cocked his head to the side, listening to Wiggles' constant barking, "Well, listen to that." Something ugly passed over the fat man's countenance. He hated to be bested. "As soon as the brew gives me back my man-stuff I'm gonna get me a piece of that skinny Indian gal."

7

THE FAITHFUL PRAYER WARRIORS

Months passed, yet Henry and Mary still faithfully prayed for their little Mary. As often as their tired bodies allowed, the decrepit old couple climbed into their ancient car and drove to their designated parking place.

Freezing cold nights and hot sultry evenings passed and when their worn-out bodies were desperately tired, the old couple climbed into their car in order to watch and pray for the one God had given them as a burden and as a promise. They prayed with hearts that broke anew each time the girl got into the car of another godless stranger.

One late winter night a girl with very short, spiked, coal-black hair stood in Mary's place. "It's her, Henry. She's just cut and dyed her hair. She wishes she were someone else. I remember when ... I can tell by the way she stands. Besides, girls don't take each other's spot. Mary always has that large satchel sitting at her feet."

Henry looked confused as he stared at the waif-like figure across the street. "She looks so skinny. I know we missed a few weeks coming here while I was in the hospital, but I don't remember her looking so skinny."

The old woman's eyes clouded with unspoken pain. Her trembling voice was a bare whisper. "I know Henry. I know. But, trust me ... it is our Mary.

That chilly night they watched as their little Mary got into a two-door gray Cavalier. They knew her life was in jeopardy.

Henry cried out with renewed faith, "Oh Lord, stop the evil man. God, put little Mary in a place where she will need to call out to you. God, we put her in your hands. We believe that you will bring her to yourself. We bless your name Lord, for you are worthy to have glory and praise forever and forever."

They returned each evening to pray for her until five months later, when Henry died peacefully in his sleep.

The frail old woman was moved into a nursing home, but her days were spent in continued prayer for the unknown girl. "Dear God," the nurses would hear her pray over and over in her weak whispery voice, "You are able to stop the evil man. You are able to stop the traffic. You are able to bring light into the darkest mind. You are able to send a good family to help her. Bless them, Lord. Keep this blessed family safe! Make your light to shine on them as they shine their light on our little Mary. You are able to give beauty for ashes. We look to you for the beauty from the ashes of little Mary's life. You did it for me! Please, Lord, care for this child."

The attendant leaned close and asked, "Would you like to sit on the porch this morning, Mary Dotty? It's warm, and there's a gentle breeze. This old place can get stuffy after a while. Let me help you to the porch for some fresh air."

Even as the attendant rolled her to the porch, the old woman continued to pray for little Mary as she and Henry had done hundreds of times before. Curious, the worker asked, "Who's little Mary? Is she your great granddaughter?"

The gentle woman shook her head and smiled. "No, not my granddaughter. I haven't any children. Little Mary is a prostitute, like I once was." Seeing the doubt in the caretaker's eyes, Mary continued, "It's true. I see you shaking your head, but it's true. Once I was a terrible, terrible sinner just like the little Mary I pray for. My little Mary will soon hear of Jesus' forgiveness and become my heavenly sister. God is doing for her what he did for me. She will soon be his. Little Mary will be made clean. God told me."

OLD MARY

Smiling, the attendant gave Mary an affectionate smile and a pat before she turned to walk back into the building, telling another attendant what Mary had said. The nurse shook her head as she said, "Poor thing. That sweet lady wouldn't know terrible sin if she fell into it up to her neck."

The angel standing nearby readied himself to dispatch her prayers heavenward. His form was large and powerful. He smiled after the ignorant caretaker. *Little does she know.*

The invisible warrior of God now leaned over the old lady, ministering comfort to her heart. *Mary, just keep praying. Mary Magdalene still needs your prayers.*

Mary's weathered face glowed with certain peace as she smiled brightly at the surprised angel. Her dimmed eyes saw him clearly. She responded, "Oh! I will! I will!"

Be not forgetful to entertain strangers:
for thereby some have entertained angels unawares.
Hebrews 13:2

8

*Ye shall not need to fight in this battle:
set yourselves, stand ye still, and see
the salvation of the LORD.*

II Chronicles 20:17

OMAR'S HEART, FRIDAY, APRIL

In the distance, Omar saw the girl standing beside the road at the intersection of two country highways just east of town. Her arm sagged as she held out her thumb for a ride. She might have gone unnoticed, but today there was an unusually long line of cars. Traffic had slowed. Impatiently, Omar flipped open his phone to see if there was coverage. Of course, there wasn't. He spoke out loud as if he were able to talk on the phone to his friend concerning tonight's meeting. "Asher, you might get to teach if these cars don't get moving." He slapped his phone shut. His eyes were drawn back to the pathetic girl.

"Skinny ... Hunnee child, you are skinnier than Cheyenne ... and that is skiiiiiiiiinneee." She couldn't be more than sixteen, yet her stance and expression showed a tiredness beyond her years – bone dog tired. Watching from the line of cars, Omar shivered with an unexpected chill.

Turning his face to the rear view mirror, he began to review the text for tonight's meeting. He would be teaching on Hebrews, chapter 4. He softly quoted the passage.

> *Let us therefore fear, lest, a promise being left us of entering into
> his rest, any of you should seem to come short of it. For unto us was the
> gospel preached, as well as unto them: but the word preached did not
> profit them, not being mixed with faith in them that heard it.*

"I'll bet some of those skeptics are ready with their questions to-night. Yessiree, I sure like to be prepared when I meet with folks who don't believe the BOOK. They worship their edumacation. It's good to know God's irrefutable truth. God help me tonight …" Omar stopped talking to his Savior, for he knew when something was hindering his prayers. The passage from Luke 10:27 resounded in his consciousness.

Thou shalt love the Lord thy God with all thy heart, and with all thy soul, and with all thy strength, and with all thy mind; and thy neighbour as thyself.

He looked up again at the road ahead. In the distance, the girl was still there. She continued to hold out her thumb in a way that seemed to expect no one would stop. "Lord, that white girl is PALE. I do be-lieve that is the whitest white I ever did see. Sick, Lord, she looks sick. Help her, Lord."

And one of you say unto them, Depart in peace, be ye warmed and filled; notwithstanding ye give them not those things which are needful to the body; what doth it profit?

It had been years since he memorized James 2:6. Now it came to him unbidden.

Omar continued to wait in the long line of cars. He checked his watch and muttered, "Ten minutes. I'm supposed to be teaching He-brews in ten minutes! This line looks to go on forever." The line inched forward at a snail's pace. "Lord, where are all these cars coming from? We're out in the middle of Nowheresville! Can't you just push them along a little faster?"

Normally the county road was empty. Today there was a steady stream of cars at least a mile long coming from the southwest. Maybe there was a bad accident up on the highway and they had diverted traf-fic this way to bypass it? Omar sighed in frustration.

Sticking his head out of the car window, Omar called to the man in the truck in front of him, "What's going on? Was there a wreck on the highway? Where's this traffic coming from?" The man's face registered puzzlement as he lifted his shoulders and shrugged, not knowing.

As Omar's dark eyes moved over the line of traffic. His gaze was drawn continually back to the pale, empty eyes of the girl, provoking him to call out to God on her behalf. "Somebody help that poor girl! Lord, send someone to help her ... God, somebody needs to pick her up. God, I'm asking in Jesus' name. You said we have not because we ask not, so I'm asking you right now. Thank you, God. Amen and Amen."

> *Also I heard the voice of the Lord, saying,*
> *Whom shall I send, and who will go for us?*

Isaiah chapter 6, verse 8. By now he had given up trying to recall his notes on Hebrews. Glancing back up into the mirror, Omar saw tears on his face. He grimaced with intense emotion. "Lord, someone helped my own sweet Tess when she was a young girl in trouble. Thank you, Lord, that you caused somebody to help my sweet wife."

Again he checked the traffic ahead. The girl looked miserable as she clutched her baby tightly to her chest. He groaned, "Lord, she is way too young to have a baby! That's a fact. Help her. Help her!"

As though the other drivers could hear him, he began to speak to each driver that passed the girl. "Okay, You. You, in that yellow bug, stop! Did you hear me? I said stop, and help that girl!"

Five cars ahead, an old lady with beauty shop smooth hair was driving a blue Lexus. The fancy blue car with the sweet-looking woman neared the young girl. At the first opportunity, the old woman sped off. Omar watched the driver depart and slammed his hand down on the steering wheel in frustration. The girl drooped against the light pole.

"That is so wrong ... so wrong! Okay, now, you. Fine Christian family up there with your head coverings and car full of young-uns. I see you with that over-sized van. Pick that poor girl up! I tell you to do what you know is right!" Omar's voice had taken on the cadence and swing of an old-timey preacher. Yet the large van slowly pulled into the oncoming traffic, forcing the line to break to let them onto the highway.

Vexed, Omar put his head down. "Care, people! Care! God said go into the highways and byways. Well, this here's a highway, and we are stuck on a byway, so pick the girl up!" He turned his attention to the next vehicle, featuring a bumper sticker declaring Repent or Perish. "Can't you see she won't repent unless somebody preaches the gospel to her? She sure ain't gonna hear you with your windows rolled up! Pick the girl up!"

But he, willing to justify himself,
said unto Jesus, And who is my neighbor?

Looking into the mirror, Omar knew well the verse from Luke chapter 10 that came unbidden to him. The mirror reflected the same tormented look he had seen on the girl's face now etched in his own. "Lord God, please don't make me pick up that girl. You know I already spent ten years behind bars. Please, God, not again."

Roughly, he ran his shirt sleeve over his face.

"Lord, you know how much is at stake. TLP is at a critical time in the publishing. Remember Malachi's dream, Lord! And Asher, Lord, he told us how thousands of Hmong are just waiting to hear. This is just one rebellious girl who's probably heard the gospel a thousand times and rejected it. If I pick up a white girl, it could jeopardize the whole project. A million Muslim souls are at stake and all it would take is one lily-white teenaged girl crying foul. The whole thing would be derailed while everyone at The Last Publishers tried to defend me. God, you know she is going to cry foul! Are you listening? I've just got this feeling."

Omar recalled the discussion he had with Malachi this past week. He could clearly hear Malachi saying, "A blessed life is full of big things and small things. It is having a vision to reach the whole world and spending time fishing with your three-year-old son. It is caring for the masses, and it is having a hungry person over for dinner because you know he needs food and someone to care. The key is not to confuse your Christian social life—which is just a form of entertainment—with ministry. Don't lose sight of the big or the small opportunities in ministry."

At the thought of Malachi, Omar put his forehead down on the steering wheel, "God, I know I never would have learned to forgive and grow as a man without his strong example and solid Bible teaching while I was in prison. God, thank you for Malachi Freeman. I guess it was a very good thing that I did go to prison, 'cause I would most likely be dead and burning by this time if I hadn't got put in prison and heard the gospel. God, thank you, thank you, thank you."

He that findeth his life shall lose it:
and he that loseth his life for my sake shall find it.

Again the word of God came to him. This time from Matthew 10:39. Trembling, Omar prayed, "You know I got a sweet wife and four small children. God, this is Parson County, and White Suprema-cists are everywhere, in every political office. God, please, Malachi says a man of God must be wise. It would definitely not be wise for a black man with a criminal record to pick up a young white girl down here even if she is hungry and sick." The traffic inched forward.

Nothing more came to him. Nothing else was needed.

Sitting slumped and defeated, Omar whispered, "Okay, God. I'll offer her a ride."

Immediately a large man, military by his appearance, arrived from the opposite direction. He pulled his car over, jumped out and be-gan to direct traffic. Ten seconds later, Omar's car came even with the girl's position. His reluctant eyes met hers, and he said, "Hop in if you want a ride." The young girl holding tightly to her baby jumped in without hesitation.

When she was seated, he said to her without looking her direction, "Where to?" She turned her head to look out the window and said in a dull voice, "Anywhere you're willing to take me. I'm hungry. Will you get me something to eat?"

As his car moved out into the flow of traffic Omar looked at the volunteer traffic director. Their eyes met. The large military-looking man saluted him as if in a solemn tribute and called out through the open window, "God will provide."

Blessed is he that considereth the poor:
the LORD will deliver him in time of trouble.

A sob almost sounding like laughter broke from deep within as Omar received the encouragement of Psalm 41:1.

The girl skittishly glanced at him, moving away as if suddenly afraid.

He shook his head at the incongruity of the situation. *Who's more afraid? Me or her? Probably me. She looks mean.*

Omar thought of Tess at home with their newborn. He noted how tightly the girl clutched her baby, and cautioned: "You need to let that youngun' breathe, you are holding him way too tightly in this heat."

The girl shot him a look of bitter hatred as she loosened her grip. "Her, not him."

ↀ

Several miles passed in silence. Without turning her head to face him, the girl glanced furtively at the dark man who picked her up.

Omar could feel the sweat gather on his forehead. The hair on the back of his neck prickled with the potential danger, while his mind engaged in private conversation. *Oh, no you don't! God made me pick you up, and you'd better behave yourself. I mean it. Don't you even think of crying foul. Don't you dare try and take advantage of this circumstance! I've seen that look before.* The man of God gripped the steering wheel until his fingers hurt. He drove the next five miles in silent prayer.

Omar pulled into the Herb Den's parking lot. "I have a Bible class to teach here," he explained. "They serve refreshments, and the girls here will help you." He exited the vehicle and moved around to open her door.

"Do you think any goody-goody two shoes is going to help me?" she snarled.

Omar was aware that Malachi's SUV had just pulled up. He could see Malachi was waiting for a parking spot to clear so he could park. The curious faces of the two Last Publishers employees who were riding with Malachi stared at him through the windows of the SUV.

Omar looked down at the rebellious face of the young girl, seeing her for the scared child she was. Resolve settled over his features. He spoke with sharp authority as if he were talking to one of his own children, "You wipe that sassy face off, girl, and get out of this car right this minute. You owe a little thankfulness right now, and best you remember it. And I said, stop squeezing that poor child." He was relieved that she obeyed as if she were conditioned to do as told.

Asher stared dumbfounded as he watched an edgy Omar enter the Herb Den, escorting a small, pale teenage girl carrying a tightly wrapped baby. Prayer came automatically to his heart. "Lord, he must be scared. Give us wisdom. Help us, Lord."

He turned to speak to Cheyenne. She had already anticipated the need and was unfolding her legs where she sat on the floor. With one fluid movement she bent to pick up the plate of cookies and welcomed the girl with a smile. "Hey, my name's Cheyenne. How about you bringing your baby and coming back to eat some cookies? I think I have some milk and fruit in the fridge. Follow me back, and we'll see what we can dig up."

When the girls had exited the room, every head turned toward Omar. Asher gave voice to everyone's thoughts. "That had to be scary. You okay?"

The two good friends stared hard at one another, sharing a common bond. Omar broke into a nervous smile and began to laugh in relief. "You have no idea. I think I lost ten years of my life from plain fear. Everything I love, I had to put on the line for that skinny girl, and she still might cry foul. All I can say is, she'd better be worth it." Omar sat down quickly as though his legs would no longer hold him and began to tell them about how he came to pick her up.

THE HIGHWAYMAN – As if on cue, Ben and Dusty slammed through the door and rushed into the middle of the room. Excited, they both tried to speak. Dusty, the loudest, got in first. "Sorry, Asher. We know you say to always be on time, but we're late because some guy posing as a sheriff directed all the traffic off'n Highway 64 down onto Route 7. There musta been thirty cars and trucks pulled off afore he got back into his car and drove off. He just flat disappeared."

Excited, Ben added, "Can you believe the gall of that guy? Looks like he got away with it, too. You should hear the police band. They're looking all over for that dude. You'd think he murdered someone, the cops are so mad. Anyway, that's the reason we're late. Malachi's just parked and headed in. I guess he got held up by the traffic too." The boys flopped down on the rug.

Asher chuckled and gave Omar a knowing look. "I guess God deems that gal pretty important after all. You can relax now, brother."

Omar warily replied, "Wonder what God's got in mind?" Then he smiled and did his best Paul Harvey imitation. "I guess you all would like to hear the rest of the story?"

The door opened again and was filled with Malachi's presence, trailed closely by the two TLP ministry employees. "Wait, wait. Hang on 'til we get in the door. We saw your visitor when we pulled up. I've got to hear this one. Oh! But first, I've got a quick announcement to make. We're on our way to another meeting and only have fifteen minutes. The news is just too good to keep, so we came by on our way."

Malachi stroked his long gray beard, took a breath, and spoke quickly. "You all know that we've been short-handed with less staff. I have an idea where we can get the help we need. Actually it's really an idea that Asher and Timothy Vick, our missionary in Thailand, came up with. I'll be filling you in on the details later this week, but I wanted you to know reinforcements are on the way. That should make all our lives a little easier.

"Also, the really good news is that we have had an influx of needed funds. The $222,000 Asher got from Dan's investments paid for the printing of 70,000 more books in the Hmong language, as well as 50,000 in Chinese and 20,000 in Khmer! That's enough for a few books to be sent to every Hmong village in five Asian countries. Vick has crews carrying the books into Vietnam, Laos, and Burma this week. There was even enough to pay for the shipping. This means that the first language group has been reached for Christ, for we have observed that the people freely share the books with everyone." At this, the group broke into spontaneous applause.

Malachi held his hands up to continue. "And that's not all! A few minutes ago, as I was leaving the office, I was told that a lawyer from up north called. It seems that an old Pentecostal lady named Lydia Kaye from North Dakota—a place named Devil's Lake, of all things—died this week and left a fortune designated to be used to print *God's Story* in the Arabic language. The lawyer said she left instructions for the state to give her a pauper's funeral in order that the money be used for missions. The old lady's family is having a conniption fit, but the will is firm and cannot be broken. He is sending us a picture of her quilting prayer group. How's that for a story?" Everyone stood clapping and yelling before Malachi settled them down once again.

Now it was Malachi's turn to give his version of a Paul Harvey impression. "Now I want to hear the rest of the story!" He nodded towards the back of the store where Cheyenne and the strange girl had disappeared. "Truthfully, I want to hear the whole story, but hurry because I only have twelve minutes before I need to leave for Missouri, and I'm not about to get out of here until I know what is going on."

Malachi put up his hands once again. "Wait ... I just remembered. Asher is leaving for Thailand tomorrow to help distribute the Hmong translation of the *God's Story* book. Before I leave, we need to lay hands on him and pray. Much to my chagrin, I will have to hear the rest of the story from Omar when I get back."

The older man glanced back to speak to Omar. "Omar, you will need to give teaching from Acts 6:6 about the laying on of hands to the group this evening since I don't have time."

See page 85 for more on the Hmong people.

Malachi grabbed a plastic chair, pulling it to the center of the group. "Asher, you sit here. Come on, men, and let's pray God's blessing on Asher."

The young man sat in the chair, but his face reflected uncertainty. Malachi smiled. "Don't worry, Asher. God knows we are all running on short time around here, so he is standing ready to receive and answer our hurried request. Let us hope that others are also covering you in prayer."

As the men moved to where Asher sat, Malachi glanced back to where the girls had disappeared into the back of the warehouse. "Omar," he said, "see to it that the group prays for the new girl both tonight and in days to come. I sense God's hand is upon her. Until we know her real name, just call her Mary when you pray. God knows who we are praying for."

Now he surveyed those who sat around watching him. "And all of you need to be patient. She has obviously suffered some serious pain. With pain comes anger; with anger comes a lashing out. Keep in mind Luke 7:47, '*Her sins, which are many, are forgiven; for she loved much: but to whom little is forgiven, the same loveth little.*'"

The old warrior's eyes misted. "Treat her like she is a saint until such day that she comes to love the Savior, because when she does come to know him, she will love him very, very much."

THE NURSING HOME – The nurse came out of Mary's room. "She's gone. She went with a smile."

The attendant who had grown rather fond of the old saint inquired, "Did she say anything?"

"Funny thing, just before she died she said, 'Thank you Lord; I knew you would take care of my Mary.'"

The Hmong People, a note from the author

A few years ago one of my sons took flying lessons from an old Vietnam pilot. While they were in the air the old man told my son his story.

"The Hmong people fought as allies with America in the Vietnam War. They were some of the most natural pilots I ever worked beside. I loved training them to fly and went on raids with them to blow up the elephants that were carrying supplies."

My son was shocked, "Why blow up elephants?"

But the old man only was amused, "Sounds bad, blowing up elephants, I know, but they were vehicles of war carrying supplies to the enemy. Laos had thousands of elephants and they could carry loads where no other vehicle could travel. I really came to love and respect the Hmong pilots. They were a good lot ... by far the smartest people group in the whole area."

My son was intrigued. "Did you ever contact any of the Hmong pilots after you left Vietnam?"

Leaning forward in his seat so he could stare out the window the old pilot answered, "No, much to my regret and frustration. When the USA pulled out of 'Nam, the Hmong people had to flee for their lives into neighboring countries. Their involvement in Vietnam made them a people without a land. Even after all these years they are still living in refugee camps and trying to find a permanent country to call their own. As you know, in Thailand there are several thousand, and then there are groups in Laos, Vietnam, Burma, even a large group that has made it to America. Yet they have always kept their own language, speaking and reading. Almost everywhere they have been their language is banned, yet all their children can read Hmong. They are the most homeschooled people group on the earth." ∽

But the end of all things is at hand: be ye therefore sober, and watch unto prayer.
And above all things
have fervent charity among yourselves: for charity shall cover the multitude of sins.

9

I Peter 4:7-8

MAGDALENE

"What's this place?" The girl looked around nervously. "It smells so strange."

Cheyenne laughed as she led the way down a long narrow path between high crowded shelves. "This is the Herb Den, where I make my living. That smell is the aroma of dried herbs, spices, and berries."

As they moved past the storage area, the girl looked at the high shelves staked with clear bags of what looked like grass clippings or crushed leaves. "Cool."

Cheyenne couldn't figure out what Omar was doing with this girl. She would have dearly loved being back in the meeting, hearing his story, but she planned on finding out as much as possible from the girl before she burst with curiosity.

There was a kitchenette in the back of the Herb Den that was furnished with a small refrigerator, hot plate, table, chairs, and a microwave. Cheyenne motioned for the girl to sit down while she dug in the fridge for milk, cream cheese, and fresh fruit. She knew the girl and the baby would need the extra nourishment. "Do you need any milk for the baby or are you nursing?" The girl fidgeted, looked down and away.

Leaning over with a smile, Cheyenne put out her arms, "I'll hold your baby while you eat."

The girl kept her eyes down as she frowned and pulled her shoulder away, bringing her bundle to her far side as if stating aloud, "Don't you touch my baby."

Cheyenne backed off and smiled. "Fine; hold your own baby. You know, I love to put cream cheese on my cookies. It makes them taste so good, and it helps us skinny girls fill out a little. Would you like to try it?"

As she laid out a tall glass of milk, a plate of fresh made Amish sorghum cookies and a few small packs of cream cheese, Cheyenne made small talk, gently probing for information. "Say, you know my name; what's yours?" The girl held her baby tightly as she ate her cookies, piling on the cream cheese as if she were afraid it would be taken away from her.

Cheyenne struggled with irritation as she watched the girl eat almost the whole plate of cookies meant for tonight's class.

The girl totally ignored her question and kept eating in silence. Licking cream cheese from her fingers, the girl leaned back without ever looking up; she answered, "I ... Uh, well? ... Uh ... My name is ... uh, ... It's Ann."

Disgusted by the obvious lie, Cheyenne stood up and walked past the girl. She busied herself at the counter behind the young mother. "Poor you. That's a bummer. I mean, you don't seem like an Ann. Anyways, you look more like an Esther? Or Miriam? Or ... no; you are a Mary Magdalene."

The young girl bolted to her feet, flipping over her chair, which slammed on to the concrete floor with a bang that sounded like a firecracker. In the whirl of movement, she threw her baby to the floor. With her back pressed against the table, she stared at Cheyenne and hissed, "How do you know my name?"

Startled, Cheyenne grabbed the counter behind her. Her pulse raced and her knees felt weak as she stared into the palest blue eyes that she had ever seen. But her attention quickly shifted to the cast aside baby. Her panic shifted to bewilderment when she realized: It was not a baby.

It was a tattered, dirty old doll. Cheyenne forced herself to breathe and think. Letting go of the countertop, she bent down to retrieve the doll. "Whoops, I think you lost your baby doll. Anyways, what's a big girl like you doing still playing with dolls?"

The girl was looking down with a scowl and did not reach out for the doll. Cheyenne laid it on the table. "Are you finished eating? I'm a pretty good name guesser, but next time I'm gonna' wait and let you tell me. You nearly scared me silly, girl."

Her self control and casual demeanor somewhat disarmed the stringy-haired waif. Magdalene couldn't help but grin. She slowly picked up her chair and slid into it, then wolfed down the last cookie, sucking the cream cheese packages clean. Licking her fingers, she grudgingly answered, "My name is Magdalene; I don't know how you guessed that one. I mean, who's named that?"

Cheyenne studied the top of the girl's head and then her shirt. Where she had held the doll there was a large hole in her T-shirt, large enough to expose her belly. The T-shirt and the skin looked as if she had suffered a burn. The girl was very thin and dirty. She stunk. It appeared that her hair had been cut very short and dyed black a few months back. She had about two inches of dead black hair on the ends of three or four inches of very pale blond roots—a reverse of what you normally see. The picture of street trash, the girl must have been through a rough patch the last several months. "How old are you, anyway? Seems like your mom and dad would be worried sick ... having their little girl out being hungry?"

Magdalene's pale blue eyes finally lifted. She slowly studied Cheyenne as if she was considering killing her. The older girl's mind was working on deciding what she could do for self-defense, but the younger girl suddenly relaxed a bit. "I'm eighteen and my parents are dead. I've been on my own since I came of age and was kicked out of a foster home three months ago." She grinned slightly, satisfied with her lie.

Cheyenne was quiet for a moment, knowing there was no need to challenge her. "Tell you what." She tried to sound enthusiastic. "Why don't you come on home with me instead of going into the Bible class? I'm skinny like you are, just taller, so I have some clothes you could use, though your feet look at least three sizes smaller. I have a great shower with lots of fancy natural girly soaps, creams, and shampoos, and I know how to cut and style hair. Anyways, by tomorrow I could have you looking like a fancy New York City babe. What'a you say, Magdalene? You game?"

A dirty, suspicious face looked up at Cheyenne, trying to figure out the motive behind the kindness. Disgusted by her conclusions, Magdalene asked, "You queer?"

10

... The fathers have eaten sour grapes, and the children's teeth are set on edge.

Ezekiel 18:2b

WORKING GIRL

By Monday morning Magdalene looked like a new person. Cheyenne exclaimed when the girl emerged from her sleeping cove, "Man alive! You're really kind of cute now that you're clean and that awful black hair dye is gone. I guess a couple nights' sleep and five pounds of my food helped round out the sharp edges."

Cheyenne stood behind the small teenager, staring at the beautiful, silky, pale hair swinging with every movement, glistening with golden highlights in the early morning sun. Marveling, she remarked, "You have the palest blond hair I've ever seen. Why would anyone want to cover up such beautiful hair with an ugly black dye?"

A violent jerk of Magdalene's head was the response to the question.

"Okay, but you don't have to be mean when I give you a compliment. Pass the milk and hand me a banana." Cheyenne busied herself with breakfast as she talked. "Anyways, I was telling you about the Herb Den. We have meetings there two or three times a week, like the one we were having when Omar brought you. Omar is married to a sweet lady named Tess, and they have four kids."

"Is that why he didn't want anything from me?" the girl retorted.

Ignoring Magdalene's remark, Cheyenne continued with her dialogue. "Anyways, during the day, the place where we had the Bible study is my mail order herb store. Bobbie Jo is my best friend, but she's half bulldog; she works for me. You'll get used to her. She is the bookkeeper, webmaster, and pulls the orders. The guys literally fall over their feet when she walks down the street. When we are bored, we take walks for laughs.

"Julie is my main packer, and keeps up with shipping inventory. She's a little sweetheart and a real cutie pie. You will just love her. All three of us pack orders, ship, and clean and such. Everyone calls us The Trio because we are always together. Bobbie Jo is big and tough, but she has a tender heart; but don't tell her I said so. Julie is small and has dusty blond hair that hangs just below her shoulders." Cheyenne stopped eating long enough to look up to see if Magdalene was listening, but all she could see of Magdalene was the top of her head.

"Anyways, with all the scare of rats, bird flu, and bad times, we really have a lot of orders. I have been working on some large berry orders with my mom, so it has been hectic. We hardly have any extra time to just play. We used to take ballroom dancing in Trashville, but now we don't have enough spare time; but we're going to start going to the creek every afternoon now that it is getting warmer." Cheyenne stood to take her bowl to the sink.

"Spare me your stupid conversation about your freak friends." Magdalene's nasty response surprised Cheyenne.

"Sure. I certainly don't want to waste my breath on trying to be polite by filling you in on who you'll be working with." Cheyenne's answer seemed to have no rancor, but she felt like spitting in the girl's face.

Stunned by the still-raw anger and hurt the girl displayed, Cheyenne silently prayed for wisdom. *God help us! She is so full of hate, deceit, and fear. Help us, Lord. Please cut away the ugliness from her soul, just like I cut away the ugly dyed hair, so she can see your love.* Then, glancing at her watch, she said, "Anyways, Kid, I work for a living, so we need to get moving. I have hundreds of orders to fill today, and I mean to put you to work helping me. Ready? Let's get moving."

Magdalene took a sullen stance. "Anyways," she mocked, "Don't call me Kid. I'm as far from being a kid as your grandmother."

With a pleasant expression still pasted on her face, Cheyenne spoke again, this time making an effort to drop her persistent use of the word anyways. "Well, it's time to leave if we're going to be on time. And it's your choice what we call you. Okay, Not Kid, I'll call you Mag or Maggie or girl because your name is too long. Which will it be? My mom calls me Shy. Can you believe that? Let's go."

Magdalene leaned back in her kitchen chair and twirled her breakfast spoon as if she had not heard a word spoken. At her limit, Cheyenne's face hardened and her tone lowered. "I said let's go. You can come to work with me or I'll dump you off at the local police, but I am through putting up with your attitude. You got that? Your weekend's over. Come on, Maggie."

The young girl flinched as if she had been slapped, and she quickly responded in a strange little kid kind of way, "Okay, I'll take girl ... just don't ever call me Maggie." Magdalene quickly grabbed her stuff and headed out the door, asking with an incredulous tone, "Do you really have a city called Trashville?"

Cheyenne chuckled as she walked out the door. "No ... we just always called big cities Trashville, and our hole in the wall here we call Nowheresville, and our county we call Hicksville. I never even thought about it." Still giggling as she walked on toward the drive, she asked, "Don't you just love my new truck?" Cheyenne lovingly patted the side of her truck. "I call her Pinky." She opened the door and dumped in her oversized purse. "I'll call you Girl."

As Magdalene climbed into her side of the panel truck, she shrugged her shoulders to show acceptance of her new handle. At that moment she almost seemed like a normal teenager.

"Okay, Girl." Cheyenne, much gratified at Magdalene's response, climbed up into the driver's side of the truck and started her usual morning ritual of loudly singing Snow White's little dwarves work song, "Heigh-ho, Heigh-ho, it's off to work we go, we go, Heigh-ho, Heigh-ho Heigh-ho Heigh-ho ..."

"Hey," Magdalene yelled over Cheyenne's nonsense song, "Why did your boyfriend go to Thailand?"

Cheyenne was caught totally off-guard. "What?" She busied herself shifting into reverse. "What makes you think he's my boyfriend? I never said a word, and you only had a brief sighting of him Friday night when you came in with Omar."

The young girl slouched in her seat, playing with the straps of the worn seatbelt. "Well, you knew who I was talking about … so just cut the crap and tell me why he went over there. Your big crocodile tears when you prayed for him this morning told me you have the hots for him." Magdalene threw a grin over her shoulder as she launched into her mockery of Cheyenne's morning prayer, "Lord, help him as he gets off the plane this morning to find his contact and arrive safely at the mission compound—boo whooo."

Irritated, Cheyenne turned to Magdalene. "You are a real jerk—I mean, first class, outta sight jerk. Did anyone ever tell you that you are a jerk? Well, you are." Cheyenne hit the steering wheel and took a deep breath, trying to maintain her dignity. "Anyways, now that you know that you are a jerk, he is over there to reach the Hmong people by giving them the *God's Story* book in their own language. I know you heard us talking about the Hmong Sunday morning, and you saw the *God's Story* book in English. He wanted to help with that people group because he has been praying for them for a long time, and has given a lot of money to get the gospel published in their language. So we finally got the money to pay for the printing, and off he went to help deliver the books. For your information, he paid for his own trip out of his own pocket. Any more questions?"

Magdalene took on a cynical expression. "Yeah, what gets me is why would they bother trying to reach a sub-race? They sure as h#%% are not gonna be in heaven. After all, they are only half human … like that black preacher of yours that picked me up, doing his Christian duty for the day."

Cheyenne blanched. Her voice was clipped as she trembled with rage. "Excuse me—whatever are you talking about? That is the stupidest thing I've ever heard of."

"Stupidest is not a word. So who is the stupid one?" Magdalene's smug expression mirrored her tone. "Man, it is simple information I learned in Sabbath School when I was ten years old. People of color … Africans, Asians, Arabs, they're not Arian and therefore a sub-race. You must know about the Garden of Eden when Eve fell, then she got it on with Satan, a beast, and bred the sub-race? Remember what Eve said when she found out she was pregnant? 'I have got a man child from the Lord.' Adam was not the father of Cain. She bred with someone she called The Lord. That was the beast of the field—Satan. It's right at the front of the Bible." Magdalene was nonplussed at the blank look in Cheyenne's expression. "Sheesh … you really are dumb."

Out of the corner of her eye, the young girl anxiously watched the silent Cheyenne. She could feel a nervous buzz growing in her stomach as time passed.

Finally Cheyenne responded, "Girl … the day you have one tenth the brains Omar has will be the day you leave the sub-race. Now you listen real close, because I mean what I am about to say; I don't ever want to hear any more of that foul nonsense, ever. If I do, I will take you to the police. No second chances. I can be very heartless and mean when it comes to taking up for my friends."

Magdalene suddenly lurched forward in the old worn seat, studying the rear view mirror. "Woe is us." Her voice took on a childlike vulnerability that Cheyenne had not seen this streetwise girl express before. "Hey, check out that cream-colored Passat behind us. It's a Muslim-looking dude driving. Ain't no doubt about it, he's following us."

Cold fear hit Cheyenne's stomach, but she forced her voice to be skeptical. "You can't see who's driving through those dark windows. It could be a grandma for all you know."

Magdalene's voice sounded shaky as she replied, "I saw an Arabic guy getting out of that car the afternoon the black dude brought me to the Herb Den. I'm an extremely observant person. I recognized the dent in the front of his car. Besides, that's the only cream-colored Passat I've ever seen. Has to be a re-paint job. I remember, all right?"

The dread in her voice was obvious. "Same dude, no doubt about it."

She looked over at Cheyenne to press her point, but noticed white, strained hands nervously twisting around the steering wheel. Magdalene's question carried dread. "But you already knew the dude was tracking you, didn't you, Cheyenne?"

CREAM-COLORED PASSAT – After the girls got out and went into the Herb Den, the cream-colored Passat pulled into the parking lot behind the tobacco store. The driver got out and knocked on the back door—three rapid knocks followed by two slower knocks. The door opened in a few seconds and a Middle Eastern face appeared in the small shaft of light. He looked around hastily and then moved aside to let his brother in. As the door was shut he could be heard saying, "It won't be long now; these Christian Whores will be sorry they defamed Allah. Come in, we have much to discuss. The others are already here. Saheed just got back from the Kingdom. They are going to continue financing our operation."

The door shut and the light went out.

The Kingdom of Heaven suffereth violence,
and **the violent** *take it by* **force.**

Matthew 11:12

- Muslims use several ways to proselytize their religion: Immigration, colonization and out-breeding (producing more children than others around them) are their most effective techniques. After large enough communities are established, violent threats and militant political demands become effective.
- When Muslims move to new countries they tend to become more militant, more conservative and more dedicated to changing their new home to becoming an Islamic nation.
- Islam is a violent religion. Heaven is granted to the militantly faithful.
- It is Iran's ambition to export the Islamic revolution worldwide. At the Muslims' current explosive birthrate it will become a reality within 10 years.
- Billions of dollars from oil-rich Saudi Arabia is funding the building of mosques and training centers in non-Muslim countries (including the USA). These training centers are encouraging and equipping believers to become militantly Islamic.
- Through immigration and out-breeding the Arabic Muslims have already successfully colonized Europe.
- Mohammed is the most popular name for newborn boys in many European cities. In Belgium 50 percent of all newborns are Muslim.

- Now Islam is spreading its wings and is already making itself "felt" in many Asian countries. Japan is currently a new and interesting frontier.
- In one Arabic speaking Muslim community in Bangkok, Thailand, they are over 20,000 strong. You can smell the difference as you drive by, as their cleanliness is not that of the Thai people. Locals fear the strange militant people.
- Russia and Ukraine are dealing with the same phenomena. One in five adults is now Muslim. These Muslim families average 8.11 children per couple.
- Does the Bible speak of Muslims playing an important role in the end times?
- If not, then what could happen that would so change the world that the leaders of the Muslims faith have set into place?
- Only a mighty supernatural intervention could change the destiny they have set into place. From Revelation we know who wins…but how?

friendofmuslim at *www.youtube.com/watch?v=XK1pnCldKZI* for demographics

11

YANCEY, MAY 1ST

Cheyenne got off her stool and stretched. It was still early, but the day was dragging by like it was stuck in thick mud. Long, silky, brown hair fell, touching the floor as the girl arched her back into a U.

Bobbie Jo glanced up at Cheyenne. She grunted with distain, "You skinny girls make me sick. Eat, eat, eat and never gain a pound. Having to work with three skinny-ninnies is a drag."

Cheyenne grinned as she straightened and settled back onto the stool. "Well, I might eat and eat and eat, but it is you who is stuff, stuff, stuffing a cookie in your mouth as I speak."

Bobbie Jo had just pushed an over-sized, freshly made, chocolate chip cookie into her mouth, so she could not speak, but her expression let her opinion be known.

"Shame on you, Cheyenne," Julie's fine, dusty blond hair swung from side to side as she shook her head and finger at her boss. Her dark eyes, thickly lashed, twinkled as she scolded, "You should not tease Bobbie Jo while she's on her diet."

Magdalene's snickers egged Cheyenne on.

Cheyenne took on her favorite tease, becoming a drama queen. She dragged the back of her hand across her forehead as if on stage, "There speaks my conscience ... again. Forgive me ... please ... Bobbie Jo. I am truly sorry I brought to your attention that you are indeed gorging on a cookie when you are supposed to lose five pounds."

YANCEY

Bobbie Jo was getting to her feet when the doorbell jingled.

Cheyenne, hearing noise at the store's entrance, dropped her drama nonsense and jumped to her feet with an eager, breathless smile. Asher had been in Thailand for two long, boring weeks, helping Timothy Vick pass out Hmong translations of *God's Story* books. Although he was scheduled to stay in that side of the world for at least ten more days, Cheyenne seemed not to tally reality when it came to the heart.

"Yo! What's dis place? You guys sell anything, or you just here to smell up da town?"

The stranger saw the beautiful young woman's eagerness and then the slump of her shoulders as she waved a hand in a sign of a dispirited welcome. Obviously she was expecting someone special.

Magdalene's youthful face revealed a rare softness as she observed Cheyenne's breathless eagerness and then her flushed, embarrassed response. *Poor Cheyenne*, the girl rightly surmised, *she has seriously got a bad case for the red-headed dude.* Her eyes narrowed as they shifted to the newcomer's top-of-the-line digital camera with a leg size telephoto lens hanging from a strap around his neck. Exercising her learned trait of sizing up men, Magdalene readily concluded, if he isn't a photographer, he's a very wealthy tourist.

Julie, never one to forget a misdeed, gently nudged Magdalene's arm in warning. The street girl had tried to steal from a customer her first day at work, so Julie was always on alert when someone came in with anything expensive. Besides, for some reason the kid had a special hatred for having her picture made.

The visitor had a purple and orange hat jammed onto his head, holding down a riot of wild, curly, dark hair which poked out from beneath the brim and framed his face in a fuzzy ring. On a day like to-day such hair would have been hot, but the added insulation of the hat would make it insufferable. His red face confirmed this. He appeared to appreciate the air conditioned shop.

Pulling his sticky shirt away from his chest, he ran his hand over his face like a windshield wiper, dripping sweat on the floor. "Swish ... I had no idea it could get dis hot in May. Of course, I've never been dis far South. And you beautiful goils must be da famous Trio," looking around, "except there seems to be four of you."

Cheyenne lifted her brow, showing just a tat of interest, "What do you know about the Trio?"

Pleased with her response, he winked. "Oh, us guys can't give away our secrets."

Bobbie Jo had already decided that this visitor wasn't likely to be worth the time he would take away from their heavy workload. From behind the waist-high counter she leaned down in her office chair, bringing with her a tangle of long curly hair. She quietly whispered to Julie who sat on a stool preparing small round cans of herbal ointment for shipping, "Great. Super city geek alert. Did you get a load of his orange hat? He must share Cheyenne's sense of fashion."

Julie's eyes registered rebuke, but she giggled anyway as Bobbie Jo called out, "Come on in and cool off, since you're already in."

"Gee, t'anks! My name is Reuben Yancey, and I," he lifted his cam-era as though he was stating the obvious, "am a professional, freelance photographer. I'm on assignment for American Joiney Magazine, from New Youk City."

"Really?" Bobbie Jo replied dryly as she continued to stare at the computer screen. "You might have fooled me. Sounds more like," tilting her head back and imitating his nasal whine, "New Joisey to me."

Yancey was surprised by her quick banter. Caught off guard by her tease, he retorted, "Well, I am originally from upstate New Jersey—and we pronounce it Jersey, not 'Joisey'—but I live in New York now, or I did til dis week when I started dis assignment."

Three of the four busy young women looked up and smiled. Magdalene continued to stare at him like he was a poisonous spider. The pale face, eyes, and hair accentuated the vacant stare she threw his direction, making him feel unwelcome.

Bobbie Jo fought down a grin at the man's jittery distraction prompted by Magdalene's spooky stare. Poor guy ... even a jerk deserves to be treated better than that. Bobbie Jo knew her biting sarcasm would be refreshing compared to Magdalene's hexing look, so she broke the silence with syrupy mockery. "Oh, how interesting."

The change in his demeanor indicated he was resolved to start over. "You guys are real workers. I mean, no stoppin' for anythin'." He was trying hard to draw the girls into conversation.

Cheyenne had been edgy since Asher left. Yancey had accomplished just what she expected: slowing down all her workers. "It's the daily grind. Work hard, finish the job, and then take a break. If you don't work hard, you don't finish the job and you don't get a break. Simple logic." She hoped her hint would send him on his way, or at least jump-start her workers.

He registered the remark, the tone, and the looks Cheyenne gave the other girls, and concluded, *she's the boss*.

The young white-headed girl immediately put her head down and focused on stuffing dried herbs into small bags. It was Yancey's chance to stare at her, wondering at her person. *The extreme pale eyes and white hair were unusual, almost like an albino. Young ... early teen, small, likes to stay focused on what she is doing. Good. I hope she never looks up again.* He shifted his gaze to the girl behind the high desk.

For a brief few seconds he observed the bigger, bolder, sexy-look-

BOBBIE JO

ing young woman working at a roll top desk over to the right front of
the store, just behind the lounge. The whine of the printer signaled
that she had just pulled off the day's orders.

A smaller woman with long dusty blond hair stood and turned his
way, carrying a load of bags. She plopped them down on the counter
and then turned to the side table, where she fell into a rhythm packing boxes with books and various half-pound bags of herbs. With the
smoothness of a choreographed dance, she shoved one box down the
rollers to the shipping area for processing while reaching for another
one with no wasted motion, a pleasure to watch.

The girl who seemed to be the boss was sitting at the counter
checking a stack of papers. For a few minutes Yancey stood, leaning
on the other side of the counter, watching each girl. Then he tried
again to win their undivided attention, "Yo, you guys have it set up
like an assembly line in here."

The small packer with the dusty blond hair looked up briefly as she
pushed a box down the line into the recesses of the herb warehouse to
be further filled with additional inventory. She smiled politely as she
acknowledged the comment, momentarily stalled in her work, but
glanced back respectfully at Cheyenne.

Yancey could see the compassion in her soft brown eyes. She's cute, not pretty, not beautiful, not even sexy … just cute in a sweet innocent kind of way. Yancey responded to her gentle smile with a subtle invitation in his eyes. She shyly diverted her glance as a blush stole over her countenance, quickly putting her face down, resuming her packing.

Yancey grinned. A bashful chick, obviously not used to confident men.

He turned his attention to the boss, deciding to make an appeal to her sense of social politeness. "Now dat you know my name, how 'bout tellin' me yours?"

The tall exotic beauty that had frozen him out after that first welcoming smile answered, "Sorry, we're just kinda busy, but my name's Cheyenne," waving her hand toward Julie, her voice softening, "The little blond sweetie over there packing orders is Julie." Now Cheyenne used her head to motion in Bobbie Jo's direction. "The shark at the desk is Bobbie Jo. Kiddo, back there is Magdalene."

Bobbie Jo's voice boomed from across her high topped desk, "Hey, Jules, did you get the re-order on the fifty pounds of Dr. Cinnamon Tea finished? That lady just e-mailed that she wants to add to her order, so hold it for a minute until I can get the rest of it to you. Hey, Kid, we need another big bag of that mix from the warehouse. Use the skid."

Yancey mentally noted the nickname of soft-spoken Julie. Then he began to quietly analyze Bobbie Jo. She was definitely a traffic-stopper: big, generously endowed, well proportioned; and with all that long, curly brown hair, she was loaded.

He noted that Magdalene, pushing the skid, disappeared into what looked like a larger stock room.

His eyes wandered back to the quiet Julie. Meeting her glance, he noticed that everything about her seemed straight except for the soft curls that played along her brow. Her straight, narrow skirt accentuated her small figure and perfect posture. She looked clean and well ordered. In that moment he decided he liked her. *Let the other guys fight over the exotic beauties or the man-eating sharks; I like my girl to be*

JULIE

mine, and mine alone. No ogling from other men. No competition. No reason to feel jealous.

He sidled up to little Julie to try to start a conversation. "What's deez enormous hay bales doin' back here?" The huge bales of herbs were stacked against the back wall all the way to the ceiling. Not waiting for an answer, he continued, "To see dis place from da outside it looks run down, like it's 'bout to go outta business, no flashing lights or anything. But if you guys are able to move huge bales of products, den I guess looks don't count." He casually turned a ledger around where Cheyenne had been working only minutes before. He whistled as he saw the numbers, "Geez … $289,000 worth of muskadine. Heck, I don't even know what dat is."

Cheyenne turned and locked gazes with Yancey. She slowly stood, then walked across the room to him. He stood transfixed as she leaned over him and very deliberately took the ledger out of his hands. Then, still without speaking, she turned on her heels and walked back to where she had been sitting.

Bobbie Jo had watched the interchange with concern. One stupid, nosy dude could cause a lot of trouble with the berry project. The sharp pain in her back screamed of tension. She stood, arching her back and stretching her arms over her head, trying to loosen her muscles, then yawned with a loud groan to lighten the mood of the Herb Den. Her ploy worked better than she could have imagined. Yancey's quick mind forgot everything as he stared flabbergasted at her full-figured body bent backwards. He tried to pull himself together to give Cheyenne the verbal cut he had already formulated, but his mouth was suddenly too dry to speak. Trying to avoid being seen gawking like a stupid teenager, he turned his back to the counter to look at the safe, empty, concrete wall.

Julie was watching. She saw his back flinch at Cheyenne's silent reproach. Less than thirty seconds later she watched as Yancey turned his whole body quickly away from Bobbie Jo's unintentional exhibition. Julie felt a sudden appreciation for the newcomer.

Somewhat regaining his composure, Yancey slowly turned from the wall. He was greeted by a receptive, smiling Julie. This time the invitation was in her eyes. Distracted, he asked Bobbie Jo, but kept his smiling eyes on Julie, "So what has dis place so hopping?"

Bobbie Jo had already become focused on a new set of numbers on the computer screen, so she ignored his question except for a brief blurt, "Rats."

Cheyenne kept her face down and hoped he would not continue asking questions. For over a year, no one who had any ability to search out answers had shown any interest in the brew. A chill of foreboding passed over Cheyenne as she sat listening to him focusing his inquiries on Julie. *Our one weak link ... but at least she doesn't know much ... I think.*

"Rats?" Yancey looked at Julie for an explanation. Half laughing, he asked, "Is she calling me a rat or is rats da answer of why business is booming?"

Julie's face flushed as she observed both girls' studied busyness, which forced the naïve girl to answer, because she could do no less than be polite, "Some herbs kill rats."

Yancey's responding smile seemed spontaneous as he looked at the blushing girl. Cheyenne could see he was either totally charmed by Julie's sweet, girly hesitancy or shrewd enough to see that she was the type of person that was always eager to please. In either case, his voice portrayed that he was obviously glad for the opening. "What you guys need is a cawfee shop. Dey's all over in New York, and dis little town could use some class."

Julie looked surprised at his suggestion. Her voice was full of wonder as if she thought he was really intelligent to think of such a splendid idea. "That is exactly what Cheyenne wanted to do when she put this place in. But there are mountains of health forms and all kinds of other rules and regulations that have to be followed for a food place, so she dropped the idea. Besides, we are really too busy with what we have going."

"Well," Yancey noted the furnishings, "Da place looks like you use it for a hangout sometimes wit da couches and chairs. You already have a sign, 'Da Herb Den.' Dat's cute." None of the girls immediately responded. "So what do you guys do when people come to da Herb Den?"

Julie's flushed face looked up at Yancey, then over to Bobbie Jo, who was still staring unblinking at the computer screen, although her face showed that she was well aware of every word said. Julie suddenly felt trapped, so her words came out a little twittery. "Well, everyone wants to know what God says about Islam in the last days, and about Israel. Since last year you can't go anywhere, not even to the mall, without thinking you might get blown up, so it's on everyone's mind. If that were not enough, the news is full of a dozen different volcanoes that are threatening to blow, including Yellowstone. The Herb Den

Yellowstone - Brooding an estimated six miles beneath the scenic wonderland of America's Yellowstone National Park is a vast liquid time bomb the size of Lake Michigan. Made of molten rock, thus ultra-hot subterranean reservoir of volcanic magma will, almost certainly, one day burst forth upon the world, changing our planet's history just as proto-Krakatoa did fifteen centuries ago. Yellowstone is host to the world's largest dormant volcano—a huge caldera covering around fifteen hundred square miles. ∽

gives people a place to gather and ask questions. So basically, we do kind of have a coffee shop minus the coffee and donuts. We just serve tea and cookies for free."

Yancey looked interested, yet took on a cynical tone. "Yeah, good old Father Abraham sure produced da scourge of da earth. Da*# Jews, excuse my French, ladies. Anyway, the bombin's is why I left da Big Apple. About half da population up dere have fled. Dere have been 86 bombin's in da last six months alone. No sense pushin' fate. Since nothin' has happened down dis way yet, I figure I'll sit it out in da deep South."

Everyone seemed to freeze as they all tried to decide what he had almost said. For a second he sounded very anti-Semitic. It was a touchy subject due to the White Supremacists in the area making such a big issue of their hatred for Israel. An awkward silence filled the room until Cheyenne finally muttered under her breath, "Maybe ... at least we hope not ... not yet, anyways."

Yancey's head came up like a radar. "What's dat supposed to mean?"

Cheyenne nonchalantly lifted her shoulder. Yancey stared at her, waiting, but she didn't elaborate. Again an awkward silence filled every space. Yancey seemed to be hoping that Julie would again open up to him, but she had turned her back and was packing bags of herbs into a big shipping box.

Giving up waiting for an answer, Yancey walked over to a table, picked up the Old Gent's book, *God's Story*, and began flipping through the pages. "Hey, dis is some quality artwork. The drawing looks like da same artist dat did da Incredible Hulk comics." Yancey suddenly looked up with narrowed eyes and his voice held question, "Malachi Freeman ... sounds Jewish?"

Cheyenne had been leaning down to pick something up off the floor so she missed Yancey's expression, "Naw ... . not Jewish. Lots of Christians use Old Testament names for their kids. But yeah." Cheyenne's smile showed her dimples, but her eyes remained elusive: *Why was this guy so interested in whether they were Jewish?* Her voice did not betray her concern. "My dad wrote that. It's causing quite a stir all over the world. His ministry sends out free copies to all the prisons, and he gets thousands of letters from prisoners thanking him for the message of salvation. It's also being published in many other languages. The Last Publishers Ministry gets letters from people from all over the world about how it has blessed them. Some in languages they can't read, especially a lot in Arabic."

Yancey noticed her perk up, especially at the information on the Muslims. "Why's he givin' books to da Muslims? Dey're all very religious, so he's wastin' his money tryin' to convert dem." Agitated, Yancey kicked out his foot. Bobbie Jo and Julie exchanged troubled looks. Magdalene, ever observant, pushed the heavily laden cart up to where Julie was working and caught Bobbie Jo's eye communication with Julie. Something was up.

The obvious irritation in Cheyenne's voice as she challenged the newcomer confirmed the girl's suspicion. "Have you got a better idea how to solve the problem of Muslim terrorists? It's not going to go away. There's no place to run, no country to flee to that isn't home to Muslims. Saudi money is financing their spread in every country, even right here in this podunk town in Tennessee. There is no other Muslim solution unless God does something. We are hoping to be a part of that solution. Besides, Muslim people as a whole have never been allowed to hear the truth. In some countries many can't even read. My parents want to help give them the same opportunity the rest of the world has had through this Bible story book."

Bobbie Jo had a unique knack for doing several things at once. Now she was typing away on the computer as the conversation unfolded. She abruptly shoved back her chair and spoke up in her loud, commanding voice, "You know, Yancey, two evenings a week we invite either the Old Gent—that's Cheyenne's dad—or Omar to come and conduct a Bible study, followed by a question and answer session. They just answer whatever questions people have from the Bible. The crowd is usually small, about ten to fifteen young adults, but it's a serious group. Like Julie said, we always have tea and cookies." Bobbie Jo looked down at her watch. "Saturday night is our next meeting. That's just the day after tomorrow, at 6 P.M." She glanced up at him and smiled. "You're welcome to come." Yancey flushed with the feeling of unexpected success.

The shop door opened.

HILLBILLY WOMAN – The four girls and Yancey all looked up when they heard a small, timid voice come from the partially opened front door, "Howdee. Kin I c'mon in, or yuns onliest mail order?" A young, very pregnant woman stood peeking through a small opening in the big glass door. Her clothes looked like Goodwill would have thrown them out, and her greasy hair was covered with an equally worn out old cloth—an attempt to be what the locals called an Amish wannabe. When she smiled, her teeth showed several rotten spots which screamed of bad breath. Altogether, the poor girl grabbed the girls' heartstrings as someone pitiful and in need of a friend.

Always the advocate of the downtrodden, Cheyenne moved toward the front counter and smiled with welcoming warmth at the young woman. Speaking in a friendly voice, trying to put the girl at ease, she replied, "Well, we are mail-order, but we can help you this once. Come in. I haven't ever seen you around here. Where're you from?"

Stepping in heavily and moving aside for the door to shut, the pregnant girl responded gratefully to Cheyenne's friendliness as though starved for female conversation. "Well, wees from up th'air in the hills. We ain't got no car, so we ain't out to these parts much 'cep when we gots t' lay in supplies. Then we make camp oer yonder unner the bridge with our horses."

Bobbie Jo stood up. "That's cool. Do you live near the Amish community up there? I love horses. My name is Bobbie Jo. What can we do for you?"

The girl flushed and looked down at her feet. "Zulla Mae is my name. I was a'named after some fancy movie star my daddy onct' saw. I kinda' like it. And yeahs, we live next door to some Amish, and we are plain livin' like they is. We buy and sell and work with em, but we ain't Amish. Theys German like, so theys talks funny." Now she carefully unfolded her list, then flattened it on the counter, pushing it forward. "Well, I'z a wondrin' ifen I could buy some herbs frum ye. I don't rightly know much about store boughten herbs, but I'm a studyin' on it. Shore smells good up in here … like lemons." The pregnant girl's voice was more hillbilly than Hope had ever thought to sound.

From his corner of the room, Yancey made a slight snorting sound.

"We're packing Lemon Balm today, and it does smell nice," Bobbie Jo answered with a note of sweetness reserved for rare occasions. With her eyes, in contrast, she shot daggers at the photographer. In that moment she could have strangled Yancey as he leaned against the wall behind the country woman. He caught Bobbie Jo's eye and immediately straightened up.

The country voice caught Cheyenne's attention as she asked, "Mind if I ax ye, what's it fur? That thar Lemon Balm? Whatchee use it fur? I b'lieve we gots us some-a that a growin' up the mount'n."

As Cheyenne scrolled down the list the young woman had handed her, she answered, "It's best known to help destroy the virus that causes fever blisters on the lips, but you have to add it to several other herbs and coconut butter for it to work effectively. We make a lip balm here at the Herb Den that we sell."

The pregnant lady looked highly impressed with Cheyenne. "Are you da' Indian gal folks talks about that makes a stuff that can bring folks back from da' dead?"

Cheyenne looked up, trying to force herself into laughter, although she felt faint that apparently the rumors had gone so far. "Well … that's interesting. Has someone invented something that raises folks from the dead?"

The hill woman shrewdly studied Cheyenne for a brief moment before she laughed, "Yeah … folks will say anythin'." As she spoke she cut her eyes over to the man with the camera then back up at Cheyenne. Zulla Mae widened her eyes with wonder as if she were meeting a real shaman. Her voice held a wonder that she hoped would provoke more mockery from the camera man, thus dulling his interest in what she had just said about the healing tonic. "My widder womern friend told me I oughtta set in a supply of herbs—just in case—wid all the rats. Did y'uns hear in South America theys found a whole string of villages—pert near 20,000 people—dead with sum kinder plague? Theys a thinkin' it wuz the rats that brought in the fleas. Last ev'nin' the public channel ran that special 'bout the Black Death plague. Said fleas on the rats carry plague. We knowed some folks here in town, and theys had us'ns over t' watch the TV. 'Cept my 11 month old boy cried pert near the whole way through the show, so I missed mosten it. I shore hated missin' it. It is terrible to onliest get to see a TV oncet in a year and then the baby cry all the way through."

The girls all nodded their heads in understanding. They had watched that same program together, thinking about their Amish neighbors' children who had been bitten by rats just this past week. Now even Magdalene moved in close to listen to the strangely compelling pregnant woman.

Seeing her audience was soberly listening, she continued, her big eyes full of foreboding. "I don't 'member. I just knowed I need sum Caster Beans and sum Fox Glove. My widder womern friend grew it last yaar. I ordered the seeds frum a mail order book, but it will be awhile 'foren anythin' can make fur harvest, seein' as hows it's still spring, so ... Anyways, 'bout them rats; It's the vary same thang that wuz a happenin' durin' the Bubonic Plague, and then Black Plague, as what's a happenin' now with them rats: multiplyin' with the bamboo a comin' into bloom every 48 yaars. Shorely y'uns has heard 'bout that? I like t' read, and I gots me lots uv ol' hist'ry books 'bout the dark ages. The librarian gives me more evah time I come t' town. She's real nice."

Bubonic Plague: www.haciendapub.com (old history books available)
Bubonic plague, which struck in A.D. 540, is justifiably the worst recorded pandemic to ever afflict humanity. This epidemic ravaged the populace for five decades between 540-590. It caused the death of at least one-third of the world's population.

>

CHEYENNE, MAGDALENE & ZULLA MAE

Again the girls nodded their heads as one. They had discussed this very topic only a few hours earlier, although only Magdalene had never read a history book on the subject. Magdalene pushed to the front of the counter, her interest suddenly whetted by what the pregnant woman was saying. "Are you saying that there were two different worldwide plagues?"

Zulla Mae grinned, "Honey, days been a bunch of plagues, but the one in 540 was de worstest of all time. Scientists think a really big volcano throwin' ash in the air made that one the worstest 'cause of the weather world wide being cold and no sun ashinin' … no vitamin D3, you know. Nows theys Yellerstone about to blow." Zulla Mae stopped to catch her breath before finishing her tale.

"Anyway, dey says cats helped bring an end to the dyin'." Zulla Mae shifted from one foot to the next as the extra weight from her belly bore down on her poorly clad feet. Turning her head from

Black Death struck 800 years later. The great pestilence of the medieval period was the Black Death (1346-1361), the bubonic plague caused by the then highly virulent bacterium Pasteurella pestis, and transmitted generally by the black rats. Again the plague passed from rat to rat by fleas. The pneumonic form of the plague is most ominous. In this highly contagious acute form the disease may also be transmitted directly from person to person. Up to 90% of France's population perished from this plague. ∞

side to side in her anxiousness and looking over her shoulder as if expecting someone evil to slip up behind her, she went on. "I jus' won-ert if you'uns might be able t' sell me a goodly supply of these here herbs, just in case."

"Just in case of what?" Cheyenne's face was as blank as an empty page, made so by careful practice in hiding a thousand fears. Where had she heard those exact words being used by someone not long before?

Yancey snorted again. His mockery was too obvious to ignore. All four of the young women behind the counter looked at him. He had his head down with his hand on his forehead. His other hand was supporting his elbow as he shook with laughter.

Both Magdalene and Bobbie Jo started to move toward him in de-fense of the young mother. But before anyone else could react, Zulla Mae took three long, quick steps toward the mocker, bringing her up uncomfortably close. He looked up, startled, tried to jump back, but was already against the wall, so he just flattened out, looking appre-hensive. Aggressively posturing herself in front of the shocked Yankee, she stared him in the eye and hissed with such vehemence that every-one was stunned. Yancey looked to the left and right, obviously trying to decide the most favorable direction of retreat.

"You'uns kin mock if'n you want too, but I'm a tellin' you a sum-thins' bad is a gonna happen!" Her eyes were ablaze with a strange fiery confidence. "I knowed 'bout things like this here. I gots the gift. And I smell death. Ne'er been wrong in all my bornd days, and don't spect I'm a wrong now. Might not be this month's moon ner the next, but yer gonna see death within a yaar—bodies a layin' in the streets. Maybe yer body, city boy. Write that down on yer calendar. Make yer mark in big red letters. Make shore you put my name a'side it, 'cause I wont you to 'member it wuz me that warned ye."

Yancey's mockery and his courage had failed him, and now he looked genuinely perturbed. To cover his unease and as a way to strike back, he put his camera to his eye and began taking pictures of the strange character. The pregnant woman took it to be an insult, like she was some kind of oddity. She turned her back on him with a show of dismissal and distain.

Cheyenne swept across the room and held up her hand in front of his camera. With a tone of voice and a look that left no room for argument, she commanded, "No more pictures. Shut your mouth or get out. You choose."

Suddenly cagey due to the strain he recognized in Cheyenne's voice, Yancey swung his camera down to his side but kept his finger on the button.

In the next few moments there was a tension that provoked preoccupation with work from everyone but Magdalene. She stood stock still, staring at Yancey with a strange vacantness in her eyes. Julie rushed around either side of Magdalene, gathering bags of herbs, while Bobbie Jo marked it off the inventory and made a purchase slip. Cheyenne made polite conversation with the young woman as she straightened out her crumpled dollar bills, counted pennies, nickels, and dimes. No quarters. Unseen by the pregnant girl, Cheyenne quietly added several pounds of healing teas to her bag, herbs that would aid in her carrying and delivering the child. As an afterthought, she stuffed a few smaller books and pamphlets in the bag, explaining the herbs' use. The girl obviously enjoyed reading.

Zulla Mae picked up the two big bags of herbs and repeated her previous warning. As she spoke, her eyes strayed to Magdalene, obviously feeling a kindred spirit with the white headed teen. "I smell death. I smell blood. I gots the gift. I ain't ne'er been wrong." She then aimed her look at Yancey, staring at him with mixed contempt and pity. Looking again at the older girls, she offered, "Ya'll don't pay him no mind. He's one thems deceived. I knowed that fur shore as soon as I set foot in here. Get ready. I dun smelled death for a while now." She turned, pointing her finger out the large plate glass window of the store front. "And I seened the foreigner watchin' from behind the sign near the alley. Watchin' … watchin'." She looked back, meeting eyes first with Cheyenne, then slowly moving her gaze to each of the other girls, and finally motioning with her head toward Yancey. "He knows."

12

HAVING DONE ALL ... STAND

Fireproof

It was late Sunday night as a weary Malachi and Hope drove up the lonely lane to their home. It had been a long weekend for the aging couple. They had flown out to California where they ministered to a growing home church that had adopted the Swahili-speaking people as their first missionary project. The eager young families had conducted various bake sales, lawn jobs, and even built a few storage buildings to raise money for the translation and printing of *God's Story* in their chosen language. Hope sighed contentedly and commented, "Oh, I'm tired, but wasn't it just wonderful seeing all those fine children so thrilled to help get the gospel out to a people on the other side of the world?"

Malachi was grunting his own joy when Hope's startled jerk instantly brought him to extreme wariness. "Looky there, would you, somebody left TLP ministries wide open." The light was on in the building and Malachi could see the big shipping door raised to reveal the contents inside.

"There must be somebody working," Malachi automatically responded.

"On a Sunday night?" The apprehension in Hope's voice was apparent.

Sounding wary, Malachi cautioned, "You stay in the car, and I will shut the door." Hope waited, but Malachi did not return immediately.

After five minutes he came to the door and waved for her to come in.

"What's that stink?" She asked, as she entered the warehouse. Horrified, she answered her own question. "Someone burned the books!"

In the middle of the concrete floor, ten pallets of the Arabic *God's Story* books were blackened and partially burnt. And beside the burned books was a red, two gallon plastic gas can, partially melted by the fire. Stacked tight as the boxes were, the fire had apparently gone out after the initial flammable was consumed. The whole place smelled of smoke. The ceiling was blackened but hadn't caught fire because it was high and finished with roofing metal. At the time they built it, Malachi chose the metal because it was cheaper, quicker, and quite substantial; now it served another purpose as well.

Malachi stood staring as Hope ranted, "They intended to burn the whole place down! Look, Malachi, they sprayed Allah Akbar on the front wall. Well, that makes it clear what this is all about."

Malachi stared at the wall for a full minute before he spoke. His tone expressed resignation to the inevitable. "It is starting."

Malachi pulled at the charred boxes on the outside of the pile. Unburned boxes lay beneath. The old man smiled. "By all rights the place should have burned to the ground. God fireproofed the three Hebrew children, so I don't reckon a warehouse would be any problem for him. There is nothing we can do tonight." Malachi turned as if to leave, but paused, remembering something. Turning back to Hope, he said, "Let's pray."

There beside the Devil's handiwork, God's two servants knelt and thanked God for his protection and deliverance, committing their ministries and lives to God once again as they had done many times during their fifty years together.

As they closed up the warehouse and left, Malachi said, "Tomorrow we must call a meeting. There is much to do."

Daniel chapter 3 - God saves three Hebrews from being burned alive in a furnace.

LOUISE – As Cheyenne plopped into her seat in the small church building, she slid her arm around the back of Louise's chair to give the old lady a quick hug and a reassuring smile. Asher's old friend had arrived three days earlier to find that he was still on his trip. She had sold her diner and come to Tennessee, just as Asher had suggested. The Muslim problem was getting worse by the day. The city had adopted Sharia law. She was glad to be out of the place.

Hope had put Louise to work in the kitchen within hours. Everyone greatly appreciated the wonderful meals. The last three evenings, Cheyenne had been helping the older woman clean the TLP kitchen while she listened to tales about Asher and Dan. It was almost as good as having Asher back from his mission trip. She was learning far more about him from Louise than she had learned from Asher himself.

Cheyenne's foot tapped up and down as she sat waiting for the meeting to start. She was unconsciously grinning as she relived last evening's story telling. In her mind she could still hear the thrill in Louise's strongly accented voice. "For years theys' ate breakfast evahry mornin' at my place, and evahry mornin' Dan left napkins full of writing and drawings on the table. He and Asher were always either discussing the Bible or inventing something. They would draw everything out. Us gals would always rush ovah ta look at the napkins ta try ta fig-yah out what the scribblin' meant. I think the napkin writing was Dan's way ta entertain us and let us be a part of theys life. So he left us little clues of what thems were planning. The first year Asher started coming he looked like he wahr only sixteen years old. I was sho-wah theys' were spies fo-wah the FBI or CIA tracking down terrorists, becawse of the weird stuff he wrote on the napkins. Dem' boys showah made dat bunch of waitresses' lives wicked interesting just trahyin' ta keep up with ahll thays' new adventyahz. Course, we eventually figured out most of that stuff they was writin' was just Bible charts of prophecy and end time occurrences, sometimes it was their strategy for finding the fish, but it was exictin' while it lasted."

Louise's face had been covered with tears of appreciation as she uttered her simple statement at the end of her story. The thankfulness of the older woman had a profound effect on her young listener. Cheyenne realized that she already loved this animated character simply because Louise's soul was so pure.

The sound of popping gum beside her forced Cheyenne to suppress laughter. She could still see the scene last night as Louise first spit her gum into a napkin then spit on the same napkin to swab her smeared mascara under her eyes as she looked at her reflection in the TLP kitchen window. That was when Louise had been telling her about how Asher learned to fly a plane. "Let's see ... the next yee-ah, theys' spent three months in Alaska fishin' on a boat fo-wah a living. That was the yeah Dan taught Asher to fly planes so he could work as spottahs for the fishing boats. See ... we kept up with evahthin'. We even kept a notebook of 'Dan and Asher's Adventyahz' based on da' little napkin notes. It was Dan that helped Asher be the man he is today."

Quick tears flooded Cheyenne's eyes as she remembered the anguish in Louise's rough voice when she spoke her heart. "Dan was a good man ... a really good man. I loved him."

WARNINGS – Cheyenne's attention was abruptly captured by the silence as her dad jumped to his feet. Malachi's tall, lanky frame moved quickly toward the front, speaking as he walked, "Take your Bible and turn with me, if you will, to the sixth chapter of Ephesians, verse 10." He seemed tense.

Before anyone had a chance to find the passage, and just as Malachi's long legs bypassed the steps to jump up on the two and a half foot high stage to step behind the podium, he was praying, "Lord, give us a heart to see the fields are white unto harvest. Grant us a vision of the best way to reap the crop. Guide my words. Amen ... Amen ... in Jesus' precious name ... Amen."

A small group of people sat in the humble country church building. A request had been made for church members and TLP workers to make every effort to attend. It was a low key request. Most had opted to stay home.

Through the open windows a soft breeze lifted Cheyenne's dark hair from around her face. She pushed it back as she leaned forward to where Asher usually sat. His seat was, of course, empty. She looked down at her fingers, mentally counting the days until he returned. Prayer for him came to her mind as automatically as breathing. "God, give him wisdom and grace. Help him reach those whose hearts you have prepared for the gospel."

The off-balance rocking of the ceiling fan clanged against its pull chain. *Tick, tick, tick.* A small child stirred restlessly and was soothed by his mother. Old Louise's popping gum seemed to be keeping time with the fan. Everyone wondered and waited for Malachi to unveil the reasons for this special meeting.

Malachi stroked his long gray beard and looked at his text. His bushy brows hid his eyes. He seemed to be waiting on God to move him. He looked up, scanning the many empty seats. His face radiated spiritual insight. His searching examination of the room caused others to turn and mentally note the others who were present . . . and absent. It suddenly seemed to matter who was there.

Finally his strong, authoritative voice addressed their anticipation. "You are aware of the failed attempt to burn out TLP Ministries over the weekend. God has sent his angels to encamp around about us this time." Then he looked up, and as if addressing God he said, "May he continue to be our shield."

Searching the faces again, Malachi continued, "Most of you who are here have chosen to commit yourself to sowing the seed of the Word of God. Some of you have sacrificed much, but, I fear, not as much as you will sacrifice before we have completed this journey. Our Lord said,

Whosoever will come after me, let him deny himself, and take up his cross, and follow me. For whosoever will save his life shall lose it; but whosoever shall lose his life for my sake and the gospel's, the same shall save it.

"Paul, in a letter to a young minister named Timothy, warned,

Now the Spirit speaketh expressly, that in the latter times
some shall depart from the faith, giving heed to seducing
spirits, and doctrines of devils.

"It is the latter times. Be warned;

the love of many will wax cold
and
some will depart from the faith.

"Don't be one of them.

Fight the good fight of faith.

"Are you willing to go all the way? Jesus warned,

And because iniquity shall abound, the love of many shall wax cold."

Several people leaned forward, wondering where Malachi was going with this line of thought. It sounded sort of Arminian.

"In his second letter to Timothy," Malachi continued, "Paul further warned that in the '*last days*' there will come '*perilous times*' in which those who are '*godly will suffer persecution*'. And Matthew recorded Jesus' warning that '*a man's foes shall be they of his own household.*'

"Now pay special attention to Jesus' words concerning the last days:

Then shall they deliver you up to be afflicted, and shall kill you:
and ye shall be hated of all nations for my name's sake.

"We are at that point where Bible-believing Christians are hated by the nations—the United Nations—for nearly every nation has signed on to the Universal Child Protection bill which makes it a crime to teach children the precepts of the Bible. They can teach the Koran or Buddhist and Hindu literature to their children. They can even teach their children to hate Christians and Jews, but it is a crime for us to teach children the Bible. Thankfully, at this time our government is too preoccupied with the financial crises and with terrorism to have the resources to enforce their social agenda.

"Jesus continues:

> And then shall many be offended, and shall
> betray one another, and shall hate one another.

"That means professing Christians will betray one another because they are offended by the old historical beliefs. They refer to us as fundamentalists, fanatics. They say we are hateful and a menace to the New World Order.

> And many false prophets shall rise, and shall deceive many.
> And because iniquity shall abound, the love of many shall wax cold.

"There are more false prophets in America than true prophets of God. Just turn on the TV and look at the parade of reprobates conning gullible believers out of their money. The Emergent Church movement has produced cold hearts with its reinterpretation of The Christ Spirit. '*But he that shall endure unto the end, the same shall be saved.*'

"Many are being deceived, but some are growing stronger and more resolute. With God's grace we shall endure unto the end of this great apostasy, and not just survive; we will do as Jesus commanded:

> And this gospel of the kingdom shall be preached
> **in all the world**
> for a witness unto all nations; and then shall the end come.

"We are engaged in the colossal task of preaching the gospel to the whole world. The end will soon come, and will we be found faithful stewards of the precious message of repentance and forgiveness?"

Ben and Dusty shouted, "Amen!" and several others uttered various sounds of agreement and encouragement. Cheyenne found herself wishing Asher were here; he would have loved it.

Matthew 24:10 Speaking of end times, "And then shall many be offended, and shall betray one another, and shall hate one another." ∽

"If you are willing to give your life for the sake of the gospel, you will suffer persecution like the western world hasn't seen for 400 years. Your 'Christian' friends, and even your family members, will betray you to the authorities. John recorded a voice from heaven saying,

Woe to the inhabiters of the earth and of the sea! for the devil is come down unto you, having great wrath, because he knoweth that he hath but a short time.'

"Our enemy is not the Unites States government, though it is hostile to the Christian family. Nor is our enemy the Muslim extremists who have sworn to kill us, nor the fellow Christians who will betray us to our enemies. Our enemy is none other than the old Serpent, the Devil.

For we wrestle not against flesh and blood, but against principalities, against powers, against the rulers of the darkness of this world, against spiritual wickedness in high places.

"Paul told the Ephesian believers how to prepare for and win this battle with the Devil."

Malachi's voice suddenly was filled with power as he began to read God's instructions.

Wherefore take unto you the whole amour of God that ye may be able to withstand in the evil day, and having done all, to stand. Stand therefore,

"Having done all to stand, then *stand*. It is one thing to put on the armor, train for battle, and be prepared to stand. It is quite another thing to stand, *stand*, and keep *on* standing. This will not be one short battle. It is a war with the Devil for the minds of men. We do not go to battle with guns and grenades. We go with a sword, the sword of the Word of God,

…which is a discerner of the thoughts and intents of the hearts of men."

ॐ

Even as the old minister poured out his heart, eight Muslim men huddled in the small storage room in the back of the tobacco shop, reading the latest email from an imam in New York City. "He is due to arrive in two days. He is bringing the explosives with him. Allah Akbar!"

ॐ

"Paul, the greatest missionary who ever took a beating for the gospel, said,

For the weapons of our warfare are not carnal, but mighty through God to the pulling down of strong holds.

"We will pull down the strongholds of Satan by prayer and preaching of the Word of God.

'Praying always with all prayer and supplication in the Spirit, and watching thereunto with all perseverance and supplication for all saints.'

"If we leave the devil alone, he will leave us alone, but if we go into his territory with the gospel of truth, he will come after us. As long as we stand in faith we have nothing to fear. I tell you, Jesus has *bound the strong man* and I intend to *spoil his goods*. I cannot do this alone. Are you with me? Will you pay the price? Will you take up your cross every morning, saying, 'Lord, if it please you today, I am ready to die for you'?"

Malachi paused and looked from face to face. Even the fan seemed to have temporarily gone silent. The room was as still as midnight. A challenge lay in front of everyone.

"This meeting has a dual purpose: One, to encourage those of you who do not want to be on the front lines to depart in peace. The second reason we are here tonight is to teach those of you who are ready to go forward what you must do to prepare yourself for this spiritual war.

"It is possible—I guess I should say likely—that if you continue with me in the publishing ministry, you will be risking your life, and

OMAR

maybe the lives of your loved ones. No, no one will think any less of you if you leave. This is what God has called me to do, not necessarily what he has called you to do.

"I have had a dream, a vision, if you will. I believe God has given me the privilege of publishing the gospel to the Muslim people—a vast multitude of Muslim people."

Malachi was overcome with inexpressible emotion. He leaned over the podium and began to weep in earnest.

Both Julie and Cheyenne, sitting three rows back, broke into sobs, although neither could have explained why. Cheyenne had never seen her daddy really cry, and now he wept like a baby. Even Bobbie Jo's eyes swam with tears at the sight of the strong man weeping.

For a full minute sobs echoed in the church. The small group looked around in mute wonder at the enormity of what they had heard. Cheyenne suddenly thought of how alone Louise must feel, being in a strange new place and now listening to everyone fall apart. She glanced over to the older woman but saw that the old face was full of peace.

From the corner of her eye Cheyenne saw Omar slowly moving to the front of the room. When he reached Malachi he placed his arm across the older man's shoulder, tenderly directing him to his seat. His gentleness toward Malachi and their oneness of heart spoke of a shared vision.

For a long moment Omar thoughtfully looked down at his beloved teacher. Then he, too, searched the countenances of the people before he slowly began to speak. "I think I know what Malachi wants to tell you."

Taking a deep breath, Omar's dark eyes searched the ceiling. Focused, he leveled his gaze on the gathering. "We have spent many hours praying, seeking God on this matter of safety. It is a grave decision, not just for us, but you as well."

THE DREAM – "As you know, Malachi is not a dreamer. He says dreams are the products of too much spicy supper, but he had a dream a few months ago that left him shaken. He believes it is from God. Remember, Acts 2:17 says,

> *And it shall come to pass in the last days, saith God, I will pour out of my Spirit upon all flesh: and your sons and your daughters shall prophesy, and your young men shall see visions, and your old men shall dream dreams:*

"In his dream he saw Muslim people crowded into a tight group. Then, as a camera began moving out for a wider angle, the picture revealed the group was bigger and bigger until he could not see any end to the people, and each one was reaching out his hand trying to receive a copy of *God's Story*. It was almost within their reach.

"Even as the people reached for this book of truth, other Muslims came with swords and began to slay men, women and children until they all lay dead. Hundreds of thousands of precious Muslims fell beneath the sword of their own leaders. Until that time, Malachi—none of us really—had any idea just how big Islam had grown and just how terribly violent it was in its growth.

"That dream awakened in Malachi a vision for reaching the Muslim people with the gospel. Malachi began asking God to provide the necessary funds to mass produce and distribute the *God's Story* book, and to make it available through multiple sites on the web, free of charge, in the Arabic language.

"Just think, Saudi Arabia is closed up airtight against the gospel. Anyone caught with a Bible or Christian literature would be subject to death. No missionary can go there and share his message, but we can go there, directly into the private rooms of everyone who has access to the web. The rulers of Saudi Arabia will be able to secretly read *God's Story* and understand fully the message of salvation. Our little digital missionaries cannot be arrested. If they block one website we will open ten more. As long as a Muslim has access to the web, he will have the gospel at his fingertips. Terrorists hiding in the caves of Afghanistan who have satellite web access will be able to see the gospel in a beautiful presentation. Many will be saved and the mullahs will not like it. We will be targeted. Apparently we are already in their sights, and our book is not even posted yet.

"The reason Malachi invited you here tonight is to help you understand that this coming ministry is both glorious and dreadful. He has received several phone calls and emails warning him against making this book available in Arabic.

"One-fourth of the world is now Muslim. If you add all the Christian religions together, we are not even close to their number. We are overwhelmingly outnumbered by a people residing in every nation, taught to conquer or destroy non-Muslims. There is no place for us to flee.

"Malachi wants you to know his vision and the danger that comes with it. Tonight will be the last meeting in this building. For those of you willing to spend your lives in this great cause, contact us. We will continue to have Bible studies for new believers in private homes, but we will move around a lot, never being in the same place two times in a row."

Without further comment, Omar dropped his head and began to pray. "Lord, make us wise. Cause us to daily put on the whole armour of God. Give us courage for the days to come. In the power of the precious blood of Jesus ... Amen."

Omar stood while the people quietly filed out. Then he walked back to where Ben and Dusty were now standing, quietly talking with Cheyenne and Bobbie Jo. He gave them a searching gaze.

Magdalene's whisper caused all of them to jump. "The car was here. I saw him. Only this time there were three men with him."

"Well," Omar said as he knelt to pick up his youngest son, "This is the beginning."

13

THE WAGES OF SIN

For two weeks the small community was quiet. The news reported a couple of bombings on the East Coast, but even that was less frequent than in the past. The danger seemed far away.

The cream-colored Passat was still occasionally sighted in the area, but with the passage of time the threat seemed to recede. With a sigh of relief, life returned to its happy normal routine in the shadows of the Smoky Mountains.

The moon was new. The rain had continued for three days, preventing their afternoon visits to the creek. When the weather was nice, the expanded Trio would visit the swimming hole to take in the comforting rays of the sun, but the steady rain had kept them indoors.

Adding to their discomfort, Asher's stay in Thailand had been extended. In truth, this last news only set Cheyenne on edge, but her distress was felt by the others. No one knew when he would be back.

Normally, Ben and Dusty would have brought a welcome distraction with their visits, but they were too busy to stop by the Herb Den. Yancey, however, was almost always available. He had visited almost every day that week.

Hormones, lovesickness, cabin fever, loneliness and a prying stranger: the Herb Den had become a powder keg of tension.

Once she settled in, Magdalene proved a surprisingly diligent worker. The girls, glad for the help, welcomed her into their group. Without thinking, they began to refer to her as a member of the Trio, though her addition made them four.

The new bonds of friendship weren't formed easily. Magdalene wasn't trusting by nature. She was used to surviving on her own. Initially, she tested everyone's limits.

Bobbie Jo and Julie were at the packing table taping shut huge boxes full of herbs for shipping. Bobbie Jo passed the time by telling a Bible story. While her hands were busy, her mind was absorbed in her storytelling as she built to the climax.

"Jezebel was standing close to the window so she could get good light as she carefully painted the outline of her eyes black with a mixture made of donkey dung and charcoal—that's what Bedouins in Israel use for eyeliner even today.

"Suddenly two of her trusted slaves rushed into her room, grabbed her by her arms, and threw her out the window. They yelled and laughed as she fell, splattering on the stones below. Just like God said, the hungry dogs ran in ..."

Magdalene interrupted impatiently. "I said I am *hungry*. I want to go eat, *now*."

"ROHFF! ROHFF! ROHFF! GRRRRRR! ROHFF! ROHFF!" Bobbie Jo grabbed Magdalene by her shoulders and began shaking her back and forth while barking and growling like a mad dog.

Magdalene looked like a limp, white headed rag doll in Bobbie Jo's hands. Julie squeaked with panic at the unexpected behavior.

Startled, Cheyenne rushed over to the work area to see what was happening. "Bobbie Jo, have you lost your mind?" she exclaimed in shock. No one even noticed her rebuke.

Magdalene began to whimper. Bobbie Jo's voice remained gruff as she shoved the teenager to one side. "Don't you *ever* interrupt one of my stories again. I'm through with your spoiled self-centeredness. Got it?"

Magdalene silently nodded.

Cheyenne and Julie glanced at each other. They both now understood that what had just happened was crude but necessary. Without respect there could never be true friendship. From that moment forward Magdalene realized that either she would be one of them, do her share of the work and treat others with respect, or she was out. In a strange way, she immediately bonded with Bobbie Jo.

∽

Later that same week, Bobbie Jo called out, "Hey Kid," as she tossed Magdalene a copy of *God's Story*. "Sit down and finish reading this. It's raining, so we can't go down to the creek today. Since we're going to be stuck here for a while, I'm going to catch up on the bookkeeping. Cheyenne's busy doing something for Hope, and Julie's working on shipping supply inventory. So you're free to read."

Magdalene rolled her eyes and flopped down on the couch. She secretly loved reading, but she resolved not to let Bobbie Jo know. Nevertheless it wasn't long before she was engrossed in the book.

Two hours later, Cheyenne left her office cubicle and wandered over to the lounge area. She approached the couch from behind and plopped backwards over the low back, landing next to Magdalene with her feet stuck straight up in the air. She spun around and up-righting herself with her long hair slung over the back of the sofa and one leg draped over the armrest.

"I am sick to death of working. These twelve hour work days are just wearisome. I wish Asher would come home today, *today!*"

Julie paused with her elbows on the table, supporting her chin with her hands. "It would even be a break if Yancey came to visit," she sighed.

Groaning in unison, Cheyenne and Magdalene leaned forward and pretended to gag themselves by placing their fingers in their mouths. Together they flopped backwards, staring at the ceiling while listening to the pounding rain on the metal roof.

After a few minutes, Cheyenne stood wearily to her feet, returning to her work. "Geez." Magdalene sounded deflated. "Rain, rain, rain. Why does it have to be raining? We can't even go to the creek."

"Well, the farmers are sure celebrating," Julie responded cheerfully. "I heard old Eli say this past week that he had prayed all night for rain. So he's happy."

"Oh, crud, Julie, are you always so sweet? You even think Yancey's charming. You're loony." Magdalene didn't attempt to hide her disdain. The young girl turned toward Cheyenne. "I gotta say, can't figure why all of you put up with the jerk. I mean, it's obvious that Yancey grates on you guys, yet you all treat him like he's one of the gang. Why not just tell him to get lost?"

Cheyenne smiled, but her eyes looked perplexed. She tapped her index finger against her lips as she considered her answer. "Well, Mag girl … it's hard to explain. Let me put it this way. Tess was a real jerk when she first came here. Then God reached down and saved her. Now she's the kindest person I know. A lot of our best people around here once were lost and troublesome, yet when they came looking for answers we prayed for them and treated them as friends."

Cheyenne could see that Magdalene was thoughtfully studying her. From her expression it was manifest that the young girl had become conscious of how she might also be in Yancey's category: a jerk treated like a saint until she came to love the Savior. Cheyenne had to control her grin as she continued explaining, "Dad always taught us that when someone started coming around to Bible classes or hanging out with Christians, then we needed to start praying for that person because there was a good possibility that God was doing something in that person's heart. He says treat them like saints until the day they come to love the Savior."

Magdalene's deep sigh indicated she was now bored with the conversation and ready to move on to more interesting distractions. She turned her back to Cheyenne, then leaned forward in order to peer out the window towards the alley. "Well, at least the constant downpour has the stalker seeking cover. Or maybe he was just watching Asher. I haven't seen him much lately."

Magdalene continued to stare silently out the window, listening to the older girls quietly going about their tasks. "You know," she said after a few minutes, "I met one of the young Muslim girls." Magdalene offered the information casually as if it were nothing of consequence.

"*What?*" All three older girls chorused. "When?"

Magdalene was pleased to be the center of attention. "Yesterday."

"And?" Cheyenne prompted.

Bobbie Jo's authoritative voice settled the matter. "Spit it out, Kid. This could be important."

Magdalene looked suddenly pensive. "It wasn't anything. Her parents are the folks that bought Main Street Market. She was just sitting in the car parked in the back lot. Her head was leaning forward and with all that headgear on I couldn't tell if she was crying or what.

"When I knocked on the window it really scared her. She jumped like it was a gun going off. I asked her if she was okay. Turns out she was playing a game on one of those new phones that have internet. She showed me her game and we just talked a while. I showed her our newest website with *God's Story* on it and told her to read it sometime.

"She seemed like just a regular person, so I told her where I worked and that she was welcome any time to visit us. She said thanks. That's it."

The three older girls couldn't quite decide how to respond. Had Magdalene endangered herself or the Muslim girl? Cheyenne spoke first.

"Well, Kid, you always manage to surprise me. I guess it was nice of you to be concerned."

The girls uneasily fell back into a work pattern. Their simple life in this backwoods town had become complicated.

Bobbie Jo worked with a fury spurred by frustration. She hated to be intimidated. It made her feel as though she wasn't in control. The tension of the past weeks grated on her more than she cared to admit. Now this. Since the book burning at TLP, no one had seen much of the stalkers. Maybe they got it all out of their system. But if they found out about Magdalene's conversation with their daughter ... Malachi had said that he thought the trouble was just beginning.

Chasing away the troubling thoughts, Bobbie Jo smacked her open hand down loudly onto the desktop. Tense, she stood and stretched, arching her back, which noisily popped.

She moved to the couch and raised her foot onto the armrest. With a staged bravado she pulled the hem of her loose Thai fisherman's pants up and removed her Charter Arms stub-nosed .38 pistol from its ankle holster. "Maybe the reason we haven't seen old rag-head is because he heard me through his listening device talking about my shootin' iron and how I'm not afraid to use it."

Magdalene's young eyes reflected a wizened experience beyond her years as she stared at Bobbie Jo with her pale vacant-looking eyes. Finally she answered, "I doubt that." A chill passed over the girls. They knew Magdalene was probably correct. If he wanted them, he knew where to find them.

TRUTH OR DARE – Cheyenne stood and clapped her hands together, breaking the mood. "All right! Why don't we play Truth or Dare for a few minutes to lighten the mood?"

Bobbie Jo pulled her hair band off and released her pony-tail, shaking her long mass of curly hair loose. Rubbing her scalp, she slumped into the big chair with one leg folded into the seat. "Sounds like a plan. My eyes are so tired. I've been seeing double for the last hour going through those orders." She squirmed into a better position in the worn out chair while looking menacingly at Magdalene. "But no crazy dares where the town people would see us doing dumb stuff. Got that?"

"What's a matter? You sceeert?" Magdalene teased. "Come on over, Jules, 'cause I'm gonna be first. I know just what I wanna know." She punched Cheyenne in the arm to get her attention, "Okay, Cheyenne … truth or dare … dare … dare?"

Wearily Cheyenne laid her head onto the low-backed stuffed couch. "Oh, give me a break! I'm not letting you dare me into doing something stupid. I have my dignity to maintain." Cheyenne winked.

"Okay, scaredy-cat," Magdalene challenged, "if you're scared of a dare, do truth."

Feigning a show of defeat, Cheyenne groaned, "Okay, Truth. Ask me anything, and I'll tell you the truth, the whole truth and nothing but the truth."

Magdalene clapped her hands in delight, "Okay, tell the truth: Is

Asher a great kisser, or what? Good, huh?"

Cheyenne's head came off the back of the couch with a look of reprimand. "Magdalene, shame on you! I haven't kissed Asher." A blush hotly burned her cheeks as she tried to look offended. "You know he has set himself apart for the Lord's work. When are you ever going to believe that we really do honor God in our lives? Even our private lives!"

"Oh, phew-whee ... you think I believe that? You old prude," Magdalene scoffed. "You girls make me ..." This time she really stuck her finger down her throat. At the sound of her gag reflex the girls jumped out of her way and screamed for her to stop.

"Apparently Magdalene isn't in the mood for good wholesome fun," Bobbie Jo declared, and stood. "I guess we can skip game time and just finish our work."

"Don't be such a dead-head, Bobbie Jo!" Magdalene fumed. "They obviously have the hots for each other. She gets all oogey every time someone even mentions his name, so ..."

Cheyenne and Bobbie Jo stood and started back toward their work. Magdalene yelled, beating her arms on the soft, worn leather of the old couch, "Okay, you prudes! Dare me or ask me a question. I'll do anything, or I'll tell all."

Bobbie Jo turned and slowly walked back around to the end of the couch. She folded her arms and stood with her hip to one side. Staring down at Magdalene speculatively, she ventured, "Okay, Kid, truth. You've dodged telling us anything about your life ever since you came here. It's time you tell us where you came from and how you came to be on the side of the road when Omar found you last month. Tell us everything."

Magdalene's small, pale face looked vulnerable, but her voice sounded practiced. "I don't care. I'll tell you. It ain't so interesting anyway." Then she rushed ahead with her prepared story. "Well, I already told Cheyenne that I was kicked out of ..."

"Shut up!" Bobbie Jo roared. "This is Truth or Dare ... I dare you to tell the truth for a change." She glared at Magdalene.

The girl shrugged her shoulders, sending her soft cottony hair swinging around her head. Her manner said *I don't care*, but she looked trapped.

Cheyenne slowly sat back onto the couch, while Bobbie Jo and Julie dropped into the two soft faded chairs opposite the couch. Everyone looked at Magdalene expectantly. Finally they would know.

14

A SAD STORY

"Well, you already know I was doing drugs." She paused as if she wished she could disappear. "I supported myself by turning tricks." Not meeting their eyes, she waited for the expected rejection. Nothing.

"I didn't care who they were as long as I could eat and do drugs. Last fall I was working the street when this fat, short dude picked me up. He took me to get a hamburger and coke. As a matter of fact, it was the very same day I cut and dyed my hair black.

"Anyway, this fat guy told me to sit in the car while he went in to get the food. Instead of getting anything for himself, he kept drinking out of a bottle he kept in the car. He called it a tonic or something and said it would make him my superman ... ugh!

"So, I drank my soda and ate my burger. I'm pretty sure he must have spiked my drink when he was in the burger place, because I can't remember a thing after I finished eating. I can't even remember how he got me way out in the woods! All I know is that I woke up and I was on the ground with him putting a piece of red hot iron on me.

"I was so drugged, I couldn't even fight or do anything to stop him. I felt the heat and could smell my skin burning, but I couldn't move. It was freaky. It hurt like, like I was burning in hell, but I couldn't even scream. I really did think he was going to kill me." Magdalene rubbed her midriff where the large ugly scar remained.

"One minute he had this evil look, like he was really enjoying himself, then he started puking like something exploded inside him or something. He just doubled over and started spewing his guts out. I mean, he was really sick. I saw him stagger over to his motorcycle and leave. That was one lucky break for me, him getting sick."

Cheyenne, Julie and Bobbie Jo sat in stunned, mute horror.

"I was just too doped up to move. I hurt like crazy. The pervert BRANDED me!" Magdalene lifted her shirt, revealing an ugly, three-inch scar above her waist.

Julie had seen the scar before, but hearing the story caused her to tear up. "You poor thing. I'm so sorry."

Magdalene was pleased with the show of sympathy. "When I woke up the next day, I was lying by a dead fire. It was freezing cold. I sure was glad I had taken a lighter from his car when he stopped for the burgers. I fished it out of my backpack and used it to start a fire to keep warm. Can you believe the jerk was so eager to fry me that he didn't even take my backpack off? Good thing, though."

Magdalene shifted around on the couch and fidgeted. "I tried to find my way out of the woods but got lost. While I was wandering around, I found spots that looked like shallow graves out behind the house. Stuff like that sure freaks me out.

"I decided that when he came back, I was going to kill him and take his motorcycle. I took the next several days and sharpened a dozen big sticks on rocks and laid them all around so I would always have one close if he surprised me, but he never came back."

"What town were you in when he picked you up?" Bobbie Jo asked through clenched teeth.

Julie blurted out before Magdalene could answer, "That's awful! What did he look like? Do you remember his name or kind of car? Would you recognize him?"

Magdalene shrugged and answered Bobbie Jo, "I lived in Winston-Salem, North Carolina then. I don't even remember how I got there. But I can remember every detail about the guy. I learned to be obser-vant when I was just a kid. My older siblings and I made up a game where we remembered details about people. I learned to notice and remember all kinds of things. On the street all the girls tell you to remember your man because it's the only way to survive.

"He was around 35 years old, really short, maybe five-five, must have been 250 pounds. A seriously fat dude. His head was almost bald, and what hair he did have was thin and stringy, and pale as mine. And he had a big, rotten hole right between his two front teeth. His hands were gnarled like he had arthritis in them, and he stumbled like he had a bad knee when he got out of the car at the hamburger joint.

"The car he drove was a gray-blue, two door Cavalier, probably ten years old. I don't know how he got me up to his place in the woods, because there's no way that car could have gotten up in there. I can just barely remember him driving away on that motorcycle."

In unison, the Trio exclaimed, "Derek!"

"Yeah, that's his name! While he was buying the burger and coke I went through his car's glove compartment and saw his name on some insurance papers. That's when I found the lighter. He's a White Supremacist too. I saw his tattoo ... just like my dad's—88."

Magdalene's memory was stirred at the mention of the name. "Let's see ... don't tell me ... let me remember his name ... Derek the cowboy ... his name was ... Roy Rogers ... yeah, that's right ... now I remember: Derek Rodgers. That's how I remember names. I associate them with something I can picture like a cowboy. Cool, huh? So, is the Derek you know named Derek Rodgers?"

"That's the nasty pile of dog stuff we know," Bobbie Jo confirmed. "I wonder what he was doing so far from home, though?" She hit her palm with her fist. "First thing tomorrow we'll go to the cops and swear out a complaint against Derek."

Cheyenne's shook her head. "No, Bobbie Jo. You know where that will go."

"Nowhere," Julie offered.

Some tattoos are common among skinheads, such as:
Two lightning bolts or SS bolts like those worn by soldiers in Nazi Germany.
The numbers "14-88," with 14 standing for the 14 words White Supremacists use as their oath, and 88, or 8, standing for the eighth letter of the alphabet, "H." Two "Hs" together stand for Heil Hitler.
Swastikas from Nazi Germany.

https://secure.deseretnews.com/article/1,5143,680194690,00.html ∾

"Yeah, you're right." Bobbie Jo admitted. "We all know his family runs the county." She sighed in resignation. "Magdalene, finish your story."

"Well, anyway, at that old house there was some bagged up emergency food in five gallon buckets. The labels on them said Y2K Dried Foods. Someone obviously meant to use the place as a hideout if the world had hit the fan at the beginning of the year 2000.

"My dad thought the end of time would come then too. He bought stuff and had us a cellar built for the occasion. I remember we ate that canned junk for years afterwards. But the stuff these people had stored was the weirdest stuff you could ever imagine, like dried, chopped apples flavored with cherry or raspberry. There was some dried powder that was so disgusting; I couldn't bring myself to eat it until everything else was gone. It was like powdered dog food. It was labeled a meat substitute. Phew-whee! It was gross!" Magdalene emphasized her disgust by doing her favorite gag trick, sticking her finger down her throat. This set all the girls into movement at once to avoid any potential splashing.

Bobbie Jo warned, "You do that again, and we are going to hold you down and feed you dog food! You are so gross. Now finish your story."

Magdalene smiled at Bobbie Jo's interest. She was relieved that they hadn't rejected her. "Anyway, I lived off that stuff and slept in the sleeping bag that pervert Derek left behind. Thankfully he was too sick to gather his belongings before he left.

"I was there for at least a couple months—maybe three—I lost count. The first week I had drug withdrawal, and it was bad. At the beginning I didn't start making marks, because I was sure I would find a road out of there soon enough. When I figured out it wasn't that simple, I started keeping track. Being stuck back there by myself was worse than being on the streets. I was pretty scared. But I lived, and my burn healed without getting infected.

"I got so sick of eating beans and pounding seeds." Magdalene put her finger up again to shove down her throat but noticed Bobbie Jo's eye's narrow and she didn't dare. She put her hand down into her lap.

"I did learn how to sprout seeds. Sprouted barley is really sweet, especially if you dry the sprouts and pound them with a rock to make a brown sugar looking stuff. You can use it like really sweet tea."

Magdalene bit the inside of her cheek. "I waited until it was warmer weather so I could float downriver. Besides, I was about out of food. I can't swim too good, so I had to float hanging on to an inflatable mattress that I found in the cabin. Jeepers, that water was so cold, I thought I would freeze to death. I made it down to a bridge and started hitchhiking south. It was a day later when Omar picked me up."

THE REST OF THE STORY – Caught up in the story, Cheyenne asked, "So how did you end up on the streets in the first place? Weren't you homeschooled?"

Magdalene paused. Hadn't she risked enough today already? Cheyenne was asking her to peel back some ugly layers. There were some things best left untold. The girl drew back and continued in a whiny, childish voice, "Well, my daddy beat me all my life and my mama ran off and left me when I was just a kid. I had nowhere to go and nothing to eat, so I ..."

"Oh, cut the crap! Tell the truth or I'm outta here." Bobbie Jo had a keen sense for deception and an equally low tolerance of it.

Snapping back, Magdalene stormed, "If you are going to call me a liar, then I'm not telling you anything." The small teen pulled her feet up onto the couch, sitting on them.

"Fine, Liar, get your stuff together," Bobbie Jo retorted. "I have spent several weeks trying to hide my purse from your thieving fingers. I'm tired of your drama. It's someone else's turn to put up with your duplicity. Get up. I'm taking you to the cops."

Bobbie Jo was ten inches taller and at least fifty pounds heavier than Magdalene and just as tough. She could be as mean as she needed to be, and everyone knew it. Magdalene peevishly relented. "Okay, okay.

Seed Sprouting

Nutritional research has proven that the best foods are not the expensive foods. Good nutrition means good health. Fresh fruits, vegetables and grains straight from the garden are the wonderful ideal. But what if no fresh foods are available? Then SPROUT!

You're going to be sorry, because it is one lousy story."

Julie and Cheyenne breathed a sigh of relief.

Magdalene stared at her empty hands for a few seconds. They could hear her deep sighs as she struggled to know where to begin. "This is one stinking story, but you guys asked for it, so here goes.

"My family homeschooled—really goody-goody two-shoes. We girls wore head coverings. The boys were not allowed to play Cowboys and Indians because it was violent. We were drilled on behavior and manners. Mama made sure we followed all sorts of religious requirements. Appearances were very important to Mama. I think she thought if people thought we were wonderful then so must God. She really thought she was saving her children, but our family was always bitter."

Magdalene stood up and walked around the lounge area's sofa, trailing her hand across the low backed couch. The girls' eyes followed her.

She dropped back into her seat. "There was some church trouble. I'll spare you the details. Mom rehashed the problems every waking minute. Dad dropped out of church and got more bitter with each telling. He began spending a lot of time on the internet. Then he started going to what he called Bible meetings, but didn't invite us."

Magdalene knotted up her forehead trying to decide how to continue. She shrugged her shoulders, wiggled around uncomfortably, and finally started again.

"We wanted to know what was really going on, so Ike—that's my favorite brother—got a key to the locked room and got on my dad's computer and found out it was White Supremacist meetings he was attending. Soon after that, Dad shaved his head and started slipping off to meetings all dressed up crisp and clean like a soldier getting ready for inspection.

"That's when Mom really flipped. She became the victim."

It only takes 2 days to grow a fresh supply of food—the most nutritious food on earth. Research proves that broccoli seed has 10 times the nutrition of the same amount of a broccoli plant. And that is just one kind of sprout. Other seeds also dramatically increase their nutritional value when sprouted. As an added benefit, sprouts are an exceptionally rich source of enzyme inducers that protect against chemical carcinogens.

Sprouts grow practically anywhere and require neither soil nor sunshine. Just think ... it would take 370 quarts of canned food to feed one person for a year. Translate that into dry beans, peas, lentils or other seeds that can be sprouted, and it will only take 125 pounds. And, the food will actually be completely

>

MAMA'S MENTOR – Leaning forward to scratch her back, Magdalene's face looked like she had just tasted something very foul.

"Mom started getting regular counsel from a lady named Alice who told her to ignore any unreasonable demands my dad made, and that would humble him. So Mom just stopped doing home school with us and told us kids to stay outside all day while she talked on the phone to Alice. Dad said mom and Alice were spiritual lesbians. At first it seemed like a nasty thing to say, but after a while I saw his point.

"Anyway, Alice got mom into keeping Jewish feasts and fasts, lighting candles on the Sabbath, and a bunch of other ridiculous religious junk. They even started calling each other 'prophetess'. When she wasn't on the phone, Mom was reading the Bible or down on her knees praying with this big black scarf on her head. It was really weird."

Silence filled the room. In their imaginations the girls could see the events unfolding as Magdalene related them.

"We barely saw Dad for the next year. When he wasn't at work, he was with his White Power buddies. Mom was sure that when things didn't go her way it was a direct attack on her happiness."

THE KISS OF AN ENEMY – Magdalene sighed and shifted again. She pulled her knees up, wrapped her arms tightly around them, and hugged her legs to her chest. "Anyway, the night of my sixteenth birthday, my oldest brother, Dave, came home for the party. Dave was hooked on drugs and I hadn't seen him for a while. I was thrilled and flattered that he came home just for me.

"He took me aside and asked if I wanted to slip out the window and meet him after everyone went to sleep, for a real party. I was thrilled. I thought he was finally treating me like an adult, not some stupid kid. Later, I found out that his friend promised him free drugs if he could

fresh and full of nutrition. Sprouts can be eaten in salads, on sandwiches, stirred into soups or mixed with any cooked food.

There are lots of books available and many websites that teach everything there is to know about sprouting. Learn from them and live well. Because many commercially prepared garden seeds are treated with chemicals, do not use them for sprouting. Read the labels carefully. For more information on sprouting seeds, visit: www.chetday.com/sprouts.html & www.nogreaterjoy.org/sprouting-seeds ∞

bring me to meet them. His friends liked fresh meat ... really young girls —virgins ... especially blondes." She paused.

"At the time, I was so excited to be included. At home, I was just a kid. Everyone else was wrapped up in themselves. At the party, the guys actually complimented me, and talked with me long into the night. It didn't take much to convince me that it was destiny and I was in love.

"I got pregnant, but the father was long gone. I had no idea what to do, so I finally told Dad. He just stood there and sobbed like a baby. He didn't cry because I was into drugs or pregnant, but because I was carrying a black baby. Dad kept saying, 'Pure Arian blood! You have tainted pure Arian blood!'

"That night I slipped out and never went back. Another girl invited me to come live with her. After a week she told me that I had to earn my keep."

"You said you were pregnant?" Bobbie Jo asked. "What did you do with the baby?" There was a long silence as they listened to the rain pattering on the roof.

Magdalene's head dropped. Her white hair draped over her face. Her voice sounded dead. "I aborted the baby. Had it taken care of at the clinic. Lots of people do. The government pays for it." She shrugged. "One less kid on welfare."

Tears were sliding down Julie's cheeks. She extended her hand to touch Magdalene's shoulder.

"Don't touch me!" Magdalene flinched back and grimaced. A few moments passed while she fought the sobs that threatened to overtake her. Finally she started again.

"I was really scared. I was over seven months along before I went back to Planned Parenthood. When I arrived, there was a group of pro-life people in the parking lot. They told me how the doctor would give me medicine to bring on labor, then stick a giant needle in the baby's head as she was coming down to be born. Then, he would suck her brains out and dump her in a garbage pail.

"The people that talked with me begged me not to do it. They told me they would give me a nice place to live and pay for my baby to be born and help me find a good home for her, but I went in anyway." Magdalene's voice sounded ragged. "I was done with hoping and depending on people, especially religious people.

"When I got in there, they told me to put on a gown and lay back on the table. They ran an ultrasound. The nurses forgot to turn the monitor away and I saw that my baby was a girl.

There was silence for a few minutes until in a soft whisper they heard Magdalene say, "I actually heard her cry ... for a moment ... at least, I think I heard her ... I named her Starlite."

The afternoon shadows darkened the Herb Den lounge as the girls sat in silence.

After a long pause Julie spoke softly, "Magdalene, you need to contact your daddy. You know he's worried about you. Wouldn't you like to call and tell him you're alive and that the boogie man didn't get you?"

Magdalene jumped to her feet, overturning a lamp. The lamp shattered with a loud crash, plunging the room into darkness. Everyone startled in alarm.

Bobbie Jo was the first to recover. She stood and turned on an overhead light. Cheyenne's churning emotions left her feeling as if she had been run over by a train.

Magdalene had hit her breaking point. The memories surfaced like bile. Dark purple circles set deeply into the tiny, ghastly white face, surrounding her pale blue eyes. Tears had made paths, leaving two vivid red streaks down each cheek.

Magdalene's face twisted into a snarl in response to Julie's advice, "You are such a stupid freak to believe such a lie. Do you think I will not pay? Nobody gets away ... nobody! You have no idea just how bad the boogie man did get me!" Magdalene jumped to her feet and rushed to the door.

Agile as a cat, Cheyenne jumped over the low couch, loped three long steps, and reached the door in time to shut it before Magdalene could open it further. Catching Magdalene by both arms, Cheyenne swung her around and wrapped her arms tightly around the small girl, holding her still. She looked down at the top of the pale head.

"Be still, girl." Cheyenne's voice was full of conviction, authority, and compassion. "You are through running. It's time to understand once and for all that Jesus didn't come to call the righteous, but sinners to repentance.

"You definitely qualify for Jesus. Where sin abounds, grace much more abounds. It's time to get started on some of that grace. Besides ..." Cheyenne placed her hand under Magdalene's chin and lifted her tear-streaked face. "I believe the Bible teaches that your baby will live again in the Millennium and have her chance to grow up and come to love the Savior. You can't leave until you know all about what the Bible has to say about that."

Cheyenne began to pray aloud, sorrowing over the sin and rejoicing with hope, knowing God had the victory.

God was listening and had been listening for over a year to the prayers of two faithful old saints for this lost soul.

There were no dry eyes in the Herb Den that day.

A tiny spark of hope had been kindled in Magdalene's young soul.

15

WHY BLOOD?

"I'm telling you, it was the best day ever. I had so much fun clearing out the brush for the new fence.

"It was so cool how the bulldozers made the path, but I was glad the area needed a little hand work. It was such perfect weather.

"Didn't you just love the food Louise packed? You should have heard Dusty groaning. He thinks she likes him special and fixes food just for him. Crazy kid. Anyways, it was so good ... don't you think the picnic in the woods with just your crew was a good idea?" Cheyenne's excited, ceaseless chatter was annoying Bobbie Jo as her hands clattered over the computer keyboard.

Suddenly, her fingers stilled. This silenced Cheyenne and prompted the other girls to look up. Bobbie Jo stood menacingly with her hands on her hips. Now she had their full attention. She turned and leveled her gaze at Cheyenne.

Her voice was thick with sarcasm. "Okay. We know Asher is home from his long trip. We all enjoyed the brush clearing thing on the hill." She raised her voice. "We know it was perfect weather, perfect food, perfect everything, except for poor Magdalene here who was sick as a dog, and she was part of your foursome crew. But that didn't seem to keep you from celebrating big time. We know ... so now will you just shut your trap and work? Since we all skipped a workday here to help with Asher's project, we've got two days' worth of orders to catch up on and … and … I cannot think when you are gushing endlessly over Big Red."

Julie, Magdalene, and Cheyenne stood frozen for about 10 seconds. Then they all exploded with screams of laughter. Their voices chimed in together as each shouted their opinion. "She's jealous. She wants a man! Did you hear her? She's a girl, after all."

Bobbie Jo took a menacing step forward, causing the girls to scream again amidst their giggles. Following their boss's lead, they all fell to their knees, still giggling, pleading for forgiveness.

As usual, Bobbie Jo was right. Play time was over. They had a lot of work to catch up on. Boxes were piled all over the counter, floor, desk, and on the rollers heading to the shipping area. It would be a long day, and lunch would have to be eaten on the run.

Magdalene seemed to feel better, but she was making a lot of mistakes in the orders. Julie called out for the fourth time in less than twenty minutes, "Mag, you feel okay? You put five pounds of bilberry in this order. It called for eight pounds. Bilberry is expensive, and the lady would think we were trying to cheat her. You'll have to pay closer attention. It's a good thing Cheyenne set up a double check system, or we would have already sent out four wrong boxes."

"Yeah, I almost feel back to normal today. I was just thinking …" Magdalene's voice was cheerful, as though she hadn't registered Julie's chiding tone.

Excited with her own train of thought, she boomed, "Hey, do you know why Jesus is called the Lamb of God?" Before Julie could again caution her to keep her mind on the work, Magdalene excitedly continued, "I know!"

Magdalene's rediscovered childlike wonder was refreshing. She had spent the week studying Scripture in a great rush—she was drinking in the information like a thirsty sponge. She just couldn't seem to get enough. In addition, it appeared that she had chosen to set aside the past.

The other girls were relieved to see the change. Magdalene's sense of humor kept them laughing much of the day.

Bobbie Jo, always ready with a story, launched into a narrative of the first lamb that was killed, by God himself, "a perfect picture of the covering for sin ..."

"Hey, you interrupted me. It's my story. It's your time to listen." Magdalene objected.

Bobbie Jo put one hand on her hip and another hand over her mouth. "Well, excuse me, Miss Know-It-All," she mocked the younger girl. "Although I can't think how a discombobulated Baptist could tell a decent Bible story."

Magdalene rose to Bobbie Jo's bait. "Are you trying to make me look dumb with your big words? It so happens I am not the one who is discombobulated," she retorted, walking fearlessly towards Bobbie Jo.

"Cool it, you two." Cheyenne warned. "If you girls want to argue, fine. Just keep working while you do.

"Besides," Cheyenne pretended to take offense, "Asher is a Baptist too, if you recall." Then she lightened the mood with her imitation of a southern belle, "Theyafoah Ah simply will naht brook insults in that regahd." She fanned herself and fluttered her eyelashes for emphasis, "I sincerely hope that someday in mah very near future, Ah too shall be a Baptist."

Bobbie Jo's answering snort spoke of how highly she regarded that possibility.

"Okay, Miss Old South," Magdalene's patience was running out. "Now how about you cork it while I tell my story?"

The girls welcomed the distraction of a good story while they worked. Magdalene, usually the observant listener, was now venturing into the spotlight.

Magdalene hesitated just a moment, organizing her thoughts. "Jesus is called the Lamb of God because like a lamb he fully followed his shepherd, God the Father. Like a lamb he was humble ... an example to us ... something present company still needs to learn." She made a dramatic pause before continuing.

"He was called the Lamb of God because he was willing to die without uttering a complaint. He was called the Lamb of God because he was harmless and passive, never defending himself. He was the perfect example for us to follow." She ceased her monologue with a satisfied smile.

Cheyenne and Bobbie Jo exchanged a look of disappointment. They knew from Magdalene's story that she had not yet understood the gospel. They had been praying for Magdalene's salvation especially since the day she gave her life's story.

Please, Lord, let her find peace today! Cheyenne silently prayed

"Good job, Kid. More like a sermon than a story, but pretty good." Bobbie Jo walked over to lightly punch the small girl's arm. "Of course, not the quality of the pro here, but you are getting there." She winked. "Could I ask you a question about your story?"

"Well ... I don't know. Since when do you ask me questions?" Magdalene answered uncertainly. "You are always the smart aaa—I mean the smarty pants."

Bobbie Jo grinned. "My, my, my, aren't you the touchy one today? I was just wondering why do you think God rejected Cain's beautiful offering of fruits and vegetables but accepted Abel's bloody offering? Was Cain not humble? After all, Cain was sincere and was trying to worship God. He obviously thought his offering would please God. He did the best he knew. Why was he rejected? Why was God pleased with killing and shedding blood?"

Julie had been down on her knees counting bags of herbs. Now she quickly scribbled down her count and rose to her feet. This subject had troubled her in the past. She wanted to be certain to hear the answer. Her Mennonite background was strong in the teaching that the meek would inherit the kingdom of God.

With a critical tone, Julie inserted, "It does seem strange. Cain was trying to make God happy. I mean ... being God ... it seems God could have accepted anything he wanted to accept. It seems cruel to kill a sweet little lamb when God could have just chosen to accept fruits and vegetables."

"Yeah?" Cheyenne stopped filling out forms and casually chewed the end of her pen. Finally, even Julie would be forced to see truth. *Thank you, Jesus*, she breathed quietly, then, "Why, Mag? Why did it have to be blood?"

Magdalene stood at the packing counter, taping down boxes they had filled earlier. She secured the last long piece of tape across a box before answering. Her face looked perplexed. "Well, because Cain's offering was like good works, and Abel's offering pleased God, because God said offer blood. He obeyed God and Cain didn't."

"That's not good enough," Bobbie Jo pressed. "It's just a parrot of what you've heard all your life. Think about it. Why would God require a death? How can you prove Abel was obeying God? How do you know God told them to offer a lamb?"

When Magdalene didn't answer immediately, Bobbie Jo challenged, "What do you say, Julie?"

Julie slid up to sit on the counter, pulling her legs up to hug them to her body. "Well, the reason is because sin is such a terrible thing, killing something would show how really bad it is?" Her voice lacked conviction. "Why not let Cheyenne answer?" she questioned, being evasive.

Cheyenne bit the insides of her cheeks as she considered how best to answer. "Cain and Abel had both sinned. Abel sensed in his spirit that his sin deserved death. We call that conscience. He knew there was nothing good he could do to make up for his sin.

"All sin results in death, now and forever. The Bible says that the soul that sins will die. No one needs to be told this; our own guilt leads us to sense our impending doom.

"Cain ignored his conscience and tried to appease God with his praise and sacrifice that said, 'I have sinned. I am unworthy. Please have mercy upon me.' God saw Abel's heart of repentance and faith and was pleased with the blood sacrifice, for it pointed to the time when God would offer a blood sacrifice to atone for all sin. Jesus is God's sacrifice that pays the price of all sin."

As the words sank in, Magdalene and Julie were silent.

After a pause, Cheyenne invited, "Bobbie Jo, tell them about how you felt when you first moved here."

Bobbie Jo put her hands over her face. She hung her head. Slowly she lowered her hands and sighed. "Before I finally understood forgiveness … sometimes at night when I felt guilt for my sin, I wished I could do as the Jews had done, go out to the barn yard and get a lamb, take it to the priest and say, *offer this blood to God in place of my blood.* The Jews had it so easy. They didn't have to struggle with this thing of repenting and believing with all your heart; they just had to believe enough to offer the lamb.

"I would have gladly done that if I could. Instead, I was never sure if I had repented correctly or if I had believed enough. Was I sincere? Had I surrendered to Jesus as my Lord? On and on such thoughts tormented me."

"Oh God, I hate being scared!" Julie uttered with unguarded emotion. Gone were her careful words. The others were a little surprised by her uncharacteristic openness.

Magdalene walked over to put her arm around Julie's shoulder. "Hush Jules, don't get so upset. You are one of the nicest people in the whole world. If anyone is gonna make it in, you will. The Bible says all you have to do is to ask forgiveness for your sins every night. Isn't that right, Bobbie Jo?"

"Nope." Bobbie Jo's response was immediate and decisive. She addressed Julie with concern. "Sister, you better hope that's not what it says. Have you always remembered to ask forgiveness of all your sins? Do you even know all of the sin that is in your life? Have you ever learned something was sin after doing it all your life? If confession is the catalyst for forgiveness, then you weren't forgiven until you confessed. Do you think there has ever existed on this earth a man or woman other than Jesus who was righteous enough to even recognize every sin? All is a very big order. If that is what it says, then I sure missed the boat."

Magdalene was incredulous. "Jeepers, Bobbie Jo! You're the one that's always telling Bible stories. Are you playing dumb or something? Everyone knows that's what it says. I heard it often enough from my mom. It says you must repent of all your sins and confess them to God daily."

"She's right, Bobbie Jo." Julie's voice sounded strained. "It does say that. I can't recall exactly where, but I know it's in the Bible somewhere."

Magdalene looked at Julie with frustrated compassion. "Bobbie Jo's just exaggerating. Don't let her get to you, Jules. You know that God is merciful. If repentance is in your heart, God will see it. I know that's right!"

Reflex provoked Cheyenne to pick up the ringing phone, and then with her hand tightly over the mouth piece she addressed Magdalene, "Wrong answer!" She dropped the phone back on the receiver, mumbling, "They can call me back."

Bobbie Jo's attention was diverted. Concern was written across her face and etched in her voice. "Shy ... that was the secure line. Are you sure you need to let it go? We haven't been able to get in touch with ... for a few days."

Cheyenne shrugged away the inquiry, as if the call was of no consequence. They both knew better.

Julie's eyes narrowed. *What secure line? In touch with who? Yancey was right ... something is going on.*

HE'D NEVER LOSE ONE LIKE YOU – Magdalene continued trying to grasp the subject. "Okay, okay, I got it." She was trying to reconcile the current discussion with her preconceived notions. "Say, someone like Julie gets saved when she's twelve, and then after she's saved, she stays confessed up ... that way all her sins are forgiven ... right? Besides, if she doesn't flat out mean to do a sin, but just kinda accidentally does one, then it's not the same." Magdalene smiled with satisfaction.

Julie pulled her focus from the telephone call back to the conversation. The eternal issue they had been discussing was no longer front and center in her mind, but she was able to answer Magdalene. This particular question had been on her mind for a long time. Glancing at Bobbie Jo, Julie agreed, "You're right. How could anyone even know all their sins? So do you stay saved if you don't confess and forsake every sin? Besides, there was a time when I was 17 years old that I had a secret boyfriend. I know there was a whole lot of really bad sins that were not accidental. If I really meant it when I asked Christ into my heart, why did I sin so much?"

Again, Magdalene put her thin arm across Julie's shoulder in a comforting gesture. "God would never lose one like you. Tell her, Cheyenne."

"Sounds like Magdalene Theology 101 to me." Cheyenne supported herself on the counter with her elbows and spoke with grave seriousness. "Bobbie Jo, tell them about how you finally got peace with God."

BOBBIE JO'S STORY – A smile split Bobbie Jo's face from ear to ear. "Whew! Wasn't I a basket case? At night I could just feel the old devil stirring his finger around in my soul, wanting to get a death grip on my heart. I'm not being overly dramatic; I was really scared.

"Every time Malachi taught on end times I would be too scared to go to bed because I was afraid Jesus would come and I would be left behind. I was so scared of death, I was sick. I would have this heavy feeling of fear on my chest and I could hardly breathe. I was nearly convinced that even if Jesus didn't come back, I'd die of heart failure and be unprepared."

Cheyenne chuckled. It was true; she was one nervous ninny. "Hey, BoJo, tell them about the day you got left behind."

Grabbing her head with both hands, Bobbie Jo moaned, "Man … was that a day! About two years ago, I was sitting here at the computer working while Shy was filling out forms. We had been having a conversation very much like this one only a few hours before.

"Because I was still learning the accounting program, I didn't notice that she had gone to the bathroom. While she was in there, she changed into her sweatpants and sweatshirt because she was cold. Then Shy got sleepy. Since I was around the corner, I didn't notice that she had laid down on the couch and covered up with that brown blanket, you know, the one that's the same color as the couch. Well, she goes to sleep. Meanwhile, I'm still working. Of course, Shy's so skinny that when she laid down she just sorta disappeared, sank into the couch and was like ... gone.

"I don't know how long she was there, but it was long enough for her to be in a deep, solid sleep. At some point I got up to stretch and noticed that she was missing. I called for her, ran back to the kitchen, then up and down the aisles. You know she sleeps like the dead, so she just slept right through me yelling my head off for her.

"I jerked the bathroom door open, and there were all her clothes lying in a pile, including the shoes she had on that morning. I just knew she'd been raptured and my worst fear had come true. I was left behind.

"Well, I just freaked and started bawling. I was so upset I stumbled over to the couch and fell over the back and landed on top of that flat rascal."

Cheyenne couldn't suppress the giggles that poured out of her. The others didn't even think it was funny.

Bobbie Jo rolled her eyes at Cheyenne as she continued, "I knocked the breath clean out of her, besides scaring her half to death. She came up scratching like a scared cat, but I was so glad to see her I cried even louder and tried to hug her."

"That's the day I did my study on repentance and faith. I was through with all that hoping-I-was-saved stuff. I had to know."

Bobbie Jo finished with a smile. "That's also the day I went and bought the red blanket for the couch. No more shocks to my system."

"If I had died two years ago, I would have split hell wide open. That's a fact."

"Hey, look!" Magdalene jumped up from the couch, her eyes glued to the floor in the area by the door. The other girls stood to look over the back of the couch. Magdalene walked over to the door then swooped down, grabbing something. "Check this out. It just slid in under the door!" She held up a yellow envelope for the other girls to see the big M written on the front.

Cheyenne was still distracted with the conversation and wished Magdalene had left the card on the floor. "Just open it and see what it is."

Magdalene ripped it open and pulled out a single sheet. "This is weird."

Something bad is going to happen. You need to leave. I'm sorry. Your Friend

As soon as she heard the words, Cheyenne jumped to her feet and raced to the door, jerking it open. No one was there. She ran out to the road in time to see a young Muslim girl, with a full head covering, hastily ducking into the old Main Street Market two blocks down. Cheyenne recognized her as the daughter of the new owners.

She slowly walked back into the Herb Den. As she re-entered the store she heard Bobbie Jo say, "You know, we have to take it to the police."

"No, we can't," Cheyenne disagreed. "You know our cops are as corrupt as the devil himself. We have to think. Anyways, it's probably just an attempt to scare us."

Magdalene walked up, taking the note out of Cheyenne's hand, "I think you forgot the big M that was on the card. It was obviously my note, and so it's my choice about what to do."

The girls hesitated. Magdalene continued. "You know that if we squeal, then whoever wants to hurt us might hurt her for warning us. We've all read about Muslim honor killings. You know what I'm saying is true. We can't endanger her. We'll just have to protect ourselves."

Cheyenne used the moment that Magdalene glanced down at the note to exchange looks with Bobbie Jo. Maybe the kid was right. They would decide later.

Honor killing is a murderous act that Muslims use to control their families into maintaining strict codes that are approved by Islam. Teenage girls who date non-Muslim boys, wives who seek divorce from an abusive husband, and even Muslim girls who are the unfortunate victims of rape are in jeopardy of being killed, all in the name of family honor.

www.foxnews.com/story/0,2933,493645,00.html

16

DELIVERY DAY

Asher was sitting on the front steps of the Herb Den when Cheyenne arrived early the next morning. He came forward to meet her as she got out of her big pink truck. His red hair glistened in the early morning sun. His face looked haggard.

Cheyenne could feel her heart begin to race. This time it was not his presence, but dread. Since the warning note the day before, she had been living in expectation of horror. To her own ears, her voice sounded strange as she attempted to sound calm. "What has happened?"

He shook his head from side to side, signifying nothing had happened—then pulled her into a full, hard embrace. They stood there locked together, rocking back and forth almost as if they were dancing.

In public!

On Main Street! Just when respectable folks were heading to work.

So many times she had complained to the girls that Asher was like an onion. Just about the time she made an absolute verdict about who and what he was, off came another layer and he did the unexpected.

This day he broke all records.

She could feel the beat of his heart through his thin shirt and at his neck where her forehead lay. She could feel the bristle of his day-old beard against her forehead when he held her. Taking a deep breath, Cheyenne's anxiety was suddenly overridden by a strange sensation. He smells sweaty. Totally male. Almost nice smelling ... yeah ... *I like it.*

ASHER & CHEYENNE

Recovering her wits, she started to pull away, but she succumbed to his embrace when his deep voice full of emotion began to pray, "Oh Lord God, I ask from the depth of my heart, Lord. God, please, I am asking for your protection against the evil man. Lord, send your angels to defend and watch over her. Lord, cause us to watch and pray to be ready to seek a safe place. Lord, please."

Cheyenne felt him shudder.

She couldn't even rejoice at his tender care, knowing it was something other than a romantic embrace. She was at a loss to understand

Scientists at the University of Pennsylvania and the Monell Chemical Senses Center in Philadelphia have found that exposure to male perspiration has marked psychological and physiological effects on women: It can brighten women's moods, reducing tension and increasing relaxation, and also has a direct effect on the release of luteinizing hormone, which affects the length and timing of the menstrual cycle.

www.upenn.edu/pennnews/article.php?id=47 ∞

what prompted such passion.

Abruptly he held her at arms length. He searched her eyes as if she held some deep hidden secret. He spoke at her, but, it seemed, not to her. "I have to have faith that God will answer my prayer. I have done all that I can do. Remember who our real enemy is—that old devil—and he is defeated." Then, as if giving a blessing, "God, give her grace!"

Cheyenne stood in mute confusion, trying to collect her thoughts. His odd behavior left her trembling.

"Yeah, well," she ventured shakily, "Um, what's ... going on?"

With her keys still in her hand, she turned to insert them into the lock and opened the newly painted door. He followed her through.

He looked disheveled, as though he had not slept a wink. In addition to his unshaven appearance, his shirt was wrinkled. He didn't look at all like his normal tidy self.

Her lips curved into a grin with the memory of that day in the Hope's cellar, when he learned about the brew. She quickly sobered. "Okay, Asher, you have never bear-hugged anyone that I know about. I doubt you even hugged your mother the last time you saw her. Now, what's the deal? How come I suddenly am the recipient of such ..." Now she threw her shoulder up in a teasing way, trying to lighten the tense mood, dragging our her vvvvs and rrrrrs, "Vigorous ardor?"

He finally smiled, but his tone remained serious. "My contacts in the government—"

"Your contacts?" Cheyenne interrupted, her brows up in surprise. "In government?" Her voice held a tinge of mockery.

He had the grace to grin. "Okay, my brother's roommate works for the Feds, so I have my brother watching out for us. Anyways—as you say—my brother told me the same evening as the fire that it's possible that the Muslims were planning something in this area. They intercepted a coded communiqué that caused them to believe it involved the Trio. All of that plus our lurking watcher adds up to trouble.

"I just talked to Malachi. We don't want you four girls here in town with no one to watch the place. You're just sitting ducks. Besides—this sounds weird, I know—but right before Dan was killed, I knew he was

in danger. Instead of praying for his safety, I begged God to show me
what was going to happen. I know it was crazy … I just didn't know
… I didn't understand how this knowledge worked. Now I know to
pray and not worry about understanding everything.

"That day at your mom's lab … I knew danger was there. I knew!

"Then last night, I felt that same knowledge. Your life is in danger.
I prayed all night long for God to intervene on your behalf. Cheyenne
… I know what I know. Do you believe me?" His voice trailed off, but
his gaze was penetrating, pleading.

Cheyenne stared at him, drinking in his concern for her. The fact
that he cared so deeply seemed more important at the moment than
any danger she might face. That he cared so much that he would step
out from around his carefully constructed wall, was tantalizing.

A soft smile played across her face. "Okay … well, we need to fill
our orders to stay in business. Maybe we could hire a couple men
who are out of work to stand guard at the front door and the loading dock. Anyways, if the Feds think we're a target, why don't they
do something?"

The young man was accustomed to precise military compliance
upon command. He looked frustrated and sounded irritated. "There
are hundreds of possible targets. They do what they can, but until they
have hard evidence, they can't act. The ACLU would be all over them.
They informed the local police, but that's like telling the house cat that
the alley cat is chasing mice."

Asher put his hands flat on the counter, his shoulders hunched over
as he spoke. "You are going to have to move into TLP's old warehouse.
Today."

Cheyenne was shaking her head as he spoke.

Asher grabbed her by her shoulders as if he was going to shake her.
"Don't say you can't. You can do what you need to do! We're spread
too thin to watch here and TLP ministry."

I Corinthians 12:8 "For to one is given by the Spirit the word of wisdom; to another the word of knowledge by the same Spirit." ∞

Realizing that he had again grabbed hold of her, Asher released his grip on Cheyenne's shoulders. He continued trying to make her understand.

"I've been through this before. Just four months ago, I buried the best friend I ever had. I smelled the rotting flesh of scores of Sunday School children who were blown to bits while singing. No one thinks it will happen to them. But it does.

"The Gideon Band will move you. It has to be done. All the men are agreed. We can better know what is going on and protect you behind the fence."

Cheyenne's head was still shaking no while Asher filled her in on the details.

"It should only take about four trucks if we also use the large goose-necked trailers. Of course, you won't have all your nice shelving, rollers or office stuff. And the huge herb bales can stay here in storage until you need them. You can make do until this crisis is over. We can always run over to pick things up as you need them."

Cheyenne sighed.

Asher began walking to the door. "Within an hour a crew will be here to help get you ready for the move. The trucks will be here by noon. You girls can fill today's orders here. Some men will keep watch until the move is complete. Tonight you'll be at TLP."

He turned to look at her to make sure his words registered. Then his expression softened and the tension seemed to diminish. He winked, spun on his heels and left in a hurry.

Cheyenne's knees could no longer hold her. She dropped onto her stool and put her elbows on the counter, holding her head in her trembling hands. Her fingers pulled through her hair in frustration as she spoke to the room. "That man has no idea what he does to me!"

NECESSARY SUPPLIES – Less than an hour later Cheyenne was listening to the rattle of a hundred loose parts on the old pink panel truck as she drove down the winding road. It matched the jangling of her nerves and emotions. Her face grimaced as she looked around for her small CD headset player and realized Bobbie Jo had it. No music even. Bummers.

She was surprised how strained her voice sounded when she spoke aloud to herself. "Boy, I wish Magdalene was with me; I could use a laugh." Her brows knitted. "And I wish I had remembered to tell Asher I had to get supplies today." His name evoked a deep emotional shiver. This morning's intense display of affection—of passion—would not be soon forgotten.

She sighed as she picked up her phone to check for reception. Still nothing.

The lack of phone service was troublesome. Her brows knit in concern for the brew; still no word had come from Rob Cohen. Cheyenne's mind played back to the phone call a few days earlier, when she hung up the secure line. She chided and defended herself at the same time. It was worth missing the call. *Magdalene might have been distracted from understanding the gospel. I had to hang up the phone.*

Still, every day for months she had talked to Cohen. He was good at keeping in touch with the latest updates on the China brew. The last few weeks he had shown some concern over a set of volcanoes just off the coast of China. One had erupted, causing terrible problems in the Hong Kong port where the Pearl River opened into the sea. Their barges would be carrying the brew down the Pearl River into this port.

A week! Cheyenne checked her watch to determine the date. It had been a week today without a word from him, unless you count the phone call she had ended. She had not been able to get through since then, no matter what time of day she tried.

The young woman's hands wrung the steering wheel as her mind replayed the news from the computer. Her voice was a bare whisper, little more than merely mouthing the words. "Oh Lord, what will we do if something happens to the brew? We've put everything into this project! So much depends on it. Help us, God!"

She felt the burden of uncertainty settle down upon her. "Please let us hear today."

The early morning sun was warming the countryside as she turned off the narrow side road onto the county highway. Cheyenne glanced at the gas gauge, steadily sinking as if to match her mood. She heard her teeth grating together before she could stop herself. "Can't even buy gas in my own town anymore without being scared. At least Pinky can carry everything, so I can get it all in one trip. Lord, help me make it to town on the little bit of gas I have in the tank. God, how could I have known when I bought Pinky that this truck drank like a fish?"

She didn't notice the car that had been following her at a distance.

The shining ones saw it.

They were ready.

The car trailing her turned into the Super Center's lot moments after the young woman coaxed Pinky into a remote spot on the far side of the parking lot. Her lack of parking skills required that she select a space that allowed some room and a gentle slope. "There," she muttered as the engine shuddered to a stop, hitting on a couple cylinders after she turned off the key. "Now if it won't start, I've got enough room to get a rolling start out of here." She gave the dashboard an affectionate pat.

⁓

As Cheyenne checked off the last item on her list she could feel the heavy ball of hair bound on the top of her head sliding down. Making a face, she slowly turned to walk toward the grocery section, hoping her hair would re-plant itself. It didn't. She looked around, embarrassed to be publicly redoing her long hair. Quickly she re-looped her thick, drooping hair, winding it into a higher knot, then securing it with the two hair sticks that Asher had brought her from Thailand.

Checking her watch, she picked up the pace, pushing the largest dolly she could find, piled high with supplies. She wanted to get enough to last several weeks. *So much for getting back in time to oversee the move. It's already ten o'clock. The girls should be able to get the orders out with the extra help from the guys doing the moving.*

HealthDay News, Jan. 26 – Almost half of tested samples of commercial high-fructose corn syrup (HFCS) contained mercury, which was also found in nearly a third of 55 popular brand-name food and beverage products where HFCS is the first- or second-highest labeled ingredient, according to two new U.S. studies …

>

She turned the heavy, awkward dolly toward the dairy section. *A snack ... I need food right now ... before I starve.*

Checking the labels of all the different kinds of yogurts, her brows were knotted as she considered the dizzying array of options. She read the ingredients and shook her head. "No wonder everybody's coming down with toxic gut, fatty liver, high sugar, heart disease," she muttered. "Dead-at-40 disease! Geez! That nasty corn syrup concentrated into an unnaturally high fructose is in everything, even the stuff that says 'all natural.' That's a hoot!"

She sighed and picked up plain yogurt. *So much for yummy ... gotta take care of the tummy.*

The young woman moved back from the case and was shutting the glass door when her ear caught a sound that was both familiar and odd at the same time. It sounded like someone had snuck up behind her and was talking to her in another language. What language?

Cheyenne froze. Her whole body tingled as survival instinct kicked into high gear.

Her heart thudded in her ears. What was wrong with her?

Again the man's voice rattled off a stream of unfamiliar sounds. *Definitely not Spanish, French, German, Russian, Japanese, Dutch ...*

Still holding onto the glass door, she swept the area with her eyes, intensely alert. Black eyes met hers. She struggled to reconcile her alarm with what she was hearing and seeing.

He stood over forty feet away holding a cell phone to his ear. When he realized she had seen him, he dropped his head to stare down at the floor.

She turned back to the dairy case. The sound of his voice again bounced off of the open glass dairy case door, making it seem right next to her.

"Mercury is toxic in all its forms. Given how much high-fructose corn syrup is consumed by children, it could be a significant additional source of mercury never before considered. We are calling for immediate changes by industry and the [U.S. Food and Drug Administration] to help stop this avoidable mercury contamination of the food supply," the Institute for Agriculture and Trade Policy's Dr. David Wallinga, a co-author of both studies, said in a prepared statement.

www.washingtonpost.com/wp-dyn/content/article/2009/01/26/AR2009012601831.html

Arabic!

Of course! It was the same dialect as the Muslims were speaking at Main Street Market. Shaky hands knocked over the stacked yogurt, then fumbled to right the mishaps.

Don't freak … He has a right to shop, talk on the phone, be here … calm down. She took a deep breath, trying to clear her mind.

She intentionally avoided looking into his face, but she checked his buggy contents with her peripheral vision. The cart was nearly full of paint thinner and paint remover. *He must have a big project.*

Still, he seemed out of place in the store. He wasn't from the community. He appeared to be watching her out of the corner of his eye, just as she was watching him.

The hair on the back of her neck prickled. She was nearing panic. *God, help me calm down and not act like a silly drama queen. It's just Asher's visit that has me discombobulated. Breathe. I need to focus.*

It didn't work. Her pulse accelerated. Cheyenne gave up trying to control her emotions. She shut the door with a loud 'thwack' as the magnetic strips slapped together. She grunted, pushing the heavy dolly hard, and started back down the aisle in a fast walk. She felt stiff, like a wooden doll.

She grabbed at her awkward cart to make the turn. The act of hurriedly pushing the heavily laden dolly towards the front of the store helped her compose herself to some degree. Thankfully her list was finished. As she passed the infant strollers, she heard someone call her.

"Hey, Herb Gal! 'member me?" Cheyenne pulled the heavy cart to a stop. She stared with a vacant look.

"It's me, Zulla Mae. I done comed by y'uns back yonder in tha spring." The little woman stood, leaning on a cart. Her belly was bigger than any pregnant woman Cheyenne had ever seen. Memories forced themselves forward. It was the day Yancey had first shown up. Death … the hillbilly woman had said she smelled it.

Cheyenne struggled to respond with a feigned interest. "Well, hello again. Of course I remember you! I thought for sure you would have had your baby by now."

Zulla Mae laughed at Cheyenne's startled, polite greeting, but she could see and hear that Cheyenne was tense. "I know! You ain't the onliest person who's eyes pert near popped out seein' my belly. I reckon this youngun's half growed, or I got me a half dozen in thar."

Cheyenne's nervous strain caused her to laugh loudly—uncomfortably. She stumbled around as she searched for the words. "I'm sorry for gawking … It wasn't polite. But you are so big! Surely you must be way overdue? I thought you were due when you came to the Herb Den."

Zulla Mae's eyes narrowed in consternation as she studied the cagey young woman. It was obvious that something was greatly troubling Cheyenne. Yet Zulla Mae answered in a causal manner, "Naw, 'twaren't but 'bout six months or thar 'bouts then. Hey, I shore got me a nice herb garden a growin'. I seed you put a bunch more herbs in mah sack that day, and best of all some seeds. It were a real nice surprise when I got back up on the mount'n."

Unable to suppress her anxiety, Cheyenne looked over her shoulder. Zulla Mae's eyes followed her lead. Her voice was calm but full of authority. "Whachee lookin' fer?"

Relieved to have found a confidante, the panic stricken girl stepped closer to Zulla Mae and grabbed the expectant woman's arm with her own trembling hand. "You'll think I'm crazy, Zulla, but I just saw a Muslim man over in the dairy section. He was talking on his cell phone, but it looked like he was watching me. I left, but I'm still not sure he wasn't following me. Strange, huh?"

Zulla Mae's hand suddenly clamped down over Cheyenne's, signaling her to silence. The two young women stood silently waiting. The man passed by them, hurrying down the next aisle—without his shopping cart.

Whispering, Zulla Mae told Cheyenne, "I seed him little time ago where the plants be. He had on a worker's apern. Hizn cart were full of paint thinner. He wuz messen 'round with them furderlizer bags. This ain't good. My man uses nitro furderlizer mixed with diesel gas to blow rocks too big fur him to move by hand."

The strange man was very aware of his surroundings. He seemed surprised to find Cheyenne standing talking to someone. In spite of his efforts to remain casual, he did a double take and veered off onto the next aisle. Cheyenne stood frozen as another wave of dread washed over her. She heard Zulla Mae begin to breathe loudly. Concerned and momentarily distracted, she turned toward the woman. "Are you okay? What is it?"

Zulla Mae's eyes were wild. Cheyenne remembered that look ... burning with a weird fire from deep within. Zulla Mae bent forward, leaning heavily over her cart in obvious distress. Cheyenne put her arm around Zulla Mae. "Are you in labor? Should I call for help?"

As if speaking to herself, Zulla Mae groaned, "Deayuth ... I ... I smell it. He dun gots the evil eye. Doers of darkness dun follered you hyere, Herb Gal. Mah bones tell me of a truth."

Cheyenne shivered, but shook her head as if refuting what she was hearing.

"No, Zulla. He's just some creep. I think it might be time for your baby to come. Let me help you towards the front. They have benches there and I can call ..."

The fire in Zulla's eyes intensified. "LAWD help us! Lan's sake, Gal!" Her eyes widened with a sudden knowing.

With a short gasping breath, the heavily pregnant woman leaned over further, whimpering with the struggle of her inner war. She righted herself and gasped, "They's gonna blow this place."

Zulla placed her hands on Cheyenne's shoulders. She locked eyes with her and said, desperate for Cheyenne to believe her, "I knew, this very day I knew I wuz a'smellin' death."

A slight ringing of a phone at the opposite end of the aisle caused both women to turn in time to see the same Arabic man looking straight at Cheyenne. There was recognition in his eyes. He answered the ringing phone. Both women heard the words clearly as he spoke in English, "I see her. I am sure."

Then he sprinted for the front door.

The wild-eyed mountain woman stood up straight as if a hundred volts had run through her body, "He knowed you … He knowed you! Go … go! Leave yer cart. Run! Fast! Get outta this here store. Now!"

THE BOMB – As the Arabic man sprinted away, Cheyenne suddenly realized Zulla Mae was right. *Fertilizer; paint thinner. It couldn't be … but it was.*

Time seemed to stand still.

A low vacuum filled her ears.

In one glance she saw teenaged girls giggling as they looked through the bathing suits, a mother trying to soothe her newborn, a father and son walking down a far aisle carrying fishing gear. People laughing, shopping, rushing around … living.

Then she heard herself screaming like a crazy woman. Over and over, screaming, screeching, waving her arms wildly to force people to take notice; then grabbing those nearby trying to shake them from their indecision.

"RUN … GET OUT … BOMB! HURRY! GET OUT!!"

Satisfied that the avalanche had started, Cheyenne grabbed Zulla Mae's arm to move her, but the pregnant woman was again gasping as a new spasm gripped her. She could not move.

"Noooo," Zulla Mae groaned as she moved her head from side to side. She grabbed her belly again in pain. "Run … I move too slow … go. God's hand is on you. Go!"

Suddenly the screams and the running people seemed to fade, then disappear. There was nothing else in the whole world but her and Zulla Mae and the task set before her. Never had Cheyenne felt so focused, so alert, so confident that God was with her.

Cheyenne turned quickly and shoved the supplies off the flat low-riding cart. "Zulla Mae, get on the cart," she commanded. "We're leaving together."

The laboring woman panted as Cheyenne half picked her up and heaved her onto the low platform of the awkward dolly. Cheyenne grabbed the push bar with both hands and began running the cart, pushing it like it weighed nothing. Zulla Mae struggled to remain on the speeding cart, lying on her back, both hands gripping the bars.

Several shocked people had stopped to watch. Cheyenne yelled, her voice full of panic, "Are you *crazy*?! Run! It's a *bomb* ... run! Get out! *Fast!*"

As she ran her consciousness seemed to pass into a strange new dimension, like riding a fast flowing river ... moving swiftly ... shoving her forward as if being carried by an unseen hand.

As Cheyenne passed through the front glass doors the dazzling sun restored her to mental clarity. She instantly calculated the best path to Pinky amidst the running people and moving vehicles. Thankfully, the slope of the parking lot was in her favor as she sprinted toward the panel truck, never slowing until she was on the other side of Pinky. Then she dug her feet into the pavement, swinging the cart around the big truck. Then a sound filled her ears, something between the roar of a train and rolling thunder— only much louder, earsplitting, as if it burst forth from inside her head.

The ground vibrated as though a terrible weight had been dropped onto it. Then there was a forceful blast of hot air that punched the truck like a giant fist. Both women were kicked to the ground by the concussion. There was pressure all around them, like having hot weights pressed against their flesh. For a moment, the breath was sucked from their lungs.

Cheyenne felt a dark veil cover her vision. The roar intensified.

Then there was silence.

She could still feel the heat. The veil cleared somewhat and she could see the heavens filled with various sized pieces of what used to be a super store.

Then debris started falling all around them. Hot burning chunks fell on them and stung their skin. The smell came next, a strange odor, acrid, chemical. The air stung their lungs. They both coughed, but she didn't hear—she couldn't hear anything.

And then all was still, except the smoke and dust.

So completely silent.

Through the clearing smoke, Cheyenne saw two partial walls still standing. Mangled things lay all about that used to line the shelves of the store. She could see some of the metal roofing hanging in the trees beyond.

In the grey haze she saw a man, or maybe it was a woman, mostly naked, red with blood, staggering along aimlessly. Someone else was lying on the ground some distance away, making clumsy attempts to sit up, but falling back each time. It was like watching a special effects movie with the sound turned off.

Cheyenne felt movement under her. Zulla Mae jerked in the grip of a new pain. Cheyenne was dazed and half conscious. She realized that this was no movie, no dream. It was real.

Now she understood what Zulla had said when in the store. She smelled it too …

Death.

She could see Zulla Mae's mouth moving as if she were talking, but Cheyenne heard no sound. She had to read the screaming lips. "The baby … it's a comin' … *now* … oh! … oh! … Help me, Lawd o' Mercy, *help me!*" Zulla Mae's body contorted on the hot pavement.

Sitting up, Cheyenne waited for her head to stop spinning and for the nausea to pass. She reached up, shoving the overturned cart off them. Then she pushed her hair bun back off her forehead where it had flopped forward.

Slowly her mind seemed to settle into some semblance of understanding and remembrance. Not even able to hear her own voice, she called out, "God … please, God, help me help her. Show me what to do!" She looked around seeking help, but saw only smoke and chaos.

Cheyenne put her hand on the hot pavement to try to get to her feet. Her head spun as she fell back down on her knees. The lack of hearing left her befuddled. She forced her mind to focus, and her body to obey.

Standing to her feet, she staggered to the back of Pinky. Leaning there a few seconds, Cheyenne threw open the double doors to the cargo area. The back of the box truck was over half full of bathroom tissues, paper towels, boxes of office paper, packing material, tape, an ice chest full of peaches she had picked up from a local farmer at her first stop, and a variety of other supplies.

Cheyenne crawled in and began to shove things aside to make room for Zulla. Ripping open the huge packages of paper towels, she made a cushion for the birthing woman to lie on. Within 3 minutes she had a haven off of the hot payment and out of the burning debris. Cheyenne bent down, speaking softly to Zulla Mae, compelling the young woman to make the effort to move for the baby's sake.

Getting no response, Cheyenne began to heave and drag the suffering woman the few steps to the back of the truck.

A man holding a cloth to his bleeding head came over. Cheyenne could see his mouth move but could hear nothing. He helped lift the pregnant woman into the cargo bay of the truck. Without even looking at his face, Cheyenne handed the man her truck keys.

THE BABY – She climbed into the back of the truck beside the laboring woman. The man shut the double doors. Inside the truck, it was dark. For a few seconds Cheyenne could see nothing, neither could she hear. Her world was suddenly very, very small, until she felt Zulla Mae's body wildly writhing.

The truck shuddered, then slowly moved forward. She had no idea where the man would go, but hoped for the small hospital at the edge of town. Anywhere was better than here.

The tiny back windows were blown out by the blast. The bay was vented near the roof. A small amount of fresh air stole into the cargo area of the truck. The smoke began to clear. Cheyenne's ears made a small popping noise. Then she could hear just a little.

Zulla Mae's screaming was shrill and terrifying. Cheyenne almost

II Timothy 2:15 "Notwithstanding she shall be saved in childbearing, if they continue in faith and charity and holiness with sobriety." ∞

wished for deafness once more. "The baby ... my *baby*! God, *please* take care of my baby!"

Cheyenne jerked the young woman's long skirt up, yanking her panties off in one movement. Even in the limited light, she could see that the woman's legs were already bloody. "Lord, I ask you for divine help. Bless this mother who has honored you by continuing in faith and sobriety."

On a few occasions, Cheyenne had helped Hope deliver laboring mothers in home births. Her mind struggled to recall all that she knew. *The blood is supposed to come after the birth, not before. Something's wrong.*

She had watched Hope check for the baby's head, but never once had she put her hand forward. Now she functioned as if she had done this a thousand times. Ripping open a bag of paper towels, she scrubbed hard at her hands, then spread the woman's legs wide, propping them on huge sacks of soft toilet rolls. The labor pains seemed to be one on top of the other. What's holding the baby back ... *the cord! It must be around the neck.*

Cheyenne was ready when Zulla's next scream ripped through the closed truck. She pushed her fingers into the woman's birthing canal, feeling the hard head of the baby less than two inches inside the opening. The dim interior of the truck provided little light by which to see. But she didn't need to see for the job she had to do. She waited for the contraction to subside and then willed her fingers to squeeze in around the baby's head, searching until she felt the cord wrapped tightly around the child's neck. Her muscles tightened and Zulla Mae yelled at her to stop. Cheyenne thought the mountain woman might kick her away.

"Zulla, listen!" Cheyenne screamed. "The cord is around the baby's neck! I've got to unwind it or the baby will suffocate!"

Again she waited for the contraction to subside and the muscles to relax a little, and then, without hesitation, she plunged deeper into the tight spot, disregarding Zulla's pleas to stop.

Her heart raced as her finger found the cord. She hooked it with her finger and slowly worked some slack into it until she could pull it over the tiny chin. Yes! It slid easily around the head.

Cheyenne sat back on her heels, relieved. Seconds later the next contraction hit and Zulla Mae screamed anew. Still the child did not come.

When the contraction subsided, Cheyenne, her face running with tears and sweat, plunged her now experienced fingers back into the woman. Cramming her fingers again up around the child's head, she discovered yet another loop of the cord wrapped tightly around the child's neck. Moving as quickly as she dared, Cheyenne worked the strained cord over the bony chin of the unborn.

With a rush, the head and then the whole body slid out in an unexpected forceful gush of warm water. The baby lay as limp and unmoving as did the mother.

Cheyenne could see in the shady light that the baby's head was purple. "Oh God, it is so terribly hot in here. Oh, God, I need you to help me. Steady my hands. Give me wisdom to deal favorably with this child." Cheyenne's heart beat loudly in her own ears.

She sat back on her heels again and laid the baby on its side across her lap, rubbing the tiny chest and back with both of her hands. Time seem to stand still as Cheyenne rubbed the tiny chest, waiting, hoping, praying. Losing her balance as the swaying truck made a turn caused her to grasp the child with greater pressure than she meant.

Still no response.

She pushed back her hair with her forearm. She gently stuck her bloody finger into the child's mouth, trying to clear the airway. Her other hand pushed ever so slightly against the tiny back. The baby sputtered, took a breath and whimpered.

"Thank you, God ... *THANK YOU!*"

Cheyenne wept with joy as she pulled half a roll of paper towels free, creating a makeshift cradle. Laying the newborn into the nest, she cooed at the child, "That's enough, sweet thing. You don't have to cry. Just a little whimper will suffice. Thank you, Lord. I bless your Name, the Most High. What can I tie the cord with, Lord?"

Cheyenne cast around until her eyes lighted on the plastic grocery sacks. The baby, cord still attached, among the fluff of paper. "The cord can wait. We'll be somewhere with help soon."

The exhausted mother stirred, causing Cheyenne to get up higher on her knees to look at her face. "Zulla Mae? Your child lives. You have a baby girl." No response. A shaft of light played across the mother's still face. Again Cheyenne spoke, this time with urgency, but still no inkling of acknowledgement came from the mother. Glancing down, Cheyenne noticed with relief that the bleeding had stopped even without the aid of the baby nursing.

The slow moving truck came to a lurching stop, throwing Cheyenne forward. She caught herself by putting out her arms on either side of Zulla Mae's head. Suddenly the pale, still face of the new mother contorted.

Cheyenne saw Zulla's eyes fly open. Another loud anguished, almost growling, sound came forth, "There's anothern'!"

Quickly Cheyenne righted herself to help. The child came before she had a chance to even register her surprise, almost without effort. The younger twin emerged, screaming her protest.

The first sight for the second baby girl was in dazzling light as the double doors were thrown open, revealing paramedics. Clean, pure air rushed in over the exhausted foursome.

NEWSPAPER CLIPPING:

Three men were arrested as part of the investigation surrounding the terror bombing of the Cedar Creek Super Center yesterday. A coordinated team of terrorists set off a series of explosions that destroyed the small community's Super Center store during the morning hours.

So far, ten deaths have been attributed to the blast and at least 30 injuries. Authorities say it could have been much worse, but that alert individuals noticed the men and sounded an alarm in time for many early morning shoppers to exit the store before the blast was triggered.

Police have not released any details about the alleged bombers. Meanwhile, searches have continued at a Muslim community center in nearby Chattanooga after the arrest of a third man in connection with the attack.

The Muslim community released a statement indicating they are shocked by the events and that they will cooperate fully with police investigations into the attack.

Federal investigators are still searching the scene for forensic evidence. They have determined that chemicals and supplies within the store were assembled to ignite the volatile ingredients in an elaborate scheme that likely involved precise timing and several individuals. Damage from the explosion is said to have rendered the store a complete loss.

"This was done by an expert—someone who knew just what they needed and how to mix it in order to bring about the greatest devastation," said Detective Jay Smith, who is leading the county's investigation.

No official comments have been forthcoming regarding the motives behind the devastating explosion, but there is speculation that the attack was in retaliation to the distribution of literature to Muslims by an extremist Christian group located nearby.

"The hearts of Americans everywhere go out to the victims of this terrible tragedy," said the President this morning. "Too many honest, innocent people have lost their lives because of religious extremism.

"Steps will be taken to ensure America's place in the world as a land of tolerance, not of violence," the President asserted.

17

NOW I SEE

In the week following the bombing, the girls did what girls do when something happens more traumatic than their emotions can handle: they lived in denial. The only thing Cheyenne would talk about was the babies. The other three girls stared at her off and on during the day with looks of horror.

The trauma of the close call lingered like a foul odor. They were now working out of the warehouse, behind the fence on The Last Publishers' property. None went home to their own apartments. They all piled up in the corner they had designated as living space, some sleeping on the couches they had brought from the Herb Den, others sleeping on air mattresses. The closeness was comforting. Their brush with death left them all with an acute appreciation for the fragile uncertainty of life. They focused on eternal matters—their personal relationship to God, and the eternal fate of their loved ones.

All four girls were shoulder to shoulder packing, taping and labeling boxes when Magdalene announced, "I want to send my little brother, Ike, a *God's Story* book as a gift. He'll know it's from me, but no one else will know. When I first got into trouble, he was really concerned about me, and I was mean to him."

"That's great, Kid." Cheyenne was relieved that the silence was broken, and that there was now something positive to concentrate on. Magdalene reaching out to her family was icing on the cake. Cheyenne

CHEYENNE &
BOBBIE JO

offered, "I have some extra copies right here, so we can drop one in a small box and ship it out with this group of orders." Glancing at her watch, "UPS will be here in 15 minutes."

Magdalene took the book and walked over to the desk, muttering, "Girl, not Kid."

"Of course, anything you say," Cheyenne's sweet response to the rebuke was uncharacteristically surrendering.

Bobbie Jo's face soured. Too weird. The girls lapsed into awkward silence again.

In an attempt to make conversation, Julie looked over Magdalene's shoulder. There in the top corner of the inside cover of the book Magdalene was carefully etching two small symbols. "What's that?" she asked, suddenly intrigued. The other two girls walked over and looked. One looked almost like a flower, and the other, a sun disk.

Magdalene smiled. "You remember me telling you how us kids invented spy games? Well, we made up a sorta code that we used to tell each other stuff without our mom knowing what it meant. She was so nosey going through all our stuff and even opening our mail, so we created these signs. When I was going out, I would simply leave my sign on my brother's bed, and he would know to cover for me. With small lines added, going up or down, it would let us know if we would be out all night or just out for a while.

"This is my sign. This is his. When he sees them, he will know that I sent it especially just for him, and that I don't want the rest of the family to know who it's from."

"Well, hurry, Kid." Cheyenne handed her an overnight shipping box. "I hear the truck backing up to the dock." Cheyenne still sounded normal.

Bobbie Jo sighed.

REPENT OF WHAT?

Late that afternoon, Magdalene finished up a few late orders, then straightened her area. The pressure of work held the attention of all three of the older girls as they prepared inventory for the next morning's orders.

Since the bombing, Magdalene had given a lot of thought to their conversation about blood sacrifice and repentance. She took seriously Bobbie Jo's challenge to figure out for herself what God requires. She recalled how her family was so unhappy in their struggle to please God.

It was time to find an answer.

Magdalene sat in front of the old laptop and opened the Swordsearcher Bible software. She typed in the word *repentance* and started her own word study.

After some time, the others heard loud, frustrated muttering coming from the corner where the laptop was set up. "I know it says somewhere that you have to repent of your sins. This program couldn't have all the verses on it."

Bobbie Jo called out from across the shop, "Find the verse that tells you what to repent from ... or toward?"

There were a few moments of silence before the expected smart-aleck reply came back. "Why don't you guess, smarty pants, since you obviously already know?"

"Julie? What do you think you have to repent of?" Bobbie Jo's voice boomed.

Julie was behind one of the stock shelves counting bales of herbs. Her muted answer could barely be heard. "Oh, not this conversation again. I already told you the other day. It says you have to repent of your sins, of course. Isn't that right, Magdalene?" Julie's tone seemed to beg for confirmation. She had spent a nervous week wondering where she would go if she died.

Pause.

"*Wroooong!*" Magdalene shouted back. "The word repent is in the Bible 112 times, and not one time does it say 'repent of sin.'"

Julie stepped out from behind the storage shelves with a perplexed expression and looked down the long aisle between the racks. Her voice carried frustration. "Well, Magdalene, what does it say you re-pent of?"

Magdalene typed *repentance* from into the search box and scrolled down the results. Suddenly she shouted, "Dead works! It says repent from dead works! I see it now!"

Running back down the aisle, she grabbed Julie by the hand and pulled her to the front where she had the program open with Hebrews 6 on the screen. She plopped Julie down into a nearby desk chair.

Magdalene was bouncing with excitement. "Julie, I see it! I see it! We've been trying to please God with our confessions. No wonder we've both been scared out of our wits. Confession of sin is just dead

"It is intuitive and filled with helpful commentaries, dictionaries, Greek and Hebrew aids, nineteen Bibles in the Textus Receptus line, and other books that aid the student in understanding the Bible. Anyone can oper-ate it. It is ready to use when you first open it.

>

works! Don't you see? We have been trying to be good enough for God … and that's dead works which kept us lost! Just like Cain offered a bunch of squash and beans, we were offering our works!"

Leaning over Julie and searching the computer screen again, she said, "And over here in Acts 20 it says, '*repentance toward God and faith toward our Lord Jesus Christ*'!"

Magdalene sprang back up out of her chair and spun around to face the girls. She opened her arms wide and exclaimed, "We must repent from dead works and toward God! We don't have to deal with our sins. Jesus already took care of them. We just have to quit offering our good fruit, like Cain did, and just accept God's blood sacrifice! Wow! Where have I *been*?"

NOW I KNOW

"I was never saved … so I never lost it! Neither were you, Julie. Salvation is knowing God. We only knew religious teachings and hoped it was enough!"

Magdalene was bursting with joy. Julie remained seated, still struggling to understand.

"Julie, my repentance was super classic dead works! Just like Cain, I've been bringing my vegetables and fruit to try to appease God, but God has provided Jesus' very *blood* to cleanse me, sick sinner that I am.

"Hey!" In her joy, Magdalene interrupted her own thoughts. "Now I know why Jesus is called the Lamb of God!" Magdalene called with glee. Then she screeched out like an excited small child would, "I know! Oh, Jules … this is wonderful!"

Magdalene threw her arms out wide again and spun around, laughing like a little girl on a playground. "Now I understand why he is the Lamb of God!"

She stopped and clasped her hands with still unrepressed joy. "I kept thinking I had to be sorry, really, terribly sorry for my sins. I had to think back and confess and confess with great sorrow. But I have sinned so bad and so much I was always worried I wasn't sorry enough. I thought my real, real sorrow was proper repentance, but my wanting to be really, really sorry is just dead works!"

Cheyenne and Bobbie Jo had quit their work and stood grinning with pleasure, tears running down their faces. The thrill in Magdalene's soul was bubbling forth like cool, clean water. It was life ... it was wonderful. It reminded them that God is still on his throne and that life is a wonderful gift.

Magdalene stood, holding her head like it was going to burst with the newfound knowledge, trying to explain what she now knew. "That's why some days I felt saved and some days I felt lost. It all depended on how sorry I was feeling. I was trying to repent my way to God, and I thought repentance was being sorry enough to appease God."

Dropping into a nearby chair, Magdalene's expression suddenly sank as she looked up at Cheyenne. "Oh, Cheyenne! This is what's wrong with my mom. She's trying to appease God. She's spent her entire life in a super sorry state! This explains my whole family! No wonder we were sad and defeated all the time. No wonder she tried to control us all into being good. It was the only hope she had for us to get to heaven."

Magdalene stood again and raised her hands, palms upwards, in a gesture of surrender. "Now I understand what it means when Jesus said, 'It is finished.' Salvation is *done*. His blood covered my sins. I don't have to keep getting forgiveness ... he paid it *all*. Past, present and future, I've been forgiven!"

Tears streamed down her face. "I don't have to worry at night whether or not I've remembered to confess every sin. I don't have to be sorry enough, because I'm just a sorry old sinner to start with, and my only hope is that Jesus has already paid in full for all my sins!"

Magdalene grabbed Julie's swivel chair and turned her around to face her. Overcome with the wonder of it, the one time servant of Satan blurted out, almost singing, "Julie, I am *forgiven* ... God has forgiven me ... for everything ... *EVERYTHING!*"

PEACE WITH GOD – Julie burst into tears. She pulled roughly away from Magdalene as if offended.

Cheyenne put her arm around Magdalene and whispered, "Give her time. She needs to understand for herself and not just jump on an emotional bandwagon." The girls silently prayed as they waited.

Julie finally spoke. "Okay, I admit it ... I am not really saved. I want to get saved just like Magdalene. Right now. This minute. All my life I've tried to have peace with God. Everyone thinks I've been good all my life, yet I've been scared out of my wits because I knew what I really was. A few years back I swore to my dad that I was innocent when some church leaders thought I had stolen something. He believed me; he always believed me over everyone else. He even broke with the church over it. Three days later he died of a heart attack. I never admitted to anyone what I did. So I thought I was stuck with unforgiven sin, and it's been a nightmare.

"Every night I begged God to save me over and over, and prayed, trying to remember every sin I committed during the day. Especially this week it's been awful. With the bombing I kept thinking about what if I died. I've always known that God was not real to me.

"Being around you," Julie looked up at Cheyenne and Bobbie Jo, "made me realize that I really didn't have a personal relationship with God. Now I can see why. Sometimes, it would almost make me mad, because I felt like I was a better Christian than you ... but you had peace and were excited about God. I didn't know why I couldn't have peace." She glanced at Cheyenne. "Even when you thought you might die, you were thinking about saving someone else."

Julie looked embarrassed as her tears started to fall. "I'm tired of the whole thing. Just tell me what to do. I want to be saved."

Magdalene's face was full of joyful light. "Just turn from your old dead works of trying to be good. No, that's not right. Quit turning yourself and just look to what Jesus did for you. Jesus is the only way for bad girls like me ... and for good girls like you. Jesus paid the full price for sin. Oh, how much he had to pay and suffer for my terrible sin. I am forgiven!" Magdalene shouted with her fists thrust high into the air and her feet doing a happy two step.

As if remembering Julie, Magdalene came down to earth and focused on the distraught girl with a melted look of complete compassion. "Oh Julie, if you just trust and believe that Jesus is your only hope, then He will be there." In her overwhelming relief of sins forgiven, Magdalene pulled Julie up from her chair and both girls began dancing around and around yelling. "Jesus is our only hope!"

Cheyenne laughed as she watched the girls dancing, but she was troubled at Julie's own words, "Just tell me what to do."

Oh, Julie, I do hope you haven't reached for false hope again.

Bobbie Jo joined the other two dancing, laughing girls. Then she turned to grab Cheyenne's hand, dragging her into the frolic. "Come on, Pokey," she ordered, exasperated at Cheyenne's lack of joy, "let's rejoice with all of Heaven."

ANGEL OF LIGHT – Yancey stepped inside the warehouse. He heard the girls' excited voices but didn't see them anywhere. Something was wrong ... different. At first he was concerned, but it was soon obvious that what he heard was uninhibited hilarity.

He slipped down the aisle between boxes for a better vantage point. From there he captured their expressions of joy with his camera. He didn't know what he would do with the pictures, but this was not the kind of joy that someone could generate for a posed shot.

This is real.

What if I've been wrong? What if that weird Zulla Mae is right ... am I deceived?

The change in Magdalene was breathtaking. She looked radiant. "Angel of Light," he murmured under his breath as he slipped back out the warehouse door.

18

IT IS DOABLE

The back room at The Last Publishers' warehouse was set up for a meeting. Tonight, in just a few minutes, Asher and Omar would be presenting a new concept in missions. It would take this visual presentation to convince the old veteran missionaries that this was truly a better way to reach the world with the gospel. Several of TLP's team had worked for weeks to make this possible.

Asher stared at, yet didn't see, the huge liquid crystal display screen mounted on the wall. It had been a gift to the ministry from a businessman. He'd called it second rate, but it was first rate as far as Asher was concerned. He reached out, running his finger down the coast of East Asia. His hands still trembled.

The young man shook his head as if to clear the nervousness that had settled over him since the bombing. Trying to still the trembling, he made his hands into fists.

"She didn't even tell me about the threatening note from the Muslim girl. God, girls can be so dumb sometimes. Lord, help her to learn wisdom and discretion from all this."

Asher recalled the surprise of the investigators who questioned her after the explosion. The four girls had been warned, and none of them told a single person. He barked a short laugh as he remembered the Yankee saying, "Gee, I thought women couldn't keep a secret for anything. Four girls knew and none of them told. A weird bunch of dames." Even to his Pacific Northwest ears, the accent sounded like it was from another world. Zulla Mae sounded more normal.

The thought of the hillbilly woman brought back fresh memories of Cheyenne and Zulla Mae sitting crowded together on the hospital bed, huddled over the twin girls.

Smiling, he thought, *Cheyenne would have nursed one of those babies if she could have.* He shook his head again, trying to make sense of the strange new Cheyenne.

Asher glanced into the adjoining room, hoping to catch a glimpse of her, to hear her girlish laughter. His eyes dropped as the realization hit him. *She doesn't laugh like that anymore.*

He looked out of the window. Death has a way of making you see things differently. He turned back to look at the digital map, reaching out to touch an area of the world where no translation had begun. "God, send us to the man or woman who will translate your message for these people."

He read the list of languages down each side of the map. On the left side were the languages in which *God's Story* had been published and distributed—in some instances by other mission organizations. The right side, and across the bottom, was a list of the languages that were yet unreached by *God's Story* book. That list was long, too long. Many of those languages did not have so much as a New Testament in their native tongue.

Asher glanced down at his watch. Security was holding up the show.

The cream-colored Passat with the dent had disappeared. The Main Street Market, the only gas station in the small hick town, was still owned and operated by a Muslim family. The local townsfolk avoided the place like a plague. Even though the store was open for business, it looked abandoned. The Feds made a show of watching the place. With them crawling all over, the general population clung to a sense of relative safety.

Asher pushed his hair off his forehead as if trying to push away his apprehension. Something gnawed at the back of his mind. It was as if he knew something very important, but the information would not surface to his conscious mind.

His eyes narrowed as he considered every possible thing that the terrorists might be planning. "God, I can't see it ... but I know ... I know they are not finished with us. Help us to be ready."

A tear rolled down Asher's face, dispersing in the new beard he had started growing the day of the bombing. *So close ... God, it was so close. Can I bear to lose her?*

He walked quickly across the room, trying to outrun his emotions and force his mind to refocus on something else.

This meeting has eternal implications. I have to keep my mind on the future of this ministry.

But his thoughts turned back to safety issues.

Asher's eyes narrowed as he considered the fence he had constructed since returning from Thailand. It had been completed none too soon. A twenty foot strip all the way around the TLP property had to be cleared with backhoes and bulldozers. After the fence came the surveillance system, including motion detectors and infrared heat sensors. It had cost a fortune, money that could have been spent on publishing.

Asher mulled over the new security gates as he waited for the missionaries to arrive. Two entrance gates 100 feet apart, with armed guards in place around the clock. It had worked out well. Every semi-truck loaded with books was checked before passing through the second gate.

A sophisticated computer program kept tabs on the perimeter fence, alerting the building's occupants if anyone approached. Twice during the first week it had been set off by deer. Now an electric agricultural fence kept the deer, or any other wild creatures, from approaching the security fence. Still, a person determined to breach the fence line ...

Isaac, the Freemans' oldest son, had organized a group of young men, ages 16 to 28, that called themselves Gideon's Band. These men and boys put up four camouflaged tree stands at strategic points around the perimeter of the 20-acre enclosure. During times of high alert the boys manned the observation posts. Every stand was equipped with night vision goggles and general mobile radio service in addition to their cell phones. Their primary responsibility was to alert the guards and the local police if they spotted anyone attempting to breach the fence. Each watch was four hours. The boys passed time at night by observing wildlife through their night vision equipment. They loved it.

For tonight's meeting, the Trio's foursome had set up the back room with over 100 folding chairs. The employees spilled over to watch a screen in Louise's huge kitchen and dining area. The Last Publishers staff had already been briefed on the meeting.

Thanks to Asher, Louise and her girls had joined the TLP staff a few weeks after he had arrived. At first they had volunteered their services in the kitchen and as cleaning help. All they wanted was a house on the grounds, but Malachi would have none of it. He said the worker was worthy of his hire and deserving of payment. Malachi bought a used mobile home, in fair condition, and placed it under the trees behind the warehouse. Now the ladies were paid low wages, but they put most of it back into the ministry.

Tonight, Louise and the girls made tiny sandwiches stuffed with creamed spinach, chopped new onions, and cream cheese. The spinach and onion had come from Hope's garden, as had the lemon mint tea.

Asher glanced through the lighted kitchen window. He was just in time to see old Louise raise her painted eyebrows and slap Bobbie Jo's hand away from the treats. The young man's face lit up when he saw Cheyenne grin mischievously. Everybody loved Louise. No matter how evil the day, seeing her was like coming home.

JULIE'S INDISCRETION – Cheyenne suddenly remembered that she intended to try a call to Rob Cohen before the meeting. Hopefully she would get through this time. For security reasons, e-mail was not used for the berry brew business. The phone calls were planned at

The General Mobile Radio Service (GMRS) is a land-mobile radio service available for short distance two-way communications to facilitate the activities of an adult individual and his or her immediate family members, including a spouse, children, parents, grandparents, aunts, uncles, nephews, nieces, and in-laws (http://wireless.fcc.gov/rules.html).

http://wireless.fcc.gov/services/index.htm?job=service_home&id=general_mobile ✎

different times, using a disposable phone and prepaid long distance card. They were careful to use the proper botanical name for each herb they referenced, instead of the common name. Although it was their custom to speak daily, more than two weeks had now passed since they had gotten a call through.

The world news had reported on the volcano, but it seemed to have little impact in the area where Cohen was working. If they didn't hear from him soon, Malachi was considering sending Isaac over to check out the situation as soon as planes were flying into the area. Even Asher's well connected brother had not been able to offer any information.

Cheyenne exited the kitchen and headed to the first empty office to make her call in private. She hit the switch, flooding the dark room with light. She came up short, shocked and embarrassed. "Oh! I'm sorry. I hope I didn't interrupt. I think ... I'm sorry?"

Julie jumped away from Yancey, who was half sitting against the office desk. A strange buzz passed through Cheyenne as she turned on her heels without another word. Bobbie Jo, standing nearby, noticed Cheyenne's strained face and quick retreat.

Two minutes later Bobbie Jo and Louise watched as Julie stepped out of the same office with her head down, quickly turning away and busying herself straightening up things which weren't out of place.

Then Yancey emerged from the same room, looking completely cool and businesslike.

Louise and Bobbie Jo exchanged a knowing glance.

Bobbie Jo considered Yancey's better qualities: cute, witty, intelligent ... but something about him wasn't on the mark. *I would never even consider him as a mate.* She shook her head. But obviously Julie thought him a worthy catch.

The big girl bit the inside of her cheek as she made a quick decision. *Julie is 25 years old. She needs the freedom to prove what's in her soul. It's not my place to persuade her otherwise.*

Bobbie Jo looked back at Louise, seeing in the lined face the same resolve. Without a word the kindred spirits knew Julie would do what was in her heart regardless of anyone's caution. Louise leaned over whispering to the young woman, "A girl seeks out her own …"

Bobbie Jo looked back at her with an unspoken question.

"Your soul seeks out what you are, Bobbie Jo," Louise explained. "The pure of heart is attracted to the pure of heart. The strong woman wants a strong, confident man. So is the case with the others …"

Bobbie Jo's heart caught for a brief moment. Thoughts of Julie fled as she considered her own heart. Since the bombing it seemed to be important to get life going soon … just in case. She thought of all the men in The Last Publishers ministry. None really fit her, none really interested her. The closest to what she liked in a man was young Ben, but he was eight years younger and five inches shorter. He would be a fine catch someday for someone. His mind was sharp. He loved a challenge. He wasn't a leader, but he was a doer. He quietly considered a matter. He seemed solid, real.

Bobbie Jo sighed in defeat. The inches really didn't matter, but the age was a problem. *Unless I'm willing to wait for a few years until he is ready for marriage, and if I wait … it might be too late.*

A sense of hopelessness surfaced. *Who will I love? Who will love me?* "Lord, you know I got a lot of loving … a great big lot of loving in this big girl's body. I need me a man able to handle the whole of me. Hear me, Lord?"

Bobbie Jo watched Cheyenne walk out of another office, then through the kitchen to the glass door.

She watched as the slender girl pressed her nose to the glass door to peer into the meeting room where Asher and Omar waited. Bobbie Jo's head turned so that she could gaze out the big kitchen window. The two girls unknowingly shared the same thoughts. *Where were the missionaries and preachers for whom this whole event was planned?* Ever since the bombing, everyone was nervous, always expecting something terrible.

WAITING – Cheyenne unconsciously clasped her hands and looked down. She could feel the fabric of her shirt pulling against the scabs on her elbows. She scratched the slowly healing spots, marveling that she had never even felt the wounds until the day after the bombing.

She leaned into the glass door again, watching Asher. He was different since that day. He had a haunted look, a distant remote sadness that made everyone stop talking when he entered the room. He had never been more focused on the task than now. He slept little, worked late and came in early.

Cheyenne wrapped her arms around her body. Her eyes closed. *I am different, too. My girlhood was stolen from me ... I am old.*

When she opened her eyes, she could see Asher looking down at his watch again, then nervously over at Omar, who sat nearby studying his notes. The men had divided up the evening with Omar taking the Bible message, as he was the obvious preacher, and Asher taking the mission strategy.

Cheyenne went to yet another office, trying her call for the fourth time in just a few minutes. There was really nothing else to do about the brew except wait and pray. The labor intensive time was over. Even the print ads and commercials were made. It was a plan waiting to happen. Yet not hearing from Rob Cohen had everyone nervous. What if ... something had happened?

Except for that Sunday morning several weeks ago when Hope's private stash of the brew was stolen, nothing else had happened to slow the progress of the brew operation. Not even the Muslims could do that. Ben had heard from his geek friend that worked in the county courthouse that the local politicians and White Supremacists were hatching a plan to seize The Last Publishers' ministry property when circumstances were right. He had learned they were messing with the tax records and zoning codes. Obviously they knew about the expected China deal. Cheyenne's hands knotted. *Bunch of low-class, dumb, brainless bigots.*

Cheyenne knew that Asher had lawyers already making themselves familiar with the issues. She sighed. *More unnecessary expense.*

Her heart cried out to God for his provision. "Lord, these people coming here tonight could assume the financial burden of these things

ARABIC PAGE FROM GOD'S STORY

now ... at least some of it. They could pick up the cost of the languages ready to print. God, help us tonight to explain to these men how they can help get your message to the masses. God, help them hear."

This time she heard her own deep sigh and grinned. "I sound like I'm in an old folks' home—all those old folks with tired, worn-out hearts, sighing in unison."

Her grin faded as she thought of the measures her dad had gone to just in case the White Supremacists did cause problems. Malachi had web designers set up different sites where the books, movies, tapes, everything would be available online. Free.

Not even old Sheriff Hog Jaw himself could take away free ministry. Cheyenne lifted her shoulders as if trying to shake off the worrisome thoughts. She reminded herself, as she had a hundred times this past two weeks, *We wrestle not against flesh and blood. Pray and watch. God will send help in time of trouble.*

Trying to outwalk the disquiet, Cheyenne walked through the stocking area up front. "Hey."

Her voice broke the strained silence, causing both high-strung men to startle. Obviously she was not the only nervous person here tonight. "Are we going to be stood up?"

Cheyenne watched Asher pull up his sleeve and look at his watch. She could see he didn't really see the time; it was only a nervous habit. Omar barely lifted his head her direction as he answered. "Somebody's plane may have been late, or they could have been held up in traffic."

"Louise has snacks ... care for a cup of coffee or something?" Cheyenne asked. Neither man seemed to hear her. Both the men turned toward the open valley, where a string of car lights could now be seen heading up toward the office.

THE MAP – The room quickly filled. Some of the missionaries were too busy to come, so they had sent their wives or pastors in their stead. Many of the missionaries could not travel halfway around the world to come. For those, Asher had set up streaming video so they could watch from remote corners of the world. Everything possible had been done to have a representation of each country of the world. In the event some missed it, they were recording everything for future download.

Time had been wasted, so Asher did not wait for niceties or introductions. There would be some who had to catch planes this evening.

As soon as the majority was seated, Omar opened in prayer and Asher illuminated the big screen with the world map.

It was like looking from space, except the map was spread out flat. "We have asked you here to introduce you to digital missions," Asher began. "A way to reach the world for Christ in less than a year, hopefully in less than seven months, which is our working goal." Several of the older men laughed, thinking what he said was preposterous.

Asher motioned to one of the workers. "Turn the lights off, please." In the darkened room the world map gave off a faint glow. "Those who can read English have more gospel available to them than any other language in the world." America, Canada, England, South Africa, Australia, New Zealand, Belize, and a few other places in the world were illuminated with blue light.

"You will notice Australia's light is dimmer, as are most of the European countries, although the Bible is available there. Few people in these countries have actually heard the gospel."

Orange lights backlit Central and South America, and another dozen areas of the world. "Spanish is widely read in these countries. You will notice the dimly lit sections of the Spanish world. Although the Bible is published in their language, most of the people have never seen a Bible."

Over the next twenty minutes Asher covered the globe, discussing each country as it lit up with different colors in ratio to its saturation with the gospel. Each language group within the borders of a country was treated separately. Areas were lit according to the present availability of Bibles and literature among the masses. There were pinpoints of light here and there in most countries. A ripple of conversation could be heard as people recognized the area where they ministered illuminated by a tiny light.

Up came a list of languages on the right side of the map. "These languages represent tens of thousands of people, yet they still have no published gospel." He read the list of 213 languages. As he read, he pointed to the black, unlit spots on the map they represented.

Then he turned the light off behind the names and asked the men to look at the map. "You will notice the room in which we sit is still in shadows, for there is very little light coming from the large world map." Asher motioned again. "Turn the lights on.

"Since the days when Jesus walked this earth over two thousand years ago, the effect of our efforts to evangelize the world is that over 50 percent of the world's population has never even heard the gospel message —not one time. Even a greater number have no access to a Bible.

"If we had enough volunteers today and enough money to support them, it would still take twenty to thirty years to learn all these languages and translate Scripture into each one.

"It is estimated that the average foreign missionary has an outreach to only 5,000 people during his entire tenure. And that sounds high to me. At that rate, we would need to send a million more capable missionaries to the field this year. That's not going to happen."

PUBLISHED GOSPEL – Omar stood to his feet as Asher stepped back. The two men seemed to function as one. "God says in Matthew chapter 13, when asked concerning the end times: '*And the gospel must first be PUBLISHED among all nations*'. We may be among the last publishers before Jesus' return. The job that has not yet been done is now ours to do.

"God commanded us to '*go into all the world and preach the gospel to every creature*'. Yet for two thousand years people have lived and died without ever having a chance to hear.

"It is clear that the world will never be reached with our present methods. We must change our strategies. This is why you are here."

Omar stepped back as Asher picked up the flow. "You are all well acquainted with the 247 page, illustrated *God's Story* book that Malachi wrote a couple years ago. Many of you know or have heard of the missionary Timothy Vick, who is our foreign representative working out of Thailand. Vick has been instrumental in helping us get this book translated, published and distributed into 42 different languages. Another 60 languages are in the final stages of translation. For those of you who have been praying for this old soldier ... you need to know that his health has taken an amazing turn for the better."

Incredulous expressions covered many of the faces as they considered the old worn-out missionary. Asher grinned as he reassured them. "I was over there working with him for almost a month just recently. He worked me into the ground, trying to keep up with him. His doctors say it's nothing short of a major miracle. We are profoundly thankful, for it would have really been difficult to replace this faithful brother. Forty years of experience in missions and gospel publishing is hard to find."

A chorus of surprised *Amens* filled the room. Asher knew this personal information did much to win the hearts of the men to this project. He continued, much encouraged.

"The Last Publishers ministry has received thousands of amazing testimonies from all over the world in regard to the *God's Story* book. It is effective for two reasons. First, it's readily received and read, without the prejudice that Christian literature sometimes generates. It goes where Bibles and even missionaries are not allowed. Secondly, it teaches as God chose to teach: through stories of God's working among men. God's history, if you will.

"This has been the most successful preaching method of all time. This chronologically told Bible story book is a missionary that will not grow weary and quit, will not be distracted with sick kids, will not pause to eat, will never get malaria or dengue fever, does not have to pay rent, can live in a village undetected, can go to a country closed to the gospel, is willing to work day and night, and gives a clear and accurate message again and again for years to come. If a hostile government destroys the book, it can be replaced for three dollars or less."

Now Asher looked back at the dimly lit map. "But I have already illuminated the areas where either a Bible or our paper missionaries

193 million is the number of people today still waiting to hear or read the gospel story in their own language. There are over 225 languages with not one verse of Scripture and no story of what God has done on their behalf. For more information go to:

www.wycliffe.org ✐

have gone. As you can see, the greater percentage of the world still has not heard. We cannot reach the masses with page and ink alone; our methods must be broadened. Here is what we have in mind."

THE GEEKS – "Fellow ministers, may I present the men who will get the gospel to the whole world."

Now a group of very young men stood up to be introduced to the older, wiser ministers of the gospel. These were not sophisticated or fashion conscious individuals. None looked rugged or brave. They looked bookish, nerdy, definitely not frontier missionary material. After an awkward silence, the geeks sat down.

There was a shift of movement among the audience, not a positive move. Murmurs of dissatisfaction could be heard. Had they traveled all this way for a waste of time? Where was Malachi? Why had such weighty matters been entrusted to untried youth?

Asher stood his ground. He looked at the men with the sobriety of a prophet of old. "For the younger generation the internet is a constant source of information. We're publishing *God's Story* on the web as each translation is completed. In English there are millions of websites competing for attention. That's not the case with the other languages of the world. The young people getting on the web will be looking for anything in their language. They will find the gospel story."

Asher shrugged his shoulders to emphasize his words. "Ah, you say … not many people have a computer in the country I work in, and even if they did, who knows how to use the web or find a site?"

It was the young geeks' turn to laugh. Asher answered, "You, my dear old missionaries and ministers, are behind the times. Things are changing and moving ahead at a rapid pace. Technology is advancing by the hour. There is not a country in the world that does not have web

Bruce Smith, associate of Wycliffe (the largest translation organization) said, "… terrorism threatens Christianity in this era, so the word of God is the ultimate tool to change the life and the world." He went on to report about the challenge of reaching out to the places where terrorism is active. Dozens of translation teams in various parts of the world have had to be either relocated temporarily or permanently in order to avoid security concerns.

www.christiantoday.com ∽

cafés. The youth of the world all know how to access computers and can use them before they are able to read."

Cheyenne moved over by the door and peered out where she stood, thinking to herself, *It's not working, Asher. These old guys are yelling no inside ... I can hear their cries.*

Asher wasn't finished. "To prove my point I will demonstrate. Cut the overhead lights, Shy." Cheyenne's heart leaped. *He used my pet name in public!*

The room went dark with only the map showing a feeble light. Asher stood like a dark shadow as he continued to speak. "We have tried our new ministry idea in several countries, including those with Arabic speaking people.

"Every light represents at least a hundred people opening up a site displaying *God's Story* book. We only count those hits where we know someone has either downloaded the book or stayed on the site longer than an hour. Now watch."

The map began to light up. Color by color started to fill certain sections of the map.

"Jesus said that he is the light of the world."

There was an audible response. Asher used his laser to point to the different areas. "Notice these areas here and here. All Muslim areas. We have had as many as a hundred thousand hits in some of these areas where colleges are located.

"This is only the beginning. Your faces were once in shadows, they are now bathed in light—all the light coming through internet publishing.

Good and Evil

It takes many people years to translate the entire Bible; in contrast *Good and Evil* is a book in comic format which chronologically retells the major Bible stories and themes and can be translated by one person in about three months. Those unfamiliar with the Bible can gain an overall grasp of its message and understand what God has done in the 336 page comic novel. It also includes many verse references to aid those who want to dig deeper into the stories and subjects contained.

Due to its short read time, inviting illustrations, encompassing content and quick translation time, *Good and Evil* is an incredible tool for ministry and missionaries, often capable of reaching people and places where the Bible can't. More information on *Good and Evil* and the vast translation project concerning it can be found on:

www.nogreaterjoy.org

"The gospel has a new way to be published and we are going to make it happen. We need wise men to set up prayer chains. We need missionaries to help us find translators that can be trusted to do a good job. We need printers, storage buildings, and people on the ground who can see to the distribution. We need money. We need more young geeks who walk in truth and are willing to be the new missionaries for today. Will you stand in the gap?"

Omar stood with an open Bible.

> "'And when the day of Pentecost was fully come, they were all with one accord in one place. And suddenly there came a sound from heaven as of a rushing mighty wind, and it filled all the house where they were sitting. And there appeared unto them cloven tongues like as of fire, and it sat upon each of them. And they were all filled with the Holy Ghost, and began to speak with other tongues, as the Spirit gave them utterance.'

"Skipping to verse 7,

> "'And they were all amazed and marveled, saying to one another, Behold are not all these which speak Galilaeans? _And how hear we every man in our own tongue_, wherein we were born?'

"Let us pray that they will hear because we will be faithful to give them _God's Story_ in their language. Lord God, give us a vision of publishing the gospel into every language of the world. Let this be the dawn of world redemption. Amen!"

19

CHECKERBOARD FLOOR

Pink

Before Asher had turned onto the highway, he was grinning. Dusty poked Ben in the ribs at the same time, making a motion with his head to check out the silly grin on Asher's face. The truck cab was too small for their antics to get past Asher without notice. "What? Why are two boys giggling like girls?"

"Pink," Ben answered, trying not to grin.

An involuntary blush stole over Asher's features. Playfully he slammed his hand on the steeling wheel. "Okay, so that silly pink Wonder Bread truck makes me smile. I confess. You have to admit, it is a silly looking truck."

"Uh-huh. That truck can really speed up the old heart and get the endorphins flowing, all right," agreed Ben.

Dusty perked up when he heard the unfamiliar word. "Whad'chu say he has flowin'?"

Asher took his cue and began to moan. "Oh, oh, oh, I gotta have water. Oh, it just squishes my heart something *terrible*. Help me, my endorphins are flowing and *flowing*."

"Ya'll," Dusty's opening word sent the other two into a fit of laughter, "just stop right there ... you're making fun of me just because I like to learn new words. Words are beautiful, and that endorphin word really has a nice sound. I bet it has something to do with ... well,"

Dusty flushed as he realized he had put himself in an embarrassing situation. He started again, trying to get a satisfying answer, "What does it mean, exactly?"

They passed through security and drove around back of The Last Publishers' main warehouse where the Herb Den was now operating. Asher pretended to be serious as he responded, "Why don't you ask Magdalene, or better yet, ask Bobbie Jo?"

Ben tried hard not to laugh. It was good to have Asher getting back to normal. He had been so uptight for the last month since the bombing that it was difficult to be normal around him. He grinned as he thought of the girls. *I bet Cheyenne is real glad too.*

The three young men crawled out of the truck and looked up at the open dock to see what the girls were loading. Dusty got in one more crack. "Well, I know it has nothing to do with the pink truck, but I can durn guess it has a lot to do with the sweet thang that drives it."

Asher growled and made a face, indicating for Dusty to hush, but reached up to tussle the tall, thin boy's shaggy brown hair. "No durns. It's just a polite way of saying damn. Scripture says, *'let your yea be yea and your nay be nay'*. By the way, you need a haircut."

Hearing their voices, Bobbie Jo stepped out of the shadows of the warehouse door. She pushed her long, heavy hair back out of her way, calling over her shoulders, "Come here, girls, and see what the possum dragged up."

All the girls materialized as if by magic, calling out their welcome. Cheyenne's voice caught their attention. "Hey, we just pulled a tray of cookies out of the oven. Want some? We heard some of the missionaries are stepping up to bat and getting translations printed. We want to hear all."

The group squeezed into the small makeshift kitchen to eat and talk. The old concrete floor had been recently painted a black and white checkerboard. The small red enamel table seemed suddenly cool instead of just a yard sale reject.

Dusty's deprived upbringing caused him to really appreciate classy. He followed the red painted hallway floor to the front of the warehouse. "Man, you have the whole floor painted like it's different rooms. Cool. When did you girls find the time for all of this?"

Bobbie Jo chuckled. "One of the locals needed work. Actually, it was Yancey who gave him the layout and colors for the design. Talented fellow, that Yancey. The guy who painted the floor only followed the computer printout design. Like, fill in the squares with paint kind of thing. You should see the concrete rug up front. It matches the couch and chairs with little flowers all over it. When I walked in this morning, I thought it was a real rug!"

Cheyenne smiled as she passed a fresh cookie to Asher. "Well, you really knocked 'em dead at the meeting. I mean, when the last colored lights all came on, it was so cool. I have to admit I cried. Your light show really drove home the point. I hear money is coming in by the thousands, and dozens of languages are being handled by churches that are funding translators, webmasters, and printing."

Ben answered before Asher had a chance to clear his cookie from his mouth. "Man, yeah. There'll be prayer chains set up all over the world by next week. One of the preachers even offered to support me full time so I could finish helping Joseph with the uploading of the languages that require more space in the bubbles. So I'm out of construction and into full time computer work. How's that for a trip?" Ben's obvious enthusiasm made everyone break out with laughter.

The impromptu meeting soon ended; there was always work to be done. The boys stayed only long enough to load Cheyenne's truck with eight 50-pound bags of mixed herbs she was taking to her Amish friends' house for them to pack into cute retail bags.

PRAY AND WATCH – As Asher left, he reached out and took Cheyenne's hand. She felt as if she had brushed the electric fence. Her breath caught. He was looking at her again ... that look that made her feel like melting. But he was still not given to touching.

Asher was both embarrassed and amused at her response. His eyes reflected both, which somewhat sobered her. "Bobbie Jo told me about the conversation on repentance and then why it takes blood to cover sin. We sure have prayed long enough for the girls to understand the gospel."

Cheyenne squeezed his hand. "It is amazing that someone who has never heard has an easier time of accepting the gospel than someone steeped in trying to work their way in. I can see that coming to know who God is, instead of trying to figure out who He isn't, is their problem." Her brow knitted. "Do you know what I mean?"

"Well, kinda." He chuckled. "It sounds like your knotted lace work talk again. But I came by in person to tell you … well."

He dropped her hand in order to shove his own into his pocket. His face and tone suddenly changed. He turned away, clearly distraught. "Cheyenne, I just wanted to say that the Gideon Band guys have seen several strange cars and trucks in the area, and they caught sight of one man checking out the area with binoculars." His eyes were moist as he grabbed her hand, squeezing it once more, then turned to leave.

Cheyenne stood at the door of the warehouse watching them crawl into Asher's truck. Her hand still tingled where he had held it so tightly. Now she *knew*.

He loved her.

He was scared he was going to lose her.

20

FEDS

Dusty lurched forward. "Look at that. Ain't that the feds?" Three large black SUVs had just pulled off the county road onto the lane that led to The Last Publishers ministries. Clouds of dust billowed behind the big vehicles as they traveled down the chert drive.

"What are they doing way out here? There's nothing but TLP ministries down this road." Ben voiced what they all were thinking.

Asher gripped the steering wheel, trying to control the sense of panic that was washing over him. "Obviously something's up. I guess we'll find out soon. I sure wish we had phone reception here."

The dark SUVs pulled up to the security gate, and Asher pulled in right behind them. Dusty hooted, "Look at Joe. He's so nervous he's jerking around like a crazy man. He can't even get the gate open."

Asher spoke with irritation as he watched the guard's spastic motions, fumbling, trying to open the gate. "What kind of security do we have? He didn't even look in the vehicles. Just because they look official is no reason to ignore protocols. With those tinted windows, there's no way of really knowing who or what's in the vehicles."

Joe looked weak as water when he waved Asher on through. By the time they got up to the parking lot the feds were already exiting their vehicles, obviously in a hurry. Barking like a maniac, Wiggles succeeded in being loud and annoying but not in slowing their progress. Two of the men immediately headed to the warehouse where the Herb Den operated.

When the young men piled out of the truck, the rest of the feds were waiting for them. Glancing at Ben and Dusty, Asher saw that they were nervous. He could appreciate their feelings.

Asher moved, trying to skirt the men and go find the girls, but two agents blocked his path, saying, "Sorry, sir, we need you here to answer some questions; then you can go."

After a moment, the four girls came to the door with the two agents. They looked alarmed, puzzled and afraid. Cheyenne stepped forward, her voice sounding stronger than she felt. "Wiggles, quiet!" She commanded the dog. Wiggles trotted back to her place under the loading dock. "Could I be of assistance?" Her voice lacked the same confidence when addressing the officials.

There was a long moment of silence as the men stood staring up at the girls on the dock. Finally a small man dressed in a dark suit that appeared smaller still walked up the steps. He flipped open a leather wallet displaying his badge, as he addressed the girls standing in the open warehouse door. "My name is Agent Zich. We are part of a special anti-terrorism task force working to unravel a few incidents in the area. Mind if we have a private talk with you girls?" His head motioned forward. "Inside."

Cheyenne stepped back away from the concrete steps, making way for the man to follow her inside.

Asher's troubled gaze followed the girls as they disappeared into the shadows of the warehouse. The men stood in silence, watching the huge door slide into place. It was clear to Asher that he was being detained until they finished questioning the girls.

Ben studied the men. They all looked amazingly alike. He realized he could be one of them. He wasn't too tall or too short. His hair, unlike Asher's, was nondescript. He knew that he could blend in as effectively as they did. The sound of his voice was shocking to his own ears. It was high pitched and strained as he asked, "Why now? It's been almost a month since the bombing and you guys never came here before … so why now?"

The men's faces were void of emotion. Nothing indicated that they had heard the question. Then, with practiced precision, one of the men pulled out a paper and held it up for the three young men to see. It was a picture of a young Arabic looking girl.

The three young men stared at the picture of the unknown girl. Asher's throat felt dry as he asked, "Who is she?"

The man folded up the paper and put it back into his coat. His nonchalant movement seemed to suggest that it was not really that important, but Asher knew better. "It's her, isn't it? The girl who put the note under the door?"

Most of the feds just stood around the big idling vehicles, ignoring the question. The young men waited for an answer.

Finally one of the men responded, "We thought the girls might be able to tell us."

Asher felt a sudden breathlessness. His bass voice came out as a forced whisper. "She's dead ... isn't she?"

The agent glanced at the three young men, but never answered.

Fox News, Wednesday March 11, 2009
Muslim war protesters disrupted a homecoming parade for British troops Tuesday ... Anjem Choudary mocked the parade for the 2nd Battalion Royal Anglian Regiment in Luton, England, by posting a message on an Islamic extremist website joking about British soldiers killed by friendly fire in Iraq. He leads the group Islam for the U. K., an organization trying to make Britain an Islamic state ruled by Shariah law. ∞

21

YOU DONE YET?

Cookies

Magdalene sighed with pleasure as she finished washing the dishes in the Herb Den's small kitchenette. It was good to be back at the Herb Den, even for a day. Asher was a hard taskmaster, making the two girls promise to keep the doors locked and the lights out, making the place appear still empty and unused. But Asher had recognized that Bobbie Jo had reached her end of tolerance; she needed time out from the confinement.

Magdalene grinned as she leaned back against the counter, thinking of that first evening when Cheyenne had brought her back to sit at the little red table.

Pulling off her heavy rubber gloves, Magdalene stared at her tiny hands, unconsciously using them to count. Her brows knotted as she tried to remember the date of her arrival. *May ... May. It was a Friday afternoon ... yeah, now I remember. It was May the 2nd. Only four months, almost five months ... how amazingly different things are now.*

The young girl lit up with delight. *I scared that old Cheyenne silly when the chair hit the concrete floor, making a bang loud enough to raise the dead.*

Her giggle echoed in the tiny room. She drew in a deep, gulping breath. Sighing with pleasure, her head fell forward as her mind drifted. *Mmmmm ... cinnamon and spice and everything nice ... it smelled so good that first time, just like now.*

The young girl's mouth watered as she recalled her first taste of Cheyenne's cookies with cream cheese piled high. Oh! Those delicious, warm Amish sorghum spiced cookies. *I was so hungry. I was so scared.*

The timer buzzed. She picked up a hot pad and bent to open the small oven that had been salvaged from an old camper. *And here I am cooking those same famous cookies for tonight's meeting.*

She pulled the last tray of cookies out and set them on the stove top. The heavenly fragrance of cinnamon, cloves, and ginger filled the kitchen.

"Magdalene, where are you? Are you done yet?" Bobbie Jo's booming voice could clearly be heard from the front of the store. She didn't need the intercom.

Magdalene stepped over to the intercom and pushed the button. She whispered now into the speaker, "What's the matter, BoJo? The delicious spicy aroma of these cookies wafting up to you? Oh, they smell so good and taste even better when they are hot, fresh from the stove. Mmmmmm, I can almost *TASTE* them!"

Magdalene laughed when she heard Bobbie Jo screech her name.

"Whatsa matter? Too much for you? Can't wait five more minutes? Hee...hee ... hee. I'm not done, but the cookies are done. Tsk, tsk, tsk ... you always forget your manners and your grammar when you smell cookies coming out of the oven."

With a practiced hand Magdalene slid the cookies off onto the blue mat to cool, then turned to hang her apron on the hook by the doorway.

BABY DOLL – She glanced back toward the stove. Magdalene's shoulders sagged as memories from that first night stole in uninvited. In her mind she could still see a tiny brown stain on the floor where the doll had landed.

Thoughts of her baby doll brought back an old sadness that she hadn't visited in a while. In her imagination, Magdalene conversed with the baby doll. *Sally, you landed right on that spot. The girls still don't*

Amish Spice Cookie recipe can be found on page 216.

know about you, Sally. They wouldn't understand why I need you with me.

The soft white hair hung forward, hiding most of Magdalene's face as her pale blue eyes stared down where the small stain once graced the floor. Magdalene trembled with the memories. She revisited the old house where Derek had taken her.

Her arms automatically created a cradle, and she softly hummed a lullaby. That was how she had comforted herself those fearful days and terrifying nights. She had clutched the doll while lying alone on the dirty floor.

Night after night she had listened in terror to the sounds of animals scuttling across the floor of the old abandoned house. Many nights she had awakened with spiders crawling across her face or arms. Magdalene trembled and cooed as if she held a child. *My baby ... my little baby, you were always with me.*

The young girl laid her head against the door frame and struggled to banish the awful thoughts.

And the peace of God, which passeth all understanding, shall keep your hearts and minds through Christ Jesus. Softly she whispered, "Thank you, God, for such a great forgiveness; you even gave me a new heart. *Old things have passed away; behold, all things are become new.*

"Oh, but God, I long to see my own sweet baby girl, Starlite. Take care of her. Someday when I see her I will tell her how sorry I am. How I wish ... if only I hadn't ... let her know, Lord, that I am so ... so very sorry. Tell her Lord, tell her." A sob rose, almost choking the young girl as she struggled with remorse. Finally Magdalene sighed, "Thank you, God, for forgiving me. So much has changed. Thank you, God, for saving me and giving me peace. How different I feel now that I really know you. Thank you, Lord, for making me your own."

COOKIES – Bobbie Jo's loud voice broke into the quiet and echoed over the intercom. Magdalene jumped with a start. The air was filled with Bobbie Jo's demands. "Mag girl! I know you're finished. Bring me a cookie ... no, three cookies. You'd better hurry before I come back there and body slam you," Bobbie Jo teasingly threatened. Magdalene's reverie evaporated.

Pressing the intercom, Magdalene whispered her response, "You're going to blow the intercom's speakers yelling like that. The cookies are ready. I'm coming, but no cookies until tonight's Bible study! That's the rule, remember? Shy made us all agree after we cleaned out all the cookies two times in a row before anyone even got to the Bible study."

Reaching up, she grabbed a napkin and wrapped the largest cookie in it while muttering, "Just one little ol' cookie for BoJo. Shy won't care that much." As she walked out the door into the warehouse, she looked back at the spot on the floor. Then, as if saying goodbye to her guilty past, she closed the door.

"Hey, thanks, Kid." Bobbie Jo's glad face reflected pure happiness as she eagerly bit into the warm cookie, making moaning sounds as she enjoyed its soft chewy goodness. "I'll remember you in my will. Hey! Clean up this while I finish up this inventory list. Then we can leave. I know you want to take Tess' kids to the herb pond to play. If we hurry, maybe we can finish early enough today to go."

Magdalene stood staring at Bobbie Jo, causing the big girl to stop and look menacing at her. "Excuse me ... did you hear me say clean up?"

"Yeah, I'll clean up, but I ... did you know ... well..." Magdalene looked down nervously.

"Well, spit it out. I haven't got all day to wait on your lollygagging." Bobbie Jo's words sounded gruff, but her face showed some concern.

"Tess and Omar say I have to call my dad." Magdalene made the announcement like it was a death sentence.

Bobbie Jo quickly looked back at the screen. "Yeah, well, Omar and Tess are wise folks. If they think you should call, then you should. You can't put off contacting your parents forever. Besides, Tess has really taken you under her wing since we've all lived at TLP. You spend all your free time with their family. I think you should do what they tell you. If they told me to do something like that, I sure would."

Magdalene dropped to her knees to begin cleaning up. "Yeah, well ... I'll think about it. You know my dad is a White Supremacist. My dad believes mixed race children are mongrels. Remember he wanted me to kill his own grandbaby … and he doesn't believe in abortion. I don't think they really know just how much White Supremacists can hate. The fact that I love and respect Tess and Omar makes me not want to obey them in this matter."

"Geez, Mag," Bobbie Jo's voice held disdain, "Your dad lives 300 miles from here. He's not going to hurt Omar's family. You worry too much. Besides, that humongous fence and the Gideon Band will keep out a bunch of stupid White Supremacists. You know … you met Derek. Man alive, if he is any example of the rest of the pack, they are all way down on the bottom of the intellectual ladder. He is so gross … he is barely a humanoid as far as I'm concerned. They will not get past that fence."

Magdalene still stood, staring at Bobbie Jo. "What is it now?" Bobbie Jo demanded. "Geez, Kid. Stop standing there staring at me like that. Just spit it out so I can finish my order."

"I'm going to work for The Last Publishers ministries. Do you think Shy will be mad?"

The older girl stopped and turned away from her computer. She was genuinely surprised at the announcement.

Magdalene rushed into an explanation. "I mean, I really love helping you girls pack herbs, but I want my time on this earth spent helping people to come to know Jesus. Oh, I know Cheyenne has been the one responsible for buying all the berries for the brew made in the China factory. I know that the sale of the brew will fund the publishing of *God's Story* for the Muslims, but she says our part of the project is almost finished, even into next year."

White hair flew in a circle as she threw up her hands in a dramatic finish. "Besides, the berry thing seems so far removed from missions. It's like it's happening to someone else. Even Cheyenne doesn't have much to do with the actual manufacturing. That part is in China. I want to see the letters the people write wanting a Bible. I want to spend my whole day making it happen. I don't want to wait until the funds come in."

Bobbie Jo was still perplexed. "Why does everything have to be soooo present for you ... like today? It's not like you couldn't decide about this later. You're not scared about end times like Julie, are you? Anyway, you already live at TLP, so what's the difference which job you do?"

"No ... it isn't fear. I just want ..." Magdalene stumbled, looking imploringly at Bobbie Jo. "I want to give to others the same chance that I've had ... but I would like it to be now, this week. I want my life to be used to get *God's Story* into the hands of those who don't know Jesus, especially young Muslim girls. And now more than ever, especially after the feds came with that picture of my friend."

Magdalene's deep sigh revealed how deeply troubled she was concerning the young Muslim girl's disappearance. Her question sounded as if she were seeking reassurance. "Bobbie Jo, do you really believe her parents might kill her for reading about Jesus, or if they found out she gave us the note? I mean, I know her daddy is not the dude that drives that Passat. Both her parents seem so friendly and kind when I go in to buy something. I've been in their store lots of times since I talked to their daughter that day and they talk to me like I'm their friend. They are always so nice to me, even though Cheyenne says they give her the heebie-jeebies. I believe if they thought their daughter might be in trouble they would hide her away in a secret place."

The older girl sat there looking miserable. It was not possible for her to hide what was on her mind. Now she turned away to avoid answering, but Magdalene's persistent stare seemed to burn through her.

Bobbie Jo's deep sigh signaled she had something to say. "Nice has nothing to do with honor killings. It's a matter of commitment to a religion. The Bible teaches us that we are to love our enemy, to do good to them that hate us, to forgive those that misuse us. We are taught to give the gospel to everyone, even if it means giving our life for them to have a chance to hear the truth."

With a teacher's tone, strangely free of emotion, she continued, "The Qur'an teaches just the opposite. Islam asked believers, are you willing to kill for Allah? Are you willing to bring harm to those who are your friends? Will you misuse those who do you good, even those you dearly love? Will you for Allah's sake kill your own beloved child? Then Islam helps the believer go through with these evil deeds by teaching them to fear, not to obey."

Bobbie Jo fell quiet for just a minute before she finished her thought. "The average Muslim person is trapped into obeying or being in jeopardy of losing their life. Terror works to control their own people just like it does with those who are not Muslims. Believers are kept faithful through fear.

"It is a sad fact that the average nice Muslim uses to his advantage the fear the terrorist instills to get what he wants."

Magdalene looked confused, "What do you mean by that?"

Bobbie Jo's face showed strain, "Think about it, Magdalene. People like us, the non-Muslim community, are scared to stand against anything Islam demands, so laws get changed without effort, newscasters neglect to tell the whole story, school textbooks are changed to include Islamic teachings, officials give over to Muslim holidays and all the many other things the immigrants change in a community when they move into a new area. They let terrorists help them take control, even while fear controls them.

"Fear. Your young friend was afraid … I remember you telling us how tense she was when you showed her the website, how she jumped when a car door slammed. She had a reason."

Magdalene's young face looked stricken as she listened to Bobbie Jo tell what she already knew. The older girl almost faltered in finishing what she had decided to tell. The two girls sat looking at one another, one waiting to hear, the other dreading to tell at the risk of taking hope away from the new Christian.

This time Bobbie Jo's voice was full of anguish. "I hate to tell you what I think … but I can't help from remembering. You are too young to really remember 9/11, but that morning when we found out it was Muslim terrorists that hijacked the planes, I was still living at home. We had a family staying with us. We all stood around the TV watching that morning. The visiting man was so upset, but he kept saying,

'Remember, these are only a handful of evil, crazed men who did this terrible thing. They do not represent the Muslim people in any way. We have many Muslim neighbors and they would never tolerate such atrocities.'

"Later we were sitting at the lunch table when someone from his home town called him. I will never forget his stricken face as he held the phone. He just dropped the phone onto his plate full of food.

"Then he stumbled to his feet and left the room. We all just freaked, knowing something even worse had happened. His wife jumped up to follow him out to see what was going on.

"We were still sitting around the table when she came back in a few minutes later. Her eyes were red from weeping. She said, 'They're dancing in the streets ... our friends in our neighborhood are dancing in the streets'. They said the news says that Muslims are dancing in the streets all over the world celebrating this terrible crime."

Bobbie Jo's eyes momentarily dropped as she finished. "To my knowledge the news never clearly let it be known how widespread the rejoicing was in the U.S., but ... we do know that in our friends' neighborhood there was dancing." She looked back up into the apprehensive eyes of young Magdalene.

They stared at each other, considering how this might relate to Magdalene's young Muslim friend. Magdalene's head dropped first. Her voice was but a whisper. "I still can't believe that nice family would hurt their daughter. She's just a kid, like me. I'm just not going to believe they would do it."

Silence filled the room. It seemed to go on and on. Bobbie Jo returned to the computer and began robotically typing up orders.

"I know I did the right thing in giving her the gospel." Magdalene's voice was steady now. "When I think ... what if I never gave

The Buffalo News, February 17, 2009

The gruesome death of Orchard Park resident Aasiya Zubair Hassan—who was found decapitated—and the arrest of her estranged husband are drawing widespread attention, as speculation roils about the role that the couple's religion may have played.

A teacher of family law and Islam at the University at Buffalo Law School, Shahram said that "fanatical" Muslims believe "honor killing" is justified for bringing dishonor on a family.

>

her the website with the translation of *God's Story* because I was scared? What if she had never had a chance to hear the gospel? What if she lived here so close to us and no one ever took the time to tell her how she could come to know Jesus? What if fear kept me from telling her about Jesus?"

Magdalene's young voice dropped to a whisper as if she were afraid to say the dreaded words aloud. "No matter what, I'm glad I gave her the gospel, but I'm also glad we didn't tell about her note. I think I would be scared for her if we told about the note ... but we didn't, so I think it's okay. I know it's kinda late now to start praying for her safety, but since the feds came I've really prayed harder. All along I've been praying and praying for her to understand about what Jesus did for her."

Moving a few steps to where Bobbie Jo sat, Magdalene squatted down by the desk and looked into the older girl's eyes. "Bobbie Jo, I just want to pour my life into helping girls like her hear the gospel. From this day forward I want to personally be a part of what God is doing to make that happen. Do you think Cheyenne will say yes?"

Bobbie Jo's eyes looked suspiciously moist as she pulled Magdalene over to tousle her hair. "Well, sure, Kid, it's your life. She'll be glad to see your heart is so toward missions. She's like that too, you know. We're sure gonna miss you! You seem like you're my own kid sister. You sure look weedy today," Bobbie Jo added, reaching to lightly touch the girl's cold white cheek with her finger. "Geez, Kid ... you do look rough. You have dark circles under your eyes and you're so skinny I can see clean through you. I think you worry too much. You're too young to think about life and death. Your friend will be fine. Now, eat a cookie."

Magdalene grabbed Bobbie Jo's hand. "Thank you, Bobbie Jo! Thank

In some interpretations, the Quran allows husbands to punish "disobedient" women, Shahram said, adding that this is a minority view.

Orchard Park police Monday continued to investigate last week's death and remained quiet about its details.

www.buffalonews.com/home/story/581540.html

you so much! If I had a big sister like you in my life, things would have been so different."

Tears spilled over the big girl's cheeks, causing her to wipe at them disgustedly before shoving Magdalene away. "Man ... you can turn me into a sop better than anyone I know. I'm gonna be glad to get rid of you before you tarnish my name. People will think I'm turning into mush. Now eat the cookie. I can't even swallow mine with you looking like a skeleton."

STARLITE – It didn't take Magdalene long to finish straightening the rest of the office and lounge area. As she waited for Bobbie Jo she trailed her hand over the back of the worn, dark velvet couch as she walked back and forth.

Finally she spoke up. "Bobbie Jo, did you know that I asked Malachi what the Bible says about what happens to the children who never live long enough to believe and be saved? I wanted to know if what Cheyenne said was true about children being raised from the dead to grow up during the Millennium. Especially babies that were aborted. I needed to know."

The clattering fingers stilled over the keyboard. Bobbie Jo stared at Magdalene, waiting for her to continue. When no response came after ten seconds, she said, "So? What did he say?"

"He told me how to do a word study using the Sword Searcher Bible program to find my answer. He said since it was a heart issue for me, I needed to get an answer straight from God's Word for myself.

"I read a lot in Isaiah 65. Hope says it's one of her favorite chapters in the Bible. It's all about the Millennium. The reason she likes it best is because of that verse that says God's people will have days as long as a tree ... like a thousand years.

"Hope says her and Malachi will finally have time to build a house, garden, rock walls, and all the other stuff they like to do, and they will be able to live long enough to enjoy the fruits of their labor. You know it talks about people living a thousand years.

"That chapter also has a strange verse about different groups of people living different lengths of time. It indicates a group of children will be from some other time to grow up in the Millennium. I looked up words from that chapter, plus phrases like '*the streets of the city shall be full of boys and girls playing.*'"

Bobbie Jo's face reflected confusion at the unexpected Bible dissertation. "What's any of that got to do with anything? Just say the answer. Are miscarried children raised to grow up in the Millennium or not?"

The young girl put her head down, spilling her white hair around her face, hiding a smile. "Oh, Bobbie Jo, you are so impatient. But, yes, from what I read, they do. They really will be brought back to grow up during the Millennium. Besides, just knowing what we do of God through what the Bible reveals of him, I can't believe he would just leave those little souls hanging suspended as if they never existed. He wouldn't send them to hell, and they haven't been born again, so they can't go to heaven. What else is there for the little ones who die? The Millennium will be an opportunity for all those children, and the mentally handicapped as well, to grow up naturally and make their own decision to love God or not. We know that many people rise up against God in rebellion at the end of the Millennium, so they have to come from somewhere."

Bobbie Jo was captivated with the idea. "That would give answers to a lot of questions. You're really loving studying the Bible, aren't you, Kid? I never saw anyone change so much as you have in the last few weeks. It's like you're older than any of us. I guess it's all the Bible study you've been doing."

Magdalene mumbled something too low to be heard. It was obvious she was distracted as she trailed her fingers across the soft texture of the couch. Bobbie Jo continued typing, but remained intrigued by Magdalene's excited tension.

Finally Magdalene plunged ahead. "I had a dream last night. It was the best dream I could ever imagine. Do you believe God speaks to people through dreams? I just have to tell somebody about it!"

Something in the young girl's yearning tone caused Bobbie Jo's eyes to mist. She quietly got up from her office chair and walked over to join Magdalene, who sat balled up on the couch. "Yeah, I think he does on rare occasions, but it has never happened to me; and yeah, I'll listen to your dream. I needed a break anyway; my bones are all stiffening up."

Magdalene looked pleased as she laid her head back against the low couch, closing her eyes in preparation of the telling. Her young body was relaxed as if she were very tired, but her voice was full of joy and utter peace.

A FORETASTE – "In my dream I saw a beam of sunlight, and then in that light I saw just my hand as it reached down and clasped a child's tiny brown hand. Then I could see me running through a meadow of white and red clover, holding hands with a small girl. I could hear our tinkling giggles, sounding so full that it would take a thousand wind chimes dancing in the wind to equal the beauty of our laughter and joy.

"The little girl fell into the soft clover, rolling over and over, then lay still looking into the sky. It was then I knew her. She was Starlite, my own baby, but now she was a little girl about 5 years old. Her long ringlets of jet black hair spread like a halo across the clover. We lay there together, our heads close and our fingers intertwining. Her eyes sparkled with delight as she handed me a long-stemmed clover and ask me to teach her how to weave a crown for her head.

"Oh, Bobbie Jo! No words can describe my happiness. Never in this life have I ever known such joy!

"She ran about, picking clover to bring to me. I poked my thumb-nail into the stems to make tiny holes in order to thread another stem through it until I had made chains of red and white clover to wind around her head.

"A honeybee landed in my hair, and she laughed, and I told her how honeybees once had stingers. I told her how I was stung once and used an herb to bring healing. She wanted to know which herb, so I found some plantain growing nearby. I chewed the leaves then showed her how we put the slime on the bee's sting. She laughed with delight as we talked. Then we found some mullein, and I told her how the big, soft, fuzzy leaves were used for toilet paper all down through the ages. Right next to the fresh young mullein plant was an old dried mullein. I broke off the tall dried stock and told her how people of old would light them, using them as torches because the oils in them would burn for hours. That's why the British call their flashlights torches."

Magdalene fell silent. Bobbie Jo wanted to speak, but could find no words. They sat quietly, neither willing to break the spell.

Finally, Magdalene leaned forward and took Bobbie Jo's large hand into her own small ones. "Bobbie Jo, I believe God gave me a foretaste of how it is going to be in the Millennium. I believe that God will let me bring up my own little girl, Starlite. I think it will be from my own voice that she will hear the beautiful story of Jesus' grace and forgiveness. I know I have been forgiven from my terrible sins, and now I believe God will give me this wonderful gift of raising Starlite to learn to love him like I do.

"He says in the Bible that he will wipe away all tears from our eyes. In my dream I wound the wreath of clover around Starlite's head, and she looked into my eyes with such trust and love. At that moment, I felt … I really felt God's own thumb wipe away my tears.

"He is the God of new beginnings. Just look at Omar and Tess. He has made everything new in their lives. Sometimes in this life God makes things new, and sometimes we have to wait just a short time for him to make everything else new. I know God wanted me to know the joy he has in store for me in my very near future. And, Bobbie Jo, He wants you to know so you can tell the others."

Plantain (exceprt) - http://www.bulkherbstore.com/articles/plantain
"She came flying out of the car. Before I could even get over to her, she was on the ground chewing plantain leaves—as many as she could fit into her mouth. She had green slime running down her chin like it was going out of style. Before I knew it, Dr. Deb (Mom) had plastered that green slime all over my face. I looked like I was getting a French facial. In a matter of minutes the swelling from the bee stings had begun to subside and the pain was only a memory."

Plantain - www.bulkherbstore.com/Plantain-Leaf-Cut
Mullein - www.bulkherbstore.com/Mullein-Leaf-Cut

Magdalene cupped her tiny hand and held it out. With a gentle touch she seemed to place something invisible into Bobbie Jo's palm. Then she carefully folded the larger hand and held it closed with both of her small white hands. Both girls stared at Bobbie Jo's closed hand.

Magdalene spoke quietly and reverently. "Bobbie Jo, I have given you a jewel of my future. Keep it safe and fresh until the time that others need to know."

Crusty Bobbie Jo dissolved into unabashed tears, falling in great drops from her big brown eyes. Something eternal had just happened.

Amish Spice Cookies

Make dough in evening, refrigerate overnight, bake the next morning. Sift dry ingredients together.

9 cups of flour
1 tsp salt
4 tsp baking powder
3 tsp ginger
2 tsp cinnamon

Cream butter and sugar, add eggs, beat well. Then add sorghum and vanilla, then soda water. Mix dry ingredients into cream mixture.

2 cups of butter
2 cups of sugar
4 eggs
2 cups sorghum (syrup)
2 tsp vanilla
6 tsp soda in ¼ cup hot water

In the morning roll small balls of dough in a plate of sugar (spoonful) and put on cookie sheet. DO NOT PRESS FLAT. Bake at 375 degrees, 6 minutes on bottom rack then 6 minutes on top rack. Makes 8 dozen.

22

OUR REAL ENEMY

The sharp odor of fresh garlic, onions, and steaks sizzling together made Malachi's mouth water as he sat at the head of the long table, quietly talking with Ben while Hope and the girls finished putting the last of the dinner on the table. The side bar was loaded with fresh salad, cilantro, avocados, olives, tomatoes, and cheeses.

Dusty sat at the end of the table with his head twisted backwards, trying to watch the girls as they bustled around. He was groaning and complaining for them to hurry, for he was a growing boy and "pert near to starvin'."

Asher's eyes strayed to the kitchen as well, although it was not food that stirred his hunger. Cheyenne, grinning, glanced up to acknowledge Dusty, but caught Asher's unmistakable gaze. Her light smile disappeared and was replaced with a quiet, shy shiver of joy, mingled with a strange, pleasurable fear. She felt vulnerable, in a cozy, secure way.

When he turned his gaze away, she came to herself and was aggravated that his mere glance could so shake her usual defenses. Her finger touched the side of the hot pan, bringing her painfully back to what she was doing. She stuck her smarting finger in her mouth before spooning the last of the black beans into the serving bowl.

Hope liked a full table every Sunday after church. Cheyenne smirked. *Mom was probably happy a lot lately.* There was nowhere to go these days since everyone deemed a possible target for the terrorists had moved to the Freeman property. Books had been stacked to create walls in the warehouse in order to make hasty living quarters. It had been fun for two, maybe three days. Now it was a chore to find someplace to have an independent thought. Showers were scheduled. It was not a spa experience.

"How's your scout troop going with their drills, Asher?" Yancey asked between mouthfuls of food.

Asher stole a fleeting glance toward Yancey. Opposite him, Cheyenne could see that Asher had little use for Yancey. Today he appeared down-right disgusted at him. Cheyenne mentally made a note to tell Asher about Zulla Mae's pronouncement of Yancey. They had all laughed about Zulla Mae's stories of rats as they told the boys of her visit, but somehow it was hard to tell him about what she had said about her foreknowledge. Suddenly it seemed important. Zulla Mae had been right about death.

Asher continued chewing until his mouth was empty. His face looked like flint, and when he finally spoke, his tone was icy. "They are Gideon's Band. And things are going according to plan. The boys have a prayer meeting everyday. They are really growing in the Lord with such good leadership. We are each doing our jobs."

Cheyenne shifted her eyes to Malachi. It was clear Malachi was surprised, maybe even shocked at Asher's rudeness while sitting at Hope's table. Cheyenne checked to see her mother's expression. Obviously Asher had a devotee. Hope looked pleased as punch with the way the conversation had turned.

Cheyenne felt Bobbie Jo nudge against her leg, so she turned to her. Bobbie Jo whispered in her ear, "I'll tell you later." Cheyenne felt her insides chill. What on earth is going on that I don't know about, nor does Dad?

"... his number is six hundred threescore and six"

In the year A.D. 95 (1914 years ago) God used John, an apostle of Jesus Christ, to write the book of Revelation, a prophecy of things to yet to come. Chapter 13, verse 18 states, "Here is wisdom. Let him that hath understanding count the number of the beast: for it is the number of a man; and his number is six hundred threescore and six."

• Antichrist's name will equal 666
• The Qur'an equals 666.

OMAR'S REVELATION – Asher seemed to have slipped into a world of his own. He was obviously not following the conversation, and contributed nothing. Yancey, on the other hand, amused everyone with a constant run of stories from his life in New York.

Asher didn't hear Yancey's funny stories, because he was reviewing what Omar had told him early this morning before church.

The two men often met to pray before church. They didn't have regular church meetings anymore, but split up into smaller groups and met in homes. It was safer that way.

Today, instead of praying, they talked. Omar was clearly troubled when he walked with practiced quietness into their prayer room at the office. "Hey brother," he asked softly, as if he thought someone might overhear, "did Yancey ever tell you anything about his assignments in the Middle East?"

A sick feeling engulfed Asher as he recalled the conversation. He put his head down. This kind of information was ... revolting. He tried to slip back into the spirit of the meal, but he couldn't remove Omar's burning eyes from his thoughts.

Asher could still feel Omar's intensity as he explained, "He was there for several months covering a story about a Syrian Jew named Mohammed who was raised in a Catholic convent. You know he says he does religious news pieces. I found the story last night when I was doing some research on the internet. Yancey was credited as the photojournalist for the articles on Arabic news sites."

Asher remembered his naïve response. "You're kidding ... a Syrian Jew raised in a Catholic convent? How do you know it was this Yancey? Maybe some other guy has his name?"

Omar had almost kicked him. "Oh, give me a break! How many professional photojournalists are named Rueben Yancey? It was him,

Around A.D. 653/654 (259 years after John wrote Revelation) the first edition of the Qur'an was completed. In 1974 mathematician Rashad Khalifa, using a computer, discovered a series of numbers that appeared to be a part of the Qur'an. It was his study that revealed the number 666 equals The Qur'an. Khalifa's research was not embraced by the Muslim world. In 1990 Khalifa was stabbed to death. Truth has a way of not going away.

After his death, interest in Khalifa's work took a turn for the positive. Many Muslims began to proclaim 666 as a holy number that identified their faith. It was heralded as a glorious miracle that Allah used the number 666 to trick people who believed the Bible into believing that it was an evil number.

>

all right. With that wild hair, I could spot him from a satellite image. Besides, his name is all over the news concerning what the Muslim people call the Happenings. I've read everything I could find on the Happenings and a good portion of it was under Yancey's byline."

Asher swallowed some hot tea, trying to stop the unbidden recollection, and almost choked. Cheyenne studied him from across the table. Clearly his mind was busy with something very troubling.

Asher stabbed his salad and chewed while his mind continued to turn over the information Omar had given him early this morning.

Thirty years ago a beautiful thirteen-year-old Jewish girl got pregnant. She came from a family that has one of the oldest unbroken lines in Israel.

Her family was in an uproar and demanded that she 'get rid of' the pregnancy, as it would disgrace their family and ruin her future prospects. She refused to get an abortion because she said a light came to her and told her that she carried the divine son of God. She said his father was Mohammad.

Asher unknowingly groaned at the table as his heart prayed, *God … do we have a terrorist at our table? A Judas? Is he setting us up? Is he passing information?*

Everyone at the table stopped talking for a brief moment. Asher caught himself and covered. "This food is delicious! Nothing like a home cooked meal. Thanks, ladies," he offered weakly.

"Glad you like it, Asher," Hope beamed. "Just eat up."

Cheyenne dropped her eyes to her lap as Yancey began another tale. She knew Asher's distraction was due to Yancey. Asher was a complicated person, but so was Yancey … maybe more complicated than Asher. *Who was he really?* He just dropped in and made himself one of them.

Cheyenne leaned over as if she needed more taco shells. She noticed Julie's face. Her eyes were fixed on Yancey and she wore a smitten look.

From Muslim Unity by Maulana Zeeshan Abidi
General Knowledge of Qur'an
- There are 6666 verses in the Qur'an
- The word peace appears 666 times in the Qur'an.
- Greek symbol for 666=Bismillah which means "in the name of Allah."

www.Israelinbibleprophecy.com

She had been warned.

Cheyenne sat back, pushing her food around in her plate. *What if he's using Julie?*

She sat listening to him go on and on with his tales. She remembered the first day he had showed up at the Herb Den. He went for little Julie right off. Cheyenne's eyes narrowed. She glanced across the table at Asher, but he was still locked in his troubled world.

Asher felt her eyes on him, but his mind could not separate from what was gnawing at him. Omar had told him that according to old Arabic newspapers, as the young pregnant teen wandered the old parts of Jerusalem, Muslims began to fall down before her, claiming that they could see a light emanating from her and a high clear sound like music.

She asked someone to take her to a convent in Syria, where she gave birth and has lived with her son for many years.

Asher's hand automatically kept putting food in his mouth, but he tasted not a thing.

Omar had found some old video clips posted on the internet that shocked him. One was of Mother Uressa bowing with her face to the ground before the young boy and his mother when he was around eight years old. The caption quoted Mother Uressa as saying that he is the chosen one of God. "Now I can die in peace. He has come."

Asher considered the facts:

His mother says Mohammad sired him.

The people refer to him as the Living Qur'an and The Healer.

No one except his mother and a very old nun know his name.

The numerical value of The Qur'an is 666.

The number 666 is now being revered by Islam.

His brows knotted as he searched his mind. *Was there an obscure verse*

When I (author of this novel) started to research this subject for my book, the internet was full of Islamic websites advocating the number 666 as a Muslim holy number. Many of those websites seem to have disappeared in the last few months (spring of 2009). Perhaps when you read this, most of the sites will be gone. Obviously sentiment has changed. ∞

that indicated the Antichrist will be a Syrian Jew? No ... ? Yes ... ? I can't remember.

But the Antichrist is not supposed to be revealed until after the Tribulation. But then, he hasn't been revealed, has he? No one even knows his name.

What do we know about this Syrian Jew?

He speaks every language effortlessly, without study.

Even before the person in front of him utters a word, he greets them with a blessing in their own language.

There have been published claims of healings while in his presence.

Now even the Pope is hailing him as a blessed one, the Man of Peace.

Muslims, and now the Catholics, are calling him Blessed One.

His mother has not aged, she looks like a young woman, and is incredibly beautiful. She only answers to the title 'His Mother'.

The Happenings. They call all the miracles ... the Happenings.

Asher suddenly looked up from his meal and stared at Yancey. Asher recalled the scared, vacant look in Omar's eyes. It echoed as if it had sound. Omar had told him, "I saw a video of Yancey kneeling before this woman, kissing her hand. He looked like he was in a trance."

The scrape of Malachi's chair being pushed back caused Asher's hand to jerk, spilling his hot tea. "Oh, I'm sorry, Hope."

Cheyenne stood and reached over, mopping up the spill with several napkins. "Fixed."

Malachi cleared his throat. "Thank you, Cheyenne, for your quick response. Well, I wanted to read just a short portion of Scripture before we all find a place to nap. Ephesians, chapter 6, verses 12 through 16.

> *For we wrestle not against flesh and blood, but against principalities,*
> *against powers, against the rulers of darkness of this world,*
> *against spiritual wickedness in high places. Wherefore take unto you*
> *the whole armour of God, that ye may be able to withstand in the evil*
> *day, and having done all, to stand. Stand therefore, having your loins*
> *girt about with truth, and having on the breastplate of righteousness.*
> *And your feet shod with the preparation of the gospel of peace.*

Above all, talking the shield of faith, wherewith ye shall be able to
quench all the fiery darts of the wicked.

"It is not the Muslims that set fires and detonate explosives that are our enemies. Nor is it the local White Supremacists who have been writing us nasty letters and charging us more and more outrageous taxes.

"Our enemy is Satan, and he is defeated. He just doesn't know it yet. It's nice to know God's heavenly army is fighting our battles. The Scripture says for us to stand still and see the salvation of our God.

"Okay, enough said. You all have a nice afternoon; enjoy doing the dishes. Hope and I are going to snooze."

The phone rang just as Malachi came to his feet. He walked over to pick it up while the group at the table began to clean up. Asher heard the shock in Malachi's voice. "What?! Okay. Thanks for letting us know."

Malachi still had the phone in his hand as he hurried to the recliner, where he'd left his laptop. Asher followed him over. "What is it, Malachi?"

The older man briefly looked up at Asher while waiting a few seconds for the news station to come up. His face looked haggard. Cheyenne, Bobbie Jo, Julie and Magdalene pushed in to see what Malachi was opening up on the computer.

The screen came alive with a video clip obviously shot by a local amateur. The shaky camera swung across a wooded area, then centered in on the faces of a young weeping couple who were concluding their account of how they came upon the head.

The camera shifted to a local authority carrying a large tarp. For just a split second a clump of bloody black hair dominated the screen.

Honor Killing comes to America
www.huffingtonpost.com/irshad-manji/honor-killings-come-to-am_b_111549.html

First tribal Arabia. Then Africa. Next, South Asia. After that, Europe. Last year, Canada. Now, America. "Honor crimes" have arrived in the land of the free and the home of the brave. On the outskirts of Atlanta, a South Asian man has been charged with killing his daughter. She reportedly wanted to leave her arranged marriage. But under the code of "honor" – an ancient cultural tradition by which hundreds of millions of contemporary Asians, Africans and Arabs live – divorcing your husband means shaming your entire family. That's an act of "dishonor." And that's a crime worthy of severe punishment, including death. The catchy phrase for it is "honor killing."

>

The tarp was quickly laid over the grisly scene as the newscaster's high pitched voice filled in, sounding sickened, to give the details.

"The hikers who took this video footage told CBC News that they made the gruesome discovery about one hour ago. The hysterical couple said they literally stumbled across a young woman's head near the Rock Creek Gorge, northeast of Chattanooga off Highway 411. Last Wednesday the beheaded body of a young girl was found near Coker Creek Gorge, just twenty miles east of here.

"Officials on the scene say they will give a statement in a few minutes, although the local authorities told CBC news that the slaying is thought to be what some radical Muslims refer to as an honor killing."

The screen switched to the face of the local sheriff. Tears rolled down his rugged face as the man's broken voice told the listeners, "How anyone could use the word honor in connection with the brutal killing of a child is beyond decent human understanding."

Magdalene's childlike voice shrilly cried out. "No … couldn't be!"

Then she hit the floor in a dead faint.

Culture of death? Palestinian girl's murder highlights growing number of 'honor killings'
They kill their own, too. And the world expects "peace"? ABU QASH—Rofayda Qaoud—raped by her brothers and impregnated—refused to commit suicide, her mother recalls, even after she bought the unwed teenager a razor with which to slit her wrists. So Amira Abu Hanhan Qaoud says she did what she believes any good Palestinian parent would: restored her family's "honor" through murder.

www.sullivan-county.com/id4/honor_killings.htm
www.sullivan-county.com/id4/cul_death.htm

Maintaing Family Honor - Jan 20, 2003
by Al Skudsi bin Hookah, roving reporter and foreign correspondent for The Gaza Gajeera.

I am very unhappy. Our way of life is under attack. And we are not fighting back. Deep down, we know that when a woman has disgraced her family, nothing will restore honor except by killing her. This is understood in Jordan, Syria, Yemen, Lebanon, Egypt, the Gaza strip and the West Bank. So why are we Arabs telling the Western press that honor killing is cultural, that it is not really part of Islam? Our way of life is based on maintaining our honor. And make no mistake about it: a woman does tarnish her family's honor by engaging in pre-marital sex, or by getting herself raped, when she seeks divorce and when she marries against her family's wishes.

Why are we pussyfooting? Are we ashamed of what we do? Why are some of us trying to play it down? (go to the site to read full article) ∞

23

BLESSING, I WILL BLESS THEE

Asher stood on the hill where The Last Publishers offices were located. Below he could see Cheyenne sitting beside the rock herb pond, dangling her feet in the icy spring water. She had changed.

He recognized in her the same feeling of destiny that he had experienced after his mission trip. Seeing life and death up so close purifies one's perspective, purging out the mundane and irrelevant, leaving only the eternal. A melancholy came over him as he realized he missed her childish antics, her flirtatious nonsense that came from always assuming that life would just keep on being the same safe, happy place that it had always been.

The bombing and births, and then the murder of the young Muslim girl had taken something from Cheyenne … from all of them. Young Magdalene looked like a scarecrow; Bobbie Jo was often visibly sad. Even Dusty and Ben seemed subdued. It was like eating of the fruit of the tree of knowledge of good and evil. Until then they had only known good folks. Now they had stared evil in the face, heard his scratchy voice, and seen his deadly deeds.

Work called.

The young man turned to walk back to the office.

Cheyenne knew he was watching her. She had felt his eyes on her many times since the bombing. She wished she could reassure him that she was not sad, stressed, or even in need of time to recover. She stood up and walked over to the patio recliner beside the herb pond and plopped down on it. *If I could just explain that I have not felt this much peace and relaxation in months. I wish I could tell him that I feel like I've been to hell and survived. Life ... all of life is precious to me now. Even the sounds.*

She rolled over, shoving her hair out of the way so that the sun could pour down on her face. She felt tears sliding over the side of her nose and dropping off to wet her cheek, pressed against the rough surface of the recliner. Where are these coming from? She wiped them roughly from her face.

Cheyenne mumbled under her breath as if she were trying to understand a parable. "Magdalene is the only one that really understands ... and she's just a kid. That is really weird."

The dinner bell rang. Louise didn't like anyone late. Cheyenne stood, gathering her towel and other things before loping up the hill toward the dinning hall.

Bobbie Jo and Julie had been crammed into the backside of one of the warehouses packing her herb orders while she lollygagged in Hope's herb garden. She grinned. *Oh well, the perks of being boss.*

YANCEY'S QUESTION – Before Cheyenne even got close to the dining room, she was assailed with inviting aromas. Fresh, whole wheat yeast rolls were piled high in a huge crock. Soft homemade butter was in the bowl beside the crock. A salad made from every conceivable vegetable occupied the other end of the counter.

Louise hummed as she hovered over the food bar, moving spoons and preparing the entrees. A quick glance confirmed that all the tables were already occupied. As she filled her plate, she could hear Yancey's voice over the others. He did not live here at The Last Publishers ministries, but he was usually here for lunch.

Cheyenne felt her face flush with irritation at the mere sound of his voice. *I wish he would get a job somewhere on the other side of the planet.*

Yancey was either hardened to people's lack of affection, naively oblivious to their feelings, or he was driven by something more powerful than acceptance. "Yo, Malachi, I've been wondering about da passage dat speaks about da USA, Russia, and Israel in prophecy."

Cheyenne noted an instant lull in the buzzing conversation as everyone waited to hear what Malachi had to say. She sat on the stool at the bar and began to eat, keenly waiting for his reply.

He didn't answer.

Yancey pursued. "Yeah, I looked up all dose woids you listed, and it appears dat da good old USA might be in for some hot lava. I found verses in Jeremiah 50 and 51 dat seems to say dis. So, whaddya say?"

Now the room lay in silence, waiting.

Malachi took his time, which seemed to intensify everyone's need to hear his answers. Finally he cleared his throat to answer. "The passage you're referring to in Jeremiah 50 and 51 prophecies of a nation that is the *hindermost of the nations*, which means that it is the youngest of the powerful nations. It says it is *the hammer of the whole earth*, that is, it is responsible for nation building, and it is populated with what is termed *mingled people* ... many different nationalities forming the citizenry.

"Verse 13 of chapter 51 says it is a country of *abundant treasures* and the end comes to it because of *the measure of its covetousness*."

Yancey spoke, "Yeah, so how is dis nation suppose to be destroyed?"

Malachi looked up. "Did you read the chapters?"

Yancey waited, blank-faced.

"Okay," Malachi scooted his chair back and picked up a toothpick. "The Bible says that a great nation from the north will war against this other great nation. The passage continues to describe a great drought overtaking them. They are also hit by terrible plagues. God says he will overthrow them like Sodom and Gomorrah, and rocks and mountains are described as coming down. The interesting thing about this passage is that it never dates this event as the last days or the times of the end;

Jeremiah 50 and 51, and Ezekiel 38 and 39 speaks of Persia (old name for Iran), Ethiopia and Libya coming together with Gomer (Possibly Germany) and Meshech and Tubal (this army comes from the north ... assumed to be Russia) to attack Israel. Verse 8, speaking of Israel, says, "and they shall dwell safely all of them." God says in verse 22 of Ezekiel 38 that he will fight against those that come against Israel in the latter day, "And I will plead against him with pestilence and with blood; and I will rain upon him, and upon his bands, and upon the many people that are with him, an overflowing rain, and great hailstones, fire, and brimstone. ∞

nothing to suggest this happens at the end of the world, which makes some theologians think it could happen before the Tribulation."

MUCH GIVEN . . . MUCH REQUIRED – Bobbie Jo's brow was wrinkled with concern. "Do you really think it's the United States?"

Malachi shrugged his shoulders. "I didn't say that. I only told you how the Scripture describes the nation."

"Why us?" Bobbie Jo's voice was strained. "Why America? Most all other nations are more wicked than we are. We are the salt of the earth."

Everyone in the room waited for Malachi's answer. "The Scripture says in Luke 12:48, '*For unto whomsoever much is given, of him shall be much required: and to whom men have committed much, of him they will ask the more.*'"

He waited for a few seconds. "Remember Asher's mission map? Many areas of the world had no light, some had a little light, but only one place on earth was lit up with full opportunity to hear the gospel. It was America. We here in America know truth. America is the number one producer and consumer of child pornography in the entire world." Cheyenne could hear the anger in his voice.

"Abortion is an acceptable form of birth control, and our nation finances abortions in developing nations around the world. We are not content to kill just our own; we pay to kill babies wherever we can find them.

"God says concerning those who offend these little ones that it is better for them to be cast into the sea with a millstone tied around their neck than to cause such offense."

Malachi looked at the young people sitting at the table. "A nation is often judged by its leadership. Every president this country has had since 1949 when Israel became a nation has been a good friend to Israel ... until now. Our nation is pulling back from its support of Israel.

"God starts right off in Genesis promising to bless those that bless

Israel and curse those that curse Israel. We, as a nation, have erred, and we will be judged; it is a promise from God. God kept his promise to bless us while we blessed Israel, and in 200 years we became the greatest nation in modern history.

"Now, as a nation, we daily betray Israel. Now we can know for a certainty that God will keep his promise to curse us. If our nation continues to turn its back on the nation of Israel ... then we may soon be facing what is described in Jeremiah 50 and 51.

"We worry about Muslims, White Supremacists, volcanoes and such. But these fears are trifles compared to falling in the hands of the angry God."

Everyone sat in sober contemplation for about 30 seconds until they were rattled out of their somber reverie by Louise's exuberant response.

"AAAAMEN. I am glad God is a God of justice and judgment. Now, eat, 'cause the food is g'tting' cold!"

Genesis 27:29b records the special blessing given to Jacob, who was later called Israel. "...cursed be every one that curseth thee, and blessed be he that blesseth thee." ∞

24

BLUEBERRY HILL

Blueberry Hill was located on the west ridge of Malachi Freeman's property, the high point of the whole farm. The view was wonderful, especially at sunset when the very last rays of the sun lay over the land and ignited the reds, oranges, and yellows that reflected off of every exposed surface. It was here that everyone had retreated for a picnic.

Cheyenne lifted her long ponytail away from her sweaty back. "Good game of volleyball, but I'm out until I cool down."

Bobbie Jo grabbed up a towel. She stood wiping her face in agreement. "Why don't the married couples play against the Gideon Band guys this time? You guys are killing us girls." She pulled a bottle of water out of the bucket of ice before turning to follow Cheyenne out of the gated court. The remaining players regrouped for the next game on the court.

Cheyenne noted the setting sun at the top of the far ridge. "Hey, Ben! Better turn on the court lights. You'll need them before this next game is finished."

Cheyenne eased herself down onto the bench of the nearest picnic table. Bobbie Jo joined her, lying on the table top.

"Hey, you." Cheyenne poked Bobbie Jo, who responded by rolling over onto her side. "I've been dying to show you these pictures." She pulled a stack of photos from her back pocket and handed them to Bobbie Jo.

BOBBIE JO & CHEYENNE

"Cool. Oh … the twins?" Bobbie Jo tried to sound interested. Her curiosity was more piqued by logistics. "So how did you happen to get the pictures? It's not likely that Zulla Mae has a camera. They'd have to come to town to mail them. So?"

"Dusty and some of the boys took the horses up the mountain last week. They were surveying the area for suspicious activity. I made sure they took a camera to bring me back some shots." Cheyenne took the pictures back, re-examining each one carefully.

"Man!" Bobbie Jo complained as she rolled onto her back, "I never thought we'd be free again. How long have we all been living here at

TLP? No TV, no movies, no swimming at the creek, no going bowling, no going out to eat. We are talking prison.

"Bunch of stinking, murdering Muslims!" Bobbie Jo's tone bordered on a curse.

Cheyenne's rebuke held little conviction, "Watch it, BoJo."

Bobbie Jo took a cleansing breath. "Well, at least tomorrow we finally get to go somewhere. I heard Omar is taking his family home tonight. I know they'll be glad to be a family again. It's hard on the big families living communally."

Cheyenne reclined back onto the bench. "Yeah, but being up here on Blueberry Hill is almost like being out of prison, you know? I love it up here."

Cheyenne sat up, then leaned her head back on Bobbie Jo's arm as she reminisced. "I remember when dad cleared this part of the hill. I must have been about ten years old. I helped him plant the blueberry bushes. It makes this afternoon's berry picking all that more special. Now my nieces and nephews run around picking his berries.

"I helped a little while Dad and my brothers laid the cross ties for the volleyball court. That was the first thing we did up here after we cleared the trees. That was B.F.G.—before Freeman grandchildren." She chuckled at her own joke.

"We put up the tall fence after the first game when the ball kept rolling down the ridge." Cheyenne rotated, then lay down on the narrow picnic bench.

With her arm now free, Bobbie Jo propped up onto her elbows and looked over the area with new eyes. "Makes sense." She turned her head to study the children's play area. It shared the south fence boundary with the court. The railroad ties continued around the playground, keeping the white sand from migrating.

Cheyenne followed Bobbie Jo's gaze and rolled over onto her side, watching the children playing in the sand just twenty feet away. Eight little boys were at one end building a fort. On the end closest to where the young women reclined, about the same number of small girls were playing princess. They clustered around a plastic castle. The toddlers were playing around the swings.

Cheyenne put up fingers as if to count. "Man alive! Mom and Dad have a lot of grandkids, and I haven't even started yet. I bet they end up having thirty or more."

Bobbie Jo's mind wandered.

MAGDALENE'S DREAD – "Hey." Bobbie Jo's foot dropped off the table, nudging Cheyenne's behind, "Hey ... Shy, what's going on with Mag? She looks like she's crying."

Cheyenne sat up and glanced over towards the gate to the play area. Magdalene and Tess, Omar's wife, sat talking. Tess looked up in time to catch Cheyenne's eye. She waved them over.

The friends approached tentatively. They had expected Magdalene to go to pieces over the beheading of the Muslim girl. Not so. As soon as she recovered from her faint she seemed to put the grisly murder behind her and move on. In fact, she seemed overly accepting of the news, as though it was expected. Bobbie Jo was anxious for the young girl.

Tess pulled her legs up off of the reclining lawn chair, making room for the girls to share her seat. Tess didn't waste words. "Magdalene needs an encouraging word."

"What's up, Kid?" Bobbie Jo's voice was light, but her eyes betrayed her apprehension.

Magdalene put her head down on her knees, her white hair spilling over her arm. "Tess and Omar want me to call my dad."

"Well," Cheyenne's tone held a slight admonition, "It has been a long time now, kiddo. Why are you making such a big deal out of calling your parents? You know what we talked about the other night, a time for this and a time for that ... remember the passage in

Ecclesiastes chapter 3: "To every thing there is a season, and a time to every purpose under the heaven: A time to be born, and a time to die; a time to plant, and a time to pluck up that which is planted; A time to kill, and a time to heal; a time to break down, and a time to build up; A time to weep, and a time to laugh; a time to mourn, and a time to dance; A time to cast away stones, and a time to gather stones together; a time to embrace, and a time to refrain from embracing; A time to get, and a time to lose; a time to keep, and a time to cast away; A time to rend, and a time to sew; a time to keep silence, and a time to speak; A time to love, and a time to hate; a time to war, and a time of peace. All this have I seen, and applied my heart unto every work that is done under the sun: there is a time wherein one man ruleth over another to his own hurt." ∾

Ecclesiastes? Well, the time has come for you to call your family. For crying out loud, after all this time they probably think you're dead. Hearing your voice will surely be a relief."

Magdalene lifted up her head and looked at the young women sitting around her. Her face was white. Her pale eyes were deep set in purple circles. The bleak, careworn face of the young girl startled them.

"I am so scared and I can't tell you why. My Daddy is a white power man just like the jerks running our town. What if he comes here and gets mixed up with them? He would then be our enemy."

Bobbie Jo's hand once again tousled Magdalene's hair affectionately. "Remember who our enemy is. Not your dad; not the White Supremacists; not the Muslims. Our enemy is not flesh and blood. It is principalities, powers of darkness, the Devil and his demons. We will pray and stand against them," Bobbie Jo encouraged. Cheyenne and Tess nodded their agreement.

Bobbie Jo pushed Magdalene gently, saying in her gruff, bossy manner, "Besides, I already told you a month ago you should call, so stop procrastinating and just call."

Tess's voice was soft and soothing as she nailed down the particulars. "Tell you what, Magdalene. Call your dad tonight from the office. Now that they have arrested the terrorists, and things with the Muslims have settled down, Omar and I are planning to go on a long awaited anniversary date. How about staying over at our house Sunday evening and keeping the kids? It will be just like before the bombing."

Magdalene wiped her eyes and tried to grin. "I would like that, Tess. I have to admit, not being allowed to leave the farm for a while has been grating on my nerves."

The girls spent a few minutes quietly praying with Magdalene.

They still had their heads down when Bobbie Jo pinched Cheyenne's bottom. "Ouch," Cheyenne whispered grouchily. "What's your problem, you knot-head? Why do you always pinch or kick me?"

"Oh, cool it. You're too sensitive," Bobbie Jo chided. "Come here, I need to show you something."

Cheyenne got to her feet, but her face still showed grievance.

Bobbie Jo's expression caused her to leave it unstated. The big girl had her finger to her mouth, alerting Cheyenne to silence. Cheyenne's stomach clenched as she whispered, "What is it?"

The sun had dropped below the distant horizon, leaving the ridge in shadows that were driven back from the areas under the lights of the volleyball court and playground.

Bobbie Jo moved forward along the shadowed tree line towards a cluster of chairs where Cheyenne's parents sat around the fire pit. They both held a sleeping grandbaby. Asher sat near them on a log, petting Wiggles. The dog was exhausted from chasing bugs and playing with children.

Life had been so strained for weeks. It was good to enjoy some peaceful quiet. Even the internet traffic seemed quiet. Asher's team of computer geeks had reported of little or no Muslim activity involving The Last Publishers. The cream-colored Passat seemed to have vanished. Everyone was feeling giddy. Free.

Bobbie Jo put her mouth close to Cheyenne's ear. "While Tess was praying," she murmured, "I heard Asher speaking to Malachi. I heard him say something about his brother, Levi. It sounded conspiratorial. Let's sneak up on them and hear what it's about."

Both girls had to silence their giggles.

They stepped in among the trees, moving up to the next picnic table and then up behind Malachi's SUV.

(B)ut if the watchman see the enemy **25**
come, and blow not the trumpet,
and the people be not warned; if the sword
come, the watchman must be taken away
in his iniquity; his blood will I require.

~Ezekiel 33:6

THE CAVE

Malachi's quiet voice was muted by his full beard, but portions of his conversation came through. "Why does he want to move here in the middle of nowhere? There's not a synagogue anywhere in this area. It can't be his religion bringing him here. Is it to be close to you? Is he scared of Muslims and trying to find a safe place?"

The girls could detect that Malachi's questions were more statements of incredulity than inquiries.

Asher's answer was reassuring. "The Muslims still have him worried. There has been some strange chatter. Israeli Mossad are puzzled because it is so different from their standard business of killing infidels. My brother says they speak of reclaiming their own, making known among their people that there is no God but Allah, and no prophet but Mohammed. He says the Israelis and our feds are keeping close tabs, and he thinks we need to be more vigilant ourselves. Although they don't think much of our fence and patrol."

Asher kicked at the dirt in front of him. "But it's better than not having any protection. I hate to let everyone go home now, but I sense that they need some time as families. Anyways, as Cheyenne would say, Levi says that the Israelis think the day of the Muslims' free reign of terror will not last forever. With the recent advances in fuel cell technology there may come a time soon when oil is no longer in high demand. Just look at what Ben's been doing while we've been stuck here at TLP. Everyone's vehicle now runs partly on water, and even TLP's electrical power is operating independent of the utilities. Without the money from oil, Muslim countries will quickly degenerate back to camel riding tribesmen, drinking mare's milk and warring over water holes and date palms. The world will no longer acquiesce to them."

Hope sounded stunned. "It is so strange how fast world events ... terror ... life can change. One minute they hold all the aces, then things change. Surely God is in control."

Asher concurred, "That's true. Nothing will change for a while, but if the money ever does stop flowing from Saudi Arabia, immigrants will be on their own."

Malachi enjoined, "Although they could get more desperate when they see their financial support gone and hope for Islam conquering the world fading."

The girls sat in silence, straining to hear every word. Asher's deep bass voice suddenly caused both of the girls to jerk, startled. "Yellowstone is what's bringing him out here. Levi is a volcanologist who works for the government. He really thinks that a Yellowstone eruption is imminent."

The crackling fire kept Asher from hearing Bobbie Jo's groan. Cheyenne, standing in front of her, clearly heard her whisper, "Oh, brother, another new and present danger. Just what we need."

Cheyenne poked Bobbie Jo to shut her up. They could both hear trepidation in Asher's voice as he continued. "Levi is planning a lot of things around such an event. He has studied caves and mountains, wind currents, weather patterns and all that stuff. He thinks the large caves here in this area would make a good survival spot if they were properly outfitted. Plus, he knows from me that the folks in this area know how to grow food and maintain animals. He figures to establish a safe haven for a few select professionals as well as a few locals."

Yancey and Julie quietly walked up behind the girls. Yancey had his arm around Julie. Any other time, Bobbie Jo and Cheyenne would have been fuming, but now they all looked at each other in awkward silence.

Cheyenne's eyes met with Julie's as she stood leaning against Yancey. Cheyenne recalled the day at the creek when Julie was so upset, thinking she would never have a chance to marry.

Never have a baby.

Those memories came back in vivid detail. For a split second, Cheyenne's soul grieved for her own loss. She clearly remembered asking her mom, will there be time for me to be loved?

WHY DON'T YOU MIND YOUR OWN BUSINESS? – Asher glanced over his shoulder and caught a glimpse of the silent group through the glass of the SUV. He could see from their faces that they had heard. "You guys," he groaned, "why don't you mind your own business? I didn't want to scare you with this kind of talk. You bunch of eavesdropping nincompoops." His distress made what they had heard even more worrisome.

"Well, now that we know a little," Cheyenne replied, "We might as well know it all. Anyways, this isn't a good time for secrets. So come over and sit down and tell us what you know."

As Asher watched Cheyenne position the chairs, his soul grieved that he had spoken so harshly, his heart hurt with the need to just hold her in his arms. She had been through so much.

But we could be so near the end.

Educated men running for the cover of caves!

He forced his mind to concentrate on how much he should tell them, conscious that Yancey would also be hearing what he said. Everyone sat down and waited for Asher to explain what they had heard.

He put his foot up on the chair seat that Cheyenne had just moved into place. Asher leaned over, resting his forearms on his knees. "Well,

---

What's under Yellowstone? by Larry O'Hanlon

Yellowstone National Park sits atop a subterranean chamber of molten rock and gasses so vast that the region, known for its geysers and grizzlies, is arguably one of the largest active volcanoes in the world.

http://dsc.discovery.com/convergence/supervolcano/under/under.html

>

my brother Levi is thirty years old, and is, of course, a Jew. We haven't seen each other but once since I left home. He has maintained a distance from me since he heard that I had become a Christian. But recently, due to the bombing we have been back in contact. He's one of our nation's finest volcanologists."

Asher stopped when he saw the question in Julie's eyes. Uncharacteristic of him, he grinned and said, "No, a volcanologist is not somebody from another planet. It's a geologist that specializes in the study of volcanoes. Levi specializes in supervolcanoes.

"He has been commissioned by the U.S. government for the last four years to study Yellowstone. This afternoon he phoned to inform me that he has sold everything he owns, even his stock portfolio, and has used the money to purchase the farms of James, Peterson, and Holly, as well as a huge tract behind them from a Japanese lumber company. This property would include that whole section of caves, and that entire ridge on the south side of the river, over 7,000 acres.

"He's bringing in heavy duty fencing with electronic protective measures. There will be double fencing with a high speed road between them for security vehicles—military level security, if it is needed. Picture the fence around Jurassic Park. Something like that."

Cheyenne was shocked. "Where did he get that much money anyways?" Asher shot a grin at her, "Well, it's not just him. There are several men and companies involved. "Well," Cheyenne still sounded stunned, "how did he ever get Peterson to sell his land?" Cheyenne met eyes with Malachi, affirming what she was saying, "Dad has tried for years to get just one tiny spot so he would have a place to launch his fishing boat, and they wouldn't even talk to him."

Asher looked embarrassed. "I don't know, but I would not put it

Yellowstone National Park holds one of the world's largest super-volcanoes. Scientific research has shown that the ground is 74cm higher than it was in 1923. The reservoir is filling rapidly with magma. The upward movement of Yellowstone caldera floor has been 7 centimeters per year for the past three years. This supervolcano has regular eruption cycles of 600,000 years. The last eruption was 640,000 years ago. So the human race is living on borrowed time. The Yellowstone volcano could erupt with 10,000 times the force of the explosion of Mount St. Helens in 1980.

>

past Levi to do whatever it took. He's a very persuasive guy, quite the command man. Besides, we have several members of the family that are lawyers. They have a lot of influence and the ability to uncover a world of mistakes in one's business, taxes, and personal life—if you get my drift."

"So," Yancey cleared his throat, throwing his head back, his nostrils pinched in a look of nervous control, "Dat is not good. He's pretty sure it's going to blow ... Yellowstone? Nobody buys 7,000 acres unless he's pretty sure he needs it. I s'pect he paid top dollar?"

Asher was looking down at his foot as he stirred the soil with the toe of his boot. "I'm quite sure he was delighted to pay a premium price. As to your other question, I'll spare you the professional jargon he shared with me as to how they came to their conclusion, but yes, I would imagine he's totally convinced it will blow in the near future."

"How near in the near future arc we talking about?" Unnoticed in the twilight, Omar had walked up and caught the last bit of conversation. "Like tomorrow or next year or what?"

Before Asher could answer, Cheyenne spoke up with confusion in her voice. "On TV it said that no one would survive between the Rocky Mountains and the Smoky Mountains. So we're in that area ... why doesn't he move to the East or West coast?"

Asher rubbed his hands together. "The West Coast is fragile geographically as well as politically. He thinks they might fare far worse in the earthquakes that accompany the big blow. But that's another story and not what I came here to discuss. Furthermore, the worst models put East Tennessee on the outer edge of destruction."

Cheyenne wasn't finished. "What does he plan on doing with all that land he bought? I mean, if you know it's all over, why buy land?

Q: What are the likely effects of the eruption of the Yellowstone supervolcano? Bill McGuire, professor of geohazards at the Benfield Greig Hazard Research Centre at the University College of London told the UK Daily Express that magma would be flung 50 kilometers into the atmosphere. Within a thousand kilometers virtually all life would be killed by falling ash, lava flows and the sheer explosive force of the eruption. One thousand cubic kilometers of lava would pour out of the volcano, enough to coat the whole USA with a layer 5 inches. He adds that it would once again bring "the bitter cold of volcanic winter to Planet Earth. Mankind may become extinct." (Source:UnMuseum)

www.Johnbarrysblog.blogspot.com/2008/12/Yellowstone-super-volcano-eruption.html ∽

And the caves, what can he do?"

Looking at Cheyenne with a small grin that he always had just for her, Asher cleared his throat. "He can do a lot. He'll have money to invest in food storage, systems to filter the air, power generation with artificial light to grow plants in controlled conditions, plus very high tech survival stuff—all that a real backwoods survivalist would need. He plans to build a kind of Noah's ark ... with more than eight souls. And if Yellowstone decides to stay sleeping for another thousand years, there may yet be need of a safe retreat from the worsening terrorism and the possible breakdown of government."

Now Asher reached over, lightly punching Cheyenne's arm, teasing her. "He even mentioned you, Cheyenne. He asked how many thousands of pounds of herbs, berries, and seeds you keep on hand and where they're stored, how you store them, how moisture affects them, how long they're viable, how they're used as seasonings or for added nutrition. He wanted to know how many non-genetically altered seeds you keep on hand and how long they'll stay viable. Plus he wanted to know how much practical knowledge you have, how extensive your library of practical help books is, how skilled you are at applying the knowledge available for natural healing and nutrition—should I go on? Of course, he was more interested in Hope, as she appears to be quite well known among his colleagues," and grinning his understanding, he added, "for some strange reason."

Omar began to shake his head again, "I've lived worrying about White Supremacists for over ten years. Then the Muslims start acting like a ticked off street gang. Cheyenne gets almost blown away, my family is almost ..." His voice broke, but he gathered himself and continued. "And now this. It's just too much to happen in one

Catastrophe - Author and researcher David Keys in writing his book *Catastrophe* consulted more than forty scientists and scholars—astronomers, physicists, climatologists and historians—experts on cosmic collisions, volcanoes, epidemics and ancient wars. Keys explains the evidence from nature (tree rings, ice drills, rock formations, historical accountants of yellow skies, alone with three years of constant cold weather, etc) explains the mystery of what cosmic event (A.D. 537-542) brought on the centuries long period referred to as the Dark Ages. According to Keys' exhaustive research a super volcano named Krakatoa was the culprit.

>

generation. I just can't take much more. I feel like we're living on the edge of a dynamite keg and one tiny step this way and she blows, and one tiny step that way and she blows, and nowhere to sit down."

WHO ARE THESE PEOPLE? – Before anyone else could speak up, Yancey remarked, "Well said, Omar. I can truly identify. And now dat you mention identify ... Who exactly are dese people? I know Levi is your brother, but da group as a whole ... who are dey? American, Israelis ... some international group?"

At Yancey's question, Omar involuntarily jerked as if he had been tied to a string that had just been yanked.

Asher quickly answered, "No, they're not any of the above. They're just a few younger professional men who are scared and looking to survive. Who can blame a person for trying to find the safest tomorrow? Especially if you have no hope in Jesus and the rapture."

"Asher," Bobbie Jo asked, "Does your brother know about you being involved in reaching the Muslims with the gospel?"

This time Asher looked up and smiled. "Yeah, he's really happy that we've managed to help with what the Jewish people call the Muslim Problem, although their perspective is quite different. Sadly, they rejoice that the inroads we have made in the Muslim populations have created internal discord, resulting in Muslims killing Muslims rather than killing Jews. There has never been a time in the 1,300 years of Islam's history when they were so shaken by large numbers converting to another religion. It totally freaks Levi out.

"My brother is not a believer, but he is a survivor. He does not think time is coming to an end. He thinks the strong will survive, and he expects to be among the strong. He uses his mind, as he says, not his emotions. He thinks anyone who believes in Jesus is on an emotional trip."

With this sudden horrific climactic change came the Plague. The Black Plague, carried by the fleas who rode the backs of the rats, killed millions. Whole cities were left empty, everyone dead. History was changed, monarchies changed hands, whole people groups left their native land trying to outrun the death, and the earth's population was decimated.

At that time people were thinking that this was the end of time. People needed a savior. They needed a hope. Along came Mohammed. His message struck a resonance.

Islam was born. ∽

Yancey motioned to Omar. "Well, what about Omar's question? How soon are we talking about an eruption? And how long dis he say a survivor would have to stay in da cave if Yellowstone does blow? Does he have any calculated ideas of where da safest place in da world would be? Why doesn't he move to Israel?"

Asher put his foot back up in his chair and leaned over to clean the toe of his boot off, not looking at anyone as he answered, "He has tons of information and calculations, but the short and long of it is, he says world climate will dramatically change, taking seven to fifteen years before things moderate to normal. And without preparation none will survive in the areas hardest hit. He thinks the earth's disruption will break away several coastal areas, sending tidal waves all over the world, which will take out many islands and low lying areas. He also thinks this will set off a series of other earthquakes all over the world. The information's on the web for anyone to access.

"He says something like a third of the United States would be uninhabitable for months, maybe years. The other two thirds will be a mess from the ash.

"Something like this has happened before, so they have a pretty good idea of what to expect. And yes, they list all the areas of the world they believe will be basically spared this disaster.

"As to Israel, they believe there's a fault under Jerusalem which will cause the mountain on which it sits to split. They think a great river will flow from it."

"Your brother's hit on something there," Omar interjected. "The Scripture teaches that very thing. It says the river will flow down and cleanse the Dead Sea. But when did such a large volcano erupt before?"

Asher stood and arched his back, trying to relieve the tension in his knotted muscles. He sat again on the table and pulled his leg up in the chair. "The last major supervolcano, which came around A.D. 537, seems to have ushered in the Dark Ages. Without the sun's life-giving

Zechariah 14:4 "And his feet shall stand in that day upon the mount of Olives, which is before Jerusalem of the east, and the mount of Olives shall cleave in the midst thereof toward the east and toward the west, and there shall be a very great valley; and half of the mountain shall move toward the north, and half of it toward the south. ... And it shall come to pass in that day, that the light shall not be clear, nor dark." ∽

vitamin D, people's immune systems would have not been able to fight against disease. So within a year the Black Plague hit. It lasted over ten years. Speaking in terms of time, A.D. 537 is not that long ago. They've found a lot of evidence which helps the scientists understand how the big blow affected plant and animal life, as well as humans."

A sobered Bobbie Jo asked, "Will we be seeing Levi or be invited to be a part of his big survival plan? Or does he just plan on stealing the herbs when the time comes? Besides, I still don't understand why he'd stay in an area he thinks will undergo extreme damage."

Asher stood and then leaned with his hands down flat on the table, emphasizing his words. "He and others think that if one third to one half of this country is destroyed, which would include all the great farming areas of the country, those who do survive will be thrown into chaos. The ash will dim the sun all over the world, bringing cold weather, causing greatly reduced harvests for several years. Food shortages will bring violence and anarchy. The East and West coasts will be Animal Farms for real. No one will be safe. At such a time, none will venture into the dead zone, which includes our area. Here, all he will have to deal with is the elements. As a scientist, he considers the elements manageable. A crazed, hungry population is never manageable. But really … why set up his survival cave here? It's because he and his colleagues are first and foremost scientists. They want to know, learn, discover, and record for future generations how they survived.

"As to who goes in the cave … just because I'm his brother and you're my friends would not guarantee that we would be part of his survival team."

Seeing their stricken faces, he smiled. "He's not an emotional planner. If he sees you have value to the greatest number surviving, then you will be included. If he doesn't deem you valuable, you will not be included.

"Great minds or strong, young breeding stock are part of his plans. But, yes, he thinks those who can make this much difference in Islam have to be visionaries and doers. He feels that some of the doers will make good partners in survival. Like I said, he knows there are things that many of us know that cannot be found among his educated friends or in books.

"He knows he has to invite a few of the plain Amish people and their animals into his fold. He will need farmers, herbalists and more. If I know my brother, his setup will be very large. He told me that a limited number of my friends will be welcome, but no one is allowed to proselytize him. He is a devout Jew and feels a special calling from God to save humanity. He strongly feels that for him to consider Jesus or even allow someone to talk to him about Jesus would be to disavow his commitment to Jehovah God."

Omar looked at Asher with a hint of humor. "That sounds emotional to me, Brother. I can sure see why folks don't like Jews." Everyone's face reflected their startled surprise at Omar's statement.

"Well, it's true, not funny. The Jews come in here and survive. Everyone else just stands around worrying and fretting, while some devout Jew sells all he has and starts planning for the future. Then boom, she blows … and there he and his chosen few sit behind their hot wire in their safe cave breathing clean air and eating food with big iron gates and bad guns keeping out all the worriers and fretters. Can you imagine how much all those outside folks would hate Jews at a time like that? See what I mean?"

MALACHI'S CAUTION – The group sat silent as every one of them imagined the unthinkable.

Malachi's quiet wisdom brought them back to the here and now. "Do keep in mind that the world does not end in a volcano. Our mission remains the same, regardless—get the gospel out to the whole world before it is too late. We know Jesus is coming back. We do not know with any degree of certainty that there is going to be a volcano that wipes out half the United States. And, if so, it is very possible the big blow will be during the Tribulation, which will not affect us in the least. Let's not talk about this to others and create panic or worry. There is not anything we can do to make it any different. No use stewing on it."

Then, as if trying to end the impromptu discussion of doomsday, Malachi exhorted, "It's getting late. Before we leave, let's agree to keep our mouths shut concerning Levi's plans. His project is just getting started. It will take months, maybe even a year for him to set up a water supply, food, air exchange and all the other necessary things for cave survival, so he must not believe it will happen in the next few weeks or months. Is that right, Asher?"

"Yes, sir." Asher seemed relieved with this logic and the fact Malachi was insisting upon silence. "That's correct. Even with all the money he has to work with, he still couldn't make it happen for a while, so he must feel that there's still time. Malachi is right. Let's keep it quiet. Besides, if my brother does set up the caves and the local people find out, then you can bet thousands of people like Derek and his high ranking family will use force to take over the place before Levi can even get it ready to be put to use. So keeping quiet will serve us the best."

Malachi motioned with his head, since his arms were still full, holding the sleeping child. "So, Asher, that's it then?"

Asher nodded, seeing that Malachi was wanting the discussion to end. "Yes, sir, that's it."

Yancey and Julie, arms entwined, disappeared into the dark. The group saw his truck lights come on and watched the couple drive off. Cheyenne and Bobbie Jo looked at each other, communicating their hearts. Finally Bobbie Jo sighed, "All she ever wanted was to have a man to love her and bear his children. If her dream's going to come true, she better be in a hurry, although to think about caring for a child at a time like this is scary."

Cheyenne turned back to Asher. She put up her hand in the air to ask a question as if she were still a school girl. "I just want to ask one question now that Yancey is gone and he has no clue about how powerful the brew is. Does your brother know about the brew?"

The question caught them all off guard. Not being able to contact Rob Cohen had caused a lot of tension. Several big printings had been put off. The money was available for a down payment, but there was concern the brew might not make it before full payment was due. The volcano in that area of the world was still erupting. It was spewing ash at unprecedented rates. Travel to that area of the world had also been canceled. The ash in the air could destroy jet motors. No one had yet heard from Cohen.

Asher looked at Cheyenne for a long moment and then answered with hesitation in his voice, "No. Well, maybe … I don't know. If he knows, it would be from his Israeli connections and monitoring people who have been on the Israeli research website. He shows a great interest in Hope, and he did ask me how Malachi was feeling.

"You remember that Rob Cohen is from a well known, wealthy Jewish family. His family is highly connected in Israel, and they certainly know of his amazing recovery. So yes, if nothing else, Levi would strongly suspect Hope has stumbled on something more than just a little interesting."

"It sounds crazy," Asher speculated, "but sometimes I think that might be why he's settling here. I think he knows a lot."

Bobbie Jo raised her hand, obviously frustrated. "Does Levi say this is the only survival place in the works?"

"Good question." Asher looked up, surprised at her thoughtfulness. "He says that there are many such survival places being set up all over the world, but this is the closest one to ground zero."

"Ground zero as in supervolcano eruption?" Omar said in disbelief. "Man, we must be at least 1,500 miles from Yellowstone."

"Yeah," Asher's responded flatly.

QUESTIONS UNASKED – Omar looked over his shoulder to where Yancey's truck lights were disappearing, "Now that is worrisome. Like having a spider in the bed. Little … but nerve-racking."

"What's that supposed to mean?" Cheyenne demanded, sensing a new threat.

Omar, not answering, turned toward his son.

The girls sat watching Omar's youngest son come stumbling up to him with his arms in the air. The volleyball game was over. Families pulled together, each crawling into its own van.

Malachi grabbed Hope's hand, pulling her up. "Come on, Sweet Thing. I'm sleepy. Plus I need to study. I preach over the web in the morning for Sunday service."

Cheyenne, still wanting an answer to her question, pressed Asher. "I'm almost afraid to even ask what that was all about. It obviously has to do with Yancey, right?"

Asher's shoulders drooped like he was bone tired and the question doubled the weight. "Yeah, but we've had enough tonight, so let's drop it."

Bobbie Jo and Cheyenne exchanged uneasy glances. "Oh, well," Cheyenne said with a deep sigh, "we might as well go pretend life is just a bed of roses, and we are gonna have long normal lives, get married and have twenty kids each.

"Oh." Cheyenne turned to Asher. "One happy note. Magdalene is calling her dad tonight. Wanna join us as cheerleaders in about thirty minutes?"

"Yeah." Asher put his leather hat on, pressing it down secure. "I'll get Ben and Dusty. They've prayed for that girl everyday since she came here. I figure one of them will marry her someday." He stopped suddenly, looking stricken. "Well ... it's still possible we all might get married someday. The terrorists can't keep this up with the new Federal police force pursuing them so aggressively. And my brother says he could be dead wrong about Yellowstone."

26

MAGDALENE'S DADDY

"Daddy, this is Magdalene."

Magdalene was standing in the recording studio of The Last Publishers ministries. The telephone system was set to broadcast the conversation to the adjoining room. There her friends had gathered for support, watching through the large soundproof glass window.

There was a long silence, then muffled sounds as if someone was trying to get control of their emotions and only a sob broke through. "Hey, Baby! Are you okay?"

Magdalene's face glowed. She held her thumb up as she turned around to look at Cheyenne, and Bobbie Jo. She tossed Asher, Dusty and Ben a wink.

Profound relief washed over the group. At least he hadn't hung up.

They watched Magdalene struggle to control her emotions. Her voice quivered. "I'm doing really good, Daddy! I've missed you so much. Daddy, I am so sorry for not obeying you ... and Daddy? I got saved and am walking in truth and have lots of good friends that love the Lord and are busy sharing the gospel over the whole earth.

"God has been so good to me, Daddy. I'm so thankful. I wanted you and Mama to know that I am doing good and that I love you and I am so sorry for not being a good daughter to you. How's Mama and the kids? I miss them so much!"

Asher noted the tension that came to Magdalene's face when Mr. Giles told her to hold on a minute. In the dimly lit room, the group

262

listened to the sobbing sounds. A woman's muted voice, obviously Magdalene's mama, began asking questions. Then there was the muffled sound of her parents arguing.

Finally Mr. Giles was back on the line to talk, "Baby, it's been a long, long time. We didn't even know if you were dead or alive. Where have you been all this time? Did those people keep you from calling us?"

A look of dread settled over Magdalene's young countenance. She had explained her father's paranoia to those listening in the next room. It had been this way ever since he had become involved with the White Supremacists.

Magdalene's voice carried panic and frustration as she answered him. "No, Daddy! Don't be crazy! They begged me to call, but ... I don't know ... I was just scared you wouldn't forgive me or something. Oh Daddy, *please* forgive me!"

Magdalene was openly weeping. She grabbed some tissue from the dispenser. "I missed you so much, Dad. I had a really bad time. A man kidnapped me and almost killed me, but I ran away. This nice man here found me and picked me up and brought me to stay with these really good girls. They helped me get on my feet and took good care of me for the last several months. I was a mess.

"They put up with my sassing and stealing and all kinds of stuff. Most of all they told me about Jesus.

"Oh, Daddy! I am so thankful! Jesus has forgiven all my sins. I am saved, Daddy! I am really, really saved."

There was a long silence. Mr. Giles asked, "Magdalene, what did you do with the ... you were ... did you get rid of the ... Magdalene ..." Her father cleared his throat then asked in a determined voice, "Magdalene, I would like to see you. But, if you come home, will you be coming alone?" It was understood. No half-breed would be welcomed.

Magdalene's face flushed. A sob caught in her throat. "I'll be alone," she responded flatly.

They all heard his sigh of relief, "Ha ... that's good. Well. Now I can plan how to get my girl back home. It has been a long time, Maggie. I still can't believe someone didn't keep you from calling me ... ? Something smells funny, Magdalene. I need to know, so don't you lie to me. Are your new friends Arian or not?"

Magdalene hesitated for a moment, looking with frightened eyes through the glass at her friends for support. Dropping her eyes, she lied. "Yes."

Asher knew that her dad would guess that she was lying. He felt the cold grip of fear began to knot up in his stomach. "Lord, help us."

Mr. Giles let her hesitation pass. For once his desire to see his child overrode his White Supremacist notions. "Good ... good. Okay ... let me think."

She stood tensely waiting for a moment, but then burst forth, "Daddy, I'll just hop a bus or train. My friends said they would buy me a plane ticket, so you don't need to come. I could be home in 3 days."

Mr. Giles interrupted her with urgency in his voice that made her know he still cared. "No, no ... I'm coming to get you. Where are you anyway? The caller ID said you're in Tennessee? How in the thunder did you get all the way down to Tennessee?"

Magdalene looked at the group and smiled through her tears. This was the familiar, demanding, angry response that she was used to hearing. This was the daddy of her youth. In her best memories, he was always thundering this or thundering that.

Asher detected the change in the man's voice. The sag in the young girl's shoulders showed she was disappointed that her family would not be coming with him. They listened to him explain to her that it would take him several hours driving. He couldn't come until Monday morning.

"You have your stuff together, Maggie-girl, because I got to be back home for an important meeting Monday evening. It's way too important for me to miss."

A look of fear passed over Magdalene's face. Monday nights were reserved for the White Supremacist meetings.

Magdalene continued to talk, telling him all about the *God's Story* book and how they were trying to reach the Muslims.

A cold chill ran through Asher as he listened to Mr. Giles' carefully crafted questions. He recognized the direction he was going. In her naïveté and desire to see her family Magdalene told her daddy information which would enable him to know those among them who had Jewish roots. When he asked for The Last Publishers website, there was nothing she could do but comply.

With much joy and enthusiasm Magdalene continued, "Daddy, you will love all the wonderful things The Last Publishers ministry is involved in. It will bless you so very much."

Everyone present could hear Mr. Giles' short clipped response as he cut Magdalene off. "Well, then this is enough talk. I'll be there early Monday. You be ready. Don't keep me waiting." The phone abruptly went dead.

Magdalene lifted her small shoulders, smiling at the group who sat around the table, but her smile could not cover the anxiety that filled her soul, "Well, that's it then. Daddy's coming to get me. I have two more days and then I will be going home." She tried to grin. "But I'll be back."

Asher breathed a sigh of relief. The man just wants to get his daughter and leave. No hanging around getting to know everyone. Suits me.

PREPARATIONS – Mr. Giles looked at the phone he held in his hands. Before he lay it down, he hit a few buttons. His computer had been open and he had been reading The Last Publishers' website as Magdalene talked.

A deep scowl covered his face when he saw Malachi's name. "Filthy Jew, pretending to be Christian." An even deeper scowl came over him when he looked through the pictures found under the Meet the Staff section. Omar and Tess with their children were front and center. Magdalene's white hair looked like light as she stood huddled together among their children.

He whispered under his breath, "They're using her, no doubt about that. She's too young and dumb to realize the truth. Probably that

African heathen is cooking something up for her right now, or worse than that, some lousy Jew. Well, I'll be there by tomorrow and then they'll know that the hand of God will not tolerate them touching a clean white thing."

"You gonna tell me about my own daughter?" Mrs. Giles voice brought him back. She stood pensively in the doorway. "She's my daughter too, you know. I gotta right to know."

Mr. Giles continued to scowl. "She's fine. You heard that. I'm going to pick her up and bring her home where she belongs. What else is there to know? Now, get the devil out of here before I backhand you."

Relieved, the broken woman shoved her knuckles into her mouth. Her daughter was coming home. She backed out into the hall to stand leaning against the wall. She often stood there in the shadows waiting and listening.

Mr. Giles unlocked the door to the small closet-sized room where he kept his private things, as well as a more private computer. He sat down and typed into his computer the first of a long list of secret codes, then he began typing in the set of secret passwords to locate any brothers in the county where The Last Publishers Ministries was located. "Well, now, look what we have here," he whispered to himself, "This is a pleasant surprise! Look whose town you ended up in, Maggie dear. Must be divine providence."

He was surprised to see how many well placed, powerful government officials were among the KKK in such a backwoods place. There were clans of White Supremacists and a branch of Neo-Nazis in little old Mayberry.

He laughingly whispered to himself, "So we basically own that area of the world. Good. Very good, indeed."

Mr. Giles made a few calls to set things into motion. He was given the name of a man who had made it his special project to purge the area of undesirables, some of which were The Last Publishers leaders.

So, Maggie-girl, they taught you how to lie. Your new friends are definitely not Arian. Gotta get you out of there fast.

Mr. Giles pulled an attaché from underneath the bed and quickly packed his bags, working from a mental list. "Let's see ... two extra clips—48 rounds should be enough to handle anything ... my boot knife ... wilderness survival kit just in case. That should do it."

An hour later his wife walked back into his bedroom. She stood there, a drooped-shouldered testament to their years together. The thin, gray woman wrapped her arms tightly around her skeleton thin frame. She gazed at all he had laid on the bed in preparation, noting the pistol in the suitcase.

Her voice sounded whiny as she tried to reason with her distant husband. "What are you doing? You heard her say those folks been good to her."

He acted as if she were not even there, just as she had acted toward him all these months. The bile rose within her and the accusations flew. "Why are you acting like it was them that made her run off? They didn't entice her away. It was you, so full of hate! You'll be disappointed if they turn out to be whiter than you are."

He ignored her. She lashed out again.

"You really, really believe you are superior, don't you? You think you and your silly friends playing dress up in your bed sheets are the chosen of God! How did you ever get so stupid?" She faced him in her frightened state, defiant, demanding an answer.

Briefly, he wavered before responding by slowly removing and then reinserting the clip in his pistol.

She lowered her head, cowered, and left the room.

For a moment he stared at the empty doorway. Memories of children's laughter spilled from the bedroom down the hall squeezed free from the recesses of his mind. The sounds of running feet as Magdalene came to meet him. It was as if she were still there, her long white hair trailing behind her.

He shook his head free of sweet memories.

Mrs. Giles watched her husband drive the car down the lane that same evening. *A whole day*, she thought as she watched him go. *He plans to use a whole day to get down there and scout out the place. That will give me more time . . .*

WATCHING . . . WAITING – Mr. Giles rolled into the tiny town, driving a van loaded with the tools he would need. It had taken him most of the day yesterday to gather the needed materials, as well as appraise his leadership of the interesting developments. Now he did a fast survey of all the shops surrounding the Herb Den. His contact had said there was a strong connection between the store and The Last Publishers ministries. There was no traffic there at all. It was Sunday afternoon; maybe they didn't work on Sundays.

He pulled out his phone, calling his contact. The man volunteered information about a new fence that had alarms all over it. He said the church where Malachi preached was closed now, but he thought the people used The Last Publishers office building for Sunday morning meetings.

The man had suggested it would be better to wait on the main road. If he didn't spot Magdalene by 5 P.M., then call back.

Giles turned into a logging road about 500 feet from the main gate of TLP ministries and, concealing his van, he settled down to wait where he could see who was coming and going.

From his observation post about 200 feet away, a sixteen-year-old member of Gideon's Band observed the secretive move. He called the other watchers and put them on alert, and then called Malachi and informed him. As Malachi started to alert the others he noticed that Omar was already leaving by the front gate. He was starting to call Asher when he got a call from Gideon's Band informing him that the panel van had driven away.

Giles watched as a middle-aged black man drove through the gates and down the road in a small car—with Magdalene in the front seat beside him.

Hatred birthed from the loins of destruction seethed. "Just what I figured, a no good, filthy, dirty, black ni ..."

The dark forces grew stronger with the deception. They were emboldened. Now was the time.

Giles let the small car disappear down the country road before he pulled out. For the first few seconds he thought he had lost them. Which way did they go?

He smiled with an ugly sneer when he saw they had turned south. "I'll teach that cur dog his place ... using a white girl ... my pure, Arian blood. God can have mercy, but I won't."

WE SURE ARE GOING TO HAVE SOME FUN – Magdalene was on her way to spend her last night babysitting for Omar and Tess's children before she went back home with her dad. She was thrilled to be able to spend her last evening with the kids. But her emotions were mixed with sadness at the thought of leaving the people she had come to love so dearly.

The bittersweet feelings of the evening stole over her. She loved these children as though they were her own brothers and sisters. She couldn't remember loving as intensely as she did now.

I'm going to miss them so much.

Magdalene sat, silently trying to contain her tears. She focused on planning the evening. She twisted in her seat as she asked Omar, "Can we eat ice cream tonight and read the *God's Story* book? I'd like to play charades too, if that's okay. I thought about doing one about baby Moses in the basket and I brought my basket full of baby stuff."

Omar chuckled and readily approved her ideas. She was still just a kid herself. Magdalene chattered eagerly, "Boy, are we gonna have some fun!"

⁓

For seven miles Giles trailed Omar. When he finally pulled into his driveway, Giles drove slowly past, looking the place over as well as he could in those few seconds. Then he turned around to pass the house two more times, making sure he knew the lay of the land.

He was pleased to see that the home was located on a lonely county highway with a deep rise in the back, cutting off all view from the west. The cover would make it easy to use fire. By the time help was alerted, it would be too late.

I'll just call and tell her I came sooner, and to get her stuff and meet me on the road. No one the wiser.

Giles sat in the parking lot of a local store, eating a hamburger. He notified the network of local men who were complicit in his intentions. The Brotherhood liked to be a part of everything. They liked to tell and retell their stories. Besides, the local leadership would be protecting him from the law, especially if the feds got involved. They were his insurance.

He thought for a moment, chewing his sandwich. The chlorophyll would need to be handy. It would be easier to just put her out before she knew what was happening.

IKE – "Mom, I know Magdalene called. I know where she is. She sent me this book a few weeks ago. It has an address in it."

Ike's mother burst into tears, covering her face with her hands. "Thank God! Thank God! I wanted to tell you, but I was afraid something might happen and …"

Ike waited for his distraught mother to calm down.

"Ike, you have to help me be strong. I think your daddy's going to do something to hurt the people that have helped Magdalene."

The skinny fifteen-year-old boy's shoulders were bowed under the load of his parents' sins. His pale blue eyes were filled with fear, but when he spoke it was with calm authority. His wisdom came from God. He knew the hand of God was on him. After reading *God's Story*, which Magdalene had sent him, he had become enthralled with studying Scripture.

"I know, Mom. I heard him talking to some of the men and I can help you stop him, but once we begin, we can't turn back." He looked at her, measuring her response.

Again his mother covered her face with her hands as she sobbed, "I'm so ashamed, son. Bitterness and hatred have so poisoned your daddy that he cannot see good in anything or anybody. I tried to tell him, but it only made him angrier!

"Ike," She continued her accusations, "did you know that your daddy is a White Supremacist? Do you know what that means?"

Ike looked at his mother, trying hard not to feel disgusted. Even now her goal was to lay blame. She was so naïve, it was pathetic. "Yes, Mom. I know all about everything. That's not the issue right now. Let me help you warn Magdalene."

The boy used the address on the book to locate the ministry's telephone number on the internet. A call confirmed that the offices were closed. The phone was answered by an automated recording. He attempted a web search for the numbers of individual staff members, but found they were all unlisted or blocked from receiving incoming calls.

Thinking furiously, Ike suggested, "Let's try telling the phone company the trouble, and see if they will help us."

"I know what we can do!" Mrs. Giles clapped her hands as if the problem was solved. "We can call the police of that town. They can go get Malachi Freeman, and he can go get Magdalene."

The young man shook his head, sending his pale silky hair falling over his forehead. "No, Mama! We can not go to the local police. I've heard Dad talking. That county's elected leadership is full of white power members. I overheard him say that even the judge is KKK."

Ike flushed bright red at his mother's expression. "I'm sorry, but I've been using a listening device that I picked up at the pawn shop. At first, I was just goofing around to see what I could hear, but then I started to keep up with what Dad was doing. It's a good thing I did. That's how I know what Dad has been up to, and ..." He looked at her, willing her not to ask further questions, "I know what he's capable of doing."

Mrs. Giles collapsed into an emotional heap, weeping uncontrollably.

Frustrated with her display, Ike rebuked her. "Mom, your crying is only endangering Magdalene's life. It's time to start thinking about what to do. You can cry later." Then, removing the edge from his voice, Ike continued, trying to help his distraught mother to focus, "We can call the feds and tell them what we know. We can call our local police here. They're clean. We can ask them to help us get in touch with the feds. We still have time before dad gets to Magdalene. We can explain to the feds that the law in that small southeastern Tennessee town is KKK."

Ike's mother looked at him in disbelief. "They won't believe you. No one ever believes me. They'll think we're crazy."

"Mom, I can give them Dad's computer with his passwords and codes. I can send them his whole hard drive and internet history. They'll believe me; I have the evidence. Now let's get started," Ike said as he walked down the hall and through the master bedroom door towards the locked closet. Mrs. Giles meekly followed.

"But Ike," she whined, "The office door is always locked."

Ike looked at his mother. She was truly pathetic. "Mom, that's not a problem. I can get it open."

The shaken woman slowly sat down on the bed. Her legs were no longer able to hold her. She looked up at her son. "How? No, never mind. Take care of it. Do whatever it takes and we'll deal with the consequences together."

It was near midnight before the two finally made a positive contact. They sent the needed information over the internet connection to the feds. But it was the weekend and government moves slowly on the weekend.

SUFFER THE LITTLE CHILDREN – Giles' van was parked as close to the house as possible without being noticeable. He climbed into the back

MAGDALENE WITH OMAR'S CHILDREN

and set up the military listening device he had purchased through the Brotherhood. He made himself comfortable. It promised to be a long wait.

He would listen for a while and then call Magdalene from his cell phone, using the number his contact had supplied him. She might be suspicious, but she would come to the door to speak to him. That's when he would grab her. It would be better if she already had the children in bed before he acted.

The family car was gone. He could tell from listening to the conversations that the parents weren't home.

He heard the children laughing and playing as Magdalene chased them around the room. A little girl sang the ABC song, mixing it up with the *Jesus Loves Me.* A loud, high-pitched squeal from the whole group nearly made him start. He heard them chanting, "*Ice cream! ICE CREAM! WE ALL SCREAM FOR ICE CREAM!*"

When Magdalene got them settled down, she started to read from the *God's Story* book. When she got to how Jesus received the little children, she really got into her story.

His heart melted. He listened to her stumble over the reading of a passage. "Suffer ... suffer ... suffer? '*Suffer the little children to come unto me, for such is the kingdom of God.'* Wonder why Jesus says suffer? That's a strange thing to say. What do you think, Timothy?"

He strained to hear the reply from the nine-year-old boy. The kid sounded pleased with himself as he answered, "Oh, that's easy. Sometimes kids get on people's nerves when they fidget or have to go to the bathroom, which makes the stuffy old people suffer. You know, like in church when they're trying to listen to the preacher. And course, the preacher really suffers when a kid makes noise when he's telling a joke in his sermon and messes up his punch line, but Jesus said you gotta just suffer it out. My daddy says Jesus likes little kids best of all."

Mr. Giles grew uncomfortable. Unbidden memories of his own children danced at the edge of his mind. He tried to shake them off.

Magdalene was impressed with the young boy's manufactured wisdom. "That's great, Timothy! And to think I thought that must be the wrong word to use. I'll always remember when grownups want to run the kids out of the church meeting because they don't want to be interrupted, because Jesus said to suffer the little children to come unto me."

"That's exactly what it says!" Timothy declared brightly.

The evening continued with Magdalene telling stories and each child singing specials or taking turns telling whatever was on their minds. Looking at his watch, he realized he had been listening for almost three hours. Mr. Giles stretched, wishing he had just had her come home on a bus.

He shook his head in frustration. "Maggie Girl, why did you have to get mixed up with this family?"

Around nine o'clock Magdalene began getting the children ready for bed. He heard Timothy in the distance. "Magdalene, could you tell us the story of how my dad found you when you were hungry and thirsty and scared on the side of the road and took you to the Trio for them to help you? I want to hear it one more time before you go back to your family. Tina, she needs to hear it again, too. She forgets easy 'cause she's so little."

Magdalene giggled as she settled the children down and began her animated tale, "This is my favorite story in the whole world! It's the story of how someone chose to love a dirty, ugly, nasty person enough to help them become a pretty, clean, nice person."

"Did he ... did he ... did he?" a little girl's voice kept asking until Magdalene must have given her the proper attention, "Did he help your hair get white again, too?"

"Yep, he did that too. But the most important thing was that when everyone passed me by on that hot dry road, your daddy saw my need and trusted God. He was really scared. He was so scared he almost didn't help me, but he knew God loved me and wanted someone to help."

In the back of the van Mr. Giles hunched over, studying his hands. *He was scared, was he?*

Little Tina spoke up a little skeptical. "Why was Daddy scared? Did you have a gun?"

Magdalene's laughter sounded like tinkling rain. "No, you silly bug! I didn't have a gun!"

Her voice seemed so close, he felt as if he could reach out and smooth her silky white blond hair. Unconsciously he held out his hand as if caressing her head while he whispered, "That's what I used to call you—silly bug. You were my pride and joy, and my silly bug. Oh, Maggie, why this family? Why this family?"

Tina pressed for an answer. "Well, did you have a great, great big knife?" The man could almost see the little girl throw out her arms to show her measurement of the knife that might scare her daddy. He could hear laughter and then a muffled sound. She must be hugging the child. He heard his daughter answer, "No, I didn't have a knife."

The childish voice persisted. It sounded as if she were pulling her head loose from an embrace. "Well, my Daddy is big and strong and he would not be afraid of you. You're just a twerp! I heard him tell my mama. And my daddy would not be afraid of a twerp!"

Mr. Giles fought to gain control of himself. "Twerp! Mag-Girl, how many times did I call you my little twerp? You were always such a tiny little thing. My little twerp ... God, what am I doing?"

Magdalene's voice patiently tried to clear the little girl's confusion. "Twerp, huh? I am a twerp. When I was a little girl my daddy called me Twerp. I loved it when my daddy called me a twerp. Sweetie, your daddy is the bravest man in the whole world. You don't understand, but your daddy knew that if he helped me someone might get the wrong idea and maybe hurt somebody he loves. That's why he was afraid."

"Like me?" Tina's sweet little voice sounded pleased with her new-found understanding. "Hurt somebody like me? Cause my daddy loves me very, very much."

Mr. Giles heard his daughter's voice break with a sob as she tried to answer. Then, much to his surprise, he felt hot tears trickling down his own face. How could he be crying? He roughly wiped them away.

It was as if he saw himself in a dream, sitting in the stuffy truck. "Dear God, what have I done? What have I become?"

He heard the muffled sounds as Magdalene went to quiet the baby and then returned to the older children. Magdalene's voice was so soft now that he had to turn up the sound to hear her response. "That day your daddy helped me, I was so terribly sad that I had almost decided to climb the bluff there by the road and jump off. I wanted to kill myself that day because I was so tired and hungry. But your daddy, your daddy took a chance to help me. That is why I'm here today.

"I want to always be the kind of person your daddy is. I want to see a person that's in need and help them no matter how unworthy that person is or how much trouble it is for me to help them. You kids have a fine daddy, one you can be proud of. Would you like to pray and thank God for your mama and daddy?"

Mr. Giles whispered into the night, joining in with the children as he heard them answer in a chorus, "YES!"

"Oh Lord, would she ever thank God for me? God help me. What am I going to do?" His cry was softly spoken, but heaven heard every word.

It had been almost three hours. Three hours of listening to the children. They sounded just like his kids when they were small, before his bitterness had subdued and finally drained away all of the playful joy from his home. Giles covered his face with his hands, rocking to and fro.

"God Almighty!" he cried in a hoarse whisper. "What have I done? When did my children stop laughing and playing? When did they stop being my joy and delight? God, how could I have driven this precious child away with my hatred?" He sat, his head bowed in grief as he listened to each of the children pray, thanking God for their parents.

27

BURN OUT

A thundering knock on the van door caused Giles to jump, banging his head on the ceiling. His heart pounded so fast and hard it felt as if it were going to explode. As he yanked the ear pieces from his ears he heard the muffled call, "Hey, Mr. Giles, you in there?" He opened one side of the van doors. There stood a short, fat, grinning man wearing the KKK token on his sleeve. The man was casually using a large pocket knife to clean his fingernails.

In the cool, clean, night air the man's breath smelled like sewage. "You ready? I've been wantin' to get them little pickaninny mongrels for a long time. Every time I drove this way for the last four years all I could think about was roastin' them little jigaboos, but the judge said wait. Now finally the sweet night's arrived.

"Oh! Forgive my bad manners. My name's Derek. The judge sent me to give you a hand. I love to burn. I'm *good* at burning and can gair-ruhn-tee there will be no investigation—not even insurance trouble. You ready?"

Giles stood half in and half out of his van, sizing up the loathsome man. "No, not yet. My daughter's in there, and I'm thinking of doing something else. I just don't feel like burning is the right thing. Not tonight."

"Come on now," Derek whined in a patronizing tone, as he lifted the pocket knife to pick the black cavity between his front teeth. "Everything's ready. All you have to do is watch. Besides, you know the brotherhood comes before family."

The disgusting man looked searchingly as if trying to decide how much Giles might know. He finally said with a hint of conspiracy, "Man, this thing's a hell-of-a-lots bigger than this here house of Nigs. We are talkin' *big*. Ain't nothing can get in the way. Judge says it has to be clean ... real clean."

That said, he cleared his throat and spat, then said with a note of disgust, "'Sides, your daughter's been consorting with Nigs and Jews, so she's one of them. Now, let's do what we are trained to do for the greater good of the Arian race. I'm even going to capture it on film for the meeting next week. Got my rig set up right there and it is already rolling. Just do what you're told and everything will go right on schedule."

The last of Derek's speech sounded more like a threat than a request. Never one to be ordered around, Giles yelled at him in defiant anger. "No! I said no, and I mean *no*. This is my show, and it will go when and how I say. You were invited here as a witness for your brotherhood."

Derek threw up his hands in mock surrender, one hand still clutching the blade. His face was full of glee as he glanced beyond the van and sweetly announced, "Too late. Too late!" He laughed. "I already doused the place with juice and gotten her going. We got us a real hot spot right this very minute. You wanna see?"

Giles felt his heart lurch. Memories of his own evil deeds flooding his mind, mocking him like stinking ants. He had once done the exact same thing. He shook his head trying to throw off the ugly thoughts. People had died at his hands? How many families were without homes or churches due to their hatred and destructiveness? Now his own daughter was in danger. "God help me! Please, help me!"

With a roar that sounded more like an animal than a man, Mr. Giles leapt from the van and ran across the road in a wild panic. The house was already ablaze on three different sides. As he ran there was a loud explosion.

DADDY? HELP, PLEASE! – The demented father screeched for his daughter, but there was no sign of light or anyone at the window. Surely she had heard the explosion!

He knew all of the children were upstairs, including Magdalene. He began screaming her name over and over. In what seemed hours but was really only a few seconds, she threw open the window. "Daddy? Is that you? Daddy? Daddy, please, I'm scared! What are you doing? Please don't hurt us, Daddy!"

Never in his life had he ever hated his sin more than in this moment. In this awful instant he realized how much he loved his golden girl. He realized just how much he had suffered and worried about her this past year. He had been so thrilled to hear her voice when he answered the phone.

Now it looked as though she would perish by events he set into motion. He looked up and saw her young, thin body and white fan of hair. Commanding with a voice full of panic and love he roared, "Jump, Magdalene! Jump! I'll catch you!"

"Daddy, Daddy! Please, Daddy, help us!" She screamed when she saw the open flames. "The stairs, Daddy! There's too much smoke! We can't get down!"

Mr. Giles wailed, "Jump, Magdalene! I'll catch you!"

Magdalene leaned out the window holding the baby. She screamed, "I won't leave the children! Daddy, will you catch the baby? Please, Daddy, please help the children!"

Bitter hatred had consumed Giles' soul for so long. The constant drilling that he had been through had hardened his heart. Yet as he looked up into his daughter's fearful face, he renounced all of his foolishness. The only thing he hated at that moment was what he was and where it had brought his beloved daughter. His face crumpled as he yelled hoarsely above the noise of the crackling blaze, "Okay, Sweet Pea!"

All four children were crying and struggling for the air at the open window as the smoke and heat was rising from below where the fires were started.

"Okay," he got his voice to respond now, yelling above the roar of the fire, "I'll catch them! Send the older boy first so he can help me with the little ones." He extended his arms and waited.

When the chunky Timothy hit Giles it forcefully threw them both to the ground. Giles was up again in an instant, ready to catch the baby, quickly passing him off to Timothy. "Take the baby."

The four-year-old girl was next. Then they stood in the heat waiting for the six year-old to follow. Both girls sent Mr. Giles to the ground, almost winded. He screamed at the boy without ever turning their way, "Take the baby and your sisters. Get in that van and close the back doors. Magdalene, jump!" he shouted as he regained his footing, the heat becoming almost too intense to stand close any longer, even though only seconds had passed.

The flames suddenly intensified in a gust of wind. He could see the flames almost engulf her pale, slim frame as she stepped to the ledge, ready to jump. Putting up his arms to shield his face from the blaze, he could see her face. She was looking at him in a way she hadn't since she was a toddler. Her face glowed with thanksgiving that he had helped the children. Now she looked down at her him with trust. His mind caught her image as if it were a still picture. "Come on, baby girl, jump!"

In that instant time stood still. The force of the moment seemed to slow every motion.

Heat. Flickering light causing ugly shadows to appear to jump out from everywhere. Fear.

And into that awful mix a single gunshot rang out. Its sound lingered. Magdalene's light body seemed to jolt. She fell sideways. He saw her look down as if trying to understand the new unexpected pain. She teetered there as if hanging somewhere between heaven and the burning hell around her. She lost her balance, seeming to fold over, falling out of the window.

Giles was filled with a wild drumming as he watched her fall. He could no longer feel the heat. He could not move his limbs. He could not even call her name. He stood frozen, unwilling to believe this hell he had helped bring.

His mind replayed the scene over and over as if hours were passing. He could see the thankfulness in her face for saving the children. He could see her trust. He saw her face change as the pain of the bullet hit her body. He could see her twist sideways and then fold and tumble over. Her hand reached up to touch her side. A smoky haze closed in around her. He could see her falling.

She fell and fell and fell, as if falling from a thousand miles high. Finally he caught his daughter in his arms. Heat seared his skin. His ears were roaring louder and louder as he gazed at her still, sweet, young face.

He stumbled backward away from the flames licking out at them.

With Magdalene in his arms, he collapsed to his knees. Still holding her, he struggled back to his feet, stumbling backwards. He searched her pale blue eyes as he staggered away from the heat and smoke. Dropping again to the ground, he lay her down on the cool soft grass, smoothing her pale hair back away from her face as he talked to her. "Sweetheart? It's Daddy. Hey, Goldilocks. Daddy's here, Little Twerp. Daddy loves you. Sweet Pea! Tell Daddy you love him too!" Leaning down he kissed her nose as he did when she was a child, calling her name.

But she did not speak.

Stumbling to his feet, he shook his head trying to clear his thoughts to think of what to do to make this terrible nightmare go away. He looked back over his shoulder hoping for a miracle. There he saw the man who had shot his baby.

Derek was coolly waddling towards him reloading the chamber of his 30-06 rifle. He let the barrel swing slightly to the right of Mr. Giles, while leaving his finger on the trigger. He wanted to make sure the stunned man knew what was at stake.

Yelling over the noise of the fire he rebuked the grief-stricken father. "She would have talked, Giles. You know the code as well as I do. We vowed to protect the brotherhood. You just had a temporary lapse. Unfortunately it took me a few minutes to retrieve my gun. You'd better start remembering because we got us a situation here with these four pickaninies, and one of 'em half grown, plenty able to tell all."

Derek looked around, obviously trying to decide how to rid himself of the living bodies of the four children as he shouted at Giles, "I keep trying to tell you that this ain't some small town fire. This is really important! Something bigger than you can imagine is coming down. Money. Big money. The judge says the fire has gotta be clean and if'n it ain't clean we's as good as dead ourselves!"

Giles never heard a word. The raging in his soul, hotter than the burning house, drowned all else. For the last four years Giles had been practicing his fast draw. He wore his gun in an open topped, cut away holster the way he had worn it to every White Supremacist occasion since he had joined the clan. A thousand times he had daydreamed of standing face to face with the enemy, pulling his gun out so fast that it was only a blur. He had envisioned it bucking in his hand, imagined the smell of the gun powder. Now, the skill came to him without a conscious thought.

"You filthy, murdering—" He was screaming as he pulled his gun. The pistol cleared leather, bucking and roaring in his trained hand as if it were a part of his arm. Derek never had time to consider his soul or tighten his finger on the trigger of his rifle. The first bullet took him right in the sternum; the second and third took him in the neck and face. He crumpled like a dropped towel. Giles unloaded three more shots into his head. Derek's body flopped and jerked while behind them the house continued to burn hotter and hotter.

Then the stricken father turned to his beloved child. He cooed as he carefully brushed her white hair from her face, then he picked up her limp body. The distraught man staggered further away from the now raging inferno as he spoke soft words of love and comfort.

CONSUMING FIRE – A neighbor down the road who sometimes attended church with Omar saw the glow in the sky and knew it was Omar's house on fire. He called the volunteer rescue and fire, and then, on second thought, called Malachi to inform him.

Asher was out the door running to Dusty's truck before he even knew the whole story. He had done some drag racing in his youth. It took them about ten minutes, but they got there before any of the others. In the dancing light, the first thing Asher saw was a stranger staggering across the lawn carrying the limp and bloodied body of Magdalene in his arms, and beyond he saw the twisted frame of a fat man lying closer to the fire, his head nearly gone and his clothes smoking from the intense heat.

Asher raced over to the man carrying Magdalene. He could taste the fear in his mouth. Springing in front of the man, he reached out to take Magdalene from him, but the man pulled away, saying, "No, she's my daughter, my angel."

Asher then knew this was Mr. Giles, her father. What was he doing here? Then he saw the gun Giles was wearing and realized who the fat man must be and why Giles had shot him.

Over the roar of the fire Asher could hear the screaming of the emergency vehicles. He could see blue and red lights coming from both directions.

Help was here. Thank God help was here. Then he heard Omar's children screeching from the back of a van parked out by the road. Weakness from relief almost overcame him. *The children are safe.*

His own thunderous voice startled him as his soul called out, *Blessed be the LORD, thank you Lord, the children are safe.*

Magdalene's father sobbed inconsolably. "Sweetie Pie. Baby girl, Daddy's got you. Daddy will take care of you." Asher turned to try to help but the man would not let Asher touch her.

The fire could be seen for miles licking the night sky.

Omar's car had barely stopped when he jumped out and began to run and stumble towards the flames. Without pause, Omar ran straight at the inferno even though it was clear that no one could have survived.

Asher screamed at Omar to stop and dove towards him, tackling him like a linebacker. Omar turned and delivered a vicious kick to Asher's face, breaking his hold.

Rolling over to his knees, Asher felt the sting of the fire on his face.

Omar was crawling and running on all fours before regaining his feet, running straight for the burning house.

Four big rescue workers who were already rushing to intercept Omar were able to overtake him and bring him down before he could regain his momentum. It took all four to drag the screaming man back from the heat.

Asher tried to call out to say the children were safe, but the blow to his jaw and head caused his senses to reel. His last conscious thought was that of watching his friend fight like a demented fiend, trying to get loose from the men as they dragged him back from the blaze.

Asher could hear people yelling as his mind again resurfaced into consciousness. He struggled to open his gritty, hot eyes. Unconsciously he threw his arm across his face to shut out the pain brought on by the flashing lights from the fire and rescue vehicles. He peeked through the space where his arm bent. Cheyenne's face swam above him. Her eyes were red and swollen. Tears still washed down her face. He hardly recognized her, so haggard was her countenance. Flashes of memories came in a rush as if each one were fighting for predominance. He struggled to sit up, but the pain caused a surge of nausea.

His tormented mind formed the question his voice was unable to utter. Darkness again embraced him. Sounds faded. He gladly surrendered.

He awakened to a cool wet cloth on his aching jaw and head. Cheyenne's tear-covered face seemed to swim over him. Asher finally managed to sit up but was immediately pushed firmly back down.

In his confusion he could hear young Timothy's voice. "I screamed and screamed to my dad that us kids were okay and *finally* he heard me. I never saw my dad act so crazy. He kicked you clean out. Man! We thought you were dead or something, cause you've been laying here a *long* time. Cheyenne cried so bad that she made me cry. Did you know I almost squished that man when he caught me? The man told me he's Magdalene's daddy. I'm scared for Magdalene. They took her away in the ambulance. Her daddy cried really bad but the sheriff took him now. That's my dad you hear crying. He won't stop crying and crying. I wish my daddy would stop."

Asher registered the sound of continuous loud sobs as coming from his dear friend, Omar. The boy could not understand that this night was his father's most dreaded nightmare come true. Asher tried to focus his burning eyes to reassure the young boy. Somehow his body and mind didn't seem to be functioning together.

Unknowingly he lifted his hand to his head. His fingers felt as if they belonged to someone else as they explored the gash on the side of his aching head. The gooey warmth of the clotting blood finally helped him reunite the hand with his mind. Satisfied, he allowed his hand to fall.

Consciousness, and with it recollection, returned in bits and pieces. A hurting more intense than mere wounds assaulted him. Deep in his soul he felt lost, empty, broken. The sorrow made him want to submerge into darkness once again, but this time life was not so merciful.

His eyes locked with Cheyenne's, hoping she would give him any sign of hope, any hope at all. But all he saw was profound anguish. He had seen that haunted sorrow just a while ago in the eyes of Magdalene's father.

A raw dry scratchy sound erupted from Asher's parched throat. "Magdalene?"

As he called her name he could almost hear again her father gently cooing over his daughter as he staggered away from the raging fire with her in his arms, "Daddy's got you. Daddy will take care of his golden girl. Daddy loves his little twerp."

God help us ... Magdalene.

28

THE REASON WHY

Magdalene was dead.

Grief pulled them down like a tidal undertow. It was a nightmare, beyond comprehension. Every pleasure was swallowed up in the pain they bore. Sleepless nights, sobbing off and on all day, work left undone, their vision gone in the midst of despair. They had talked about danger and dying. They thought they were ready for anything. They were willing to be martyrs. But this was real—so different from their play pretend bravery and spun spirituality.

Reporters came from all over the nation to document the arrest of what seemed to be half the county. Corruption, greed, murder, and major fraud involving banks, insurance companies, local lawyers, and county tax assessors, all suddenly made known. The novelty of discovering every political leader in a three county area to be involved in a violent White Supremacist clan was worth reporting.

When they approached those who loved Magdalene, asking about the night of the fire, they were met by sobs from men and women alike. The great sorrow subdued the news hounds, making them wonder how one young girl could have provoked such devotion.

Word trickled to the Freemans that, amidst the many arrests, federal agents were discovering that some local and state officials were actively manipulating the law to seize the property and assets of The Last Publishers ministries and their leadership. It all smelled of money … big money.

The weary eyes of Malachi met the eyes of his beloved. Obviously the berry secret was not such a big secret after all. Hope briefly wondered if the lack of communication from Cohen was due to the evil men here. But grief overshadowed her worry and clouded both their minds from thinking about the conspiracy.

Then, suddenly, the press was gone. The feds were gone. The mourners were left to weep undisturbed.

Yellowstone's soon coming fury could no longer be hidden. The spitting and spewing of the earth's largest volcano was news, front and center. But for those left behind in the small Tennessee community, the threat of Yellowstone, so troubling to the rest of the nation, seemed a distant worry. The thoughts of evil days ahead could not take away the deep sorrow of the here and now. Nothing would ever feel normal again.

Those who had come to love Magdalene in the past three months now sat in the Herb Den in total silence. Magdalene's body had been taken back to her hometown for burial. None of them had been allowed to leave due to the investigation. Now Malachi had brought them together because he knew they needed closure. It had been a long week.

Tonight's group was made up of TLP office workers and a few old friends. They came because they were shaken to their very core. Every face looked troubled; not just sad, not just confused, but very, very disturbed.

Even with everything else that had happened, losing Magdalene had been the greatest blow in Cheyenne's life. Bobbie Jo hadn't stopped crying since that night; even in her sleep she whimpered. Julie had thrown up for two days.

In his grief, holding back angry tears, Dusty stood in the middle of the floor, waving his hands and directing his uncertainties toward the group. "Why would God do such a thing? Why did God let that nasty, filthy scumbag kill Magdalene? God could have turned the bullet just a tiny bit. He could have caused the smoke to cloud Derek's vision. He could have done any number of things that would have required almost no effort. Why?! Didn't he care?

"She was so young! She had her whole life ahead of her. Why would anyone hurt her? She believed and trusted! How could God allow this terrible thing to happen to her? She trusted him to protect her! We prayed ... and now she's *dead*!"

The young man stopped. Breathing hard, he looked around the room, daring anyone to answer, knowing they couldn't.

In the silence that followed, Yancey stood. "Da boy's right. Dat week we met here and prayed for her family in dis situation. What did God do about dose prayers?" Yancey's angry eyes settled on Malachi as if he were blaming him for the murder of Magdalene. A tremor seemed to engulf him. He dropped into his seat as if he no longer had strength to stand.

Physically and emotionally, they were all spent. Exhausted. The frustrated, anguished questions being shouted in this room were the same ones silently considered by every person there in the days since the terrible tragedy.

Every eye in the warehouse room turned to look at Malachi. His spirit sagged with the load of their grief, their anger, their blame, which they had unconsciously shifted toward him. Asher could see that Malachi's heart was heavy. He had seen him break into weeping several times over the last week. Now he watched the Old Gent struggle to clear his eyes and throat before he answered.

GOD'S WAYS – He looked uncharacteristically gaunt. His voice broke as he struggled to answer. With his eyes he searched out those who sat in the room.

"When *should* God have let Magdalene die? Should he have turned the bullet, this time saving her, then stopped the car from crashing five years from now?

"Should he keep her from getting cervical cancer at 45 years old, or stop her from having a stroke at 68?

James 3:1 "My brethren, be not many masters, knowing that we shall receive the greater condemnation." ∽

"Is God more merciful to let her live a long time before she dies? Is he unjust to let her die so young?

"Who has suffered here? Her? Or us?"

Malachi's hands hung loose down his side as if he were too weary to lift them. His voice dropped to almost a whisper. "What we fail to understand is just how short life really is."

Hope handed Malachi a tissue to blow his nose. Everyone waited as he cleared his throat.

"I know. I have lived a life that seems only to have started yesterday, yet it will soon be over. Where did my time go? Life is just a vapor. We appear for just a short time and then we are gone.

"Walk up to the graveyard and look at the tombstones. They all have one thing in common. It is the small dash between the date the person was born and the date when they died. On tombstones, you will see dates where that dash spanned ten days, ten years, fifty years, or eighty years, but they are all dead. No one visiting the cemetery much notices whether they lived ten years or eighty years. Now they are all in eternity, time without end.

"If any of these people could come back and speak, they would tell you that this life is just a dash between two dates, a vapor drifting upward, or downward, a blink in time. What really counts is eternity. This life is just a brief opportunity to decide your eternal destiny. It is just a testing ground, not only of where you will spend eternity but what you will be for eternity."

Asher could feel Cheyenne's grief as she sat there beside him. Her elbow bumped his arm as she lifted a tissue to her eyes. His soul burned with the need to hold her and assure her that there was still love … still life. His big hand closed over her hand. He felt her body shake as a new tremor consumed her.

Malachi's voice again grabbed Asher's attention. "Magdalene was a flower picked in early bloom. But she had made sure of her eternal home. More than all of you, she looked forward to the time when she

James 4:14 "Whereas ye know not what shall be on the morrow. For what is your life? It is even a vapour, that appeareth for a little time, and then vanisheth away." ∽

would see the face of Jesus. Many of you have been with us off and on for a number of years, yet you have never really come to know the Savior the way she did. If it had been you instead of her, would you be as sure of your salvation as she was?

"You stumble along, showing up for a Bible study or Church meeting when the mood hits you, but some of you don't truly know the Savior.

"Now, Magdalene ... she knows, and we know she knows, the living God. None of us are left uneasy wondering if she really is in heaven. We can rest assured."

THINGS MADE KNOWN – "So she went on ahead. Yes, I grieve to lose her. But our loss is her gain. Many of you did not know that Magdalene carried a very heavy secret on her small shoulders. That secret weighed her heart with great grief. She was too young to keep such a terrible thing to herself. She bore her grief alone except for Hope and I, and at our request she told Tess. She didn't want to grieve you, so she kept quiet. She wanted to protect you from sorrow.

"You remember she was fanatically clean and particular. We often laughed at her and her yellow rubber gloves and doctor's mask. She was particular for your sakes, not hers.

"During her year on the street she had become HIV positive. The disease was already advancing in her body. She knew she was living on borrowed time."

There was a shared gasp across the room as everyone sat up in unison, trying to fathom this unexpected revelation. Then the mood in the room shifted to fear as people searched their memories of any time they might have come in contact with Magdalene.

Cheyenne interrupted, "But what about the brew? Wouldn't that have helped?"

Rather than begin a discussion about the brew, Malachi responded with as little information as possible. "There seems to be some properties to this particular disease that would not respond to the brew. The brew's formula works with the immune system, building it. HIV uses your own immune system to destroy your health."

He stumbled to recover his thoughts. "Of course, Magdalene took every precaution, especially around the children, and Tess saw to it that she did. That is one reason that Tess encouraged Magdalene to contact her daddy when she did, before it was too late."

Great drops of sweat formed on Malachi's forehead. He stopped to wipe it dry, keeping the sweat out of his eyes. The emotional strain of the evening was apparent in his whole body.

"Why did God allow that evil monster to shoot our sweet baby girl? Would I have liked to have strangled him with my own hands that night as her body laid on the ground? You betcha. Is it fair? Did God answer our prayers? Does he care? Why?"

For a long moment Malachi looked down, "Is there an answer for these questions that will satisfy a rebellious, angry heart? No, there is no answer. Is there an answer to cause us who trust Him to cry out and say, 'Abba Father, not my will, but thine be done?'

"Yes, there is an answer."

Taking a deep breath, Malachi looked Dusty in the eye. "Magdalene greatly wanted her father to see the truth and turn to God. You heard her pray for her family to come to the truth every time we met together. In her last moments on earth she saw him prove that he was turning toward God by being willing to catch Omar's children. I *know* that as she floated heavenward she was praising God for the miracle of what God had done and will continue to do in her daddy's heart."

Silence came to the room as Malachi stopped speaking, his breath labored.

"God answered her prayer. We have all seen and heard Mr. Giles testify to having come to know Jesus. In prison he will be able to share his testimony of being deceived and then seeing the truth, and coming to know the Savior. He may make a profound difference in the lives of many inmates. Ike, her favorite brother, has shared with us that the rest of the family is now seeking God."

Through her tears Cheyenne noted the Old Gent looked haggard. His skin had taken a grayish tinge, reminiscent of the time before he had started taking the brew. Magdalene's death had been hard on them all, but for Malachi, it seemed to be a sickening blow.

She turned to look at Asher, because she could feel his gaze upon her. Asher's eyes were clouded with pain. He too, noticed Malachi's frailness.

MAGDALENE'S VISION – "There is another thing you should know about Magdalene," Malachi continued.

"A few weeks ago, she came to me and told me that a while back God had given her a deep burden to pray for young Muslim girls. She told me that she had had a dream or a vision of some kind and believed that God had told her that she had a special mission here on this earth, even though it would be a short mission. In her dream she said she was standing and holding hands with lots of young Muslim girls and that they were all standing in a circle singing and moving, floating in motion to the music.

"She said she heard the song they were singing. She sang it for me and it was so beautiful that it sent chills up and down my spine. I can't remember all of the words, but it was something to the effect of:

> We sing a new song.
> Jesus is Lord. Jesus is God.
> He has redeemed us to God by his blood
> out of every kindred, and tongue, and people and nation.
> He has removed our darkness,
> now we see.
> Jesus is the King of Kings.
> He is worthy.
> Worthy is the Lamb that was slain.
> Sing a new song with us.

"She felt that those girls were the ones God had given to her. She knew that many of these girls would be terribly persecuted if they trusted in Jesus. She did not take her burden lightly.

"When Magdalene came to TLP, she began to fast three days a week.

When you thought she was working, she was actually shut up three hours a day in a dark room praying, asking God to bring his word to millions of young Muslim girls who had been shut away for so long from any knowledge of the true and living, loving God. She asked us to give her a place where she could be in darkness, a reminder to her that the Muslim people have been in darkness for so long.

"The night of the fire, as I knelt by her body I had a sure conviction that God had indeed chosen her as his own for this brief moment of time. I believe that she set the windows of heaven open for the little girls among the Muslim people. I believe that even at this very moment God is answering her prayers."

Cheyenne could feel a sob rising in Asher. He let go of her hand to put both of his hands over his face as he wept.

Asher had worked with Magdalene all those weeks. He had loved her like his own baby sister.

Malachi paused to allow everyone to regain their composure. He picked up a large cup of hot tea, warming his trembling hands before taking a long sip.

"Another thing you need to know about our little sister is that she dreaded her advancing sickness. She knew that it might be long and drawn out. She had studied what to expect, and it was an awful road she had to travel. Death is always an ugly monster, but when AIDS is the vehicle it is an extended ugliness that torments over and over before it is through. She would be thankful that her friends and family did not have to go through that with her."

The old warrior of God stopped speaking. He stood staring at the floor as if there were some secret writing there to tell him what to say. When he looked up, his eyes slowly traveled around the room looking at each person, considering each one.

"How many people are in this room? Thirty? Thirty-five people? How many of you truly love the Lord? Yet, to my memory, I can not remember one of you ever saying to me how you long to see the face of Jesus. How many times have all of you heard Magdalene say just that?

She longed to see the face of Jesus.

"One of Magdalene's favorite verses, many of you will remember her quoting it, was Philippians 3:10."

Malachi smiled as he looked down at his Bible and read.

That I may know him, and the power of his resurrection, and the fellowship of his sufferings, being made conformable unto his death.

"The night of the fire was one of the saddest moments of my life. But I trust God. I love him, and so did Magdalene. I will see her soon, and when I see her I will ask her, 'Is it okay that God took you so soon?'

"I can almost hear her laughing and saying to me, 'Oh Malachi! You know, it was *perfect* timing. He spared me all my pain and gave me all his joy!"

There was a pause as everyone contemplated the words. Cheyenne looked around at the people who sat there. The Old Gent had answered well. It was strange how differently you feel when you know all the facts. She thought about how many times people become bitter with God and demand to know why he allows bad things to happen. And Malachi only knew a small part of the picture; how much better would it be when all the facts were known? She bowed her head, silently praying, "Thank you, God, that you are holy, just, and merciful."

MAGDALENE'S JEWEL – Bobbie Jo slowly stood to her feet, holding her hands cupped as if she held something in them. She tried to speak, but simply looked at everyone in a silent plea for them to understand.

Finally she forced herself to speak.

"Once, about six weeks ago, just before Magdalene started working at TLP full-time, she gave me something precious. She put it in my hands and asked me to hold it until it was time. It is time." Bobbie Jo opened her hands and held them palms upward as though releasing a balloon to float upward unfettered.

"She told me that she had a dream. She saw herself running through a field holding the hand of a little girl. She said it was her little girl named Starlite. In the dream, she said they laughed and played together in a meadow of white and red clover. She said it was the most precious moment in her life. She believes God gave her a foretaste of things to come.

"She put it in my hand and told me it was a jewel of her future to be kept safe and fresh until others needed to know."

Bobbie Jo dropped to her knees, weeping. "It's okay! Oh, Lord, I love you! It's okay. I know Magdalene would be glad."

Everyone sat silent without looking up or saying anything. Except for the quiet weeping, the silence went on and on.

THE VISIBLE MIRACLE – Suddenly the door of the office was thrown open, sending in a flood of late afternoon light. Raw terror from the tense days caused every person in the room to react with a violent jerk. Several metal folding chairs slapped the concrete as people jumped to their feet as if to flee. There was a guttural sound as air rushed from their lungs. Panic sent a surge of adrenaline through Cheyenne's extremities, stinging her arms and legs.

Dana Reed, the storekeeper from next door, stood looking dazed, almost haunted. He seemed to be searching for words. Finally the simple, kindhearted man screeched, "Turn your TV on ... just turn your TV on."

Asher leaped up like a jack-in-the-box. He hit the power button on the big screen. It was Fox News, live from Iran. There appeared to be a huge peaceful rally.

"That's it," the storekeeper shouted. "Glory to God ... it's a miracle."

Relief was audible.

The people in the room sat up, interested to see what could have so galvanized the softspoken, easygoing shopkeeper. They saw on the screen what looked to be several thousand people standing tightly grouped together, in front of what appeared to be a college campus. Many had their hands in the air. Their faces were full of joy. They were obviously Middle Eastern. Some of the women were covered head to foot in burkhas and dark robes.

The camera shifted, pulling in close to show their faces ... and something else.

Everyone in the room jumped to their feet, awestruck with what they were seeing.

Right in front, clear to all, a large group of smiling teenage girls was waving the Farsi translation of *God's Story* book. The camera panned and came in for a close-up shot, settling on one of the books. The girls began to sing in another language, but the English translation scrolled across the bottom of the screen:

We sing a new song.
Jesus is Lord. Jesus is God.
He has redeemed us to God by his blood
out of every kindred, and tongue, and people and nation.
He has removed our darkness,
now we see.
Jesus is the King of Kings.
He is worthy.
Worthy is the Lamb that was slain.
Sing a new song with us.

As the group watched, the whole multitude of people began to sing with the girls, their voices swelling like a mighty wave.

Asher began to repeat what he had said dozens of times, but this time it was like never before, because he could see the miracle right before his eyes. "It's just like we had hoped and dreamed. Our miracle has happened."

Bobbie Jo quietly whispered in a trembling voice, "Magdalene's girls? They're singing Magdalene's song!"

29

SEVEN VIALS

The pungent odor of St. John's Wort herbal tea blending with the heavenly fragrance of spice cookies made The Last Publishers' office kitchen a haven for the hungry. Voices softly hummed as people leaned over the kitchen bar, munching, waiting for the meeting to start. Since the bombing, everyone felt safer behind the fence. Except for the one meeting concerning Magdalene's death, they wanted to meet here at TLP.

When Malachi and Hope entered, the crowd quickly dispersed, heading to their respective seats. Before the last straggler had settled with tea and cookies in hand, Malachi lit up his overhead screen, showing a chart of the Book of Revelation. "Well, it's nice to do something normal again. How long has it been since we have had two Bible studies in a row? Okay, open your Bibles to Revelation chapter 13 ... verse ..."

Before Malachi was able to read his verse, Ben spoke up with a question.

"About the number thirteen and the vials you covered last meeting...I was going through some of those verses and wondered if you would go over that part of Scripture one more time?"

Cheyenne and Bobbie Jo exchanged glad glances. Cheyenne looked around for Asher, knowing he had been stumped in trying to answer this question for Yancey earlier this week. Her face registered surprise. *Where is he?*

"Okay, you remember where we are on our chart?" Malachi shook his head as if to clear his thoughts, then pointed his long stick toward the chart. "Right here is where we are."

"The number thirteen in the Bible stands for sin, death, and judgment. For that reason it is often associated with the devil. Revelation chapter 13 deals with the beast rising up out of the sea, with seven heads, ten horns, and ten crowns upon its heads with the names of blasphemy.

"The book of Daniel was written seven hundred years before Revelation and records a vision Daniel had that is very similar to what John saw as recorded here in the book of Revelation. In both books we read of a seven-headed beast.

"We have a divinely inspired interpretation of what these symbols stand for both in Daniel and in Revelation. We don't have to wonder. We don't have to guess. The angel interprets them for us right here in chapter 13."

Malachi turned a page in his Bible. "This is during the seven years of the great Tribulation. In Revelation chapter 13, we find the description of the Antichrist and of the wicked religious leader.

"They attempt to supplant Christ by presenting the world with a counterfeit Christ. The Antichrist will not speak against Christ; on the contrary, he will claim to be Christ and will try to emulate Jesus' character and miracles."

Ben and Dusty's eyes lit up. Malachi was answering just as they hoped he would. Cheyenne's eyes twinkled as she watched the boys twist in their seats with satisfaction. She giggled and punched Bobbie Jo, wanting to share the moment. Bobbie Jo glanced over, feigning disinterest. Cheyenne looked around again. *Where was Asher?*

The sober-minded in the room were glued on what Malachi was teaching, not noticing the girls. Malachi's tone was emphatic, "People will believe he is truly Christ because of his great kindness, generous heart, and ability to bring peace to so many different factions. He will have trusted religious leaders standing with him who will introduce him as being the true Christ. He will be well-versed in the Bible. He will demonstrate his power with glorious signs and wonders. Why shouldn't they trust this kind, powerful, wise man?

"All the problems we are dealing with today, such as disease, wars, terrorists, and even earth disruptions, will suddenly have solutions. In many cases there will be supernatural solutions, healings and miracles. People who thought themselves Christians before the rapture, especially those who don't believe in a rapture, will see all the wonderful things he is doing and will be relieved that Christ's kingdom is finally going to come to the earth as he promised.

"Ask yourself ... would it not make you wonder if a man who claimed to be Christ were to call fire down from heaven in the sight of thousands of people and then perform signs and wonders with extensive healings of every disease? Why would you not believe? What if he quoted Scripture and showed you how he is fulfilling prophecy?

"God intends for the people who rejected Jesus Christ before the rapture to be deceived. God helps the Antichrist to deceive people by sending a strong delusion so that they might believe a lie."

Cheyenne glanced around, trying to find Julie to see how she was responding to Malachi's answer, but Julie didn't appear to be in the room. *Man ... this is the wrong Bible study to miss.*

Cheyenne could almost hear anew Julie's seething response to Bobbie Jo's wild Bible story on this subject. Julie's face was red as she stopped Bobbie Jo, saying she would quit her job before she would listen to someone accuse God of purposefully deceiving people into believing a lie. The verses stating the fact only made Julie angrier.

Now Julie was not hearing the truth. Julie always had time for work and play, but managed to miss Bible studies and church quite often. Her excuses were always plausible. *Why was she not here this time?* Cheyenne glanced back at Bobbie Jo, but now Bobbie Jo was gone. Louise's old face grinned back at her from Bobbie Jo's seat. Obviously the older woman was delighted with the message she was hearing.

Malachi pointed to the drawings of the vials on the Revelation chart, "You remember in chapter 16 how the vials are poured out? The word *vial* appears thirteen times in Scripture, each time in a negative context. Your modern commercially-driven bibles have changed the word vial to bowl. Vials are the vessels used in laboratories that contain bacteria and disease. Bowls are for eating cereal. God sends his angels to pour diseases and plagues upon the earth from vials, not bowls.

"It is interesting to note here that just like in Egypt when the disease fell upon the Egyptians, but did not touch God's people, so God protects his people during the Tribulation from these terrible plagues. One plague leaves men covered with runny, pus-filled sores. Tribulation saints will not be affected by any of the vial judgments."

"Ha." A swishing sound escaped Hope. "Maybe it only gets the males, like in Egypt," she murmured.

Cheyenne grinned at Dusty's and Ben's perplexed looks. From their expressions it was clear Asher didn't tell them about the seven women for every man passage. Cheyenne snickered. Probably too much for the boys to think about.

Malachi grinned at his wife, knowing this was one of her interests. He looked as if he were about to respond to Hope's interjection when Ben interrupted with another question, "Are you saying that some Christians are not raptured?"

"No." Malachi looked back to Ben, pausing for a moment before settling back into his seat. "All believers are taken with Christ before the beginning of the Tribulation, but some people who never heard the gospel will become Christians during the Tribulation. The final publishers ... preachers ... the 144,000 will be the ones who preach the gospel to them."

Yancey jerked, making everyone look over toward him. He then leaned forward, pressing his point with an intense look on his face.

Exodus 12 - Speaks of the first Passover and the death of the Egyptian firstborn males. ✑

"So that means if a person does not get saved before the rapture, but knows about salvation—when he sees that the rapture has occurred—*then* he could get saved? Right?"

Louise's satisfied smack almost unseated the unsuspecting Cheyenne. The old lady grinned with obvious delight, both at unseating Cheyenne and at the answer she knew was coming. She whispered, "Here she blows … finally."

THE STRONG DELUSION – Malachi's gaze rested on Yancey. The old man's face was stern. The group glanced around at each other, surprised at the absence of the Old Gent's usual levity. Those listening had no clue that Malachi was remembering the video Omar had shown him on the internet a few weeks earlier. In the video Yancey was bowing before what the media referred to as 'His Holy Mother.' Malachi had hoped Yancey would open up to someone about his previous activities, but he had not said a word.

"No, Yancey," Malachi declared emphatically, "anyone who has heard and rejected the gospel before the rapture will be completely deceived into believing in the antichrist, and will thereby be damned."

Pausing for effect, Malachi spoke again with power. "There will be no second chances for anyone."

Malachi opened his Bible to Second Thessalonians 2:11 and 12 and read,

> *And for this cause God shall send them strong delusion, that they should believe a lie: That they all might be damned who believed not the truth, but had pleasure in unrighteousness."*

"Strong delusion. God sends something so convincing that they can't not believe."

Malachi leaned forward as he drove home his point.

"This is God's Word. Do you believe God's Word?"

"Yes … Lord … yes!" The thrill in Louise's soft praise sounded strange in the face of such a verdict, yet Cheyenne felt the same. Knowing God was so full of judgment was both dreadful and glorious.

"God has a plan that those who wait for evidence before believing will find evidence that the Antichrist is the true Christ. With God's help they will believe a lie."

Suddenly a cool breeze filled the room, causing everyone to shiver. Malachi looked up and saw Asher entering late, accompanied by a man. *Could it be … ? Yes, it is Levi.* The audience was too riveted on what Malachi was teaching to notice his brief perplexity.

THE 144,000 – Dusty, frantically searching his Bible, called out, "The 144,000 … who are they and where do they come from? How do they get saved?"

"Okay. Good question." The old teacher grinned as he looked up, uncrossing his legs, and enjoying the moment of teaching the Word to young people truly riveted on the Word. The tone in the room changed. Always sensitive to people's moods, Cheyenne could feel the room relax.

"Take note of the good numbers; chapters 7 and 14 are where we read about the 144,000. Look first at chapter 7 where it names the twelve tribes of Israel, telling us that 12,000 from each tribe are sealed. It tells us that no harm can come to them until they are sealed on their foreheads, meaning God providentially protects these 144,000 young, male, Jewish virgins.

"I never cease to be thrilled by these passages. These 144,000 will be the final publishers, the very last proclaimers of the gospel.

"I like to believe that some of these men will find our book, *God's Story*, and read it. And maybe this will cause them to want to find a Bible and read about themselves right there in Revelation.

"They will surely employ every means possible to communicate the gospel of the kingdom to the whole world. They will doubtless preach publicly, on the web, radio, and in the printed page. These street preachers and publishers will accomplish in less than three years what the church has not done in two thousand years. They

Revelation 7:4 "And I heard the number of them which were sealed: and there were sealed an hundred and forty and four thousand of all the tribes of the children of Israel."

will carry their crosses until every last one of them is killed by the governments of the world.

"It tells us that in heaven they will sing a new song, a special song, that no one else can learn. Like Magdalene's song, they will sing the song of Moses and of the Lamb."

"So," Ben summarized, "The 144,000 will be young virgin men from the twelve tribes of Israel who love and honor Jehovah God."

LEVI – From the back of the room came a loud, clear bass voice. "Sounds like me to me!"

Everyone in the room startled. "Levi?" Malachi questioned.

The handsome young man standing beside Asher made a slight bow to the crowd. "The same."

The two brothers stood, starkly different, yet strangely the same. Asher's red head stood up several inches above his older brother's coal black head. But the dominant nose and strong jaw were the same.

Levi addressed Malachi. "I would like to know what your Revelation says about Islam."

Malachi's face lit up at that. "Well, as to that, let your mind rest easy, because..."

Levi threw up his hand to stop Malachi's eager answer. "But not now."

Cheyenne saw that Asher seemed keyed-up, anxious.

Suddenly she felt a new kind of nervousness taking over her. It almost felt exciting. She wiped her sweaty hands on her blue jean skirt. Taking a deep breath, she tried to relax. Her senses told her something was up ... something had happened ... or was about to happen. Something very different.

Another movement from the backdoor caught everyone's attention. It was Bobbie Jo who had just entered the room and was standing just inside the door next to Levi. Cheyenne's jaw dropped in bewilderment. Sometime in the last few minutes Bobbie Jo had managed to slip out of the meeting and change into an elegant peach-colored, floor length evening dress. Now she stood erect, her skin glowing with a blush, her glorious hair pulled high, yet hanging in curls down past her waist, and her eyes shining like lights.

Levi turned toward Bobbie Jo in polite acknowledgement. It was as if lightning struck. Everyone watching felt the jolt.

Bobbie Jo was aglow, and her eyes sparkled as she stared transfixed. Levi's response was all male, embarrassingly so, as he stared back at the beautiful girl.

Shaking her head as if to clear her thoughts, Cheyenne tried to put what was happening together. She looked around to see if anyone else was suddenly dressed in finery. Catching Hope's troubled eyes, she mouthed her question to her mother, "What's going on?"

Hope followed Cheyenne's gesture and noticed Bobbie Jo's unusual clothing. The girl looked resplendent. Hope looked back at Cheyenne and shrugged her own wide-eyed confusion to her daughter.

Mother and daughter looked back at Bobbie Jo. She stood unabashedly staring at Levi with such a tender newfound vulnerability. The effect struck Cheyenne as breathtakingly beautiful.

In another time and place, Cheyenne would have found the whole thing hilarious: old rawhide Bobbie Jo thunderstruck. Who would have believed it could happen?

Cheyenne looked back at her mom, but Hope's attention had turned to Levi, and her expression was full of genuine concern. Cheyenne looked around at the perplexed faces of the people sitting there. She felt a knot in her stomach as her mind refocused. Why was Levi here?

Asher unknowingly broke the invisible tie between the couple as he draped his arm across his brother's shoulders. Laughingly he spoke to the crowd, although his eyes still revealed his apprehension. "This is my brother Levi. It's been a while since I've seen him. He and some of his friends just arrived a few minutes ago." Asher stuck his thumb in the direction of the hall door. "We're going to visit a while." The brothers exited the room.

Omar looked around, trying to come to a decision. Quietly he stood, moving his little girl Tina from his lap to his warmed chair. He nodded to his wife in silent communication, then exited the room. Something more than a family visit was up.

Running lightly down the steps, Omar followed the brothers to the shipping and handling area of the far warehouse. The wind had picked up. He stood for a moment in the dark, studying the sky and praying for wisdom, then moved into the warehouse. He stood flabbergasted as he surveyed the strange men with military bearing who were precisely packing the warehouse books and equipment onto pallets. "What?" Omar thundered. The two brothers turned in unison and the packers momentarily startled to alertness. The stout looking young man closest to Omar crouched and quickly grabbed at something in the small of his back, stopping when he saw that Omar was not a threat.

"Man!" Asher fumed to Omar, "don't slip up on these guys unannounced." His eyes gestured to his brother, willing him to explain what was going on.

Levi shook his head, looking apologetic as he continued to answer Asher, but turned to include Omar in the conversation. "Things have been moving faster than we thought. I told you I would let you know if I knew there was going to be an attack against TLP. Well, it's almost a sure thing. It happened fast. All this is as new to us as it is for you. I knew there wouldn't be time for you to get your people and your material out without help. I didn't want to use the phone or e-mail to tell you we were coming because we believed our communication would be intercepted. As you know, TLP appears to have a mole. I had to make a decision. When I spoke to Malachi several months ago he told me he trusted me to be decisive. He said in times of life and death, decisiveness wins. Our trucks will be here in a few minutes."

Omar was looking from brother to brother, then turned to stare at the packers as if he could not believe his eyes. "Who are you people?" he demanded. "I thought you were some kind of volcano specialists, not secret agents. What do you think you're doing coming in here and messing with our stuff?"

Now Omar's voice boomed another command as he watched one of the workers start moving his own work area. "Hey you!" Omar pointed his finger at the determined worker. "Don't touch my stuff! I said, don't touch my stuff!"

Levi motioned with his head for the worker to move to another area, then turned to the two men before him. Levi looked at his brother, then at Omar. "Right after the shopping center bombing, at my brother's request, we worked out a plan for TLP in case the ministry ever became a prime target for terrorists. Asher presented the plan to Malachi and he agreed to it. I called and talked to Malachi to make sure he understood and agreed. I believe you read the plan as well. Is that correct?"

"Yeah, I know that ... but ... man! Pistol packing strangers here, moving books?" Omar rubbed his head in frustration. "I don't remember reading that."

The pressure that came with knowledge caused Levi's muscles to ripple in tension. He took a deep breath, trying to relax as he continued trying to explain. "One of my fellow militia members works for the government in counterterrorism. You guys are targets."

Asher stood with his hands on his hips looking around as twenty or more men, who, for all the world, except for their lack of uniforms, looked like soldiers, quietly organized the shipping department for the move. The sound of plastic being wrapped around pallets of boxes filled the room.

Levi looked contrite as he spoke to the anxious preacher. "Omar, I didn't keep you abreast of the new developments these last few days because Malachi said, since you almost lost your entire family that you needed to have some sense of security and normalcy so you could concentrate on your teaching ministry. That is your first responsibility. I didn't even tell Malachi after the first alert because he told me until we know something is going to happen, just let him think about ministry. He told me that what you did was eternal and you both needed your minds and hearts free of worry. Anyway, I figured there would be plenty of time to tell you when and if something ever happened. Obviously, I was wrong."

Levi remained patient as Omar continued to glare. "Okay, Omar, a little background. When we," he motioned to the people packing, "my friends from all over the world, started getting ready for a possible

Yellowstone event, we also started organizing and planning as a private militia. We are all experts in one area or another, some as scientists, like me, and others are special forces of one kind or another. We count ourselves as patriots."

Omar dragged his eyes from watching the men pack up the warehouse, and looked at Levi in disbelief. "How can the government just let a bunch of regular guys organize into an armed militia? You're all gonna end up in trouble, and you're taking us with you."

Shaking his head, Levi answered, "Actually, it's always been legal, but now it's necessary. In the last few weeks the storms that we've been seeing in the governments of the world have become full-blown hurricanes, if you get my drift. Things are different in U.S. government now, more different than the average person could ever guess. Financially, many governments of the world are failing, including the U.S. With financial failure comes a breakdown in all areas of government, health, social, civic, and basic law and order.

"We knew the government would not come to your aid, even if they suspect an attack, so we, our militia, voted to let this be a training exercise as well as a rescue. There are militia groups forming all over the country, and none too soon."

Omar remained incredulous. "So ... so, are you telling us that your private militia is moving our entire publishing company someplace, along with all our people, without even asking?"

Levi sighed, beginning to lose his patience. "Malachi read the drill, approved of it, and knew that when I thought it necessary it would be enacted. Also, I understand that Malachi shared the basic tenets with the leadership in the ministry and they agreed. Of course, it wasn't public information because of your mole." The three men looked at one another as each assessed the other.

Asher's tone was full of dread. "I'll go tell Malachi."

"Well," Omar said to no one in particular, maintaining his defiance, "I am gonna pack my own stuff."

30

TO HAVE AND TO HOLD

Malachi watched Omar follow the two brothers out of the room. He wished he could go along. Levi's presence could only mean one thing: the time had come. When Yancey jumped up, Malachi was almost glad for an excuse not to try to teach.

Yancey stood looking very nervous but obviously excited. "I was going to wait until after the Bible study, but as we are already interrupted ... so I wonder if I could have a few minutes of your time. I have prepared something very important for dis evening!"

ETERNAL FINALE – Malachi's relaxed response had its intended effect on the folks sitting before him. "Well, I knew that Yancey had a little something special prepared, so I think now is a good time. But first I wanted to share a few thoughts with you myself." Malachi's heart was full of thanksgiving. He hoped he could convey the eternal redemptive picture he was seeing. No one, not even Hope, guessed he was summing up their time together, a sort of farewell.

"My mind has been replaying all that has gone before in the last while. Our lives have changed ... we have changed. What is coming, who can know?

"This one thing I know, and that is these last few months have been about what God is doing. It is the big picture, the eternal finale. We are *publishers* ... publishers of the gospel to a lost and dying world.

There are at least 1,822 languages that still do not have the simple gospel message, and we will see it through to the end or to the rapture. Every day we read letters from all over the world of people who have heard the gospel of Jesus Christ for the first time and have believed. Missionaries call to tell us of another people group that now have the story of Jesus.

"Asher has already put teams together to go into areas of the world that have not yet been reached. These teams are busy locating translators where Timothy Vick has not been able to explore. It is exciting to know we are a part of the big picture. Lord willing, our berry product from China will soon be here to help finance the dream of finishing the publishing work. God in his mercy and grace has used us simple people to do an eternal thing. Thank you for joining with me to make this possible."

Now he moved his eyes across the room, finding Hope. His face took on a soft yearning as his eyes rested on his lifelong lover. "Yet we are also people who love, dream, and want to enjoy the simple pleasures of life. It is such moments, it is little snapshots of life, if you will, that make up the bigger picture. Friends, loves, babies, swimming at the creek with the grandchildren … all these simple pleasures have made us rich as a people.

"I just want to say thank you … thank you all for being a part of my life, this ministry, and helping make this vision a reality."

Malachi looked toward Yancey with question in his eyes, "Well, it's Yancey's turn, so let's listen up."

Dusty moved the podium away from the front of the room.

For the first time, Cheyenne noticed that Yancey was surprisingly handsome in his attire. She looked over at Asher as he walked into the room. His face revealed no clue as to what events were about to transpire. He looked curious.

Cheyenne sighed. *Well, at least I'm not the only one who doesn't know what's going on.*

BOBBIE JO SINGS – Yancey cleared his throat and straightened his shoulders.

He suddenly blushed as he stammered, "I'm going away. Before I leave I wanted to say how grateful I am dat you were willing to share your lives with me."

Yancey continued to stand as if he were not finished. Everyone looked around anxiously, but stayed in their seats.

"I ... we ... well, what I want to say is, I would like to invite all of you to my ... dat is ... mine and Julie's wedding."

Yancey's face turned beet red as everyone exclaimed in shock.

"When?" Asher's bass voice called out with surprise and some consternation. "When's the big day, Yancey?"

Yancey put his head down in embarrassment then shuffled his feet, "Actually, we did it legal at the Justice of the Peace Friday, but Jules says she's not married 'till she wears a white dress and Bobbie Jo sings,' so dat's right now."

Half the crowd laughed in a burst of incredulity.

Yancey started again. "If you're willing to stay five more minutes, you can watch me make a big promise to my Jules."

With that announcement, one of the office doors slowly opened. There stood Julie, dressed head to foot in a beautiful white old-fashioned wedding gown, her soft hair draped in curls around her neck with a lovely old lace veil hanging over her face. There was a unified gasp from the crowd as they came to their feet in homage. She was stunningly beautiful.

Cheyenne felt as if she had turned into concrete. Her mind refused to absorb what was happening; her body felt terribly heavy. As if in a vacuum she heard music played over the sound system. Now it made sense how Dusty had set the chairs up and decorated. He had intentionally left an aisle for the bride. Cheyenne watched Julie move forward in step to the music. She watched her take Yancey's hand. *But Levi? Why did he come?*

Dusty stepped up behind Yancey and began to sing Yancey's marriage vows, which were a series of Bible verses put to music. After

JULIE, YANCEY'S BRIDE

each verse, Dusty waited for Yancey and Julie to answer with the proper, I do.

Then Bobbie Jo, still glowing and flushed, stepped up behind Julie and began to sing in her strong pure voice.

I no longer face each day alone
I have found a haven of my own
I feel alive,
Complete
Full of hope
Coming home after a long, lonely journey
Coming home to you, My Love.

Bobbie Jo didn't seem to be aware of Julie or Yancey. She didn't seem to realize that an entire room of people watched her instead of the bride. She unashamedly stared toward the back of the room where Levi now stood. Longing was written on her face. Cheyenne looked over her shoulder. Levi no longer looked like a hardened soldier ... he looked like a man. His stare was primeval. Cheyenne felt heat rising in her face. She chided herself. Why am I blushing? I'm not the one acting like ... like ... that.

Unbidden memories flooded her mind. Cheyenne's eyes glittered with a moment of silly insanity. *Crazy ... how can I think about this at a time like this?*

Once started, her psyche would not allow her to stop. Her face twitched with mirth. What had Asher told her a few months back about Levi? *Oh, yeah, now I remember.* Asher had been flushed as if embarrassed. He had also been so tickled that the girls had trouble understanding what he was saying. He told them that Levi had always said that he was waiting for an Amazon woman, a girl that was tough, big, and luscious. As of yet, he had not found such a creature.

Yancey and Julie faded into the background as Cheyenne considered her best friend, Bobbie Jo. With new eyes she speculated, considered, and marveled that she had never really seen her in that light.

Her mind snapped back to the present when she saw the bride and groom step toward each other, sealing the marriage with a kiss. Bobbie Jo and Dusty continued to sing as the couple stayed locked in a long embrace.

She glanced down, listening to the duet. Bobbie Jo's beautiful harmony wrapped itself around Dusty's full baritone, creating a splendid blend.

Ever since Bobbie Jo had been thirteen years old she had been singing at weddings. Cheyenne, always bugging her friend about her extra ten pounds, had a standing tease at every wedding. Now the thought of this silly tease seemed ominous. *It ain't done 'till the fat lady sings.*

Cheyenne's smile was stiff. No longer able to watch the embracing pair, she glanced around.

Her eyes fell on Asher. He was staring directly at her. It was only an instant, but it seemed that all his defenses had fallen away and she saw into his soul. No more pretenses.

For that brief moment it was as if he did not care that she saw the raw need he had for her. His soul seemed to be boring into her. Time stood still. He devoured her with his gaze. His face was a study in reflections of sadness, hope, hesitation, desire, longing ... all wrapped in a terrible need. He loved her. He wanted her. But he seemed so sad.

Cheyenne's gaze mirrored his.

Slowly, reluctantly, Asher dropped his head and turned his face away. She was shut out again.

Cheyenne exhaled. She hadn't noticed that she'd been holding her breath. The tingling in her hands and feet slowly faded. The pounding in her head took a full minute to subside. "When, Lord, when will it be my day? I know he loves me ... but what holds him back? What's going on?"

Cheyenne put her head down.

At that moment the face of Zulla Mae flashed into her mind. A strong shiver caused Cheyenne's whole body to quiver as closed her eyes, trying to shut out the ugly thoughts. She felt again the flash of the bomb as she knelt over Zulla Mae's laboring body. *Death ... I ... I SMELL it. Run, girl. Run!* Cheyenne, almost as if against her own will, drew in a deep breath as if trying to detect the smell of death.

Her senses heightened, she glanced back again. Levi was no longer held captive by Bobbie Jo. Cheyenne saw Levi's strong jaw tightening, his eyes flash with an absolute knowledge as he stared at Yancey. Fear caused her hands to tremble as she silently cried out to God, "Oh, God, help Julie. Help us all."

Cheyenne's silent battle raged. Why hadn't Julie sought counsel?

There was a strange sound outside; the wind had picked up howling with unusual volume. It seemed to have taken with it any semblance of calm or stability. She could hear the gusts whirling through the tops of the trees on the high ridges that surrounded The Last Publishers compound. A storm was coming.

Oh, God what is to become of us? Why is Levi here? God, I need ... I need someone to hold me. I'm so afraid!

Raising her head, Cheyenne turned to Asher. She knew he was aware that she was staring at him. He kept his face straight ahead. *God, what's wrong with him?*

Looking for reassurance and comfort, she turned her head, seeking out her mother. Hope had been watching Cheyenne's silent battle.

She met her daughter's gaze, noting her bewilderment. Trying to insert a little levity, she shrugged and held up nine fingers, rocking her shoulders and mouthing the words of an old 60s song, "Love potion number nine!"

With that, Cheyenne's taut mental state went from despair to a failed attempt to control a fit of wild laughter. She struggled to regain her composure.

Oh, my dear Asher! You're lucky Mom has other things to keep her busy. If she ever had the time to devote herself to a special brew for you, you'd never know what hit you!

A tiny giggle escaped the emotionally wrung out girl. *Mom could make a dead man laugh.* Cheyenne didn't know, but in a few short days that was exactly what Hope would do.

BEING FILLED – Without any noticeable reason, a calm like the moments before sleep began to seep through Cheyenne's body. There was a heavy limpness in every limb; a tranquil warmth filled even the most hidden corner of her soul. Every worry and fret that had ever assaulted her mind seemed to drift away, as it were, out into the deep blue ocean.

A total disconnect.

Then a strange sense of eternal destiny descended down and hovered over her, guiding her mind.

Seek and ye shall find.

Time seemed to stand still as Cheyenne's eyes slowly traveled around the room ... seeking. Her gaze moved from one to another and then another. Her search stopped as she reached the faces of Omar and Tess' small children. As she watched, young Timothy glanced up at his mom, then his eyes shifted, resting on the door where his daddy had disappeared a few minutes earlier. His face was curious but serene. Cheyenne's heart silently cried out to her heavenly Father, *Oh Lord God, how I wish I were a child and could just trust my daddy to make everything right. Life would be so much easier. All I would need to do is just watch for daddy to come back.*

As if straight from heaven's throne a voice filled her mind. "Exactly. Just say, Abba, Father, and then watch for my return." Unshed tears made her eyes sparkle like green crystals reflecting the light. Another verse of Scripture came to mind, *"And he said, Abba, Father, all things are possible unto thee; take away this cup from me: nevertheless not what I will, but what thou wilt."*

The very essence of her soul seemed to be alight with God. "Oh, LORD my God, thank you for being willing to go to the cross for me … thank you for taking the awful cup of death to pay for my sins. Oh, Lord, whatever you have for me … *I want to know you, the power of your resurrection and fellowship of your sufferings."*

Instantly Cheyenne could hear Magdalene's girlish voice quoting those very words from Philippians chapter 3, verse 10. That had been Magdalene's special life's verse. A trembling took hold of Cheyenne as her mind recalled Magdalene's cotton-white hair hanging over the edge of the stretcher as the paramedics loaded her still form into the ambulance. At that moment, as clear as light, amidst the smoke and screaming she saw Magdalene's young face, forever locked into a look of wonder, thankfulness and joy. Cheyenne unconsciously whispered, "I had forgotten. The night was so full of tragedy … I never registered that her face was so joyous."

It was as if a deep wellspring of understanding filled her soul. Cheyenne felt a tingle flood her being. The presence of God consumed her, pressed in, surrounded and compassed her about. Fear was gone. Anxiety dissipated like fog in the face of bright morning sunlight. It was as if she could hear God's voice, *"Trust in the Lord with all thine heart; and lean not unto thine own understanding. In all thy ways acknowledge him, and he shall direct thy paths."*

Her head moved up and down with a thrill of acceptance, "Yes, Lord ... I am willing, ready and glad to be in your service. I will continue serving you with my whole heart. I will not be afraid of what may come because I know you are worthy and you will win."

At that moment Cheyenne felt another tingle take over her being. Although she was still aware of what was happening in the room, none of it seemed to be of any consequence. She knew what she must do as soon as the opportunity presented itself.

For the space of less than a minute, Asher had watched her, totally captivated by the glory in her lovely face. Now she lifted her moist green eyes to stare into his. Scripture seemed to come to her as if it were a song sung by a chorus of a thousand angels rejoicing in things to come. *"Delight thyself also in the LORD; and he shall give thee the desires of thine heart."*

A soft smile touched her lips as she whispered, "Thank you, Lord."

Asher tried to read her lips, tried to understand what she might be thinking, but he had no clue. Where he expected worry, fretting and questions, he only saw peace, delight and purpose. *Does she understand what's happening?*

She turned her face back to the newly wedded couple. Julie's face shone with the brightness of a dream come true. Cheyenne bit the inside of her cheek as she pondered. *Well, Julie, you got what you wanted.*

Yancey spoke up, sounding confident and happy. "Will you, my good friends, pronounce and bless us, Mr. and Mrs. Reuben Yancey?" The crowd simultaneously responded, "We pronounce you Mr. and Mrs. Reuben Yancey."

It was the shortest wedding any of those attending had ever witnessed. It was a good thing. The spectators were ready to scatter. The storm had stolen away the last vestiges of calm.

Then the momentary quiet was filled with Hope's hillbilly twang, revealing her surprise at the turn of events. "Well, I never saw the likes ..."

Malachi leaned over, kissing the top of his true love's graying head. He responded to her where all could hear, "Well, let's hope we see more of the likes real soon."

WHAT PART DOES *THE LAST PUBLISHERS* PLAY? – Asher's loud voice rattled the fun out of those sitting before him, "Wait, before you all go."

He stepped forward. With urgency he explained, "My brother is privy to NASA surveillance of terrorist activities. He's been in touch with me in connection with the mounting terrorist threats toward this ministry. I had hoped we were off their grid, but it appears we've become a probable target. This is not from the small cell group that bombed the shopping center. This is an international group. Is that right, Levi?"

A master at assessing situations, Levi saw that the group of about 60 people would need understanding and reassurance before he would get their cooperation.

Malachi shifted his gaze to Levi, seeing in the man's face his decision to take the time to inform the people of the eminent threat. "If you'll bear with me," Levi declared, "I'll explain what's happening."

Their gaiety turned to anxious wonder as the imposing man lifted his arm to speak, his jacket swinging open, revealing the gun high on his waist. "The publishing of your web book *God's Story*, in the Arabic language is gaining converts from the masses, but it is also reaching some of the imams and even the royal family in Saudi Arabia. The backlash is tremendous. Islam has never in all its history experienced such a mass departure from the faith. Even some militant Muslims are now laying down their arms due to their newfound belief in your Jesus."

Disgust twitched his face. "Their leadership is calling on all Muslims to kill their own kin if they even suspect a family member of considering converting to Christianity. All it takes to come under a death sentence is to be found with one of your books. They have tried to block web access, but you have so thoroughly inundated the web with it that anyone who wants to can still find it. They are being encouraged to report any family member who views it. Those who don't report it are considered equally guilty and subject to death. The leaders say such murder is a kindness to save their souls before they have a chance to convert."

Levi stood with his knees slightly bent, his hands folded at waist level. Like a cat, he seemed ready to move in any direction. If they hadn't been so disturbed, the group would have noticed that he stood with his back to a wall, giving him full view of all the exits and windows.

Not one to be easily surprised, Levi was amazed—no, shocked—at the innocence of these people. They *couldn't* be the same ones that were such threats to followers of Mohammed.

"Islam is a violent religion. Now Islam has a new enemy that terror has failed to subdue—your brand of the Christian religion. In fact, it seems the more the leaders forbid their people to read your book, the more the people want to know what's in it. The violent leadership is losing their hold on the Muslim people. Those people are beginning to realize that their leadership does not care about them."

Levi's expression changed to pleasure. Seeing them gave him an even greater appreciation for the impact they were making. His voice softened. "What war has not been able to accomplish, what negotiations have only made worse, when man's efforts at friendship brought disdain, amazingly that one religious book you're distributing has Islam by the throat." He shook his head in disbelief.

"Some in the U.S. government do not like the instability you've created, especially now as the economy is failing worldwide. Others think it's a godsend. Israel will not look a gift horse in the mouth. If it works, it works to their favor, even if it's Christian. We Jews like to pay our debts. Furthermore, it's to our advantage that this movement keeps going. In the last sixty-five years, Christianity has proven to be a friend of Israel. Islam has always made itself our enemy.

"This is how it's going down. Most of you received instructions about two months ago in case there was a credible threat against The Last Publishers or its workers. I advise you to follow the instructions you received and not share that information with anyone, including friends who stand in this room. There is a mole here among you, a friend, who is not really a friend. Therefore, what we say here will be limited."

Malachi looked around, still struggling to believe this was really happening. "Do you really think it necessary to follow through with all that now?"

These people were unlike any Levi had encountered. In Israel, people jumped for cover first and hoped to live long enough to ask questions later. This was frustrating. He realized he would have to exercise a bit more finesse to capture their trust. He made a mental effort to shake off his military mindset and think in terms of people who, as a rule, lived in total peace and harmony.

"We've been monitoring internet traffic and other communications. Militant Muslim terrorists have planned another 9/11 attack. It will be series of coordinated attacks against Christian targets, all to take place on September 11th."

A stunned Malachi answered, "Against us?"

Levi was almost amused at the older man's teenage-sounding response.

"They want to make a statement to their own people saying, *Allah is more powerful than the Christians' Jesus.*

"You need to get out of here. Now."

The whole group looked to their leader. "I never thought it would come to this," the Old Gent said, "but we should do as the man says."

Levi grinned with relief. "Trust me. Having spent several years in Israel, I've become a master of survival. Now we all need to move. Quickly. We've divided you up in groups depending on your work here with TLP. Each group will have one of my team as a leader.

For those of you who did not receive prior information I would advise you to take a short holiday to visit family or friends. Leave first thing in the morning. Your job here will be over until further notice. You will be compensated for a few weeks. Your group leader will give you all the details, which will save us time now. For those of you who just came in for the Bible study, I would also advise a trip somewhere. For the rest of you, we'll show you which room to go to for further instruction. At least for the near future, these grounds will no longer be The Last Publishers ministries."

⚭

Cheyenne slipped from the room. She had to get the small jar of elixir. For the first time in her life she knew God had supernaturally visited her. She knew her task.

Hope saw her run out, and knew her mission.

Levi watched her leave as well. His men had been informed, if she or her mother did leave, not to stop either of them.

He smiled. *Good.* In this uncertain time you never knew when you might need a little miraculous help. Levi unconsciously touched his shirt pocket, feeling for the small container. Just in case. For just an instant, comfort flickered in his eyes.

FINAL LIMITATION – Omar finally finished packing. He mounted the steps two at a time as he returned to the meeting.

When he looked up to the front of the room, Yancey and Julie still stood in wedding finery.

A satisfied grunt escaped Levi when he saw the shocked horror that crossed Omar's countenance. Levi knew instantly that the black man had knowledge of Yancey's other life.

A vow was a vow; the deed was done. It was time to move.

Levi opened the meeting room door and loudly clapped his cupped hands. The sharp sound echoed in the hall, causing everyone to startle as if it were an explosion. "Time's up! Everyone out, *now!* Move!"

Most of the people came to their feet and began to scurry out, rushing to their cars in an effort to elude the lashing rain. The others looked like they wished they could escape, but instead they stepped into lines like herded animals, separating into small groups or indi-vidual families at their leader's command.

"Daddy! Daddy! Are we going somewhere?" Young Tina ran to Omar, who scooped his daughter up into his arms.

Omar's questioning eyes met Levi's.

There was a shift in the mood, a relaxing of the warrior's stance. Trust and respect showed in Levi's eyes. "Are you familiar with the story of Gideon? How God chose his army?"

Omar gave the slightest nod. "Judges, chapter seven, verse six and seven."

Levi acknowledged Omar's quick familiarity with Old Testament Scriptures. "Well, let's just say this is the final elimination before the battle." Now his tone took on more force. "There will be a battle."

Omar's eyes never wavered; his voice was firm. "Count me in. I'm ready."

EPILOGUE

SUDAN

Thursday

The small motorcycle pitter-pattered down the dirt lane, carrying two weary riders who were thankful for the cover of darkness. It was late fall and the night air was soft in the desert.

"Our mission is almost completed and no one the wiser," whispered Fadiyah to her young husband as she squeezed his sides with her hands. A large heavy box was lodged between them. It was the only one left of the 40 boxes they had been assigned to distribute. A van had delivered many boxes to selected areas over the past couple of weeks. Then teams were sent to spread the books to the countryside villages.

As the couple topped the small rise, they saw the silhouette of the last village. They both sighed with relief. It had been a tense day. Both knew if they were caught dropping *God's Story* books in Muslim communities they would be killed. It had been the reading of this simple book on an Arabic website that had made it possible for them to come to understand what God had done for them.

As they paused that morning at a road side store to eat a small bowl of rice, Rashid had whispered to his wife, "We were so hungry to have peace with God. But so many still have not heard the truth because they have no access to the web. It is worth the chance we have taken. I am thankful to have been considered for this task."

After riding for nearly twelve hours, they were looking forward to stopping for the night. Suddenly the evening darkness exploded with bright headlights from several vehicles. It didn't look good. *Why would three vehicles be parked on the road leading to the village and then suddenly turn on their lights?* Bringing the motorcycle to a stop and turning off the motor, they heard men's voices. They quickly pushed their cycle into the ditch and covered it with a thin tan cloth they used for sleeping. Rashid hoisted the box to his shoulder before they hurried from the road toward a small cluster of homes in the distance. After several minutes of hard running, Fadiyah suddenly stopped, grabbing her husband's arm as she urgently whispered, "Listen."

There was a low, distant hum of large vehicles. The sound was still a good distance off, but heading their way. "Quick," Rashid gestured as he shoved the books into the base of an old rotten tree, covering it with sticks and debris that lay around.

Turning to his beloved wife, he began to pray, "God, keep this box hidden until it is safe, then send a child to find it so this village will hear the gospel. In Jesus' Holy Name we ask. Amen."

Rashid grabbed Fadiyah's hand as they ran across the open field. The young husband hesitated for just a moment as if searching for something, then he ran up to the seventh old house in the line of houses. Not a dog barked in the whole village.

Whispering, he told her, "Look, Fadiyah, God has given us a mulberry tree as a sign of his deliverances. Remember how we read the story in Second Samuel? God told them when they heard the sound rushing through the mulberry trees that He was there for them? God will keep you safe. You must lay flat on the roof under the limbs of the tree. It will give you shade, substance and a cover should you move. Prop your legs around a limb so you do not fall off the roof when you sleep."

He cupped her chin in his hand and lifted her face towards his to emphasize his urgent words. "Remember what they told us—if one of us is taken, it will only cause greater sorrow for the taken one to see the other also taken. They are counting on us to expose each other, so you must stay hidden even if you hear. Don't get up, regardless. We must do what we know is best."

His tone softened but was still urgent. "I will take joy that you escaped and that you can give a full report of victory. Use wisdom, not sentiment. Stay still for three days, then if all is clear, go back to the safe house."

Fadiyah tried to speak, but he put his finger to her lips as if to seal away her protest. She did not want to be left in hiding without him.

The young lover forcefully held his wife in his arms. Then his hands slid gently to her slightly rounded belly where their first child lay hidden and waiting for his birth day. "If I am still free I will meet you there; otherwise, I will meet you at Jesus' feet in worship and thanksgiving."

He paused and offered another warning. "Don't dare try to get the cycle. If it is found, it may be watched.

"I have loved you, Fadiyah. I have loved you so very, very much. Take care of our little one." Rashid pulled his slender wife tightly, quickly kissing her forehead as he prayed while he smoothed her long black hair down her slender back. "God be with us. Keep us strong. Thank you that you have shown grace upon our people that they might have the opportunity to hear the precious message of Jesus. Thank you for the *God's Story* book that will bring your message to Muslims all over the world. You are worthy, O Lord. We put our lives into your hands."

The agile Fadiyah quickly climbed her husband's body as if he were a ladder, balancing on his shoulders as he stretched to give her another inch. She grabbed hold of the edge of the roof. Rashid lifted her feet as high has he could reach. She silently pulled herself up under the overhanging mulberry tree limbs. Her beloved sprinted off into the darkness. She knew he was hoping to draw any attention as far away from her as possible. Their child would live.

As he raced away, the young warrior of God whispered into the night, "God make me swift. Make me strong. Cause me, Lord, to suffer in silence so that my dear Fadiyah will not hear my cries. Thank you, Lord, that those of this village will soon know you." ∽

"And this gospel of the kingdom shall be preached in all the world for a witness unto **all nations;** and then **shall the end come.**"

Mark 13:10

Every work of God has been preceded by

PRAYER

"And I say unto you, ask, and it shall be given you; seek, and ye shall find, knock, and it shall be opened unto you. For every one that asketh receiveth; and he that seeketh findeth; and to him that knoweth it shall be opened.

If two of you shall agree on earth as touching any thing that they shall ask, it shall be done for them of my Father which is in heaven.

Ask of me, and I shall give thee the heathen for thine inheritance, and the uttermost parts of the earth for thy possession."

Psalms 2:8

Will you pray?

Matthew 7:7-8, Matthew 18:19

Berry Herbal Brew

In a gallon jug put one half cup of each dried seed, skin and juice of each berry:

Indian Goose Berries
Blueberry
Bilberry
Red grape
Powered pomegranate
Dried fig leaf and grape leaf
   (Dried mixture available at BulkHerbStore.com)

Add 9 cups of boiling water and cover with cloth. Put rubber band around mouth of jar to keep out fruit flies. Let sit until berries are hydrated (about 24 to 48 hours). Add 3 cups of sugar or honey. Knead berries with hand for about 10 minutes. Make sure you have towel over opening to keep out fruit flies. Put tight cloth over mouth of jar, set jar in cool, dark place for at least three weeks (can be months). For the first week open up and squeeze berries a few minutes, stirring up the pulp and making sure you keep out fruit flies.

   After three or more weeks siphon off (or strain off liquid) then discard pulp. Store in a clean glass jar (in cool, dark place). Take 3 ounce each evening (recipe can be doubled).

Salmon Egg Benedict

Split fresh hot biscuit or toasted English muffin. Lay small amount of smoked salmon on open biscuit (about the size of sausage patty). Cover with poached egg. Pour Hollandaise sauce over the whole. Serve.

Mock Hollandaise Sauce

¼ cup sour cream
¼ cup mayonnaise
1 tsp lemon juice
½ ycllow mustard

Stir together in a saucepan over low heat until warm. If desired, thin with a little milk.

THE STORY CONTINUES IN THE 2ND BOOK IN
THE LAST PUBLISHERS SERIES...

THE TEST

Asher Joel and Cheyenne Freeman have survived a storm of adversity—stalkers, spies, bombings, murder—and persevered through it all, driven by their mutual vision to reach every corner of the earth with the gospel of Christ.

But the test of who and what they are has just begun.

Stand with them as they battle forces natural and supernatural while struggling to survive in unfathomable conditions. Share with them as they face sorrows so great that they wonder if they can go on. Study with them as they discover the old ways of healing through herbs and berries. See the strength, love and unspeakable glories that God pours out upon those who faithfully fight the war for His harvest.

Will Asher be forced to choose between God's call and the promise of a life with Cheyenne?

What has become of the berry brew?

Who is Yancey, really? What will the uncertain future hold for Yancey and Julie?

Will threatening circumstances solidify this faithful band's commitment, or will the seeds of discontent and bitterness threaten the harvest of souls?

FOOTNOTE CONTENTS

CREATED TO BE HIS HELP MEET
&THE HELP MEET'S JOURNEY

"...Simply THE BEST book
I've read in conjunction with THE BIBLE
on being a GODLY WIFE "

- **Candace Cameron Bure**, Actress & Speaker, Growing in God Ministries

CREATED TO BE HIS HELP MEET

What God is doing through this new book is amazing! Written by international best-selling author Debi Pearl. This book has been translated into multiple languages. We are receiving thousands of letters from people giving testimony to marriages restored and made new. Also available in Spanish.

THE HELP MEET'S JOURNEY

The Journey is a 184-page year-long spiral-bound companion workbook/journal for Created To Be His Help Meet. There are extra pages for your stories, doodlings, studies, and pictures where you will create a lasting memory of the miracle God is doing in you. This is a perfect study guide for individuals or women's study groups.

THE ULTIMATE SUPER HERO COMIC BOOK!

"My children have been **POURING** over the *Good and Evil* books since they arrived...!"

- Mother of six

GOOD AND EVIL

God chose to introduce Himself to mankind, not through principles, concepts, or doctrine; but through stories of prophecy, war, mercy, judgment, miracles, death, life, and forgiveness. This is God's redemption plan told chronologically from Genesis to Revelation. Those familiar with the Marvel Comic book format greatly appreciate this classic, high-quality, color art. 336 pages, 7x10¼ inches. Also available in Spanish as well as 25 other langauges and 54 more in progress!